Dead End

Peri Jean Mace Ghost Thrillers #8

Copyright © 2017 Catie Rhodes.

Published by: Long Roads and Dark Ends Press

Cover artwork by Book Cover Corner

Content Editing by Word Webber Press

Copy Editing by Julie Glover

Proofreading by Deborah Digrispino

First Printing, 2017

ISBN Ebook: 978-1-947462-00-7

ISBN Print: 978-1-947462-01-4

Rhodes, Catie.

Dead End/ Catie Rhodes. — 1st ed.

Visit the author website: www.catierhodes.com

SERIES LIST

Forever Road (Book #1)

Black Opal (Book #2)

Rocks & Gravel (Book #3)

Rest Stop (Book #4)

Forbidden Highway (Book #5)

Rear View: Prequel (Book #6)

Crossroads (Book #7)

Dead End (Book #8)

Dark Traveler (Book #9)

Wrong Turn (Book #10)

Last Exit (Book #11)

DEAD END

PERI JEAN MACE GHOST THRILLERS #8

CATIE RHODES

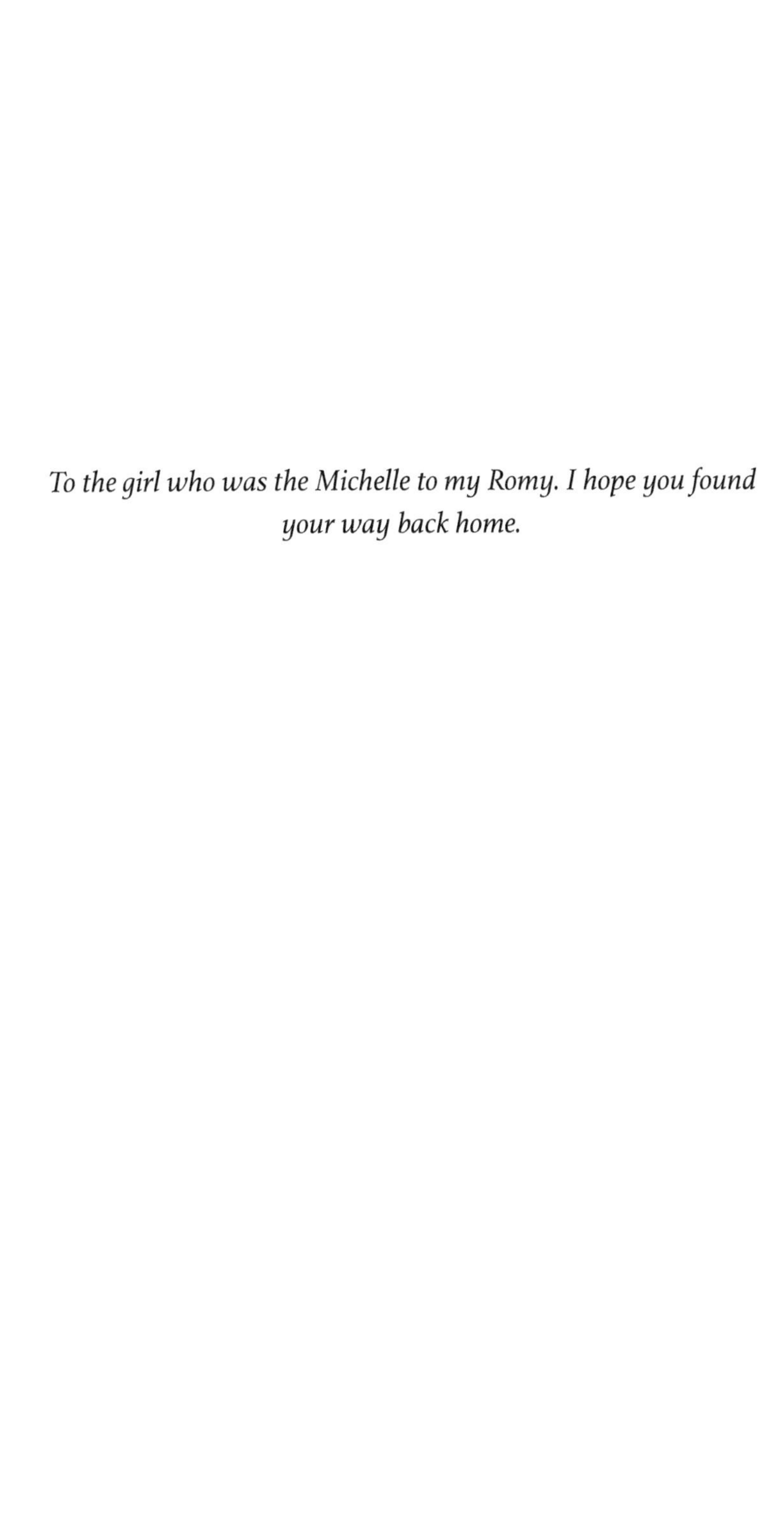

To the girl who was the Michelle to my Romy. I hope you found your way back home.

1

LATE AFTERNOON SUN streamed into the window of Gaslight City Title Company's conference room. It heated my jeans-clad leg to the point where I slid off my leather jacket and laid it over the back of my chair. For the billionth time, I asked myself if I was doing the right thing.

It didn't matter how long I waited to sell Memaw's property. It would never be easy to let it go. I'd considered keeping it, but knew I'd never live in Gaslight City again. My ugly past lurked around every corner. These city people had offered above market value for ten acres with a burned-out house and barn. I had to take it and move on.

The upside was I could see Hannah while I was in town. That would make all the unpleasantness worthwhile. We had spoken only a few words since the night I killed a man to rescue her. Things would never be as they were. But I couldn't just let her slip away, our friendship ending altogether. Maybe soon she'd answer one of the half-dozen messages I'd left her over the last week.

While the woman read from the infinite stack of closing papers, I stared out the window at the Easter decorations, eggs and bunnies in pastel colors, fluttering on the antique gaslights lining the street. A tall woman—sun glowing on her long, red hair—hurried down the street. She stopped to peer into the plate glass window of Purtlebaugh's General Store, where they still sold cups of coffee for five cents with purchase of a souvenir ceramic mug.

I sat up straighter, really alert for the first time since I sat down. *Hannah?* Perhaps she hadn't returned my call because she was coming to meet me here at the title company. My heart beat faster.

A little red-headed boy raced down the sidewalk and hugged the woman's legs. She bent to kiss his head, and I caught a direct look at her face. *Not Hannah.* I slumped in my seat and checked my phone to see if she'd returned my call since I set it to silent.

"Leave that alone." Rainey Bruce shoved a stack of papers at me to sign.

I shoved the phone in my pocket and signed the first paper. A sob crept up my throat. Relinquishing ownership of the land where Memaw raised me stabbed me right in the heart. I swiped at my face.

"You planning on staying in Houston?" asked the male half of the yuppie city couple buying the property. I finished signing and raised my head. The couple wore the kind of clothes they probably thought country people wore—pearl snap shirts, tight blue jeans, brand-new cowboy boots. I pushed the stack back at Rainey.

"Still undecided." No need to bother telling him I no

longer lived there. "What are you planning for Memaw's land?"

The woman showed me a mouthful of perfect teeth and pushed her phone across the table. "We're having this house built."

I glanced at the phone. A brick McMansion that looked like it belonged in Griff's subdivision back in The Woodlands. Deep sadness worked its way through me. Rainey passed me another stack of papers and gave me a warning glare. She needn't have worried. I was too numb to say much. I started signing again.

"We're going to get some cows and horses, maybe some chickens," the husband said. "Be modern-day farmers."

"Good luck with that." I had no reason to be angry at these nice people, but I was. Letting go of the last piece of my life here in Gaslight City stung like a bitch. I signed the last paper and pushed them back at Rainey.

She glanced through the forms. "If this is all Peri Jean needs to sign, we'll be on our way."

The title company lady, whose name I couldn't remember even though we went to school together, scowled but nodded.

I nodded at the yuppie couple and shook both their hands. Smooth as babies' butts. They sure had a rude awakening on the not-too-distant horizon.

Rainey and I walked out to her convertible Mercedes. She popped the trunk and took a sheaf of papers out of the leather messenger bag she used as a briefcase.

"The last of the jewelry and gems from the Mace Treasure sold to an antiques collector in Austin." She passed me a sealed envelope with my name on it. "This is the final sum transferred into your bank account. As agreed, I cut checks for Hannah, Wade Hill, and me, set up the scholarship fund we talked about, and paid myself back what I loaned you to buy your Toyota sedan. Where is it, by the way?" She stared up and down the street.

"I made the drive in this." I patted the huge, white truck next to me. The car was in storage, and I was considering its sale. "It pulls the travel trailer better than my Toyota would."

Rainy made a face at the truck. "I can't believe you're traveling around with a bunch of grifters and living in a *camper*." She said the word with her lips puckered.

I ignored the barb. Rainey couldn't possibly understand how wonderful it was to be around people who shared both my gifts and my blood for the first time in my life. "Did you name the scholarship what I told you?"

She rolled her eyes. "The Chase Fischer Budding Musician scholarship."

I smiled, hoping some kid like Chase would be encouraged to go to college instead of hang around this town and waste away.

Rainey set out another sheaf of papers. "This is the paperwork for the trust you had me set up for your uncle Jesse. It'll be taken out of the property sale. Very good of you. It's what your memaw would have wanted."

"This needs to cover his legal counsel and drop the maximum in his commissary account each month." I glanced through the papers. The words didn't make sense.

I was too rattled from letting go of my last tangible link to Memaw.

"You think I'm incompetent? I always get your uncle everything he needs." Rainey tapped the paper with one long, dragon lady nail to show me where to sign.

I scribbled my name. "This feels like a kiss-off. I wish we could get him out."

Rainey shook her head and stared down the street. It didn't hide the flush in her cheeks. She always got that flush when we talked about my uncle Jesse. I didn't dare ask what it was about. She might snatch me bald. I handed back her papers, and she stowed them in her trunk. When she turned back around, she had her lips pressed together and held a white envelope pinched between her thumb and forefinger.

"As you requested, I sent King Tolliver a check. He returned it un-cashed with this."

I opened the envelope. King had scribbled "void" on the check, which had been for a sizable amount. Especially since he didn't do a damn thing to help find the Mace Treasure.

The money had been a show of respect, one Wade strongly encouraged to keep King as a friend. Behind the check was a folded slip of paper. I withdrew it and read the typed words. My scalp tingled as sweat broke out.

The bill read "services rendered." The amount listed was easily five times the check I'd had Rainey send King.

"You want my professional advice?" The disdain on Rainey's face gave a good idea what she'd say.

"I don't guess it matters because I don't have this kind

of money. Not after all the other stuff I did." I folded the invoice and put it back in the envelope, offering it to Rainey.

She waved it off. "King has no right to expect anything, especially not the amount of that invoice, from you." The cords in her neck tightened, and fury crossed her face. "No right at all." She shut the trunk of her car too hard. "Where are you and the rest of your con artist family camped?" She crossed her arms over her chest and squinted her eyes at me.

"Outside Shreveport." My family had flat out refused to cross into Burns County. Our mutual ancestor had been lynched in Gaslight City by a bunch of witch haters. Her descendants feared Burns County the way some folks fear boogeymen in closets. My great-uncle Cecil, who'd taken me in like a prodigal daughter, had expended considerable hot air trying to convince me to conduct the sale of Memaw's property online. But I'd come anyway in hopes of talking with Hannah, to see if I could salvage some part of our friendship.

"Get on out of the county before dark." Rainey settled her direct gaze on me. Something in her eyes chilled me, made me sort of want to leave.

I checked my phone and shoved it back into my pocket. "I want to see Hannah, but I can't get her to answer her phone."

Rainey sucked in a deep breath and stiffened. She'd done that every time I mentioned Hannah. I didn't understand the problem. If Hannah wanted no more to do with me, why didn't Rainey just tell me? She'd never cared about hurting my feelings before.

The blat of a motorcycle echoed off the buildings. Before I turned away from Rainey, I saw her shoulders relax. What had her in such a twist? The old Rainey would have encouraged me to go out to Long Time Gone and eat King Tolliver a new asshole for sending that stupid invoice. She wouldn't have said get out of town before dark.

The motorcycle cruised toward us, sunlight winking off the iron horse's chrome. The driver's massive body came into view. Wade. My face stretched into a big, goofy smile, and I forgot about Rainey, stepped off the curb, and began waving.

Wade Hill pulled to the curb. I threw myself at him and hugged him as though it had been more than a couple of months since we last saw each other. He hugged me back, laughing into my hair.

I broke the hug and planted a kiss on his cheek. The part of his cheeks not covered by his gray-shot black beard reddened. "I thought you were tied up today with Six Gun Revolutionary business."

"I pulled a diva fit. Told King I was damn sure going to see you before you got out of town." Wade took off his sunglasses and tucked them into the neck of his leather jacket. The skin around his left eye was puffed out and beginning to bruise.

"King do that to you for coming to see me?" I didn't need Wade's confirmation. Not after seeing King's bill for services rendered. I had his services rendered. Sure did. I'd shove them right up his hairy old ass.

"Doesn't matter. We're together now." Wade glanced at Rainey, something moving behind his dark gaze. I followed it and saw something almost like fear cross Rainey's exotic features. She covered it quickly.

"I've got to prepare for court." She walked to her car and started climbing inside but stopped and turned back to speak to me. "If you need anything else, come by the office." She waved and drove off.

Wade frowned. He caught me watching and plastered a smile on his face. It didn't reach his eyes. "New fried chicken place on your way out of town. Let's go get some food. I'm about to starve." Instead of giving me a chance to answer, Wade started his motorcycle. Shouting over the thing was impossible. I started my truck and did as he said.

———

WADE LIED. The place we went to eat wasn't just a fried chicken place. They served a full country meal. I closed my eyes as I bit into my second piece of fried chicken. It actually had flavor.

"You act like you haven't eaten in a month." Wade scooped up a forkful of the creamiest mashed potatoes I'd had since Memaw died.

"You don't understand. You have to find a little hole in the wall town to get a meal like this. Restaurants in big cities have to cater to a diverse crowd. The majority of the food has about as much taste as—" I stopped speaking as a bony hand closed over my shoulder.

"Hey, girl." The nasally drawl came from behind me,

but I didn't have to see Tubby Tubman to know his voice or the feel of his skinny hand. "I didn't know you's coming to town." Tubby sat in the extra chair without being invited and grinned like a little boy up to no good.

"Why would I tell you I'm coming to town?" I finished my chicken and started on my collard greens.

Tubby shrugged and reached one skinny, tattooed arm across the table. He snagged a cornbread muffin and set about putting honey on it. Wade glowered at him but said nothing.

"Might be I thought we'd renewed our friendship after I helped you find the Mace Treasure." He ate the cornbread and licked honey off his fingers.

I thought about it and nodded. "Okay. I'll buy that."

Tubby grinned again and slid his cold blue eyes over me. "Might be you still owe me a favor."

I rolled my eyes and ate another forkful of collards. "Why can't we just say we saved each other's asses and leave it there? I mean, if you really want to be friends again."

Tubby considered it and reached for another cornbread muffin.

Wade grabbed his arm and shoved it away. "What do you really want, Tubman?"

"Talk to Peri Jean." Tubby withdrew his arm. "Heard she might be in need of a friend right now."

"What's that mean?" Wade wiped his mouth, wadded the napkin, and threw it at the table.

"Heard Peri Jean's trying to get in touch with pretty Hannah Kessler." Tubby grabbed my iced tea and took a sip before I could stop him. Good thing I was finished with it.

"Who told you that?" Wade's voice sharpened in warning. He shifted in his chair, one hand gripping the edge of the table. I stopped shoving down my collard greens to watch Wade. If I didn't know better, I'd think I saw actual fear in his dark eyes. Tubby might annoy Wade, but scaring him was another matter.

"See, I heard Peri Jean called up to the museum this morning and asked for pretty Hannah." Tubby grabbed the last piece of chicken off Wade's plate. Wade slapped at him, but Tubby hurried the food to his mouth and bit into it. "My cousin's daughter's the one answering phones there now," he said around a half-chewed mouthful of chicken.

The girl who answered the museum's landline told me Hannah didn't come into the museum during business hours any more. She suggested I call Hannah's phone if I had the number. I didn't tell her I'd been trying Hannah's phone for months.

"Okay, Tub." I tried to act casual, wiping my mouth with the cloth napkin and rearranging my silverware next to my empty plate without making eye contact. I liked to think I had experience with the right way to handle Tubby.

He and I had met the day my parents rented a cheap mobile home two houses down from his family when I was three years old. We went through school together and had a quick romance in our early twenties. After that, he stayed out of my life unless he was in trouble or wanted to cause trouble. Sad experience taught me not to fight him. "How do I get in touch with Hannah?"

"That'll cost you." His bow-shaped lips curved into that crafty grin he'd been giving since we were both barely out of diapers.

"Nope. We're friends." I patted his leg under the table.

He flushed to the roots of his hair and put his hand over mine. "Okay. Friends. You'll find Ms. Hannah Kessler out at Long Time Gone, hanging out with your good buddies, the Six Gun Revolutionaries."

Shock blossomed in my stomach and sent shock waves rolling throughout my body. I turned to Wade. Red crept out of his collar, up his face, and spread to his hairline. A mist of sweat glowed on his forehead.

"Heard she been dating King Tolliver." Tubby's voice had a gleeful ring. My food congealed into a lump of grease in my stomach. Stinging bile crawled up my throat. I put my hand over my mouth. Tubby glanced at me. Some of the light went out of his blue eyes. "That's why Mr. Motorcycle Man is in such a hurry to get you out of town. Ask him."

I didn't need to ask. Tubby was right. Both Wade and Rainey had been pushing me out of town as fast as they could. Now I knew why. Somehow I'd managed to get on King's shit list. Details clicked into place, suddenly full of meaning.

The exorbitant invoice King sent through Rainey. The deepening bruises on Wade's face. Both qualified as irritants, but they weren't anything I'd retaliate over. The invoice could go unpaid. Wade's bruised up face pissed me off, but Wade chose the Six Guns and all that came with them.

But King's taking advantage of Hannah after she'd been through hell qualified as a slap in the face. It made me see red. *Time to hit back.* I turned to Wade and raised my eyebrows. "Got anything to tell me?"

Wade ground his teeth together. "Swear to God, Tubman, you better hope you never meet me on a dark night. I will flatten you to nothing. Now get your bony ass out of my sight."

Tubby slid one arm over my shoulders and pulled me to him. I was too shocked to resist. He leaned close and brushed a kiss across my lips. A flutter went through me, shocking and horrifying me. I'd thought myself long past succumbing to Tubby Tubman's unique charm. "Later, friend." He stood from the table and left.

Wade got up and stomped to the cash register, digging in his pocket. He paid for the food, shoving open the exit door so hard it banged the building. Tires squealed as someone, probably Tubby, burned rubber getting out of there. I pushed my chair back and hurried after Wade. He stood next to his motorcycle with his head hanging. I grabbed his arm and made him face me.

"Why didn't you tell me?" I stared into the dark eyes I loved and trusted.

"I'm protecting you." He glared down at me. Streaks of red still darkened his cheekbones.

I wanted to throw my arms up in frustration and struggled to keep my voice below a shout. "Hannah needs someone to protect her right now. It's one thing for you not to want to help her yourself, but why not tell me what was going on?"

He shook his head. I noticed his eye again. It had swollen to a slit and was darkening. I knew the answer in a sudden, sick rush. Not the specifics, no. But I knew the source of Wade's silence, and it was King Tolliver.

Wade gripped my shoulders. He could have probably pulped the bones but didn't. "*You're* my priority. Hannah, bless her, is never going to be okay again. She can't drag you down with her. I can't survive that." He took one hand off my shoulder to press against his chest.

"A couple of months ago, you drove four hours to come to my rescue. You didn't know what the problem was. You just wanted to help me. Now I need to save Hannah." King beat Wade up for coming to be with me. The information flashed in my brain like a neon sign in the rain, fueling a stream of smoking fury. I closed the distance between us. "Tell me what's going on. Please." Gently as I could, I rubbed my thumb under his wounded eye.

It was too much. He jerked away from me, took a big step back. "Nothing that's any of your business. This here's between me and King." He jabbed a thumb at his face.

Anger spurred my heart into fast gear. My words came out before I thought them over. "Nobody fucks with you or Hannah. Not even if their name is King Tolliver." Just saying what I thought ignited a fire in my belly.

Wade's expression went hard and mulish. "You can't just barge in Long Time Gone and start telling King his business. It'll blow up bigger than you ever imagined anything could."

I raised my eyebrows. "You watch me. I don't back down to anybody."

Wade shook his head and gusted a sigh. "You don't understand."

I jammed my hands onto my hips, not caring if I looked just like Memaw. "Make me understand."

"All right. Have you ever stepped in a big pile of shit and got it in the grooves of your shoes?" Wade glared at me.

"What does that have to do with—"

He held up one hand. "Just bear with me. You know how you step in shit, and by the time you get it off your shoes, it's everywhere—the doorknob, the paper towel roll in the kitchen, even on the ceiling of your closet?"

I couldn't help but chuckle. "So what?"

"So that's what it's going to be like if you get in King's face. The mess is just going to keep spreading until it's everywhere in your life." Wade delivered this warning with both his hands spread wide.

"But there's one good thing about shit, handsome." I tried to smile. "It washes off."

"Not this shit." Something akin to fear moved behind Wade's dark eyes. This was the second time I'd seen it in our short visit. "You don't want King Tolliver for an enemy."

What was he so afraid of? A fight? I didn't get it. "That's where you're wrong." Pride, the fuel of every fight I'd ever had, swelled in my chest. "It's King who doesn't want me for an enemy."

"King fights dirty. Who and what are you willing to burn to the ground to win?" Wade swung one leg over his

Harley Davidson. Discussion over. Either he'd given up on me or wanted to beat me to Long Time Gone.

"I won't have to hurt anybody, except maybe King." I pulled my truck keys out of my pocket and used the remote to unlock the door. "After the amount of money he's trying to bully out of me for his 'services rendered' on the Michael Gage matter, I ain't gonna be shy about telling him how it is."

Wade shook his head and started his motorcycle. He sprayed gravel leaving the parking lot.

2

———

WADE BEAT me to Long Time Gone. He sat on his Harley and watched me try to find a place to park my huge truck in the dirt lot. The little area next to the old smokehouse that had been here back when this was a homestead was the only place it fit, where I knew I could get it out.

The smokehouse gave me the creeps. Not only did it carry an odor of old smoke and spoiled meat, it always felt alive in some way. I suspected it was haunted but never had the brass to investigate. I scrambled out of my ride and scurried toward Long Time Gone.

A strong wind rattled through the pine trees, deepening that smoke and meat gone over odor. The long, wooden building that housed the bar seemed miles away. I took the last steps running and soon was even with Wade.

"Please don't do this." His eyes, liquid obsidian, bored into my worries and shook them awake.

"I help people. Especially friends."

"Hannah's not my friend," he muttered and got off the motorcycle.

"Yeah, but I am." I marched toward the front door and grabbed the big handle to pull it open. Wade's hand slapped down on it and pushed it closed again.

"The Hannah you knew is gone." He gripped one of my shoulders. A burning current of desire shivered through me. Damn it, I wanted this man in the worst way.

I shook both the thoughts and Wade's hand off. "She ain't either. Besides, I'm here on your behalf too."

He put his hand back on my shoulder and turned me to face him. He cupped my face with both hands and tilted it up so our eyes met. His thumbs caressed my cheeks. "Michael Gage and Nash Redmond killed Hannah. They gut shot her mind, so it'll take her forever to die, and nobody can help her. I'm the same. I laid out my bed with the Six Guns a long time ago, and I deserve what I get."

"No." I pulled away and burst through the door. The smell hit me like a kick in the chest. Yeasty, stale beer and puke. I took a step backward, hand going to my nose. My eyes adjusted. I wasn't alone in the dark entry hall. Corman had both arms wrapped around Candy Pistol, his mouth against hers.

He broke off the kiss and faced me, lip curling with disgust. Wade came in behind me. Corman's eyes shot to him. "What's she doing here? She can't be here." His voice rose on the last two words.

"Because Daddy said so?" I made my voice high and sweet, enjoying the fury darkening Corman's face.

"Because *I* said so." His hand, covered in rings and

tattoos, flashed out to grab my arm.

I reached into the old boards at my feet and let a flash of magic flow through me and into Corman. He cried out and jerked his hand back. Smoke drifted from his fingertips.

"Fucking witch," he hissed.

"Pencil dick." I brushed past him and strode into the main area of the bar. Dim, neon-tinged light flickered from the bar, casting the room in gloomy shadow. The only other light came from white Christmas lights strung around the raised stage where cut-rate bands sometimes played. Nobody was playing now. Red dirt country music twanged from the jukebox.

Several members of the Six Gun Revolutionaries turned to stare. Most of them clenched their faces into the same puckered butthole look Corman had adopted upon seeing me. All conversation stopped, and the sound of pool balls clacking in the back reached my ears. I pretended to ignore them all and slowly surveyed the open, booth-lined room.

Hannah's flame-colored hair blazed in the glow of the red neon beer sign hanging over the bar. She sat spraddle-legged on a barstool, back hunched, elbows dug into the bar. The Hannah I had known would never sit like this in public. She'd sit poised and perfect like she was at one of her starched undies social gatherings. And her clothes. My Hannah would never have worn filthy jeans and a faded T-shirt four sizes too big in public. Who was this person? Dread pressing against my heart, I took a deep breath and made a beeline for her.

Five feet from her, I got a good look and stopped. Hannah's transformation shocked the righteous fury out of me. Always slim, she'd crossed the line into skeletal. Her collarbone stood out like a scythe connecting to her shoulder. Scabs covered the bony backs of her hands, mingling with mystery sores and bruises crawling up her arms.

And a tattoo. Hannah had never expressed interest in a permanent marking. This one was a wicked skull and crossbones, something I'd have never imagined Hannah getting. If ever there were a woman who'd be perfect for tattooed butterflies and flowers, it was my old buddy Hannah Kessler. Talk about alternate universes. I gathered my determination and made myself close the last couple of feet separating us.

"Hey." I touched her shoulder. My black opal flashed to life. Magic jolted through me, the force of it shoving my hand away.

Hannah turned to me. My mouth dropped open. Hannah's warm caramel eyes, usually tastefully made up, were ringed in so much eyeliner, they made my tramp tracks look like something a Sunday school teacher would wear. The eyes behind all that makeup were foggy and unfocused, and no recognition showed in them. She didn't even know me.

Hannah held a lime in one hand and a shot of clear liquid in the other. The citrusy smell of tequila hit me. We stared at each other. I saw what Wade meant. All the sweet warmth and silliness that had made Hannah herself was absent. The woman before me was a shell, a home to misery and self-loathing. She was dying slow.

Salty tears closed my throat. Seeing my dear friend like this, so broken and fucked up, sent sorrow to burrow deep in my heart. The hurt of it emanated out in waves harsher than the Texas sun.

King Tolliver slammed a full bottle of tequila down on the bar in front of Hannah. "Told you I had one more bottle of the good shit." He bared his cheese-colored teeth in a shit-eating grin, engrossed in cutting off the foil sealing the bottle closed. He popped the cork and glanced at Hannah for the first time.

His smile faded as he took stock of Hannah and followed her gaze to me. King and I glared at each other for several long seconds. I waited for him to say something, anything, so I could smart off and start the fight. Once I had feared King. But I'd seen death, shook his hand, and felt his cold lips on my cheek. We'd danced, death and I, and I survived. King was little compared to that.

"Let's have us a drink." King poured two shots of tequila, ignoring me. He and Hannah licked the salt off their hands, slammed the shots, and sucked on their limes. She set her glass down, and King immediately refilled it. His dead eyes slid over me. Warning flashed in them. I smiled at him and winked.

"Why haven't you returned my calls?" I tugged on the sleeve of Hannah's too large shirt, which I now recognized as one of King's, and winced at the odor coming off her. Unwashed body and stale hair. My bestie's skid into darkness opened a deep, empty chasm in my emotions. "Hannah?" I whispered.

She slowly raised her head and locked confused eyes

on mine. We stared at each other for several long seconds. That chasm in my emotions yawned in front of me, beckoning me to fall in, never to be heard from again. The beginnings of fear stirred in my midsection. The black opal gave me another warning ping. Hannah's eyes sharpened, their warm depths freezing into hard ice. The black opal pulsed on my chest several times. Then Hannah's eyes went dull again. She slumped and let out a relieved sigh. What was going on here? I'd had enough farting around and was about to find out.

"Take a short walk outside with me. The air might do you some good." I wrangled her off the stool and dragged her toward the front door. She staggered along with me at first but yanked her arm away before I could get her outside.

The black opal pulsed magic on my chest. I took a good look around the corners of the room, expecting to see a lost spirit. There was nothing but dust and maybe some drying puke. The black opal warmed until it burned. Magic tickled its way through my hair, making it bristle like the hair on a dog's back. Hannah. It was coming from Hannah. I focused on her, opening my second sight as much as I could in such a tense situation. Without meaning to or planning to, I leaned into her face.

That hard chill darkened her eyes again. Her upper lip curled into a snarl. A cold, oily voice issued from her dry and cracked lips. "Your own darkness will swallow you. Fuck off, or I'll make it happen even faster."

I recoiled. Where the hell did that come from? The voice, devoid of sympathy or emotion, reverberated like the last bass notes of a death metal song. It fluttered against all my nightmares and insecurities, caressing them until they hurt. There was no Hannah at all in that voice. Fear stole over me. My instincts told me to run, to get out of here as fast as I could, but I couldn't move.

Hannah's eyes flickered back to confused puddles of melted caramel, and she rocked on her feet. "I don't want to talk. I talked and talked and talked in that overpriced damn hospital in Florida." She glanced back at the bar. "I'm all talked out. I'm thirsty now."

King watched from the behind the bar, hairy arms crossed over his chest. His brows knotted up like thunderclouds boiling before a storm. It wouldn't be long before he got in on the action. Once King and I locked horns, getting Hannah out of here would be near impossible.

"Then let me buy you food. You need some food in your stomach." I couldn't quite make myself touch her again. Instead, I rested the tips of my fingers on my black opal for comfort.

"Listen to me. You escaped Michael Gage relatively unscathed. I didn't. The only time I feel safe is when I'm with that man behind the bar. The only time I can sleep is when I'm so drunk I pass out. I need this." She stopped speaking and held onto the wall, breathing hard.

"Sweetie? I got your next shot poured," King yelled. Hannah lurched back toward the bar. King raised one hand and moved his fingers the same way you shoo away a stray cat. I knew the signal. It was for drunks King wanted out of the bar. I wasn't surprised when Wade grabbed my arm and spun me around to face him.

"Get her out of here," King yelled at Wade.

"Come on." Wade stared at the wall behind me. "Don't make me force you."

"I can't let him get away with this." I tried to brush Wade's hand off. It stayed where it was.

"Please," he mumbled, still unable to look at me.

I glanced toward the bar. Hannah leaned forward and kissed King Tolliver's ugly lips. Something broke open in my heart and oozed bottomless gloom. I tore my arm out of Wade's grasp and sprinted for the bar, almost forgetting that ugly, bitter cold voice.

King saw me coming in the mirror behind the bar. The stony expression on his face never changed. He reached beneath the bar, took out the shotgun he kept there, and pointed it at me. "Stop." He didn't bother to shout. The gun did all the talking he needed to do. We both knew he'd use it.

I slid to a stop and stood still, too shocked to call on the mantle and make that thing blow up in his hands.

"Get out." King put his finger on the trigger. "You're banned for life."

"You cowardly shit. Send me a bill like I owe you something. Fuck you in the dick hole with an icepick." My shouts rang out in the quiet bar. I glanced into the mirror to see how Hannah was taking all this, praying she'd get up and follow me out. I never even saw the expression on her face. All I saw was the thing perched on her shoulders.

It was solid matte black with a hunched back. Wide, flappy ears stuck out from its head, and a long crooked nose dominated its face. Its eyes flicked to mine in the mirror. The thing's lips stretched, and it bared its jagged teeth in a smile. Fear froze me an inch at a time. The black opal sent ping after ping of magic into my skin. I stood rigid, unable to process anything.

Priscilla Herrera appeared behind me in the mirror. The thing's eyes widened for just a second at the sight of her. The two glared at each other. The magic pinging through my black opal grew. It made sense, considering the source of my power came from Priscilla's gift. The power swelled. The thing on Hannah's back hissed. Behind me, Priscilla hissed back. This was about to get so bad.

Wade gripped me around the waist and lifted me. Too shocked to fight, I let him carry me out of the bar, still slack-jawed at that awful thing riding Hannah's back.

King's voice followed me out. "Come back here, and I'll kill you."

———

Wade dragged me to my truck. He outweighed me by over a hundred pounds and was taller than me by more than a foot. There was no way I could do anything other than go. He let go of me, dug in my bag, got out my keys, and used the remote to unlock it. "Get in."

"Is that monster the reason you won't help Hannah?" I couldn't shake the sight of it.

Wade snorted. "King Tolliver saved my life when nobody else would lift a finger to help me. My loyalty to him goes beyond a broken woman hell-bent on destroying herself." Wade took in the expression on my face and quit speaking.

"I'm not talking about King." The image of that *thing* appeared again. All the spit in my mouth dried up. I tried to swallow and choked. Coughs and gags wracked my body, and I bent double. Wade pounded my back.

"What's wrong?" His voice squeaked with fear.

I pushed his hand away and dug in the backseat for a bottle of water. A few sips soothed my throat. I leaned on the seat and stared at Wade.

"You're telling me you didn't see it?"

He shook his head, confusion evident. "I don't know what you mean."

I took the black opal necklace off and handed it to him. "Put it on."

"What are we talking about here?" He made no effort to take the necklace.

"Put the necklace on, go back inside, and look at Hannah in the bar mirror. Then, come back out and tell me what you see." I pushed the necklace at him, about ready to shove it up his big ass.

"I don't..." He took one look at my face, slipped the necklace over his head, and walked back to the bar, probably to keep me from chewing him up any worse.

I lit a cigarette and watched the door. A minute passed, then two. I drank some more of my water and waited. Would Wade just leave me sitting out here? Maybe. The necklace didn't matter. The black opal would find its way home. The idea of Wade blowing me off bothered me more than anything. If he hid in the bar until I left, would our friendship end? A stray thought came into existence. If the friendship ended, it might be a relief to us both. I shook off the thought. My desire for Wade went too deep for that.

Caw. Caw. Caw. Orev, my raven familiar, flapped to a low hanging branch and perched there. He cocked his head at me.

"What is it? You got something to say?"

Orev made soft sounds.

I couldn't have explained how I knew what he wanted, but I did. I reached out to him. Our minds connected, and fragmented scenes flashed behind my eyes.

A dusty white road with a stooped figure walking. Orev flies past, swooping low. The thing twists to face him. The face I saw in Long Time Gone's mirror looms close long enough for me to recognize it. Orev flies away.

It is dusk of the same day. A dark shadow perches on an open windowsill. Orev flies closer and perches in the trees. The dark shadow turns, silhouetting the ugly sloped head and floppy ears. The thing hisses as though it realizes Orev is up to no good.

The thing climbs through the open window and steals along the baseboards until it reaches the crib. Little arms and legs kick and wave.

Its intent boils over me. I try to go after it, but Orev holds me back. This is the past, and I cannot interrupt.

The thing, now nothing more than a dark shadow, climbs up the wall and over the edge of the crib. The baby makes only one sound, a surprised squeak. Then nothing.

Time jumps again. It's morning. A woman wearing a night-gown and a bonnet comes into the room, smiling and cooing.

She leans over the baby bed and screams, long and agonizing. A man rushes into the room and lifts a desiccated husk out of the bed.

Rage fills me as I process what happened. The poor baby had no way to defend itself. That thieving monster fed on it until nothing was left.

The vision ended, and I became aware of Wade's voice.

"Wake up. I saw it." He shook me.

I jerked out of the vision, dragged my eyes open, and gasped at Wade's appearance, eyes wild, face several shades paler than when he went in. His huge hands trembled when he took off the necklace and dropped it in my lap.

Caw. Caw. Caw. Understanding flashed over me. Orev wanted Wade to see a vision of the monster attached to Hannah. I reached for Wade's hand. He stiffened and shook his head. Orev flew closer, flapping his wings in Wade's face. My friend ducked away and raised his arms over his head. *Caw. Caw. Caw.*

"You'll have to," I told Wade. Once Orev made up his mind, he didn't quit. I reached for his hand again. This time he let me.

A curvy woman sleeps on her stomach, moonlight streaming into her window, TV playing in the background. A dark shadow rises from the floor and streaks over the bed like moving smoke.

It forms into the ugly hunched monster and perches on the woman's back. It leans forward until its mouth almost touches the woman. Its sides expand as it breathes in. Then it turns to smoke again and drifts into her ear. The woman weeps in her sleep, tears soaking into the pillow.

Time jumps. The same woman, now nothing more than skin and bones, her arms covered with the scabs of a spiker, stumbles down a trash-littered street. She passes graffiti covered buildings. A car slows next to her. The person inside says something. The woman nods and gets inside.

Time jumps a few hours. It's the wee hours of the night. The woman leans against a dirt-streaked wall, belt choking the veins on one arm. Green vomit trails from her mouth.

"No!" Wade jerked his hand from mine. His chest heaved with each gasp. He raised trembling hands to his face and turned away from me.

"Did you know her?" The force of his reaction puzzled me. The woman's demise, just like the baby's, made me angry and sad. This thing had stolen their normal lives away, as though it deserved their lives more than they did. But Wade was truly upset.

He kept his hands over his face, but his voice came through. "Oh, Riley. I'm sorry I blew you off." Sobs followed his words.

Riley? Wade didn't like talking about his past. The most I'd ever gotten out of him was that he had a lot of brothers and sisters and his parents were alcoholics. Riley must have been part of that silent past.

I didn't know the right thing to do. Some men got offended if a woman acknowledged they'd shown emotion. But wouldn't sitting there in my truck like a prima donna be just as insensitive? My heart ached for whatever made Wade hurt like this. I slid out of the truck and put one hand on his back and stroked. He came no closer, but he didn't shove me away either. He took a deep breath and cut off the waterworks like he'd pushed a button.

"Was Riley one of your sisters?" Then I blurted out, "Never mind. You don't have to talk about it."

"Not my sister." He swiped a hand over his eyes and took a shaking breath. "You remember when we first met I told you my sweetie married somebody else while I was in the Marines?"

I nodded, shamefully eager to know Wade's secrets.

"Riley married heroin, not another guy. I came home on leave and found her all fucked up and skinny." He hung his head and slumped. "I just couldn't deal with it, you know? So I blew her off. Told her not to write or call any more. She laughed in my face. Got a letter a few months later from my oldest sister, Desiree, saying she was dead."

After wanting to know Wade better for so long, to learn such a tragic story, and to see the ugliness of his guilt over it, shook me.

"Hannah reminded me of the way Riley was the last time I saw her. It made me just not want to look at her. But seeing that, knowing that monster in there changed Riley from the girl I loved to a walking husk...I'm a selfish prick for not trying harder." He squeezed his eyes shut and clenched his fists so hard the knuckles turned white.

There was nothing I could say to make it better. He'd berate himself for his actions until the day he died. Regret hurts like hell when we stub our toes on it.

"I was wrong to tell you to walk away from Hannah,

and I am so sorry for that." He took another long, shuddering breath and pulled his shoulders back.

Wade could have helped me help Hannah long before now. But being angry with him wouldn't solve anything, so I shook my head to let him know it was all right. "I don't know what that thing's doing to her. According to those visions, it's going to kill her. But I don't know what it is or how to get rid of it."

Wade glanced back at the bar and made a sick face. "I think it's a hag. I remember Aunt DeeDee talking about them." Wade's Aunt DeeDee had been his magical mentor. "She said they come at night to ride their victims while they're sleeping. They can steal a baby's life force."

Cold worked its way through my body at the memory of the first vision.

"But Aunt DeeDee said they can also make their victims do all sorts of self-destructive things. Poor Hannah." Wade dragged his cigarettes out and lit one. He kicked at the ground.

Time for him to snap out of it and get to work. "How do we help her?" I said.

Wade's face creased. "I never saw Aunt DeeDee get rid of one of these things. She'd just warn people against them, tell them to put screens on their windows. I'd say you're looking at banishment. Exorcism if you know a priest." Wade glanced at Long Time Gone. Someone turned on the outside lights. He turned his gaze back on me. "We need to get Hannah by herself to help her. That's gonna be like a magic trick. King's draining Hannah's bank accounts faster than shit runs through a short pipe. He ain't gonna let us near Hannah. Worse, she's not in control of herself enough to help us help her."

I glared at the building. "Let's drag her out. I can't do it by myself, but you and me—"

Wade began shaking his head, face already closed. "If I go against King, I'm a traitor to the club."

I wanted to kick Wade, wanted to blame someone for letting this happen to Hannah. But the real blame lay on me. None of it would have happened had she not known me. Wade's foot-dragging was just an obstacle, an easily circumvented one if I was honest with myself.

Wade's phone chirped his text message alert. He checked it and rolled his eyes. "King's says he's about to call you."

My phone started ringing, and I hit the answer button but said nothing.

"Come at me again, and there won't even be nothing left of her to scrape off the floor." King kept his voice at a low growl. I guessed he was still near Hannah but trying to keep her from hearing. He didn't need to worry. She was too drunk. "Then I'll kill Wade Hill and make you watch."

Panic flashed like heat lightning in my stomach. Thunderous rage followed close behind. Six months ago, I'd have lost control and screamed threats about how I'd dig out King's eyeballs with a hot spoon, how I'd castrate him with dirty glass. Now I ended the call and put my phone back into my pocket. Because I knew I was on camera, I struggled to keep my face impassive. I wouldn't give King the satisfaction of knowing it felt like ice had formed around my heart.

Wade's phone buzzed again. "King says to make you leave now. I guess there's no use asking you to get on out of town."

"I'll be at Rainey's if she'll have me." I climbed in the truck and started it. I wanted to scream at Wade to get away from the Six Gun Revolutionaries and to bring Hannah with him. But I didn't. I had a mighty fine line to walk if I wanted to end this thing without getting Wade or Hannah killed.

Wade stomped back toward the bar and disappeared inside. I drove out of the parking lot before King sent someone meaner than Wade out to run me off. As I drove, I puzzled over what happened between King and me. He was too pissed off for this to just be over Hannah, and I couldn't understand what had changed between us. Even his refusal of my tribute money confused me.

It didn't much matter. I had to get that ugly, hatchet-nosed hag off Hannah's back without getting Wade killed. Because if the Six Gun Revolutionaries killed Wade or Hannah, I was going to kill them. Longer and harder than they dreamed possible. As it was, I might kill them anyway. Nobody fucks with my friends.

The yellow lines on the highway led me back to Gaslight City. At a four-way-stop, I saw something that gave me an idea. The nice deputy tipped his cowboy hat at me. I waved and drove straight to the sheriff's office. Dean and Hannah had been friends a long time. Maybe he would help.

3

I WALKED into the sheriff's office and stopped in my tracks. Was this the right place? The awful seventies paneling had been replaced with sheetrock painted soothing colors, the trim painted stark white. The no-color linoleum had been updated with vinyl flooring designed to look like hardwood. Someone had paid a pretty penny to make the interior of the sheriff's office match the historic building it was housed in.

"May I help you?" A middle-aged woman peeked out from behind her computer monitor.

"Sheriff Turgeau in?" I glanced at her nameplate. Cheryl Hanse. Didn't know her.

"What's your business, ma'am?" Cheryl scooted back in her chair so she could rest her mud-colored eyes on me.

"The sheriff and I are old friends. I wanted to say hi." My cheeks heated. Dean wouldn't be happy to see me. He hadn't liked me when we dated, and he wasn't going to start liking me now.

"Miz Peri Jean." Deputy Brittany Watson emerged from an elaborately framed doorway. Damn, the whole place looked like a tourist center or a high-end bed and breakfast.

"Hey, girl." I rushed to my old friend, who I used to babysit, and gave her a hug.

"What's up?" Her brow furrowed with concern. "You look upset."

"I need to talk to Dean. Think he'd see me?" I glanced toward the spot where the sheriff's private office used to be. It was still there but had been restyled with a fancy frame around the picture window. The blinds were drawn on the window, and the antique style door was closed.

"Sheriff Dean went home for the day." Brittany started to say something else but bit her lip.

"Sheriff Turgeau doesn't like us telling people he's at home." Cheryl Hanse frowned at Brittany.

I patted Brittany on the arm. "I won't tell him you spilled it. I'll just act like I was driving by."

I took a last look around the sheriff's office. Nicer than it had been, but like the rest of Gaslight City, it didn't feel like home anymore. I drove the few short miles to Dean's fifties-era bungalow and parked at the curb.

Miracles never ceased. He'd painted it a cheerful yellow with white trim. I walked up the freshly poured sidewalk and stared into the flowerbeds on either side of the front porch. Someone had cleaned them out and planted evergreen shrubs. The front door, formerly a buckled, chipped eyesore, had been replaced with a new metal door with stained glass panels. I punched the doorbell and jumped when it gonged inside the house. Damn thing used to just emit a sick little buzz like a dying water roach.

Footsteps on a hard floor approached, and a shadow appeared behind the stained glass. I fixed my face into what I hoped was a friendly smile. The door swung open. At first, all I saw was a pregnant belly. I dropped my purse and didn't even realize I had done it until I heard it clunk on the porch floor.

"Uh, honey?" The woman, whose scared eyes and puffy face looked vaguely familiar, glanced behind her.

"What?" Dean's voice came from behind her.

"You need to come to the door." She tried to smile at me but couldn't quit glancing down at my purse. I bent to pick it up.

"What is..." Dean trailed off when he saw me. "Peri Jean. Y-y-your hair's long now. You look..." He waved off whatever comment he'd been about to make and shook his head. "Why don't you come inside?" He gently guided the pregnant woman out of the doorway and stepped aside. Too weirded out to protest, I did what he suggested.

After refusing offers of everything from soft drinks to leftover barbecue, I sat on a brand new love seat in the den. Gone was the beat-up bachelor furniture. This new stuff screamed feminine good taste. The super-sized TV still took up too much of the room, but now it sat on a tasteful table, which had been polished to a warm glow. Dean and the pregnant woman sat on the matching couch.

He put his arm over her shoulders. "You remember Megan from my campaign, right?"

That's where I knew her from. I began to nod. The

teacher who'd had such big eyes for Dean, the same one I'd seen him with the night I met Nash Redmond. At least one of us had found true love or some semblance of it.

"Of course I remember you." I tried to smile and didn't have to see my reflection to know I missed it. Lying on a bed of poison-tipped nails would have been more comfortable than this encounter.

"I guess I look pretty different." She smoothed her hands over her baby bump.

I stared and tried to figure out how far along she was. Had she been pregnant when I saw her and Dean at Bug Juice six months ago? I thought so. A more horrible thought occurred to me. Had they been seeing each other before he broke up with me?

I glanced at Dean's face. He squirmed and hooked his finger in the neck of his shirt. Maybe. Just maybe. Did it matter? The image of Hannah sitting at that dingy bar, nasty King Tolliver feeding her tequila and who knew what else, came back. Nope. Didn't matter a bit. Hannah was all that mattered.

"How'd the sale of Miss Leticia's property go?" Dean tugged harder at the neck of his shirt.

"How'd you know?" I dragged my gaze off Megan's belly.

"Rainey told me this morning on our run." Dean's body looked like he still ran. For every inch of fluff Megan had gained, he looked to have gained another ridge of muscle.

I casually raked my gaze over him the same way he'd done me dozens of times. "They gave me a check. It's over."

"The way you lost the place still burns my ass." He took

his arm off Megan's shoulders and leaned forward, elbows on his legs, his usual posture when he really had something to say. "The fire inspector charged Joey Holze, his family, and his friends with arson not long after you left Gaslight City."

I knew this part from Rainey. No surprise. One of Joey's helpers had squealed out the whole story as soon as law enforcement closed in on her.

Dean, face darkening with anger, continued. "Joey ended up having to sell his house out by the lake and the one Scott and Felicia were living in to pay his legal costs. Whole family packed up and moved to some hick town south of Austin where Carly's got family."

I raised my eyebrows at the news but didn't speak. Dean was telling me this to let me know justice had been served, that I'd been avenged, but I just felt sad. So much lost—for Joey Holze, for his family, and for me.

"How can Dean and I help you?" Megan folded her hands in her lap and smiled at me. Her eyes, fish cold and nervously darting, gave away her true feelings. Did she really think Dean would jump at the chance to be with me again? She was kidding herself.

I wanted to speak to Dean alone. Telling Hannah's business in front of this stranger irked me. I bit my lip.

"Megan's my wife now." Dean's light blue eyes fixed on me. In them, I saw understanding of my feelings. We might have been wrong for each other, but we'd gotten to know each other well. "She'll keep whatever is said here to herself." He nudged his wife with his elbow. She gave me a quick nod.

"It's Hannah." I took a deep breath and spilled everything except for the hag I saw sitting on Hannah's shoulder. Dean would consider that part hocus-pocus garbage and shut down.

Dean began nodding well before I finished, his mouth fixed into a grim line. He let me talk myself out. "It kills me to say this, but there's not a lot I can do. She's a legal adult. If she wants to be there..." He shrugged.

"But what about King?" I waved one hand in the general direction of Long Time Gone. "He threatened both Hannah and Wade if I didn't fuck off."

Megan held up one hand like a crossing guard and fixed her mouth into a condescending smile. "Language."

We're all adults. And you probably screwed my boyfriend while he was still with me, you twit. I locked my mouth closed and took a deep breath. Oxygen in, urge to bust Megan's nose out.

Dean watched me, eyes narrowed. He knew my triggers. "Okay. I believe King threatened you. But do you have any witnesses? Did anybody other than you hear King Tolliver say—"

I cut him off. "No. It was on my phone." I scooted forward and glared at Dean. It was just like when we were dating. Fun times. Not.

Dean raised his eyebrows and shrugged, meaning his hands were tied.

"Hannah was lit up like a Christmas tree. Can't you arrest her for public intoxication?" Even the couple of hours it would take her to sober up and get out of jail might be enough to get that thing off her. A few hours of cold sobriety would remind her that King Tolliver was the bottom of the lake and Hannah Kessler was no catfish.

"I'm in a precarious situation." Dean held his hands a few inches apart. "The Six Gun Revolutionaries cooperate with me on a limited basis. If I start busting them—or their girlfriends—on piddly charges, they're going to make my job harder than it already is."

"So you're just going to let them have Hannah?" I glared into Dean's face and felt my power rising. If I got worked up enough, I could probably short out his big-assed TV. "She was your friend before you ever moved to Gaslight City. She helped you get a job as deputy here." My voice was rising. I forced myself to stop and take a deep breath.

"Miss Mace?" Megan spoke loudly and clearly, probably the way she did in her classroom. "I'm going to have to ask you to leave our home."

I stared at Dean. He put one hand to his forehead.

"Sweetie, how about some iced tea?" He tried to smile.

Megan narrowed her eyes and scooted several inches away from him. The tips of his ears turned red. I chuckled, and both of them scowled at me.

"I apologize for getting excited." It hurt to say the words because, really, I wanted kick Dean in the shin and fart in his wife's face. "Is there no way you can help me, Sheriff?"

Dean frowned and rubbed his mouth while he thought. "If you get her away from that sociopath, there won't be any charges filed, no matter how it goes down." We stared at each other a long second.

I stood. "I'll be in touch." I turned to Megan and held out my hand. "Keep him in line and good luck on motherhood." She gave my hand an unenthusiastic shake and mumbled a relieved-sounding goodbye.

I got in my truck and drove past Rainey's law office. Her Mercedes was gone. What was it with people in this town going home early today? I made a U-turn and headed toward her house.

———

I SPED down the two-lane highway to Rainey's subdivision, worry eating up most of my brain power. The motorcycle started out as a blip on the horizon. My body tightened at the sight of it. Had King sent someone after me? I had nothing for protection other than brass knuckles and a cigarette lighter.

The driver waved as he came closer. Then I saw his size. Wade. I relaxed. Wade passed me, turned around in the middle of the road, roared up behind me, swung around, and pulled off in front of a closed down convenience store. He motioned for me to join him.

What now? Fresh anxiety prickled the ends of my nerves, and every bad thing that could possibly have happened sped behind my eyes. Heart pounding and body burning from the inside out, I parked the truck next to his road hog and sat with him on the sidewalk running in front of the store's boarded-up plate glass windows.

"How'd you know where to find me?" I knew Wade's mojo bag probably led him here but thought he only used it when I was in distress. Though the afternoon had overqualified as truly shitty, nothing horrible or unexpected had happened.

"Figured you'd ask Sheriff Dean for help. Drove by. Sure enough, there's your behemoth truck." He gave me the kind of grin that made me want to kick him. "I knew he wouldn't do shit and guessed you'd hit up Rainey next. Came out here to wait." He winked at me.

"And King let you go running off after me?" I didn't believe it for a second.

Wade shook his head. "King sent me out on a tequila run. That bottle you watched him open? Gone."

I didn't know what to say. Across the two-lane road, an orange-burnished sun hung over an overgrown pasture, painting the grass with shadows and golden-hued promise. Sunsets usually put the day in soft focus, hinted that tomorrow might be better. But I'd learned too much on this horrible day to fall for that kind of bullshit. I stared into spreading shadows and saw nothing but darkness coming to swallow me up.

I zipped my jacket up to my neck and lit a cigarette, too aware of my leg pressing against Wade's and the heat of him. A silly fantasy, maybe brought on by the sunset, played in my head. In it, Hannah didn't need my help. Instead, Wade declared his undying love and begged me to ride off into the sunset with him. I snorted at how stupid it was. Things never worked out like that in real life.

In real life, I needed to figure out a way to tell Wade that King was willing to kill him. I needed to find a way to save Hannah. And I didn't have a solid plan for doing either one.

"You upset?" Wade's deep voice vibrated against me.

"Huh?" Of course I was upset. Two of my dearest friends were in mortal danger.

"Yeah, you are. I should have told you Dean got married to a pregnant woman. You want to tell me off, I'll take it." Ah, Wade was talking about Dean and his stupid wife. I hadn't even thought about how his marriage and impending fatherhood made me feel.

My visit to Dean and his new wife's nice little home had been weird and embarrassing, sure. But everything that happened with Dean was weird and embarrassing. It was what I got for blindly latching on to him just because he was stable, honest, and wore a pretty wrapper. And because the sex was good. Can't forget that last one. It kept me in the relationship long after I should have left.

I remembered Wade had asked if I was upset. "Why would I be upset? Dean and I have been done for months."

Wade shrugged, the momentum of it moving my shoulder too. "Don't give me that shit. It's one thing to break up with somebody. It's another to know they're having a kid with somebody else."

He was right. This new chapter of Dean's life didn't just shut the door on the relationship he had with me. It burned down the house. I let out a sigh I hadn't realized I was holding in. "Dean and I were wrong for each other in about six thousand ways. I never thought we'd get back together, but going in that house, seeing them there..."

Wade said, "You feel left behind."

I couldn't tell Wade what really bothered me. It had too much to do with him. Seeing Dean married and expecting his first child contrasted sharply, painfully, with my own nonexistent love life. If stubborn, neurotic Dean could find lasting love, and I couldn't, how much worse did that make me? Answers, none of them good, flooded my mind.

I stopped the analysis of my shortcomings midway through. There was more to life than fiascos with men. And there were worse things than being alone. Dean was a great example. "Maybe I do feel left behind. But I don't want to be where Megan is right now, on a steady diet of Dean. Can you imagine raising a child with him?"

Wade chuckled. "Peri Jean, you're teaching this baby bad habits. It's lazy parenting. Let me show you what you're doing wrong."

A loud cackle escaped me. I clapped my cigarette-free hand over my mouth, but Wade threw back his head and bellowed at the sky. We laughed until I was out of breath and holding my sides, and Wade gasped for air.

I caught my breath. "Peri Jean, you're engaging in self-destructive behavior again. I thought we'd covered this. You're not a loser. Stop treating yourself like one."

When I'd started talking, I'd meant to inspire another gale of laughter. But Wade's giggles dried up as I talked. He sat staring at the dying sunset, which had gone a deep orange red with banks of charcoal-colored clouds spreading out from it. His eyes narrowed, and his lips thinned.

He spoke softly. "You're not a loser. You're just unformed. You're still figuring out where you're going."

I stared at his profile, marveling at the way the shadows played over his face like a mask, darkening some parts, highlighting others. "What about you? Have you figured out where you're going?"

Wade twisted to look at me. Our faces were so close together, his beard tickled me. My heart picked up speed. He slipped one arm around me. My pulse thundered in my throat, almost taking my breath away. This was it. He was going to kiss me. I parted my lips. He leaned closer until our lips brushed. I put one hand behind his neck and tried to deepen the kiss. He pulled away but left his arm around me.

"I'm already where I'm supposed to be. End of the line." His dark eyes locked on mine, and he ran one rough thumb over my jawline. I shuddered from his touch, considered begging, and clamped my lips shut. He turned away. "I need to get back to Long Time Gone."

"How long did you wait to see how I fared with Dean?" I forced a smile onto my face, even though I wanted to scream at him to run far away from King Tolliver. All they'd do was lead him down a long and winding road to a dead end. But in Wade's own words, that awful man and the Six Gun Revolutionaries were his life. Anything I said to the contrary would spark an argument. Not worth it until it had to happen.

"Doesn't matter. It was worth it to sit with you, to tell you I'm glad we're friends." Wade crushed his cigarette under one giant, black engineer boot. He pulled me to him again, dodged my lips, and gave me a firm kiss on my forehead. Then he stood and held out his hand. I took it and let him pull me to my feet. He went to my truck and held open the door. I climbed inside because I knew he'd put his hands on my waist when I did. He stood in the open door, and I really thought he'd kiss me again. Okay, it was just hoping.

Instead, he said, "We need to do something about Hannah fast. Call me mid-morning tomorrow. I'll cook you breakfast."

I nodded and started my truck. He slammed the door and ambled to his motorcycle. I watched him go through the ritual of starting it, planning to watch him until he drove away. But he looked up and motioned me to leave first. I did, but watched him in my rearview mirror until he got so small I couldn't see him anymore.

A painful dart stabbed into my heart as he disappeared. *Doesn't matter.* Wade's sister had read his cards and told him a relationship with me would spell disaster. What kind, he'd never said. But he made sure we both kept all our clothes on.

It smarted because I knew in my heart of hearts we could make things work. Wade's brokenness canceled out my brokenness. He knew the supernatural world, the world I'd finally, grudgingly, accepted. Most of all, I loved him in a way I'd have never been able to love Dean or any other man. I wanted to see where that took me, took both of us.

"Not gonna happen." My voice sounded weepy in the empty truck. I turned on the radio and found Bob Dylan singing "Tangled Up In Blue" behind a snow of static. I swallowed hard and drove the last few miles to Rainey's.

4

Rainey's subdivision, Pecan Orchard Estates, had a brick drive which ended at two tall stucco archways with pitched Spanish tile roofs. A tiny, matching guard shack sat between the arches, and a metal arm blocked the entry lane. I eased up next to the guard shack.

A uniformed guard sat inside, thumb typing on his phone. He gave me a sharp glance to let me know he saw me but kept tapping away. About the time I was ready to honk the truck's horn, he swaggered out of the tiny brick building, hitching his pants up around his gut.

"Party you're here to see?" The guard, whose name tag read Reichert, scanned the inside of my truck like he was looking for contraband.

"Rainey Bruce." I considered asking what he was looking for but decided it wasn't worth the trouble.

"Need to see your driver's license." He held one hand, palm up, right next to my face as I dug in my bag for my

ID. I got it out and handed it to him. He glanced at my name and grunted. "She expecting you?"

I made a disgusted noise and shook my head. "I should have called her."

He turned and strolled back into the guard shack, sat down, and typed something on the computer. He squinted at the screen. What was the problem? Rainey had my name on her permanent visitor list. Seven long minutes ticked by.

Reichert picked up the guard shack's phone and made a call. He hung up the phone and typed some more on his computer. Finally, he came back out of the guard shack and held out my license. "You and Miss Bruce have a nice visit." He went back inside the guard shack.

The arm barring my way rose with maddening slowness. Before I put the truck in drive, I checked the dashboard clock. Ten whole minutes. By the time I drove through her subdivision, darkness had overlaid the last shadows, and a waxing moon peeped over the treetops. A chill, probably the last until next fall, crept through the truck.

Rainey met me in her driveway, arms crossed over her chest and her features sharp with tension. "Who told you where to find her?"

I leaned out the window of my truck, almost afraid to get out. Rainey's abandoning Hannah to her fate at the hands of King Tolliver made almost as much sense to me as a pig wearing a diamond studded dildo. "You knew about Hannah?"

Rainey rolled her eyes in response to my question. "Of

course I know, you half-wit. I was doing everything I could to get you out of town without finding out. Wade Hill damn sure didn't tell you. Who did?"

I slid out of the truck. "Tubby Tubman."

Rainey snorted. "I told Wade you'd find out whether or not I said anything."

My mouth dropped open. Rainey and Wade had *conspired* not to tell me about Hannah? The ache of betrayal I'd been nursing ever since seeing Hannah flared high. "How could you keep Hannah's problems a secret? I thought you, Hannah, and me were sort of friends. I thought friends are supposed to help each other."

Rainey turned and walked to her front door. When I didn't follow, she twisted around and gave me one of her nasty glares. I huffed after her. She held the door open. "My dog's supper is about to burn. Let me finish that, and we'll talk."

I sat at Rainey's monstrosity of a breakfast table while she cooked for Ugly. The formerly abused dog stood next to his mistress, stump of a tail quivering with anticipation. He barely acknowledged my greeting rub. Too focused on the damn food.

Rainey took her time puttering around the state-of-the-art kitchen and cooing to the dog. The sight would have amused me under other circumstances. But I kept coming back to my fury at King Tolliver, my hurt over the way everybody but me seemed to have abandoned Hannah. Each passing second dragged on like a bad night with a homely man. By the time Rainey sat in front of me, I was ready to chew a hole through the ceiling. The sounds of Ugly slurping down his supper came from the kitchen.

She set her mouth in a grim line. "Let's talk about Hannah."

"Sure. I saw..." I opened my mouth to tell Rainey about the jumbo-eared monster riding Hannah's back, about King's threats if I didn't stay away, and how my fingers itched to dig his skin off his face. She held up one hand to stop me.

"Let me talk first. Please?" Rainey didn't say please often. Or thank you, for that matter. Her bothering to do so meant she felt less than one hundred percent confident she'd prevail over this situation. That scared me silent. I nodded and pretended to zip my lips shut.

Rainey cleared her throat as though she was about to address a jury and started to speak. "After the incident with your mother, you and Wade cleaned her things out of the Sugar Shack to make it look like she just left town. Remember what happened afterward?"

I nodded. Wade and I had met Rainey across the county line and loaded the luggage into an old four-door beater she kept locked in her garage. She refused to say what she planned to do with Barbie's luggage and drove off into the night, her elbow cocked out the car's window.

Rainey's voice cut off the memory. "Once I knew what really happened the day your father died, I wondered how Barbie kept everyone quiet all these years. Amanda knew. And, if Barbie was telling the truth, Joey Holze knew. I had Barbie's luggage, so I..." She stopped speaking, and her cheeks darkened.

"You went through my dead mother's luggage." I spoke with mock outrage. Rainey had nothing to blush over. Not in front of me anyway. I'd have done the same.

"I found nothing useful, not even on her laptop," she said with a sour twist of her lips. "I had my PI set up forwarding on the email accounts he was able to find and wrote it off as a lost cause." She leaned forward. "But then one day about a month ago, I got an email." She drew a printed page out of her briefcase and wordlessly handed it to me.

It read, "You pulling a disappearing act doesn't get you out of giving me that tape. You will give it up or lose everything. Meet me at Bobcats, 1 p.m., Thursday." Bobcats was a liquor store right outside Gaslight City. They did a brisk business, and I'd been told they sold more than just booze. The email wasn't signed, not even an initial. I handed it back to Rainey.

She glanced over it and then placed it back in her briefcase. "Before you ask, there was no tape in Barbie's luggage. My PI and I even took the lining out of the suitcase."

"But you went to the meeting anyway, right?" I would have just to see who showed.

She nodded. "My PI and I sat there for an hour, never saw anybody hanging around."

"They were probably watching from somewhere else. You have to hide and hope you see someone you know." I knew because this was the kind of stuff my new family did.

"Gee, you think?" She waved one elegant hand at me. She bowed her head. "I'm sorry."

"You're apologizing?" This whole thing was getting worse and worse. First Rainey said please. Then she apologized. I had a bad feeling the world, as I knew it, was about to end.

"Yes, I am apologizing. I'm just mad at myself because I was stupid. My PI drove me back to my office, where I'd parked my car, and I went—alone—to the place where I'd stored the luggage. I went through it right there looking for the tape mentioned in the email. A few hours later, a neighbor called to say I'd left the door open. I knew I hadn't, so I had my PI go back with me." She waved one hand, face set in disgust.

I knew how this story ended. Someone had ransacked Rainey's hiding place after she left. Sympathy would piss her off, so I got right down to business. "They get everything?"

"That's the only silver lining. They didn't get the laptop, which I had in my office safe, or the overnight case. It was an outdated little thing, didn't match the other piece of luggage. I guess the thieves didn't realize it was Barbie's."

Ugly, having finished his meal, came into the breakfast area wagging his stump of a tail. Rainey smiled at him and patted her leg. He gave his bowl a pointed glance. Rainey shook her head. He lay down between her and the bowl and stared at her with sad eyes.

"We've danced around this long enough." I tapped Rainey to get her attention off the dog. "You said we were going to talk about Hannah. This is just a story about how somebody outsmarted you."

Rainey watched me through hooded eyes. "You've

changed. You know that?"

I shrugged. Maybe so. It hadn't made me a nicer or more patient person. "Tell me about Hannah."

"Same time all this happened, Hannah had just gotten home from the trauma survivor's hospital in Florida. I went by to see her, all shook up Barbie's stuff got stolen, and—"

I cut her off. "She wanted to help." Hannah always wanted some excitement. Had it bitten her in the ass this time? I thought so.

"I gave her the computer and the overnight bag. That was one of my weekends to visit Jesse at the prison, and it was Friday." Rainey's dark eyes softened and got that faraway look they always did when she talked about my uncle.

Jesse was serving life without the possibility of parole, the result of a plea deal to avoid the death penalty, for killing my father twenty-some-odd years ago. Jesse didn't kill my daddy, but Rainey and I had found no way to prove it and free him. The real murderer was buried in an unmarked grave after trying to take my life. The case file documenting the crime was missing, which made me think it held a clue. I suspected the former sheriff of Burns County of taking it. If he had, it was long gone. He'd probably turned the file, and whatever clue it held, into ashes.

The situation with Uncle Jesse frustrated me. He was my closest living relative now that Memaw was dead. I loved my uncle. He met me with a smile every visit and acted more concerned over my welfare than his own. His insight on life, love, and spirituality inspired me.

But Jesse was wrong for Rainey in about six million ways. For one, he was the same age as her father. For two, he was serving a life sentence in prison. Those two cancelled out the need for a third reason. Especially for a smart woman like Rainey.

She slitted her eyes at me, as though she knew exactly what was on my mind. "I left town from Hannah's. Most of the drive has spotty cell service. When I got to the motel that evening, I had a message from her saying she may have found something in Barbie's overnight bag. The message was already several hours old, and I was exhausted. I fell asleep without answering her." Her brows crinkled, and her mouth turned down at the same time. We'd known each other since the first day of Head Start. This was what her face did when she felt guilty. "The next morning I went to visitation. I was with Jesse, and I honestly forgot about Hannah."

I couldn't help raising my eyebrows. Rainey had always treated men like living condiments. Nice, possibly tasty. But completely unnecessary. Evidently this thing with Jesse had changed the landscape of her life.

She doubled up one fist, something I'd rarely seen her do. "Wipe that look off your face, girl, or I'll do it for you." I made an effort to keep from laughing. She gave me another warning scowl before continuing. "So it was the evening of the next day before I called Hannah. She answered, and two things were obvious. One: she was at a bar. Loud talking, loud music. Two: she'd been drinking." Rainey gave me a meaningful look. I nodded. We never discussed it out loud, but even before this drunken spree,

Hannah had teetered on the edge of drinking too much. "She managed to slur that she was at Long Time Gone for an open mic night to play her guitar and sing. She pretty much hung up on me." Rainey sat back in her chair and stared at the wall.

Ugly stood from his post and came and laid his head in his mistress's lap. She absently stroked it. The dog closed the one eye his abusers had left him.

"What then?" It had become clear Rainey wasn't going to say more without prompting.

She blew out a sigh. "The week after I visit Jesse is always hectic. Once I caught up, I tried to call Hannah a few times. No response. By the time I tracked her to her permanent barstool in Long Time Gone, she was so drunk she could barely speak. She didn't even know what I was talking about." Rainey clung to her dog as though it somehow made the memory less sharp. I knew how she felt because I had failed Hannah too.

"You never had any idea what she found in Barbie's things?"

Rainey shook her head at my question.

"I might not know what she found, but I think I know where it led her." I told Rainey about seeing the jumbo-eared monster riding Hannah's back.

Rainey flinched. "W-wh-what is it?"

I shook my head. "Wade called it a hag and said it would eventually kill Hannah. But that's not all." I told Rainey what King said would happen to Hannah if I didn't stay away.

She moaned and put her hand over her face. "And

Wade just stood there." She rolled her eyes.

I sprung to Wade's defense, even though his behavior confused and irritated me. "King's somehow exerting control over him." Picturing Wade's black eye, I told her what King threatened as I stood in the parking lot of Long Time Gone. The idea of King making me watch while he killed Wade sparked a mixture of horror and fury strong enough to create a breeze in Rainey's house. I fought for control.

Rainey rubbed a shaking hand over her mouth and muttered, "But wait a minute. That fits because Wade..." Her lips moved but no sound came out.

"Fits what? What did Wade do?" I tapped the table to get her attention.

Rainey broke out of her reverie. "Wade signed his cut of the Mace Treasure over to King."

"*What?*" My voice rose.

"Hannah did too." Rainey and I stared at each other in pissed off silence.

"What the fuck is going on?" I whispered. King had never hidden his inner asshole, but this went above and beyond. And it seemed directed at hurting people I loved and bullying me out of doing anything to help them. Something had changed between King and me, and I had missed it.

Rainey sat with her shoulders bent inward. "I don't know. I can't put it together. See, there's one last thing I haven't told you." She sat very still, her eyes wide and scared.

I began straightening the piles of paper on her table to

keep my nerves from going cannibal. "What haven't you told me?"

Rainey watched me, eyes flicking nervously to the door every once in a while. Finally she got up to check and make sure it was locked. She spoke with her back still to me. "King Tolliver has threatened to kill your Uncle Jesse."

My body heated, and sweat broke out all over me. It took me several seconds to make my mouth work. Even then, all I could do was say, "Wha...wha...wha?"

Rainey didn't seem to hear me. She sat back down at the table and folded her hands in front of her. She raised one shaking hand to smooth down her perfect hair. "I told you I went out to Long Time Gone to try get Hannah to tell me what she was investigating that weekend I was gone." She raised her eyebrows, silently asking if I remembered. I nodded. She said, "That day, King Tolliver told me that if he heard another word of me investigating your father's murder, he'd make sure Jesse didn't survive another day in prison. And I'd be sorry I was ever born." She sat back in her chair.

I did a slow burn. King had now threatened four people I loved. My heart kicked a few times, and heat flooded my face. King and I had business. By the end of it, he'd never threaten anybody I loved again, or I'd be dead.

"It gets better." She snapped her fingers to get me out of my head. "You remember me mentioning that Wade didn't want you to know about Hannah. I need to tell you why."

Heart thundering in my chest, I waited for the next bit of awful news.

"Wade came to see me at my office right after King threatened Jesse and me." She watched my face, anger and fear flickering in the depths of her eyes. "He's an intimidating son of a bitch when you get the business end of him."

Cold sweat popped out on my scalp. "He didn't threaten you, did he?"

She made a face. "Not at all. He asked—no, begged—me not to involve you in Hannah's situation. He said King is just looking for a reason to put a hit on you. And now you know why I kept my mouth shut."

Sharp knives stabbed at my nervous system. My mind went into overdrive. King now hated me for some reason I couldn't fathom. He was taking this into death-match level, and I couldn't see why.

Rainey yawned, turning her face away from me. "I'm sorry. I can't believe I'm this tired. I'm going to have to go bed, or I'll fall asleep right here." She stood from the table.

Once she'd left the room, and I heard her bedroom door shut, I hurried for the French doors to the backyard, nicotine demons screeching in my head. Cigarettes. The answer to every stressor in my life.

———

THE WIND, which had been bearable with the hot sun to combat its chill, infiltrated my clothes and made my worn-out bones ache. I sat at a concrete table, the coldness seeping through my jeans and freezing my butt. I tried to ignore it and lit the first cigarette. The poisonous smoke burned my lungs. I tried to convince myself it made me warmer and went back over Rainey's story.

Hannah's voicemail said she'd found something of note in Barbie's luggage. A clue. Hannah, who couldn't resist a mystery, followed it. Somewhere along the way, she'd gotten mixed up with the hag. Where?

The clue could have taken Hannah to Long Time Gone, but I didn't see it. Hannah's ordeal with Michael Gage and Nash Redmond probably made her cautious, and rightfully so, about walking into a backwoods honky-tonk all by her lonesome. She'd have waited and asked Rainey to go in with her. Which meant Hannah picked up the hag when she found whatever my mother had hidden.

That hypocritical bitch. Though my mother had pretended to hate anything paranormal, she'd worked with a witch to hide her atrocities. Barbie's pet witch could have easily used the hag to booby trap the clue Hannah chased down. It made a sick kind of sense.

Then how did Hannah end up at Long Time Gone? King didn't fit anywhere in the equation. Or did he? The email about the tape could have been from King. That whole setup fit his style. But it still didn't make sense. I drew hard on my cigarette as though that would break loose the answers I wanted.

A stray memory popped into my head. It had been the last week I worked at Long Time Gone before I went to live with Griff and Mysti. Wade and I had been talking about my father's murder and how to prove Uncle Jesse didn't do it. King overheard and screamed at both of us to get back to work or go home.

I'd thought he was just being his usual asshole self. But now I wondered if that's where it all started between King and me. That still didn't tell me why he even gave a shit about my father's murder.

I remembered the day of my father's murder in vivid detail. Full color with surround sound. King wasn't there, had nothing to do with any of it. The real killers were dead. The man who helped them cover it up was no longer sheriff of Burns County and now lived several hours away. No matter how I tried, I couldn't figure out King's place in it all.

Another gust of wind whipped through Rainey's backyard. My teeth rattled together, and a shiver ripped through my body. The answers weren't out here in the cold. I got up and went back inside.

Rainey had left a few lamps burning to guide me to the guest room. A pair of silky soft pajamas with the tags still on them lay on the bed. Bright red with maroon piping. Good grief. Did Rainey sit around this big house dressed up and all alone like the ghost of some out-of-date movie star? No wonder she'd fallen in love with my poor uncle.

I picked up the pajamas and rubbed the smooth material over my cheek. Oh well. Beggars couldn't be choosers. At least Rainey paid for luxury. I cut off the tags and dressed in the ridiculous getup, rolling up the too-long sleeves and legs.

I slid between the high-end sheets with an appreciative groan. Rainey spared no expense, not even in her guest room. The exhaustion from the day settled into my bones. My eyelids drooped, but my mind kept racing.

I came to the conclusion I might never know how or why King decided to turn on me, or what he had to do with the day my father was murdered. The focus needed to be on his threats against my friends and family.

King's violent threats scared me just as much as they made me see red. He'd carry them out in a second. No question there. The obvious solution was to put King down, but I had to get Hannah and Wade to safety first. I imagined and rejected plan after plan. Sleep came without me knowing it.

The creak of the bedroom door jerked me into awareness. I stared into the darkness, heart picking up speed. The bedside lamp was off. Had I turned off the light? I couldn't remember. Moonlight beamed into the window and lent the room a silver glow. The sound of footsteps whispered over the carpet. The black opal heated. I tried to sit up and found I couldn't move. My mouth went dry. Panic fluttered in my chest.

A voice said, "There you are." Fingers tipped with sharp, black nails appeared over the edge of the bed, and a sloped head with big, ugly ears came into view. The hag from Long Time Gone. The one I last saw riding Hannah's shoulders.

I strained to lift an arm, but I was unable to do more than moan in fear. Childish thoughts raced through my head. If I could turn on the bedside lamp, everything would be okay. The room would be empty. My body shook with effort, sweat trickling from my hairline and racing down my scalp.

I couldn't move a muscle. Fear swelled in my heart,

stacking higher with each beat. My black opal still burned my chest, responding to the magic of Hannah's malevolent passenger. The power of the mantle, crippled by an old spell but still strong enough to steam milk, bounced around inside me. It, too, was trapped.

Cold eyes rose over the edge of the bed followed by a long nose and a sinister grin. The thing climbed onto the bed and straddled me, our noses nearly touching. Its fetid breath found my nose. "Barbara Mace left specific instructions if I ever encountered you."

Blood roared in my head. My mother left this thing waiting for me, knowing I'd eventually stumble on whatever evidence of her part in my father's murder she had squirreled away. That hypocrite. That bitch. I doubled my efforts to get away but nothing happened.

The hag's cold fingers closed around my neck. It choked off my air supply, and I tried to cough. I couldn't even do that.

"Oh, how I wish I could have ridden one so full of power as yourself." Its humid breath puffed against my skin.

My lungs screamed for oxygen. So this was how it ended, with neither a whimper nor a bang. Nothing more than a hoarse hiss from me.

The thing chuckled and leaned forward. "Oh, the atrocities I could have made you commit. How rich your sorrow would have tasted. Mmmm-mmmm."

The thing sounded like it was about to slurp its fingers. Disgust and fear churned in my guts. My thoughts slowed, and my vision darkened. I hadn't thought it would end like this—me in fancy pajamas lying on nice sheets. I'd always imagined myself dying in battle. The darkness spread over my vision.

Light flooded the room. Rainey rushed in brandishing a crucifix.

"In the name of the Father, the Son, and the Holy Ghost, I command you to leave my home." Her courtroom voice woke me from oblivion.

The thing let go of my neck. I sucked in a lungful of sweet oxygen. Rainey rushed forward and slapped the crucifix against my would-be murderer. It hissed and swiped a handful of claws at her.

"In the name of the Father, the Son, and the Holy Ghost, get out," Rainey screamed.

Once the thing took its focus off me, my ability to move came back. I shoved the monster away and scrambled out of the bed. I clamped onto a current of magic inside me and channeled it. The black opal burned on my chest. Power pulsed through it.

My voice came out of my tortured throat even scratchier than usual. I sounded like an alley cat coming off a bender. "Evil spirit, I repel you from this house." My fingertips tingled with the magic gathering there. I threw some of it at the hideous little creature.

It turned to me, teeth bared. "You can't send me away like one your ghosts, little witch. I am a higher being. And I have orders. You must die."

I gathered the power again. "No. You'll die." I sounded more confident than I felt. If this thing wasn't a ghost, what was it? Wade had called it a hag. I had assumed that meant it was the ghost of an evil witch. Maybe not.

Rainey rushed forward. She stabbed the thing with her crucifix. The metal bounced off the hag's skin and clunked on the floor. A livid burn mark where it had hit formed and began to smoke. The thing screamed and ran for the window. A foot or so before it hit the wall, it leapt up and passed through the glass as though it wasn't even there.

My knees went rubbery, and I sank down on my ass and rubbed at my sore throat. "How'd you know what was going on?"

Rainey knelt beside me, breathing hard, and smoothed my hair off my face. "I didn't. Not at first. I came to apologize." She snorted. "Why am I bothering to lie? I came to talk about Jesse, how much I love him, and how scared I am for him. But I got here just in time to hear that thing say your mother sent him."

The rest fell into place for me. She'd gone to get her crucifix and came back to help. "You're in love with my uncle?"

"Oh, shut the hell up. I'm going to have nightmares about that thing. I can't even believe it was real." She clasped her arms over her chest and rocked.

My phone dinged with a text message. I crawled to the nightstand and picked it up, ignoring Rainey's disgusted groan. "It's a text message from Hannah."

"What?" Rainey crowded near.

I read it aloud. "'Sorry for today. Please come get me in the morning. King's house in the Six Gun Compound.'"

Hannah must have had a moment of clarity while the

hag was visiting me. My voice of reason spoke. *No, no, no. It's a trap. King sent that message.* The Six Gun Compound was at the ass-end of nowhere. If I ran into an ambush, there'd be nobody to hear me scream. But what if Hannah's distress cry was real? My gut twisted painfully. I couldn't just leave her there. This was a risk I had to take. Minutes later, I was dressed again, the ridiculous pajamas folded and the bed made.

"You're not going to the Six Gun Revolutionaries' compound." Rainey held my keys in one fist just out of my reach.

I held out my hand for the keys. She shook her head. I spoke in what I hoped was a reasonable voice. "Even if you're willing to leave Hannah to die, aren't you curious about that tape? It might get Jesse out of prison. Don't you want to be with him?"

Rainey flinched as though I'd slapped her. She put the hand holding my keys behind her back. "You're acting without thinking or planning. If this is a setup, they'll kill you."

Fury at the thought of King trying to kill me licked at the walls of my sanity like flames climbing over a burning house. "I'm not going to live my life under the threat of King Tolliver's wrath. Hear me?" The black opal came to life on my chest. A breeze fluttered through my hair. The nightstand light began to flicker. "And he's not going to threaten my friends and live to laugh about it."

"You're going to get yourself and everybody you know killed if you don't slow down and—" My phone's buzz cut off Rainey's words. She closed her mouth so hard her teeth clicked together.

"It's Wade," she hissed. "He always knows when you need him. Don't you dare talk to me about unrequited love and leaving Jesse to rot in prison. You're no better with Wade."

The anger worked its way up to my face and burned my cheeks. My phone buzzed again. I ignored it and stared into Rainey's face. Friendships were difficult for her. She didn't really like people, including me. But she made an effort. I needed to do that too. "What are you suggesting I do? Nothing, like you?" It was the wrong thing to say. I realized it as soon as I'd said it. But there's no delete key on spoken words. They're out there for good.

Rainey threw my keys. Hard. They struck my breastbone and fell to the floor. I rubbed at the sore spot, imagining the bruise I'd have in a few hours. Rainey stalked back through her house. Her bedroom door slammed. I wanted to go after her, but she scared me too bad. She could tear me apart without raising a finger. I snatched the keys off the floor and checked my phone.

Wade's first text message said, "What just happened to you?" The second one was more urgent. "Please answer. I can't come looking for you right now."

I tapped out a message to him. "Hannah's parasite came to visit. Threatened me."

His message came back a few seconds later. "It's gone now? I'll come if you need me."

King would be mad as an old lady with a pile of expired

coupons if Wade came right now. I sucked in a harsh breath and tapped out an answer as quickly as I could. "No. It's okay. Rainey used a crucifix on it." The message sent, and I leaned against the wall, breathing hard.

I had made a mistake when Wade and I talked earlier, and now it was eating me alive. Wade needed to know where he stood with King. He was in danger every second I withheld King's threat on his life. *Please don't let it be too late.* I tapped out another message. "We need to talk as soon as possible. But what I tell you needs to be the biggest secret you ever kept in your life."

The pause lasted so long my mind started making up scenarios where King had snuck up behind Wade and put a gun to the back of his head. Pretty soon my phone would buzz with a picture of Wade's lifeless body, chunks of brain and bone sprayed out. King's message would say, "Still think I'm kidding, bitch?" The horrific movie reel ran a nonstop loop, faster and faster, until fear and fury beat like wings inside me.

A text message popped up. "I won't be home until three in the morning. Check your email for directions. Pull your truck into the shed and put a tarp over it. Go in the house. Leave the lights off."

I tapped out an okay and checked the time. Three hours to kill. I left Rainey's house, locked it, drove back to downtown Gaslight City, and circled the block around Bullfrog's Billiards. Lights blazed from the upstairs loft. Either Tubby Tubman was up there, or someone else was using it. I hoped it was the former because I needed Tubby's expertise.

5

———

BULLFROG'S STANK like stale urine and was so dim I had to stand in the doorway for several seconds to get my bearings. The main room held ten pool tables, each with a separate light fixture hanging over it. Dirt gritted between my feet and the hundred-year-old floorboards. I wove my way through the pool tables, nodding to the people I recognized, and stopped at the bar.

Bullfrog, pock-faced and potbellied, narrowed his piggy eyes. "Tub ain't expecting you."

"I need him." I slid onto a barstool and rested my elbows on the bar. "Call him. Now."

"You don't tell me what to do, lil' bit. I'll drag you in that back room, find ways to make you scream." He spread his thin lips in a sick grin.

I recoiled. Bullfrog was Tubby's second cousin. He did things Tubby himself didn't want to do. Nasty things. Tubby once told me Bullfrog enjoyed those things. The phone behind the bar, an old-fashioned red one with push buttons, began to ring. Bullfrog made no move to answer. He stood still, glacial eyes boring into mine. The phone stopped ringing and started again.

Slowly, as though he had all the time in the world, Bullfrog picked up the phone and held it to his ear without speaking. "Yep. It's her." He listened again. "Nope. She's alone." Bullfrog listened for a few seconds, slammed the phone back in its cradle, and turned his cold stare back on me. "Tub'll be down shortly." He stalked off.

I hunched on my barstool. The back of my neck throbbed with a stress-ache. Tubby might or might not help me. It depended on what he thought was in it for him. But I knew nobody else who could figure out a way to get out of this mess. I massaged the back of my neck and thought about ordering a shot of tequila, but I didn't drink and was afraid it might make me drunk. Peri Jean Mace. The last of the hard drinkers. Not.

Long, skinny fingers closed over my forearm. I jerked out of my thoughts to find Tubby standing next to me. He smiled and drew me into a hug. I told myself I let him do it because he'd get angry if I refused, but I leaned my head on his shoulder and wrapped my arms around his waist. He moved between my legs and tightened his grip. My body responded right away, idiotic horniness running amok. Warning bells went off in my head. I'd sworn off alley-catting. The mornings after killed any satisfaction I got from them. That included a re-run with Tubby. I pushed him away.

"Wanna go up to the loft?" He gestured at the ceiling.

I searched his blue eyes for lust or trickery and saw

nothing but a guy I'd known since I was barely out of diapers. I nodded and got off the stool. Tubby put his arm around me.

Bullfrog spoke from a few feet away. "Dozen more just like her that's a lot less trouble."

Tubby waved off his cousin and led me through the storeroom and up the creaking stairs. Someone had painted the wall red since my last visit.

Tubby caught me looking at it. "We had an incident. Red seemed like the right color to redecorate with."

Imagining blood and worse on the wall, I hurried to the closed door at the top of the stairs. Getting a glimpse of what might have happened here did not appeal. I twisted the doorknob. Locked, of course. Tubby'd never leave it unsecured, not even for ten minutes. He pissed off too many people. Tubby unlocked the door and held it open.

"No crazy teenager waiting in here to scratch my eyeballs out of my head?" I smiled but stepped cautiously into the loft. Tubby's taste in companions scared me.

He barked a hollow laugh. "Naw. Might be getting old. Those little girls got boring."

He closed and locked the door, brushing around me to hurry into the little kitchenette. He came out holding up a white cloth. The smell of disinfectant burned my nose. He wiped off the leather recliner and motioned to it with a smile. "I remembered what you like."

I nodded my thanks and sat down. Tubby dragged a wooden, straight-backed chair over and sat in front of me. He dug his skinny elbows into his knees and squinted. "You go see Hannah?"

I nodded, mouth trembling as I fought tears. I swiped at my filling eyes with the back of my hand.

Tubby put one hand on my shoulder. "Hey, hey. You seen worse'n that."

I sniffled and swiped my hand across my nose. "That ain't all of it neither." My speech patterns degraded every time I got around Tubby. I told him what I saw sitting on Hannah's shoulder.

His face paled enough for me to see a spray of freckles on the bridge of his nose and a few sunspots at his hairline. "What is it?"

"Wade called it a hag." I took out my cigarettes and tried to light one. My hand shook so hard Tubby had to guide it. He set an ashtray in my lap. I exhaled a jet of smoke. "That still ain't all." I told him about King's threats to pretty much everybody I knew and loved.

Tubby shook his head and lit his own cigarette. "You in deep, girl." He stared at the window, and I thought for a second he might invite me to get the fuck out of his safe place. "I know you, you want to save 'em all, even get old Jesse Mace out of prison. Be the hero one mo' time."

It wasn't about being the hero. I wanted to see my friends safe, my uncle out of prison. And I wanted to force alligator shit down King Tolliver's wrinkled old gullet.

Tubby watched me. Whatever he saw made his lips crimp into an almost smile. "You pissed, ain't you? No, no. You *insulted*." Tubby watched me through eyes slitted against the smoke. "And you gonna go up against King, irregardless how dangerous it is."

I didn't dare tell him there was no such word as irregardless. Instead I nodded.

"And you want old Tub to help you." He winked at me. "For old time's sake?"

Good question. I shrugged. Tubby had no real reason to help me. But I somehow felt sure he would.

He nodded slowly. "Back in high school, you and Chase was my only friends."

I hunched my shoulders. I hadn't been a great friend to Tubby, hadn't even liked him very much back then. I still wasn't sure how much I liked him.

"Chase is dead." He spoke almost to himself, eyes cast downward. "You all I got now."

Tubby's confession made me sad. Other than Benny Longstreet, he was probably the richest man in Burns County. But he was lonely and adrift, just like me. A spark of kinship burned between me and Tubby. I couldn't ask him to help, risk getting him hurt or killed. I pushed myself out of the recliner. It squealed out a protest. "I'm sorry I came here. People are going to get killed over this, and you don't need to be in the middle of it."

Tubby pulled my arm until I sat in the chair again. Cigarette clamped in his teeth, he mumbled something I didn't quite catch.

"What?" I leaned close enough to see the beginnings of crow's feet around his eyes.

"I said, 'If I'm too chicken to go to war with those cocksuckers, it's time for me to retire.' You know I got business with them. Them motorcycle fellas is fucking me. Ol' Tub's piece of the pie been getting littler and littler. I can either bend over and take it nice and polite, or I can rip their dicks off for 'em." Tubby pushed a hank of his blondish waves behind one ear and gave me a firm nod. With the magnanimity of a king offering his ring to kiss, he said, "I'll strategize with you."

Anybody else might have laughed at this. I appreciated it. Tubby didn't look like much, sitting there in a wife beater with tattoos snaking up and down his arms, but he knew how people worked.

He sat back in his chair and smoked his cigarette until it burned his fingers. He stubbed it out with a hard jab. "Your challenge ain't getting just Hannah out of there. It's getting her out of there plus keeping Wade and Jesse safe. Rainey Bruce, too, but you can just tell her to get out of town."

I already knew that, but I also knew he'd get to the good stuff soon enough. I watched him think.

"They got to get to Jesse from within the prison. Unless the Six Guns got a member in there, that's pretty much contract work." Tubby raised his eyes to mine. "I'll reach out to somebody I know. Get your uncle the protection he needs."

My mouth dropped open, and I closed it with a pop. "You'd do that?"

His lips quirked, and a smile spread over his face. He raised his eyebrows.

"What do you want?" My body tensed.

"Way I see it, you owe me 'bout three big favors." I started to speak, but he held his hand up for me to let him continue. "And this'un here, me helping you save the folks you love, is huge. Prob'ly counts for at least two more."

A few months ago, I'd have sat there like I had a mouth full of shit and was afraid of dribbling it on my white shirt. Not now. "Bullshit. You just told me you're ready to exterminate the Six Guns. If we succeed, you might be able to slide back on top of whatever dance y'all are doing."

Tubby laughed and clapped his skinny hands together. He finally caught his breath enough to say, "You have really come into your own. I am proud to know you." He clapped me on the shoulder. "Okay. Here's what I want. When this is all said and done, I want us to go on a date. All debts cleared in exchange."

A yes ran through my head, got approval, and rushed to my lips. I held it back. True, things had changed between Tubby and me since he'd helped find the Mace Treasure. We'd grown past the boy and girl who'd shared an abortive romance in their early twenties. For the first time since the day I asked him not to call anymore all those years ago, he felt like a friend.

Dating Tubby might have a few perks. I missed the company of a man, but I didn't miss the meaningless encounters. Even so, my loneliness had gotten so big I could practically dress it up and send it to school. Buy cute lunch boxes. Pay for piano lessons. But I didn't want to go boyfriend hunting because my heart belonged to Wade.

An occasional date with Tubby might be the answer. Any relationship we developed would have to just be sometimes. His illegal enterprise was rooted in Burns County, and I never planned on moving back here. And

Tubby himself? He might want me, but he'd never love me. He was too calculating and selfish. I remembered the physical side of the relationship we shared in our twenties. Talk about fireworks.

The biggest bonus? Going out with Tubby might give Wade a dose of cold water to the face. Tubby would make sure Wade knew. He might see himself losing me and change his mind.

That I wanted to use Tubby to make Wade jealous told me all I needed to know. Shit might be fine for a teenager, but I knew better. It had the potential to blow us all to smithereens. I shook my head. "I can't. It's Wade."

Tubby's eyes dulled with disappointment. He slouched and turned away from me. "He don't want you." His fair complexion reddened. "I seen him hanging all over a dozen different women since you been gone."

"I know. But it doesn't change how I feel," I said, cheeks flaming. The admission of Wade's womanizing made me feel just as miserable as Tubby looked. "I think I got a better idea than going on a date."

Tubby faced me again, interested. He nodded at a closed door I knew led to a bed he kept up here.

I shook my head. "Tub, I've known you all my life. I'd rather be your friend than your sometimes booty call." I thought Tubby and I had already renewed our friendship, but he liked for everything to be a deal signed on some imaginary dotted line. So I'd make it that way for him. "So let's do this. Never mention me owing you again. Let's really be friends."

Tubby bit his lower lip and squinted at the floor. His

eyes moved back and forth as he thought it over. It would have been so much easier to go on a date with him and then blow him off. But Tubby, weird as he was, qualified as my friend. I wanted to treat him like a friend instead of using him. "What's in it for me?" he said to the dirty floor.

"If you're my friend, I will do anything for you. Look at what I'm doing right now for Hannah." I paused to let the words sink in. "There's no way I'd do this if she didn't mean the world to me."

Tubby began shaking his head before I finished talking. "You come up here, and I tell you I'm done with the crazy bitches. Then I tell you I want us to go out. What do you think I'm talking about?" He stared into my eyes, and his meaning hit home. Tubby thought he was ready to settle with one woman. Me. He thought I meant the world to him, and this was his way to celebrate it.

Highlights of a life with Tubby flashed through my mind's eye. The good would be very good. The bad would be like a vacation on the outer banks of the River Styx. Life with Tubby would never be boring, but it would often be heartbreaking. Then one day, we'd both have enough and go our separate ways. Never talk again.

Had someone asked if losing Tubby mattered before I sat down in this room, I'd have said no. But now I knew different. The permanent loss of him would cut me deep.

Tubby knew me, had known me all my life. He'd shared some of the good stuff and had carried me through some of the bad stuff. When the ordeal with my ex-husband blew up, Tubby pulled me out of the smoking rubble and helped me find the will to go on. I owed him more than a half-assed attempt at a relationship we both knew would fail.

I curled my fingers through his and squeezed. "Did you know I never even see Chase's ghost? He's lost to me, and it hurts so much. I don't want that with you."

"Who says it has to end that way?" His words came too quick and with too little conviction. The words of a man used to winning who saw a victory slipping from his grasp. I rarely noticed Tubby's eye color, but right then I took in the brilliant cornflower irises, looked past the craftiness and down into Tubby's fears. He didn't want to be alone. Who does?

"A relationship between us won't work. You know that. Then what? We don't talk for another five years?" I pulled his hand to my lips and kissed it, the smell of cigarettes and heaven-knew-what-else stinging my nostrils. "I want things to be right between us."

Even as I spoke the words, made the commitments, I asked myself if I really wanted this level of Tubby's friendship. The boundary issues, the obnoxious intrusions, the nosiness would be worse if he considered me an unconditional friend. *But what about the fun stuff?* I gave his hand an extra squeeze and tried to ignore the tears filling my eyes.

Tubby nodded slowly, brow creased. He pulled his hand out of mine, stood, and leaned over me. I stiffened, worried what he might do, but he wrapped his arms around me and squeezed hard. "Nobody wanted to be my friend before. Least not anybody I believed." He kissed the top of my head and let me go. "But I really thought I was gonna get laid." He watched me as though I might take off my clothes right there. I shrugged and shook my head. He let out a sigh. "All right. Done. We friends, and it goes both ways. So here's a friendly question. Are you gonna tell Wade that King is willing to sacrifice him to keep you in line?"

"Later tonight." I didn't tell Tubby about the opportunity I'd had to tell Wade and blown it because I was too busy angsting over my lust for him.

"Good. Wade's gonna be our inside man for this job. No matter how loyal he is to the Six Guns, nobody's that loyal."

I was still lost. "What's he going to do for us?"

Tubby rolled his eyes. "I thought you's smart. Only way we're gonna win is to ambush the Guns wherever they got Hannah. You even know where that is?"

"The compound."

Tubby groaned and threw back his head, making his Adam's apple jut out. "They've got an arsenal up there."

"So what do I do to keep Wade safe?"

Tubby jammed a cigarette between his teeth and passed his lighter over it. "You and me don't need to worry about nothing other than getting Hannah out safely. Wade'll figure out his end." His grin reminded me why, friends or no, I'd have to be cautious every step of the way. The same way I would if I had a lion for a pet. Didn't exotic pets sometimes eat their owners? The skin on the back of my neck prickled.

"You going in with me?" Raw nerve endings burned all

over my body. Now that I knew I was going to rescue Hannah, the severity of it sank in.

Tubby blew smoke in my direction and nodded, his grin cold as an alligator's. "In addition, I'll provide transportation to and from and a place to hole up. King Tolliver'll consider this an insult. Be after us."

I shook my head, still puzzling over how King went from being a sort of friend to my archenemy.

"You wondering why he don't like you no more, ain't you?" Tubby's grin chilled me all the way down to the tips of my toes. I nodded my yes. "Dunno. But I do know King Tolliver put out the word you're no longer under club protection and talked to me about arranging a hit. I refused, of course, and told him what would happen if I found out he'd done such a thing."

My mouth dropped open. "When?"

"Right after you was cleared of charges over Michael Gage's death and it became clear you wouldn't be prosecuted for beating the Jesus out of Joey Holze and family."

My brain did whirlies. Wade must've known, but he never said a word. Why hadn't he warned me? We weren't as close as I'd tried to pretend. All of a sudden, I didn't feel so bad for not telling him earlier that King had threatened his life. Questions about what that meant in terms of the romance I wanted with Wade flooded my mind. *Not the time.* I let them go and asked Tubby the question I couldn't let go of. "What started King's vendetta against me? Any ideas?"

"Not a one," Tubby said. "But the only things that matter to a snake-eyed sumbitch like King Tolliver is his motorcycle club and staying out of prison. Whatever you did might be somewhere in one of those." Tubby checked his phone and frowned. "Now you get on out to Wade's. Take you longer than you think on those dirt roads. Make sure don't nobody follow you."

Tubby walked me out to my car. I let him give me a chaste kiss on the cheek. The vein throbbing in his neck gave me a good idea how much more he wanted, but he stroked my cheek with one thumb and didn't ask.

I sat in my truck, body too hot for the chilly night, almost regretting my decision not to hook up with Tubby. Might have been my last chance to get laid before I got myself killed for good.

———

TUBBY WAS RIGHT about the dirt roads. I traveled down some of them at less than ten miles per hour, despite being behind the wheel of a heavy-duty pickup truck. The directions Wade had sent to my email ended at a clearing barely big enough to hold a cabin and a carport.

I did as Wade instructed, parking my truck in the carport and covering it with a filthy canvas tarp. I tiptoed to the cabin, struck by the way the moon sparkled on the rippling water of Piney Lake. I hadn't even known there were houses on this side of the lake.

Using the combination Wade gave me, I unlocked the padlock holding the front door of the cabin closed and went inside. My nose, honed from years of cleaning houses, picked up the telltale smell of mildew. I left the lights off and crept through the silent house. Moonlight streaked into the kitchen, brightening it enough for me to see a table and chairs. I sat down, put my head in my hands, and listened to the drone of the frogs singing outside.

On the drive over, I'd thought of all the ways I could tell Wade he was expendable. Wade could be mule-headed. He might decide to win the argument by crossing his big arms over his chest and shutting down. There had to be a way to convince him. Fatigue scratched around in my brain. I laid my cheek on the table so I could think better. My eyes fluttered shut, and I slipped into a tense doze.

A floorboard creaked. My eyes shot open. A figure stood in a doorway off the kitchen. I half-stood, already calling to my magic even though I didn't have a spell prepared.

"It's me," Wade rumbled. "Don't do whatever you're planning."

"I don't have a plan." I tried to push the magic back where it came from, but it came a lot easier than it went. Finally, I aimed it at a plastic jug of water and let it fly. The water in the jug began to bubble, rocking the jug back and forth. After a few seconds, it burst. Water cascaded over the floor.

Wade cursed and flicked on the overhead light.

"I'm sorry." I went for the paper towels.

"No. Use these." He tossed several frayed bath towels at me. "There's no garbage pickup out here."

I knelt on the floor and sopped up water. "It's so quiet

here that you could hear a mouse fart for a mile. How did I not hear your motorcycle?"

Wade grabbed one of the towels I wasn't using and helped. "I hid it about a quarter mile from here and walked the rest of the way."

I kept working, thinking about the implications of what he'd just said. It made sense he didn't want anybody knowing I was here. But he lived here. Why hide his presence?

"King offered me this place right after you left town. I was supposed to cut you off in exchange for it." He wadded up the towels and went into the laundry room off the kitchen. The washing machine's lid squealed open. Wade threw in the towels. They landed in a wet thump.

He came back into the kitchen and started a pot of coffee. We sat down at the table. "Obviously I was unable to cut you out of my life." He reached out to touch me but drew back his hand. "You look beautiful, you know it?"

"That mean you've changed your mind about us?" I winked. In the words of William B. Travis regarding the siege on the Alamo, I'd never surrender or retreat. Wade was the only man I wanted.

He heaved out a sigh. "You know the reason I won't. That card reading my sister did—and her predictions—are no joke." His voice rose on the last couple of words.

I held up one hand. "Sorry I asked." Not for the first time, I wondered what, exactly, his sister had seen in her fateful reading of Wade's and my future. I didn't dare ask. Not after Wade had already started holler-talking.

He growled and got up to get us coffee. While he

poured, I told him about the way Hannah's parasite attacked me and about Hannah's plea for me to come get her.

"Yeah. Right about the time your mojo bag let me know something was wrong, I saw her go lucid." The corners of his eyes crinkled into a smile. "She pushed King off her and ran off to the bathroom. Puked *all* that tequila up."

Must've been around the same time she sent me the text message. "She say anything?"

"She came over and said to tell you she couldn't keep it off her. It had gotten too big."

"Too big? Meaning too powerful?"

Wade nodded slowly. "I called my sister Desiree earlier about Hannah's situation and to let her know what was going on with me, what I was about to do. Desiree said those nasty little things feed on their hosts. Some feed on fear. The more they can scare their hosts, the more they have to eat. The more they eat, the bigger and stronger they get."

That made sense. But what was Hannah's parasite feeding on? Fear was one thing. It was pure energy. But Hannah didn't seem scared. She seemed incredibly depressed, intent on destroying herself.

The visions Orev had showed me returned to my mind. The parasite had outright murdered a baby and driven Wade's fiancée to kill herself.

Wade gripped my forearm and gave me a shake. "Tell me. I'm in this too."

"I'm trying to figure out what this thing—Hannah's parasite—wants." The answer seemed right on the edge of my mind. "I—I think maybe it eats life forces. It drives the hope right out of them, feeds on it. But then what?"

Wade shook his head. "Does it matter? Isn't that horrible enough?"

I gave him an impatient head shake. "Knowing how something operates, or why, is the key to beating it. You know that."

Wade sipped at his coffee, maybe thinking, maybe wishing I'd shut the hell up. Finally he spoke. "Souls can be captured and used. Look what Amanda did to your father."

Hot anger rashed over my skin. Amanda, a witch, had imprisoned my father's spirit in a mirror. She'd made him her ghostly flunky.

Wade didn't look any happier about the idea than I was. "We get it out of Hannah, we'll find out what it's up to."

"Did Hannah stay lucid all evening?" My biggest worry was her not wanting my help by the time I could get to her. She was taller than I and weighed more. It wasn't like I could pick her up and carry her. Especially if she fought.

"I think so. About the time I left, she and King got into a fight." Wade rubbed one hand over his beard. "She wanted to go home. He belted her one."

Hot fury rushed over me. "What'd you do?" I saw the answer in the way Wade flinched and ducked his head. I narrowed my eyes.

He glared at me. "I'm in a real shitty position here, you know it?"

I nodded but didn't let him see any sympathy.

"Damn it." He slapped the table. Coffee sloshed out of his mug. "I can't help Hannah without looking like a traitor to King. He helped me when nobody else would. He—"

I finished the sentence for him. "Saved your life. Right."

Wade's irises, so dark they barely stood out from the black of his pupil, flashed even darker with anger. "I was up on a murder charge. Had the Six Guns not gotten involved, I'd be sitting on death row, or dead, right now." He bared his teeth at me. "You and me woulda never met."

So he was still glad we knew each other. That stopped me from saying anything mean. Instead I took his hand. He frowned but let me do it. "Do you know what King said to me today on the phone?"

Wade got still, his only movement the rise and fall of his chest. "Threatened Hannah."

I mirrored his stillness, confirmed King's threat against Hannah, and then told him about Jesse. Wade, who knew I loved my uncle, paled and started to say something. I held up my hand. Time for the scum on the toilet water. "There's more. King said if I didn't buzz off, he'd kill you." I paused for effect. "And make me watch. Tubby said King's asked about hiring a hitman to kill me. So I assume me dying figures somehow into your murder." The very thought called my fury. My magic rampaged through me, ready to hurt something.

Disbelief passed over Wade's face as the words soaked in. Hurt followed. The fight drained out of him, leaving behind a big, lonely man who'd just realized he'd put his trust in the wrong person. "But I..." He shook his head instead of continuing and stood from the table, knocking his chair on the floor, and stumbled from the room. A door slammed.

My heart throbbed for him, but I let him stew alone. King Tolliver was going to pay. I don't take sass from an over-the-hill outlaw, much less death threats to my friends. King just thought he didn't like me. He was about to find out what a crazy bitch looked like.

The sound of Wade blowing his nose filtered into the kitchen. A door opened, and his footsteps shook the house. He'd taken off the Six Gun Revolutionaries T-shirt he usually wore and replaced it with a plain white one. He grabbed his leather jacket off the chair and jerked the vest, which bore all his club patches, off it. He slung the vest onto the kitchen floor. It slid into a corner.

Wade sat back down in his chair and faced me across the table, chin down, eyes raised to mine. "I'm done being loyal and won't fight you anymore. What's the plan?"

I took the last sip of coffee. "Ain't really much of one. Tubby's got protection for Jesse in prison. He said we're going to war with the Six Guns."

Wade slowly nodded. "We are. First thing, call Rainey. Tell her to get somewhere safe. Her parents too."

I made the call. Rainey answered as though she'd been awake. She wanted to know who, what, when, where, and I told her. Then I told her to hide herself and her dog and keep her phone nearby. She blew up.

"You've got to be kidding me," she shouted over the phone. "How dare you cut me off like I'm some delicate flower?"

I closed my eyes. "I can't protect both you and Hannah."

The argument went round and round. By the time I hung up, Wade's impatience had him fidgeting in the chair, shaking the whole table.

"King expects you to make a move for Hannah. Trench Coat and Corman are guarding him now." He checked the clock on his phone. "When I left, I had until nine in the morning to get back there. I'm how you'll get in."

Tubby had been right. Wade had disavowed the Six Gun Revolutionaries on the strength of my word. How did Tubby know what people would do?

"But we've got a problem. Normally, if a person is ridden by an evil entity, you want to get it out as quickly as possible. But this is different." Wade stopped speaking, eyebrows rumpling into a frown. I let him take his time. We sat in silence for several minutes. "Hannah's hag can come and go as he pleases. You have to trap him inside Hannah until you can get to safe place to perform a banishing ritual." Wade set a tiny leather bag on the table between us.

"What's that?" I touched it with one finger. It felt warm and pliable, almost alive.

"Aunt DeeDee taught me to make these when I was a teenager. We sold them to people who wanted protection from evil spirits." He pushed the bag at me. "Go on and put it in your pocket. Let it charge from your magic. It won't take much."

I did as he said but still didn't understand how something intended to repel spirits would keep one inside. Wade chuckled.

"I see that look on your face. You're wondering how this'll work."

I shrugged. Wade knew his stuff, different stuff than Mysti Whitebyrd taught me. I had no call to question him.

"You can tell the bag is a living thing, yes?" I nodded at Wade's question. "Spirits can enter the human body through the eyes, the ears, the nose, the mouth, the genitals, even an open wound."

"Disgusting." The bag felt warm and twitchy in my pocket. It was disgusting in its own right.

"This bag works with the person's body chemistry. It creates a coating over the skin that's hostile to spirits. It'll keep the spirit from passing out of Hannah's body. I hope." He waited for my questions, but I shook my head to let him know I had none. "You put this in her pocket as soon as you can. Get her to safety and do the banishing ritual quickly." He slid a paper across the table. "Here's what I can remember of what Aunt DeeDee said about this. She's been dead now for twenty years, so I might have forgotten something. I asked Desiree when I called earlier what she knew, but she didn't know anything else."

The question of Wade's sister wormed around my thoughts more than it should have. He was so secretive, and this was the sister who told him not to be with me romantically. I filed away the thoughts for later, took the paper with the instructions from Wade's Aunt DeeDee, and put it in my back pocket. "But you'll be there to help."

His face darkened. "Sure will. But keep it anyway, all right?"

This was Wade's admission he might not get out alive. The possibility worked its way through me like a disease. Horror came with it. I wanted to call a halt to our plans. Walk away. But I couldn't. In life, there are fights that must be fought. They all have consequences.

"Let's talk about the mission now. You need to understand the layout of the compound." Wade grabbed a fast food napkin and began to draw on it. "The time you visited, all you saw was the clubhouse. King's got a house out back of that, and there's a barracks near it." He drew sloppy boxes for each building. "The ones in the clubhouse will be so drunk at nine in the morning they won't be able to stand. But they'll still be armed. The barracks might be full or not. I didn't pay attention to who-all was staying tonight."

"Hannah will be in King's house?" I leaned forward, trying to figure out which box that was.

Wade nodded and marked an x on one of the boxes. "She'll be in the bedroom alone, sleeping it off. King gets up early and cooks himself and Corman breakfast."

How homey. Just a couple of abusive assholes enjoying some bacon and eggs. "Are we going to kill them?" It wouldn't be my first killing. After the way King treated Hannah, it wouldn't even be the most difficult. But Corman was supposedly Wade's best friend. King had helped him beat a murder charge. I asked the question to see how far Wade would go.

"If they get in the way." Wade's eyes rested on the wall behind me, empty of their usual warmth.

There was nothing left to talk about. We sat in silence as the sun began to peek over the horizon. My phone dinged with a text message.

It was from Tubby: "You about ready?"

I passed the question on to Wade. He pushed the napkin at me, and I folded it into my jeans pocket.

I texted a yes back to Tubby.

Wade spoke as soon as the phone made its message sent sound. "Tell him we'll meet him at the Big Star Truck Stop. We can leave your truck there." He cleared the coffee cups off the table, slipped his leather jacket on, and grabbed his vest off the floor. He held it between his thumb and forefinger like it was tainted. I guess it was for him.

I started typing in Wade's directive, but the phone dinged with another text message. "He said he'll be here in ten minutes."

Wade gave me an angry scowl. "You told that freak of nature where I live?"

I made a face right back at him, not sure why I felt defensive about Tubby. "Hell no. He already knew."

Wade shook his head. "That guy's creepy."

I didn't want to defend Tubby, but I didn't want to talk bad about him. Tubby's and my official declaration of friendship had changed my feelings about him. I hoped with all my heart I wasn't betting money on the wrong horse. But I couldn't talk to Wade about Tubby. Time to change the subject. "Thank you for helping me. I know I don't tell you enough, but you're one of my favorite people."

Wade knelt in front of me, folded me in his arms, and squeezed tight. I pressed my face against his chest and inhaled. His smell comforted me no matter what was going down. He let go of me. "Let's meet him out there. We still need to take your truck somewhere other than here."

6

———

WE LEFT my truck at the nearest convenience store, and I rode the rest of the way to the Six Gun Compound with Tubby. Tubby's Chevy Caprice looked like he'd bought it at a police auction. There were holes in the console where something, probably a laptop stand, had been bolted. The car also carried a certain odor, the kind no cleaning product would ever quite mask. The heater didn't work either. That sucked because it was one of those cold, dank spring mornings.

I sat huddled on the bench seat, my arms wrapped around my chest for warmth. "Can't you afford a nicer car?"

Tubby grinned at me. "Can't be traced back to me. Plus, Bullfrog said it runs fast."

And it did. The speedometer hovered near the one hundred mark as Tubby struggled to keep up with Wade's Harley. Wade pulled onto the soft shoulder, slowing fast and putting both feet down quickly. Tubby whipped the ex-cop car off the road, jammed on the brakes, and slid to a stop behind Wade's motorcycle. "Bullfrog forgot to tell me the brakes don't work."

I got out of the car without answering and hurried to stand next to Wade. "What now?"

He'd been staring into the woods hiding the compound from the highway, but now he faced me. Excitement lit up his dark eyes, but I thought I saw fear there too. The Six Gun Revolutionaries killed their enemies. No questions asked. Traitors probably got worse. He waited to speak until Tubby joined us. "You got your map?"

I unfolded the napkin Wade had used to illustrate the layout of the Six Gun Revolutionaries' fifty-acre compound.

Wade laid one finger at the main entrance. "We're about five hundred yards south from this point. It's right down this road. I'll use the keypad to let myself inside. Trench Coat'll get the alert and see me on the surveillance camera, but he won't know what I've got in the saddlebags." *I* didn't know what Wade had in the saddlebags. He wouldn't let me watch him load them. He'd made me wait in the car with Tubby. "Where are the two of you supposed to go?"

Tubby crowded close, pointing, but I spoke up. "Back entrance." I dug in my pocket and held up a key. "No keypad. I'll unlock it with this."

Tubby let out an impatient snort and bumped my leg with his. "But first we kill the surveillance."

Wade nodded. "If they're watching, they'll come find you, and that'll be that." He swallowed hard. "But I'm thinking if we time it just right, they'll be focused on me coming in and miss you."

Tubby let out a maniacal cackle. He must have liked that.

Wade rolled his eyes. "What then?"

I traced our route on the map. "Follow this until we get to the burned-out mobile home. Walk the rest of the way to King's house. It's just around the next bend, past these train cars." I tapped the spot on the map. "Wait for your signal. What's that going to be anyway?"

"You'll know it when you hear it." Wade glanced at Tubby, who nodded. The two shared some secret. Had I not been so keyed up, I'd have angled for it. But we didn't have time. Wade turned his frown back on me. "Then what do you do?"

I took a deep breath. "Use the key you gave me to unlock the back door. Go in, get Hannah, and you'll meet us outside. We'll ride out together."

Wade stared at Tubby. Something else I couldn't interpret passed between the two men. Tubby nodded, and Wade clapped him on the shoulder hard enough to rock him on his feet.

I gripped Wade's arm. "Thank you for doing this."

He pushed off my hand and shook his head. Then he grabbed me in a back-popping hug. I hugged him back, wishing for the zillionth time it could be different, wanting to tell him how I loved him. At least Tubby was looking on. Otherwise, I'd have turned into a big, mushy mess.

Wade let go of me and put both hands on my face. "Show no mercy to any of these fuckers because they won't show it to you. Do what you came to do and leave alive." He nodded to Tubby.

"Come on." Tubby led the way back to the car and started it. We drove a few yards and turned off on an unmarked dirt road crowded with woods on both sides. Tubby slowed the car to a crawl, both of us looking for a dirt driveway with a bunch of junk piled in it. We found it and got out to push the crap out of the way. It went fast until we found the lawn tractor with no wheels. Tubby hooked his fingers under the frame, and I pushed at the front.

"I can't believe you're going into the compound with me." My feet slid in the loose sand, and I almost fell face first into hunk of junk. Tubby shook his head and kept pulling, cords standing out in his neck. The lawn mower finally began to move. We got it far enough out of the way to drive around it and stopped, both of us breathing hard.

Tubby's skinny chest heaved inside his ribbed white T-shirt. Chill bumps made the hair on his arms stand straight out. He motioned for me to follow him. "Text message Wade and tell him we're ready to go in."

I did, and Wade came back with an okay. I heard his motorcycle rumble to life a short distance away. We counted thirty just like he'd said. Then Tubby crept down the drive and pointed at a surveillance camera hidden the trees, pulled a can of paint out of his pocket, and handed it to me. "I'll lift you up, and you spray the lens." He bent and motioned for me to climb onto his back.

Using the tree for balance, I climbed until I stood on his shoulders. Tubby trembled to hold my weight but didn't make a peep. I spray-painted the camera's lens with florescent orange paint. Tubby let me down, and I unlocked the gate and got back into the car.

I couldn't leave it alone. "Why are you doing this? You could have just let me and Wade go in alone." I turned in the seat to stare at his profile.

"You even see that surveillance cam 'fore I pointed it out? How you think you gonna survive, much less get Hannah out, if I don't help you?" He grinned at me now. "We friends, ain't we? I told you I don't have many of those."

I flushed and said no more. We reached the burned-out mobile home and got out of the car, King's house visible through the trees. It wouldn't be far to run once we had Hannah. The bass throttle of Wade's motorcycle came from the other side of King's house. I dragged my tongue over my dry lips, wishing I'd peed before we left. The motorcycle cut off. Several seconds went by. My bladder felt like I'd drank six gallons of water.

A voice I didn't recognize yelled, "The fuck is he doing? Hey Mojo, what are you—"

A low whoosh interrupted the speaker. There was a moment of silence before a bang shook the earth beneath my feet. Then the shooting started. My throat closed. It took everything I had not to double over coughing and gagging because, all of a sudden, I couldn't breathe.

Tubby gave me a shove in the direction of the house. "It's time. Go!"

We crept to the back door. I unlocked it as quietly as I could. Tubby elbowed past me, a semi-automatic pistol in one hand. He went inside, gun raised. He looked around and tipped his head for me to come inside. We stood in a laundry room full of filthy clothes perfumed with a combination of beer, sweat, and cigarettes. I recognized a few garments as Hannah's. The sounds of King's and Corman's surprised shouts came through the door. Another explosion shook the house.

I put one hand on the laundry room's doorknob. Tubby gripped his pistol tighter and tensed his legs. As softly as I could, I turned the doorknob and swung the door open. We were in a dark hallway. Wade had said the kitchen was to the right and the master bedroom to the left.

Heart in my throat, I stepped into the hallway. The smell of smoke and gasoline filled the house. Men shouting, cursing, and screaming came with it. I tried not to think about how things were going for Wade. My mind supplied a few awful pictures of him lying on the ground, his blood spreading around him. *No.* My lungs tightened until it felt like I wasn't even breathing. I fought for control. Tubby motioned with his head for me to go get Hannah.

I tried to walk softly, but my footsteps sounded like rumbling boulders going down the hallway. Vomit burned the back of my throat. My heart thundered so hard my vision shook. With every step, I wondered if I was going to wet my pants.

Then I stood with my hand on the doorknob to the master bedroom. A million possibilities raced through my head, all of them bad. Hannah could start screaming. She could fight. By now that awful thing had found its way back to her. It wouldn't want me stealing its gourmet dinner, or whatever it saw Hannah as. I took a deep breath and turned the doorknob.

———

Hannah was sprawled across the bed, naked. Her sides moved with the rhythm of intoxicated sleep. I remembered seeing Chase this way too many times not to recognize it.

"Hannah?" I whispered. "You got to wake up."

She didn't even stir.

I gathered clothes that looked like hers and dropped them on the bed next to her. Then I shook her. "Hannah. Wake up now."

She grunted and coughed. I winced away. Her breath smelled like the results of a tequila enema. I steeled myself and shook her again. One eye cracked open. When she realized it wasn't King, her eyes widened, she sat up on the bed, clutching the sheet to her chest. "Get out."

I shook my head. "You told me to come get you."

"You're lying. Mind your own business." She hissed the words through clenched teeth and dropped the sheet. Both breasts had bruise handprints on them. She stood, naked. I dropped my gaze to the filthy carpet. I didn't want to see this. Hannah grabbed her rumpled clothes and yanked them on, all the while ranting. "How dare you come in here like this? King'll kill you."

A war waged outside, perfectly audible. Hannah didn't seem to hear. She dressed, giving me a hateful glare the whole time. "King?" she yelled.

I rushed forward and grabbed her arm. "Shh. Check

your phone. You sent me a text message around eleven last night."

She shoved me away and smirked. "I did a lot of things last night."

Tubby appeared in the door. The fire alarm blared from the kitchen, and the smell of smoke was closer than ever. "Come on. Now."

I didn't want to have to drag Hannah out of here, but Tubby was right. We had to leave. I closed the distance between Hannah and me, reaching for her. "I know what's got hold of you. Come with me. I'll help you get rid of it."

She giggled, belly vibrating with her laugh. I glanced in the dusty mirror attached to the dresser and gulped. The trollish wraith hunkered on Hannah's shoulder, bigger than it had been the day before. It leaned to whisper in her ear. All my hopes of her leaving peacefully died a tragic death. I'd never reason with her like this.

I pulled on the mantle, what control I had over it anyway, and aimed fire at Hannah's passenger, watching in the mirror. The magic knocked the ugly little thing askew. It turned its black-hole eyes on me and hissed. Hannah stiffened. She shook all over as the burn of my magic flooded through her. I tried to pull back, using all my strength. As it had been at Wade's, the magic came out a lot easier than it went in.

I strained so hard I could feel the pressure behind my eyeballs, but the magic finally went back where it belonged. My body shook from the effort, sweat dampening my back and armpits. Hannah relaxed as the fire left her. Then she opened her mouth and let out the most piercing scream I'd ever heard.

Time stood still, then it sped up beyond what I could manage. Footsteps crashed through the house. The doorknob turned. Whoever it was pounded on the door. "Why's the door locked?"

I froze at the sound of King's voice. While I'd worked for him, I'd seen him do a lot of scary things. I'd come here thinking I could confront him fearlessly. Now here I was, about to piss my pants, knees shaking like a kid on the way to principal's office.

Tubby ran to the window and yanked the cord on the mini blinds. We stared at grime-covered glass with bars beyond.

"Open this door. Right now. " King banged on it. "Am I going to have to show you who's boss again?"

Hannah cowered at the voice. I thought about the handprints on her breasts. Now I saw even more finger marks on her arms. Sweat sprang out on my palms, and my heart slammed against my ribcage.

King kicked the door several times. "Open this motherfucker. Now."

Tubby flinched. Hannah tried to go around us to open the door. I grabbed her arm, and she clawed at me. I defended myself as best as I could but took a good scratch to the cheek. King started kicking the door again. The frame cracked. Tubby raised his gun. The door flew open, and Tubby pulled the trigger. The blast shook the room.

King came from behind the door frame where he'd pressed himself to the wall and rushed into the room, gun already up and pointed at Tubby. Hannah tried to claw at me again. I slapped Hannah's face harder than I wanted and shoved her behind me without waiting to see her reaction. I had time to smell fear sweat, probably my own, and to hear Tubby's panting breaths next to me. Something moved in the dark hallway behind King.

Wade's face came into view. He raised one fist and let it fly at the back of King's head. The impact sounded like a melon getting dropped on concrete. King Tolliver's cold eyes closed, and he slumped to the floor. Wade took off his club vest and dropped it on the president of the Six Gun Revolutionaries.

I turned to Hannah. "Let's go. He'll never hurt you again."

She launched herself at me, kicking and clawing. "You sorry piece of shit. It's all your fault." She began to cry in ugly gulps, still clawing at me. I wanted to double up my fist and knock the shit out of her, but still felt guilty about the slap I'd delivered earlier. Hannah took full advantage, screaming, "Bitch. Whore. Your fault. Your fault."

Wade stepped forward, his mouth set in a grim line. He spoke to me. "I'm sorry for what I'm about to do, but we have to go now." He slammed one huge fist into Hannah's cheekbone. She folded like a puppet with its strings cut and dropped to the floor. I slipped the little leather bag into her pocket.

In my sixth sense, the part of me that saw and heard the paranormal world, a howl rose. My gut said it was Hannah's hag trying to escape. Bully for him. Wade winced as the shriek reached a high enough decibel to make the mirror in the beat-up dresser shake. He picked up Hannah and slung her over his shoulder like a bag of laundry.

"Grab King's gun," he said to me. "And make sure the safety's off."

Wade stalked from the room carrying Hannah. Tubby hurried to open the door for him. Both men cut across the backyard, heading to the spot where Tubby had parked the car. My lungs screamed as my short legs struggled to keep up. I grabbed at the stitch forming in my side.

Someone shouted on the other side of the house. Wade and I froze, eyes wide. Tubby raced for the car. Wade motioned me ahead of him, but I couldn't leave him and stopped every few steps for him to catch up. We finally got within sight of the car. Cheerful spring sun winking off its chrome bumper blinded me. Tubby sprinted toward it, motioning frantically at me to come on.

A gunshot shattered the silence, and a low hum filled my ears. Someone cried out. My chest tightened with terror. The ringing in my ears increased in volume.

Ahead of me, Tubby glanced down at his body. Then his gaze fixed on something behind me. *No.* Nerves sizzling, I turned around, dreading what waited for me.

Wade sprawled on the ground, arms and legs splayed out. Hannah lay motionless on the ground a few feet from him. A guy I knew only as Trench Coat, stalked toward Wade, a double-barrel shotgun held at waist level. His bald head gleaming in the sunlight reminded me of the way the sun had reflected off Tubby's Chevy Caprice. I stared stupidly at him, just watching him come.

Wade raised his head, black eyes full of pain. His mouth quivered. "Go."

I took a couple of running steps toward him. Trench Coat pointed his shotgun at me and pulled the trigger. It clicked, empty. I raised my own pistol and squeezed the trigger. Trench Coat ran behind a rusted-out truck on blocks. He dug two more shotgun cartridges out of his pocket, jacked open the shotgun, and fumbled both of them into the overgrown weeds covering his boots.

"Fuck!" he screamed and dropped to retrieve them.

Tubby ran back to us. "Which one?" he asked, meaning did I want him to grab Hannah or Wade.

"Her. Now." Wade pointed to Hannah. Without another glance at me, Tubby helped her to her feet. She was so dazed from Wade's punch, she let Tubby drag her to the car without protest.

"I can't leave you," I said to Wade. Reaching deep, I searched for my magic, but I'd used it all to trying to burn Hannah's parasitic rider. All my magic did was give me a weak ping. It reminded me of a car with a dead battery.

"Does anybody see them?" King's roar came, the proximity of it bringing new waves of fear.

"I got 'em," Trench Coat yelled. "They're back here." He finally fished one of the shotgun cartridges out of the overgrown grass and loaded one of the shotgun's barrels.

"Go now," Wade yelled.

A shout of refusal tried to beat its way out of me, but I knew he was right. "I'll be back for you."

He shook his head. "This is it. Goodbye."

Trench Coat snapped the shotgun shut and raised it.

Leaving Wade was betrayal, the worst kind. I howled my rage as I ran.

The boom of the shotgun came from behind me. Pellets peppered the dirt around me, but none found its way home. I rounded the burned-out mobile home. The car sat where we'd left it.

Tubby sat in the driver's seat staring straight ahead, Hannah next to him. Her eyes were fixed on some point in the distance. I opened the back door. Corman popped up like a jack in the box, pointing his gun at the back of Tubby's seat.

"Surprise," King's son yelled.

Suddenly I knew how I'd get Wade back alive. I raised the pistol and pointed it at Corman's forehead. "Move."

He snorted. "I'll shoot Tubman. And Hannah."

I let the gun drop a bit, like I was thinking about it. Then I pulled the trigger. The pistol bucked in my hand, the force of its discharge surprising me, no matter how many times Wade had forced me to practice. Corman fell backward on the seat, screaming, hand gripping his arm. I snatched his gun away and climbed in on top of him. Tubby started the car and sped back to where we'd gotten inside, dirt fanning from the back wheels and kicking up a cloud of dust thicker than any smoke screen.

"Now call your father." I pushed the both guns' barrels into Corman's forehead. "Tell him I'll trade you for Wade. Alive."

Corman just stared at me.

"Do it. Do it. Do it." I screamed the words in his face,

enjoying the way his eyes, already squinted in pain, fluttered every time I yelled.

The car careened onto the main road, engine roaring. Corman took out his phone, punched a few buttons, and began speaking.

7

BULLFROG's doughy face showed no expression as he loaded Corman into the paneled van marked with the imprint of a well-known power tool brand. The pain had set in, and Corman yelped every time Bullfrog yanked him. I clenched my teeth, and my hands curled into fists as I imagined Wade screaming in pain somewhere behind us.

Tubby, seeing the expression on my face, snatched one of the pistols from me and marched over to Corman. "Get in without making another sound or I will shoot both your feet and your hands. Give you bullet stigmata."

Corman, trembling all over, climbed into the van. Bullfrog followed and used zip ties to bind his ankles and wrists.

Hannah watched the whole show open-mouthed. She didn't even flinch as Bullfrog put a hand on the back of her neck and forced her into the van, giving her the same treatment with the zip ties as he'd given Corman. Tubby climbed into the van and held one hand out to me. I took it and let him pull me inside. We sat against the van's wall facing our prisoners. Tubby put his arm around my shoulders. At first, I pulled away but then I leaned my head on him and wept as though it would cure the hollow sense of loss growing in my chest.

"Go ahead and cry," Corman crowed. I raised my head to glare at him, and he curled his lip in a sneer. "Wade's a dead man. And you caused it."

Sobs wracked my body. Having heard Corman's side of a six-word conversation with King Tolliver, I was ready to believe Wade was already dead. King had said for Corman to tell us he was coming to kill us all.

"Shut up." Tubby pointed his pistol at Corman.

The other man simply laughed. "You're not gonna shoot me in here. Even you're not that crazy."

Sirens blared in the distance. "Five-oh coming," Bullfrog called from the front seat.

"Just keep the speed steady and act right," Tubby returned.

A couple of Burns County Sheriff's cars, followed by a volunteer fire truck raced past, heading toward the Six Gun Compound. A white unmarked sedan followed. Dean. Maybe Dean could get Wade.

I took out my phone and called him.

He picked up on the first ring. "You get Hannah? Everybody all right?"

I nodded even though he couldn't see me. "You just passed us." My breath hitched on the last word. "We've got Hannah, but they've got Wade. He needs medical attention."

Dean drew in a breath. He didn't like Wade when we were dating, and he probably didn't want to help him now. "I'll look for him, but don't be surprised if..." He trailed off. It was just as well. I knew what he meant.

"Get him if you can, okay?" I winced at the pleading in my voice.

"I will. And I'll keep my end of the bargain. My official understanding of this situation is that Six Guns have gone to war with another motorcycle gang. You and your people get out of sight and stay there." He hung up without waiting for my answer.

Bullfrog drove the speed limit all the way to Gaslight City and pulled into the alley behind Silver Dreams Antiques and Dottie's Burgers and Rings. He cut the engine. "End of the road, kids."

Tubby got out and unlocked the back door of Silver Dreams Antiques. I sniffed for the heavenly scent of Dottie's greasy spoon cooking. Tubby caught me and shook his head. "She retired a coupla months ago. Sold the building to my development company." He held open the door and motioned me inside. I stared back at the van.

"What about Hannah and Corman? We have to put Hannah in a circle as fast as possible in case the hag has tricks I haven't anticipated." My phone began to ring, but I ignored it, waiting for Tubby's answer. He shook his head and waved me off. I took my phone out. Mysti. Last we talked, she and Griff were on an important job. I answered. "You okay?"

Highway sounds came over Mysti's end of the call. They seemed to have an echo. "Are *you* okay? I got a call from Wade Hill last night insisting I come to Gaslight City to help you with Hannah. I'm sitting in my car in front of the museum, which is closed. Where are you?"

I walked out of Silver Dreams and skirted around Tubby and Bullfrog wrestling Corman out of the van.

"Where're you going?" Tubby let go of Corman, letting him fall on the nasty asphalt and chased after me.

"Wade called Mysti into this. She's at the museum." I hurried out to the sidewalk, ignoring the curious stares from passersby, and raced down the block toward Mysti's car. As I drew close, I realized two people sat inside with her. A man who wasn't Griff, and a shadowy figure in the back seat. The man twisted in his seat and stared out the window at me. I gasped.

What was my Uncle Cecil doing here? He told me he'd never set foot in Gaslight City. He feared it with an almost religious fervor. A shadow moved in the backseat, and my cousin-by-marriage, Dillon, leaned forward and waved.

Tears closed my throat. My family was willing to go against their core beliefs to help me? And there sat Mysti in the driver's seat, faithful as ever. The rush of gratitude brought me back from the edge. Maybe everything could be made okay. I launched myself at them. Cecil managed to get out of the car and hold his arms open to me.

I grabbed him in a hug, already sobbing. "They got Wade," I choked out. "Shot him. I had to leave him or they'd have gotten me, Tubby, and Hannah too." I wept harder.

Cecil stroked my back. "All right, all right. Settle down. Let's get off the street. Out of sight."

I swallowed my tears and swiped a hand across my face. "See the sign that says Silver Dreams?" As I asked, Bullfrog's white van exited the alley. He and Tubby must have gotten Corman and Hannah inside the building. A shadow appeared in one of the upper windows. I made out Tubby's face. He stood with his hands in his pockets, watching us. "Go in the alley and park there."

A few minutes later, we were in what used to be an upstairs storeroom and breakroom for the antique store. That is, before a nasty spell cast by a bad witch got hold of Silver Dreams's owner, and she killed Memaw and then killed herself. Tubby'd moved a scarred but heavy table, probably a castoff from the former antique store, into the kitchenette and pulled mismatched folding metal chairs around it. Someone had made coffee. Cecil was the only one drinking it.

Hannah had been bound to a chair and placed a safe distance from the table. She growled through her teeth at us. Tubby stood a short distance away holding a paper towel soaked in alcohol to a spot where she'd bitten him.

Mysti, chalk in one hand, held out a worn, cloth-bound book. "Peri Jean, get up and help me. It's time to put Hannah in a protective circle."

I slowly got up from my place at the table and took a long shuddering breath, the kind that come after a long bout of crying. The tears had left my cheeks dry and raw. Wade had known he wouldn't come back and helped anyway. The vise of grief tightened again. Was this the prophecy in his sister's card reading coming to pass? If so, she'd been right. Getting involved with me had ended Wade, the best man I'd ever known.

I came close to Mysti but ignored the book. "What did Wade say when he called you to come here and help me?" I choked out, ready to bawl again.

"If we don't get him back, I'll tell you. But let's do this right now." Mysti's tone left no room for me to argue. She pushed the book at me again. This time, I took it.

The book's weight caught me off guard. I nearly dropped it. As I fumbled, the magic of this book seeped into my fingers. My black opal heated, and the mantle crouched inside me, ready for action. A breeze from nowhere moved my hair. Mysti watched me with her mouth open in shock. Magic was like a muscle, and I exercised mine almost every day. It had grown stronger than when we were last together.

She put on her professional witch face and started giving orders, which was what she did best. "Wade said to use this exact pentacle. It's supposed to terrify spirits you seek to control. Hopefully, that and the mojo bag he gave you can keep this hag in place until we banish it."

The book's print, handwritten and red-tinted, seemed to vibrate. I glanced up at Mysti, silently asking if she'd seen the same thing. Her pinched face gave me my answer.

She said, "I'm going to draw the circles, but you're going to have to give me instructions. This is not my kind of magic."

Our work went slow. I told her how to spell the Four Names of God and directed her in drawing the grid in the middle of the circle. Hannah's growls and hisses increased as the circle took shape.

Mysti glanced at Tubby. "Help us pick up Hannah's chair and put her on top of the circle before I close it."

"She done bit me. You can't expect me to..." Tubby let out a frustrated grunt and stood.

Mysti went back to her witch bag and withdrew a black satiny sack. She approached Hannah. Seeming to know what was about to happen, Hannah whipped her head side to side. Mysti slid the bag over her head with enough expertise that I guessed this wasn't a cherry popping experience for her.

Tubby counted off, and the four of us picked up the chair and lugged it into the circle. Hannah screeched like an animal the entire time. Mysti whipped the bag off Hannah's head and leapt away from her.

The monster inside Hannah was either angry or distressed. Hannah's eyes bugged out and rolled in their sockets. The skin underneath her eyes had darkened. Spittle flecked the corners of Hannah's cracked and dried lips. She yowled again, sounding more animal than human.

Tubby backed away, face waxy. "She gone batshit. Ain't seen no evidence of a troll or nothing on her shoulder."

I walked away from the group to a far wall where a mirror hung. I took it off the wall, walked back to where everyone else was, and called to Cecil. "Papaw." My great-uncle turned to me. "Will you hold this up where Hannah's reflected in it?"

He put aside his coffee and took the mirror from me.

He stood several feet from Hannah, maybe afraid she'd spit on him if he got close enough. I walked back to Tubby, took his hand, and concentrated on Hannah. He needed to believe in what we were dealing with or he'd be more hindrance than help.

Hannah's image in the mirror flickered, and a dark shadow took shape on her shoulder, its skin the color of a cancerous mole. Its size had increased to the point it looked like a baby gorilla squatting on my friend. The hag hissed at us, but the sound came out of Hannah's mouth. Tubby jerked his hand from mine. He backed away, mouth open, shaking his head.

"No," he muttered and turned to Cecil. "That ain't real."

Cecil shrugged like someone who'd seen it all twice.

Tubby's phone rang. He answered and left the room speaking in a low voice.

Dillon approached me and held out her hand. We went through the routine again. She leaned forward and squinted at the passenger. "Damn, that thing's ugly."

I held out my hand to Mysti. She shook her head. "I see it for the same reason you do. I've already got the dark outposts in me." She looked at me as though I should have known. I hadn't. She dismissed me. "Let's talk about what we're going to do."

***

MYSTI WENT INTO THE KITCHENETTE, dug in her purse until she found one of her homemade tea bags, and set about making herself a cup of tea. Tubby came back into the room and pulled a stool next to my chair.

He leaned his head near mine and spoke into my ear. "That was my contact in the sheriff's office. Six Guns are claiming a gas stove blew up. They told the fire department and the sheriff's people to get the fuck off their property."

I didn't care what lie the Six Guns used to get the authorities off their property. Only one person mattered. "Wade?"

Tubby shook his head. "My contact never saw him. Said King had a short conversation with Sheriff Dean, and they all just turned around and left."

My stomach dropped to my feet, and my skin went hot and then cold. Of course Dean just left. He didn't care what happened to Wade. One dead member of the Six Gun Revolutionaries was one less problem for him. He'd hired his biker exterminator, and it was me. He'd be happy as long as he didn't get shit on his shoes. I was running from a human tornado, outlaw style, and I was just as disposable as the people I'd come to do away with. The magnitude of it crushed against me. I could almost feel its pressure on my skin. I caught Cecil watching me. He tipped his chin in a nod, one I understood. *You can do this.* I pulled myself together.

"Where's Corman?" Having not heard him since I came into the building, I worried he might have bled out or died of shock.

Tubby jerked a thumb at the stairwell leading back into what had been the store. "Downstairs. Tied up and stoned. Bullfrog gave him some hillbilly heroin." He giggled.

I didn't quite know what to do about Corman. If Wade had been here, we'd have healed him and kept him out of the way so he'd be a good trade. I didn't have Wade's powers. Maybe I needed to call Doctor Longstreet or see if Tubby knew someone with medical training. Then it hit me that the Six Guns were probably just letting Wade bleed and hurt. Thinking about Wade made me want to cry again. I turned my focus to Mysti. She'd have answers. Mysti sat down at the table, stirring her tea. It smelled like burnt pubic hair. Only Mysti would drink something that smelled so awful.

I tried to wait until she took the first sip but didn't quite make it. "What did you mean about being able to see the hag because you have the dark outposts in you?" I leaned away from the awful smelling brew, and my back bumped into Tubby. He put his hand on my hip. I didn't bother to make him move it.

Mysti glanced at Tubby's hand, frowning. "When you were looking for the Mace Treasure, I told you that sometimes things from the dark outposts make their way over here."

Tubby spoke up. "Yeah. I remember you saying that. I figured it was vampires or werewolves. Not gargoyles."

Mysti stared into her tea. "I don't like those terms to describe the things I see. They're the product of scared people trying to explain what they don't understand and are not wholly accurate." She bit her lip frowning. "But we do need to find terms you'll understand to talk about this." She gestured at Hannah.

A low growl came from Hannah's chest. It turned into a wail like a lost cat might make and went on and on. Dillon pushed her chair back from the table and said, "I've had enough." She walked over to Hannah, rolling her neck on her shoulders.

"Don't get close," I called after her. "You get bit, you'll still have your kids to take care of while it heals."

Dillon ignored me but stopped several feet from Hannah. Her growls increased, chest pumping air with each one. Dillon fixed her eyes on Hannah's face and said, "Be quiet."

Dillon's trick worked on a lot of people. I'd seen her take jewelry, get out of paying bills, and even get her kids free medical care. Hannah took a deep breath, and her eyes seemed to clear. Then she let out a sound I'd never heard come out of a human. It sounded like a train's whistle. The walls shook, the windows shook. Hannah snapped the zip ties holding her arms together, leaving bloody strips on her wrists. Dillon backed away, the confidence that made her seem older than her twenty-two years gone.

"Shit." Tubby jumped off his stool and ran to Hannah. I followed.

Hannah bent forward, trying her best to break the zip tie around her ankles. Tubby grabbed one of her arms and pulled it back. I did the other. Hannah snapped like an animal, her teeth clacking together.

I glanced back at the table to see if Mysti was going to help. She rummaged in her witch pack. Great time to play with her stuff. Cecil stood from his seat, eyes swallowing his face, and slowly approached.

"Tubman?" Mysti spoke without looking up. "Do you have any more drugs on you?"

Tubby shrugged. I glared at him. His cheeks reddened around the stubble. "Over the sink in a plastic bag."

Mysti opened the cabinet and rummaged around. She dropped two packages of braided nylon rope on the counter, dug around some more, and finally withdrew a plastic bag full of multicolored pills. She raised her eyebrows at Tubby. He held out one hand in answer. Mysti gave him the bag, and he picked out two pills and dropped them into her waiting hand. She spoke to Dillon. "You'll have to help me hold her mouth open."

Dillon shook her head. Cecil stepped forward. "I'll do it."

With Tubby and me holding Hannah's arms, Mysti and Cecil somehow got a pill down Hannah's gullet and forced her to swallow.

The whole time, Mysti spoke soothing words to Hannah. "I know you're still in there, and I know this is miserable. But we'll help you. Just rest and get ready to fight."

At Tubby's direction, Dillon found the package of zip ties, and we got Hannah bound again. She had already calmed a great deal. Her chin dropped to her chest, and her eyes stared unfocused. Mysti patted her and led us back to the table where she picked up her teacup as though nothing had happened.

"As I was getting ready to tell Tubby, terms like

vampire, werewolf, or even gargoyle don't adequately describe what we're dealing with here." She gave Tubby a gentle smile. "The things I've seen are not like creatures from mythology or monsters from popular television or books. But in every lie there's a little truth. If you know the concept behind an incubus or succubus, then you have a vague understanding of what that hag riding Hannah is doing. It feeds off her."

"Sexually?" Tubby leaned forward, very interested. It both impressed and amused me he knew the terms Mysti threw out, especially when he didn't even know irregardless isn't a word.

"I'm not completely sure. It could be feeding on any aspect of Hannah's darkest heart." Mysti chewed her lip and frowned as she tried to pick her words.

"Darkest heart?" The phrase grabbed my interest, made something move around in my subconscious.

"That's actually Griffin's expression." She stopped speaking and gripped my arm. "By the way, Peri Jean, Griff wanted to be here. He's just having some personal issues with his mother. She's challenging..." She cut herself off and shook her head. "Now's not the time." She let go of me and clapped once, lightly. "Darkest heart. We all have a shadow side, a side of us where our good qualities become bad ones, minor quirks grow into neuroses. Mostly you just glimpse a person's darkest heart every once in a while."

Mysti's words burrowed deep into my mind. I'd killed other human beings to save my own life and the lives of my loved ones. The experience made me question myself, who

I really was. Killing them hadn't bothered me the way I thought it would. In some dark corner of my mind, I'd considered their threats against my loved ones and me a declaration of war. There were no rules in war. Not for me anyway. Was that my darkest heart? A shiver worked its way up my spine.

Mysti watched me with an odd light dancing in her eyes. "If someone's darkest heart takes over, it eventually causes them to self-destruct. Now I'll try to answer Tubby's question about what Hannah's ugly passenger eats..."

Tubby broke in. "That ugly little shit eats feeds off the sorrow that the host feels as they self-desctruct."

Mysti nodded. "It gets bigger and bigger as the person becomes weaker and weaker. Then when the person finally dies or commits suicide, the thing absorbs their life force."

The hair on the back of my neck prickled with revulsion and maybe a little fear. "What does it do with the life force?"

Mysti drew in a deep breath and stared at Hannah. "Live on it until they find the next host." She shivered and rubbed her arms. The gesture made me wonder what she'd seen in her investigations with Griff. They called me in on ghost stuff but never anything involving an actual monster.

"So can we kill this thing?" I glanced at Hannah. She snoozed, chin dipped toward her chest. A thin line of drool dangled from her mouth.

"We can't kill it." Mysti shook her head. "We'll be lucky to get it out of Hannah without it killing any of us. It's low level compared to some of the beings you've already met, but it's still way more powerful than mere mortals. And you'll get to watch your back the rest of your life. Our stealing its meal is going to piss it off." She turned up her cup and drained it. "Wade prepared me well for what I was going to see, so I've got all the supplies we need."

The mention of Wade stabbed into my heart. He'd known he was living his last hours. I didn't want him to be dead. I didn't think I could go on living if he was. The coming days and weeks of knowing I'd gotten Wade killed stretched out in my imagination, frightening as anything I'd ever faced. I rubbed the aching ball of stress in my shoulder. I had to do something to take my mind off it. Doing a ritual, using my gifts to banish this awful parasite from Hannah, might help. "I'm ready to get started now."

Mysti smiled at me. "Good. But we're waiting until three in the morning."

"The devil's hour?" Tubby asked with a straight face.

Mysti rewarded him with a tip of her chin. "Very good. Rest now. We'll need everybody's energy if we're going to make this work."

8

———

I GOT up from the table, not sure what I was going to do with the hours between now and the ritual. Tubby stood and tapped my arm. "Let's go check on Corman and smoke."

We descended the stairs in silence. Now that we were in a holding pattern, my mind had nothing to do but get up to mischief. The moment of Wade's shooting played on endless loop. My throat ached with the need to cry, but I held it back. This had been my hare-brained scheme. I didn't deserve the luxury of crying over it now.

Mysti'd said each of us had a dark heart, a shadow personality. Hannah's both scared me and made me sad. This manifestation of her was like the anti-Hannah. She'd always liked her drink and her men, but the old Hannah kept it classy. A glass of scotch and soda at a reception. A well-heeled yuppie on her arm. People who didn't know Hannah probably didn't see how many times the scotch and soda got refilled or notice how the man on her arm was never the same. Or if they did, they saw only a wealthy young woman with impeccable manners enjoying herself. This Hannah, the one who sat in Long Time Gone slamming tequila shots with King Tolliver? That Hannah was crawling on the bottom of the septic tank.

The parasite riding her shoulders had taken mostly harmless behavior and turned it into the blackest, coldest night of Hannah's life. Was sitting on that barstool in Long Time Gone wearing a too big shirt, bruises covering her arms, and kissing a nasty piece of human garbage like King Tolliver what really lurked in Hannah's darkest heart? The jump unnerved me. It also brought my mind around to my own darkest heart.

Right then, my darkest heart, which I still thought was my penchant for violence, strained on its leash, begging to bathe in the steaming waters of brutality. I'd make Trench Coat feel like he was burning from the inside out until he lost his mind. He'd never shoot anybody again. King Tolliver. The very thought of him set off fireworks of anger in my brain. My vision wavered. Before this was over, King would beg me to leave him alone. The Six Guns had declared war on me, and I'd fight them until I won or died.

Tubby's fingers closed around my arm. I jumped and let out a yelp. He held up both hands and tried to smile. "I ain't never gotten used to bad scenes like at the Six Gun Compound neither. You keep thinking over what you did wrong, maybe even thinking you shouldn't have got involved in the first place."

I stared at the dark circles under Tubby's eyes and waited to see what he'd say next.

"You did the right thing, going to get Hannah. You're doing the right thing for your Uncle Jesse. And for Rainey too." He giggled. "That girl's got it so bad."

I cocked my head at him. Tubby watched me with an almost sympathetic look on his face. This time he did manage a smile. He slipped his arm around my waist and pulled me to him. I resisted. After his request for a date and my refusal, I didn't want to give him the wrong idea. He strengthened his grip, overpowering me, and whispered in my ear. "Rainey and your uncle got a lil' sumpin' sumpin' going on." He drew back, really grinning now. Had I been thinking straight, I'd have noted that Tubby was sharing secrets with me and not asking for compensation. But Wade dominated my thoughts. I didn't have time for Tubby's diva act. He pouted. "Ain't you gonna axe how I know?"

I shook my head, smiling in spite of myself. Tubby's enthusiasm for gossip was endearing in a scary way.

"So I told you I got a contact at the prison. One thing he brought back to me, just because he knows Rainey's from Gaslight City, is that she and Jesse touch each other ever chance they get. Which ain't much at a prison, but the way he says they look at each other..." Tubby shrugged. "Anyway, you know prisoners' mail is monitored, right? My contact says their letters ain't just legal correspondence. If you know what I mean."

My cheeks heated. How would I ever look my sweet Uncle Jesse in the face again? He was the same age as my father would have been, had been my daddy's twin in fact.

And he was talking dirty to a woman my age who used to be Miss Texas? Oh my.

A grin spread across my face. Tubby's laughter hissed through his teeth. He clapped one hand over his mouth. I put my hands over my face and laughed until my side hurt. Tears streamed down my face. Some of my guffaws sounded more like sobs, but it still felt good.

Tubby patted my back. "You gotta let it out some way. Otherwise, it'll drive you crazy."

I wiped the tears off my face. "It's driving me crazy anyway. I knew why Rainey wanted Jesse out of prison so badly. I can't let her down." I got out my cigarettes. "It's just that everything has turned to shit."

Tubby lit his own cigarette and motioned me to follow him. At the back of the store, near the bathrooms, Corman Tolliver sat tied to a chair. He raised his head but made no other effort to acknowledge us. Tubby took a phone out of his pocket and snapped a picture of Corman. He fiddled around with the phone. A few seconds later, I heard the sound of a text message being sent.

Tubby stuffed the phone back in his pocket. "King ought to like that, the bastard."

I turned away from Tubby and voiced my worst fear. "Wade's dead. That's why King hasn't contacted us." We walked back to the stairs and sat down to smoke.

"Hard to say." Tubby leaned against the wall, smoking and staring into the darkness. Without warning, he reached into his mouth and pulled out a row of teeth. I drew back from him before I could stop myself. Tubby, ignoring my disgust, held up the bridge for me to see. "Remember this?"

I flinched at the sight of it. Tubby'd worn the bridge so long, I'd forgotten about the day he showed up at school, his mouth all swollen. The memory of how long it took our teacher to realize something was wrong with him, that he wasn't just being a little asshole, made my heart hurt.

Tubby stared at the false teeth. "You remember what happened to Roger?"

I remembered. Tubby's evil stepfather. Roger beat the sass out of Tubby about once a month, bad beatings, until Tubby was in his late teens. A hunter found Roger in the National Forest leaning against a tree. He'd died with his hands laced over his stomach where it had been cut open. He must have been trying to hold his guts in. Roger's murder went unsolved.

"This here is a reminder to never eat shit from assholes like the Six Gun Revolutionaries. We can't change what they've done to Wade, but we will give them back everything they've dished out and more." Tubby put his teeth back in his mouth. What was his darkest heart? Maybe the Tubby I sat shoulder to shoulder with was the dark one. Maybe he had no light.

A phone began to ring. It wasn't my ringtone, so I didn't even take mine out. Tubby dug Corman's phone back out of his pocket and answered. "Yeeeesss." He listened, a grin growing on his face. "She's right here, boss." He held the phone out to me. "The boss wants to talk to you. Very important shit."

I took the phone. "What?"

King's shout blasted through the speaker. "If my son's dead, you freak of nature, I swear I'll—"

I hung up on him and set the phone back in my lap, anger sizzling in my veins. I couldn't let myself get into a shouting match with King Tolliver. The phone rang again. I hit the answer button and held the phone to my ear. King's heavy breathing came over the line. "You finished hollering?" I glanced at Tubby to find him watching me, eyes half-lidded, almost smiling.

"You stupid bitch. You got no idea what you done stepped in." King didn't holler, but his voice was like hot pavement at the end of summer, rough and unforgiving.

I lit another cigarette and closed my eyes. My mouth felt too full of spit, and I wanted to swallow, but I didn't want King to hear. I counted to ten and swallowed as quietly as I could. "Let's save the pillow talk for some other time. Tell me if Wade's still alive."

King barked out a dry laugh. "I don't even know if Corman's still alive."

I stood and walked back to where we had Corman, Tubby scurrying after me. The phone had a video call function, and I switched to it. King accepted, and I had the pleasure of his ugly, hollow-cheeked face. At least he wasn't baring his dingy teeth at me. "Here's Corman." I turned the phone and held it near Corman's face. His eyes moved as I got near him.

"Son?" King's voice came from the phone. "Where are you hit?"

"Shoulder." Corman's sluggish voice dragged the word out. "They doped me."

I turned the phone back to my face. "Now Wade."

King laughed at me. Actually laughed.

"Show me Wade, or I'm going to kill Corman right now." I paused, glaring into the phone's camera. "Then I'm coming to kill you and everybody left in your shitty motorcycle club."

King bared his nasty teeth in a grin. "You better be real sure who you're threatening."

I smiled even though I wanted to scream in frustration. "I am. Are you?"

King turned the phone away from himself and showed me a view of Wade curled into the fetal position, facing the camera. My heart thudded faster as I took in the blurry image. Wade's eyes were closed, his sides moved with his breaths. Alive. He was alive.

Behind Wade was a wall of rough-hewn boards, smoke blackened and dingy. They'd put him in one of the structures that got burned down. Jerks. At least I had an idea where he was being kept. Some of the stress holding me upright released. But a million questions followed right behind. Chief among them was how long Wade had left before he bled out or died of shock.

King turned the phone back to his wasted face. Both of us waited for the other to speak. The seconds dragged past, each one full of poisonous fears. Finally King coughed. "Here's my deal. You deliver my son with no further injuries and Barbie's tape about your daddy's murder. I'll let you have what's left of my former friend."

I glanced at Tubby. He shrugged. I spoke into the phone. "But I don't know where the tape is."

King started laughing. "Ask that stupid whore you carried out of my house. She had all kinds of ideas about it when I first met her. You got twenty-four hours." He ended the call.

The facade I'd used with King dropped away. My knees buckled. I pushed the phone at Tubby and grabbed onto the wall. The floor tilted, and black spots danced in my vision. Fear stung every pore on my skin. I hung on for dear life and tried not to puke. So many things could go wrong.

We might not get rid of the hag so we could talk to Hannah. Corman might die. And hours were passing. Wade could die while we bumbled around trying to find the tape. Why did King care so much about it anyway? I stumbled sideways. Corman chuckled from his seat. I shot him a hateful glare.

Tubby stepped in next to me and held me upright. His nasally drawl crooned in my ear. "Come on now. You gonna have to get it together."

I turned to him. "Say Wade's going to be okay."

Tubby shrugged. "I can't."

"He won't be," Corman slurred. "Fucker signed his death warrant when he clobbered Daddy upside the head."

I spun and shook off Tubby's arm, hurling myself at Corman in three running steps. I doubled up my fist and hit him in his bullet wound. Corman squeezed his eyes shut and howled. I delivered a flabby roundhouse to his jaw. Tubby grabbed me around the waist and dragged me away.

He threw me on the wood floor and stood over me. "Don't break your bargaining chip."

I glared at him for a second and then picked myself up. "You're right." Killing Corman would mean I'd never see Wade alive again. *May not anyway.*

A scream built in my chest. I spun away from Tubby and ran into the building's darkness. There, in a dusty corner, I cried myself into a fitful doze. Hours later, a little before three a.m., Dillon woke me to get ready for the spell work.

———

WE GATHERED in the kitchen to learn what we needed to do. I sat off to the side, slugging down coffee and trying to shake off the fogginess my nap had left behind.

"This'll be a two-step process, plus a backup plan." Mysti stood in front of us as though she was teaching a master class on witchcraft. Maybe it was a master class to her.

Cecil raised his hand. I bit my lip to keep from smiling. Must have seemed like a class to him too.

Mysti gestured at him. "Mr. Gregg, you don't have to raise your hand."

"I'm going by Gregson today." Cecil smiled. Mysti pealed out a coquettish giggle so unlike her that I had to stare hard to make sure she hadn't been replaced by some carbon copy of herself. Cecil laughed with her for a few seconds, then spoke. "I'm sorry to interrupt, but I'm not a witch. Ever since my big heart attack, I'm not much of anything unless I'm borrowing power from Peri Jean. Are you sure I won't do more harm than good?"

Mysti began nodding before he finished his question. "Everybody here has energy, and you, Dillon, and Peri Jean are able to combine power. This rider Hannah's picked up is old and powerful. We're going to need all the juice we can get just to detach it from her, let alone secure it somewhere it can't harm anyone else." She motioned to me to join her. She handed me a blue bottle. "Go on and start the consecration process."

"What's the bottle becoming?" I got into my own witch pack and removed a special blessed lemon and hyssop cleansing solution, some sunflower oil, and a black cloth.

"A witch bottle to house the entity." Mysti took fingernail clippers out of her witch pack and passed them to Cecil. "Fingernail trimmings from everybody."

Across the room Hannah's head jerked up.

A low growl issued from her. "You can't keep me in that."

Mysti ignored the guttural voice, and I did too.

I washed the bottle with soap and hot water, rinsing it well as I repeated three times, "I cleanse you." Once it was finished, I dripped the cleaning solution over it and rinsed it again. A drop of the oil went on my finger. I used it to make an even-armed cross. Feeling the weight of someone's stare, I raised my head to find Tubby watching. He winked at me.

I dropped my head and went back to my task with an extra tremor in my hands, entombing the bottle in black cloth. Tubby had agreed to my suggestion that we just be friends, but his actions said the opposite. Tubby went for what he wanted with a ruthless single-mindedness and wouldn't be dismissed easily. I hoped we wouldn't have to have a big, ugly moment of truth over it. Hurting his feelings didn't appeal to me.

I lit the incense and a candle, hand shaking harder, and got out my holy water and pure earth. The dirt came from an old growth forest in Canada where Mysti said the bones of the gods lay. The idea of earth imbued with something older than time calmed me. I looked up again to find Tubby still watching. We exchanged a small smile. I could handle him.

I rebirthed the bottle to its new purpose by pulling it from the black cloth. The heft of the bottle had become more solid, and it radiated cold prickles up my arm. I sprinkled some dirt on the blue glass. "I bless you with the element of earth." A few drops of holy water came next. "I bless you with the element of water." I passed the bottle through the candle flame. "I bless you with the element of fire." Then the incense smoke. "I bless you with the element of air." The smoke whistled in the bottle like a hard wind.

Nobody was listening to Mysti talk about energy any more. They all watched me. Dillon's eyes were the widest. She'd never admit it, but my ways scared her. I didn't mind. They scared me too.

"I name you witch bottle." I tapped my finger against the bottle. Its cold nearly numbed my fingertip. "I charge you with the duty of imprisoning the spirit hurting Hannah Marnie Kessler." A sheen of color, almost like the oil on top of coffee, washed over the bottle. Then it faded, and the cold left the bottle. I swept the fingernail clippings inside. They'd attract Hannah's passenger. I hoped.

"We need a box large enough to fit this bottle." Mysti spoke to Tubby. Without answering, he left the room. The sounds of him rustling around downstairs came back. Corman said something to him, his voice fuzzy and slurred.

"Shut up." Tubby's voice sharpened like the crack of a whip. He thumped back up the stairs, a wooden crate held in front of him and a cigarette clamped between his teeth. "This do?"

Mysti nodded and motioned for him to bring it to her. She began the process of consecration on the box. When she got to the rebirth and purposing, she dipped a craft paintbrush into a tiny bottle of paint and drew a straight line with several connected crosses on it. She caught me watching. "This is a protective sigil I developed for problems like the one Hannah has."

So that's what she called the hag? A problem? Looked more like a hell monster to me. I reminded myself again not to get mixed up in any of Griff and Mysti's more intense cases.

Mysti named the box. "You are the witch bottle house. As you deteriorate, so will the bottle's contents."

Hannah let out a particularly fierce growl at that. Mysti rose from her task and stared at the thing riding Hannah's hunched shoulders. "You know, you can go home when I banish you from Hannah."

Hannah raised her head. Slobber slicked her lower

chin. "You stupid little witch. I'll bite open your bones, suck the marrow out." Hannah's mouth made a wet, slurping sound.

I turned away. "Do you really think we can defeat that thing?"

"Yes." Mysti raised her chin. "Do not doubt yourself. That parasite feeds on self-doubt and hurt. He'll use it against you. Know you are stronger. Know you can wield your power over him."

I stood straighter, but the sounds Hannah was making had me scared. They were somewhere between a bad horror movie and a public restroom.

Mysti set the box and the bottle aside and addressed the group. "Let's talk about what we're going to do. When I first got here, I cast a circle around Hannah's chair to keep her parasite from fleeing before we're ready to banish it. Before we start the banishing, we'll cast a circle around that circle." She waited a few seconds for questions. Nobody asked any. "We'll complete the banishing. Hannah's passenger will likely reveal itself once separated from Hannah. So be prepared for that. "

"I got a question." Dillon, usually so tough and unafraid, barely spoke above a whisper.

Mysti smiled politely. "Now is the time."

"W-what happens if this goes wrong?" Dillon looked like she knew.

Mysti's nostrils flared as she took a deep breath. "If we can't get it out of Hannah, it'll likely kill her so it can absorb her energy and keep us from banishing it."

"What then?" Some of the fear left Dillon's posture, but her freckled face was still the color of grits.

Mysti, unable to maintain her professional demeanor, paled too. "It'll force its way into one of us. Probably it'll kill that person too, absorb their energy. It'll waste the pleasure of killing them slow for the power. Then…" She glanced at me and shrugged. "It'll take corporeal form and eat us."

Silence filled the room, and we all exchanged uncomfortable glances. This was no game.

Mysti settled her gaze on me, eyebrows raised. I nodded. Consequences accepted. I was about to risk friends and family for Hannah. I wasn't a good person, but I couldn't help myself. Mysti jerked her chin in acknowledgment.

"Peri Jean, you will rush to get this protection amulet on Hannah's wrist once the parasite is out of her." She removed a metal object from her witch pack and held it out to me. I came close to see it was a tarnished, open cuff bracelet with a pair of raised hands cupping a blue topaz. I slipped it on my wrist. It vibrated with power. Mysti probably spent hours blessing and consecrating it. "While all this is happening, the rest of you keep speaking the banishing incantation I'm going to teach you. It's simple and short." She recited the chant and repeated it several times. We practiced until we all had it. Mysti dug out her chalk and the candles to represent the elements for the circle. "Let's begin."

Hannah lifted her head and smiled. The hair on the back of my neck stood up.

"What about your backup plan?" I bit my lip.

Mysti stopped walking and spoke with her back still to me. "If this goes wrong, call your contact from the dark outposts." I opened my mouth, but Mysti shook her head. "No. Don't say his name unless absolutely necessary. If that time comes, say his full name, not the one you call him."

"I can't pronounce it." I heard the whine in my voice and hated it. But I didn't want to call Sol. He scared me and always wanted favors in return. His claim that he'd worked with my family for centuries only made the whole thing freakier.

"Yeah, you can. Just focus your energy. Tell yourself that's what you want, and it'll come out." Mysti walked to Hannah's chair, chalk pinched between her thumb and forefinger. A low, bubbling growl came from Hannah. "You have a choice in this." Mysti said the words in a firm, clear voice as she drew the outer circle.

I motioned everyone into the circle before Mysti closed it, and then I went behind her sprinkling sea salt over her chalk mark. She was waiting with the candles when I finished. I set down the green candle for north, lit it, and whispered my blessing. "I call upon the Guardian of the North. I call upon the element of earth. Bless us with your presence."

The lights flickered. The wood floor hummed to life. Hard energy rose up my legs and over my body, and the smell of freshly turned dirt filled my head.

I went to the next compass point, east, and set the yellow candle. The guardian of the east let its presence be known with a blast of air that swirled around the room and dried the sweat on my face. I set the other two candles, calling to the elements of fire and water. The circle rose around us. My skin shrank into goosebumps. Static electricity crackled through my hair.

Mysti pointed her athame at the edge of the circle and spun deosil three times. I knew she was picturing the light of the divine filling her, traveling through her body, and coming out of her arm to form the edge of the circle. She chanted in a voice deeper than her normal. "Lord and Lady, Guardians…" She paused for me to say my part.

"And the spirit of the raven." I concentrated on my raven familiar, heard the flapping of his wings, his guttural cries.

"Bless this circle and protect us," Mysti and I said together. "Keep us safe from unclean beings. Hold this circle in divine light." The edges of the circle lit like the brightest sunlight for a second and then dimmed.

"Let's start the incantation." Mysti pointed her athame at Hannah. The growls rumbled in my poor friend's chest. Sometimes she followed them with yips, reminding me of dark nights and coyotes. "On three." She counted off. All our voices rose together.

"Power of Earth

Power of Air

Power of Fire

Power of Water

Life in the Blood

Expel this evil from Hannah Marnie Kessler

Let it plague her no more."

Hannah opened her mouth so wide the lips split in the

corners. Blood trickled from the torn skin. She began to scream. I had expected this. But I hadn't expected the way it sounded, raw and wild.

"Again." Mysti motioned with her free arm.

We said the incantation three more times. Hannah convulsed in her chair. Foam dripped from her mouth. Teeth bared in a snarl, she glared at us. Mysti motioned us to do it again.

The flapping of raven wings filled my head. I left off my chant and moved toward Hannah. Just beneath her skin, I saw the monster, its cancer-colored skin writhing as the incantation pulled at it. My hand came up, and before I knew what I planned to do, it turned translucent and dipped below Hannah's skin. The thing writhed and slipped from my grasp. Hannah howled louder.

Mysti changed the chant. "Power of the four corners, alight this daughter of spirit." The others followed. They said the words over and over, as I tried to get my hand around the entity and ignore Hannah's screams. The flapping of wings came again. My mind slowed, and some forgotten animal part of me anticipated the parasite's next move. I grabbed for it. My fingers locked around its rubbery skin. I dug my fingernails in, pulled as hard as I could, and threw it to the ground where it fell with a wet splat.

"Oh dear God," Cecil muttered.

The slimy creature, resembling a hairless winged monkey, scrambled for Hannah.

"The bracelet," Mysti yelled. "The bracelet."

I took it off my wrist and clapped it to Hannah's. She

raised her head, eyes finding mine. The gratitude I saw there scraped over my heart, leaving it raw. I gripped her shoulder in response. She turned away from me and leaned her head against the chair, taking big, exhausted breaths.

We surrounded the hag. I held the bottle. Mysti pointed her athame at the monster. "Second part of the incantation."

We spoke as one again. "We send your evil to dwell in this vessel where you'll be unable to harm any other soul. We banish you. So mote it be."

The winged creature trembled on the ground. It raised its head to stare at me, thick lips split in a smile showing its fishy spiked teeth. I turned away, heart pounding.

We repeated our incantation three more times. I searched for the beat of the raven wings but heard nothing. The creature crawled to his feet and stood before us. Dillon broke off mid-chant and took a step backward. Cecil caught her arm and kept her inside the circle.

"I'm not going in the bottle." The rider's cunning whisper came from every corner of the room. It stared at the bottle, its chest rising and falling. The glass heated to burning in an instant and jerked in my hand. It burst into a gazillion pieces, shards flying like shrapnel. Cecil yelped as one found his skin. I wanted to scream, to run, to do anything but stand here and see what this monster had in store for me.

Mysti pointed the athame. "I banish you to the realm of darkness forever. You are never to return here."

The thing ran at her, sharp teeth bared. Mysti stabbed

at it with her athame. As soon as the knife made contact with the parasite, Mysti's body arched and began to jitter as though she was being electrocuted. I took a running step and pushed her off the thing. The athame clattered to the floor.

"It doesn't matter how long you delay." The rider's flat eyes found mine. "I will have a host, or I'll kill all of you."

Time for my trump card. I pictured Sol, my contact in the dark outposts, and tried to remember how he said his real name. Then I screamed, "I banish you in the name of Sol." Weird squeals came out of me when I got to his name.

The rider began to laugh. "I know—" It spoke the name. "He is no authority to me." It took one step toward me.

Before I had time to defend myself, the thing leapt at me. It hit me hard. I fell backward out of the circle and landed on my ass.

The rider's claws sank into me, and a black funk like no other I'd ever felt spread through my emotions. A depression so deep that it hurt settled over me. Behind it, the hag spindled my life force and began gulping it down. It was preparing to kill me, just as Mysti had predicted.

"No!" I shoved the bad feelings aside and called on the mantle.

It rose, monstrous and raging, and pushed at the parasite. Shit. The mantle was trying to get inside this thing. What would it do then?

The question became less important because the beast screamed inside my head. My ears began to ring. Still the scream went on. My back teeth throbbed, and pressure built behind my eyes. The scream continued. I couldn't stand much more. It was about to scramble my brain. I'd either have a stroke or bleed out from an aneurism. I'd done this to people but never realized how it felt on their end.

"Stop," I croaked out, unable to control the mantle in this state.

The mantle ignored me and pushed again at the beast, looking for a point of entry. But the monster dug in, its talons stabbing in deep. It felt like my insides were being chewed up. My body went limp, and the floor rose up to meet me. Someone grabbed me under the arms and broke the fall.

"*You can't kill me. Stop trying,*" the hag whispered.

"You're wrong. I'll kill us both if I have to," I growled back.

The mantle gave up trying to get inside the monster, wrapped itself around it, and began to squeeze. The hag panicked, its grunts echoing in my subconscious. I gave all my energy to the mantle. The rider unhooked its claws from my psyche and prepared to disengage.

In a flash, I realized that couldn't happen. The thing was bad inside me, but at least it couldn't hurt anybody else. I had to keep it where it was until I could find a way to banish it. Head throbbing with the effort and wetness I suspected was blood leaking from my nose, I held the monster in place.

"Shit, look at her eyes. All that's showing is the whites." This came from Tubby.

Someone began to pat my face. The scent of Cecil's aftershave flooded my senses. "Peri Jean?" Cecil's voice quavered.

"She's fighting," Mysti said. "Go on, Peri Jean. Get it out of you. We'll deal with it."

But they couldn't deal with the monster. We'd already seen what happened when we tried. This little horror would end up getting into someone else, and we'd start all over. The thing had to stay in me. There was no other way to keep it contained. I felt my body seize.

"Cecil, Dillon," Mysti said. "Let's combine our power and see if we can't push it out of her."

Her words hit me like a jolt of electricity. No. I couldn't let them put themselves at risk. I used the last of my waning strength to crawl to my feet. Fast as I could, I stumbled into the bathroom. I slammed the door, locked it, and leaned against it, fear pounding in my chest.

9

I STARED at my reflection in the bathroom mirror. The thing perched on my shoulders staring at its reflection over my head. Now that we were no longer fighting, I could feel the thing probing inside me, searching for my darkest heart. Little did it know, I didn't mind letting the murderous side of me out of the bag.

As though it could read my thoughts, the ugly little hag began to smile. "You don't know everything about yourself."

I ignored it and said, "You're leaving this plane. Now."

The bathroom's doorknob rattled. Both the rider and I jumped. Mysti's voice came through the old wood. "Come back out. There has to be a way to get it off you."

"What then? It'll just jump into one of you," I yelled at the door.

Mysti said nothing for several seconds. It was as good as any answer she could have given. She had no idea what to do. She'd risk her own safety to help me. Not happening.

"I've got an idea," I yelled at the silence, the lie as smooth as foam over latte. The only idea I had was to hold this thing inside me so it couldn't hurt my friends, combined with vague plans to figure out what to do next.

"What is it?" Mysti asked.

Caught in my lie, I said nothing.

"I'm going to do some brainstorming." Mysti didn't sound too sure of herself. For once, my mentor couldn't just snap her fingers and fix it all. That scared me more than the thing inside me. I turned away from the door and stared into the mirror again.

The hag wore a smug grin on its face. "You won't be as hard to defeat as you think you will."

I smiled back and let the mantle squeeze the little jackass again. The effort made every bone in my body ache, and a fatigue like nothing I'd ever known spread over me. I gripped the sink, poured everything I had into it, and waited for the rider to start screaming again. But something else happened.

Deep inside my psyche, where I never went, the rider slashed something open. It stung like a paper cut, and my own poison began to work its way through me. Emotional exhaustion crushed against my resolve, drowning it. Then the thoughts came.

I was sick of life, sick of being a freak, sick of being alone. The worst part? There was no end in sight. My own nature would always set me apart. Battles like this one would end only when I died.

The rider's will pushed my hand to the mirror. *Take it off the wall and break it. Cut your throat with one of the shards.* My fingers found the plastic bracket securing the mirror to the wall and began to pick at it. The lethal creature whispered into my soul, blowing life into the truth I kept locked away and pretended did not exist.

"Be stronger than this." A figure appeared behind me in the mirror. Priscilla Herrera's eyes blazed determined fire. Her strength bolstered me. I got hold of myself. Using my free hand, I forced my fingers off the mirror and curled them around the edge of the sink.

Another knock came on the door. "You all right in there, baby?" It was Cecil.

"I'm okay. We're working it out." My voice shook. Cecil loved me in his way, but he didn't have the strength, magical or physical, to help me. This thing riding me was a stealer of life and happiness. It had to stay as far away from friends and family as possible. I sifted through my mind, trying to think of how to handle this, but the buzz of a fly splintered my ability to concentrate.

The fly moved around my face, so close it tickled my skin. I swatted at it. The sink came on full blast. I jumped and backed away from it, glancing in the mirror. My pestilent passenger sat hunched on my shoulder. I expected to see it smirking at me, proud of scaring me, but its dark eyes widened.

The old plumbing in the walls let out a pained screech. The water rushing from the faucet turned bright red and then stopped. The sink rattled on the wall. I pressed my back against the opposite wall.

"Tell him to go away," the passenger hissed in my head.

Tell who to go away? Sol? He didn't answer my call for help earlier. Was he coming now? I opened my second sight and searched for Sol's magical essence, but he was so far beyond human, and I was so exhausted, I felt nothing.

"I said make him go. Or I'll kill you now. I'll..."

The hag would kill me now? That was a regular laugh-a-thon. "Eat my ass. You're going to kill me anyway if you can."

The faucet, an old-fashioned metal one, let out a groan. The hag stiffened. The metal rippled and bulged as something moved through it. The first tingles of fear pricked at my back. A dripping black-shoed foot forced its way out of the faucet's mouth. More like liquid silver than metal, the metal stretched even bigger. Another black-shoed foot came out. The smell of brackish water filled the room. The faucet stretched further to birth two legs covered by soaked black pants. The rest of the man slithered from the faucet, his head taking shape only after he was free of it. The smell of wild beasts joined the dank water smell. Sol, my contact from the dark outposts, straightened and adjusted his tie.

"You're late." I tried not to stare at Sol's pruney skin. Otherwise, I'd start calling him Pruney again, instead of his name. He might use his sharp teeth on me if I made him mad.

"It's the fault of that witch in there." His voice carried a piggy squeal, which fit because I'd seen him transform into a big, pink pig on occasion.

"Her name's Mysti," I muttered, trying out every

scenario I could think of to keep from having to make a deal with Sol. He'd had my blood, taken locks of my hair. I owed him an unspecified favor. What would he ask for now? The fly returned to circle my head. I waved it away.

Sol snorted. "You and I both know that's not her true name. The witch put holy water around the corners of the building. We couldn't come in the door like regular people."

The "we" gave me a start. Who had Sol brought with him? I'd seen other things from Sol's world. I didn't want to play with any of them.

Sol's teeth, ugly needle tipped things, flashed in the bathroom's bright lights. "Do you understand how disgusting the interior of a plumbing system is?"

I shook my head, still focused on the "we."

Sol disregarded me and stared into the mirror, body tensing. "Here he comes now."

My stomach hardened. The fly hummed, the sound maddening. Another fly joined it. They gathered on top of the mirror. A third joined. Then a fourth. And more after that. The hum became so loud it made the air vibrate against my skin. Still they came, black shadows in the harsh overhead light. Before long, I couldn't see the mirror through all the flies covering it. The mirror bulged out in the shape of a head with horns.

My mind scrambled madly through the things I'd seen with horns like this. All of them scared me. The fly-covered horns emerged from the mirror. Now a fly-covered head pushed through the glass, which stretched more like bubblegum than something breakable.

Sol reached into the mirror and pulled out a furry hand tipped with short black fingernails. Flies swarmed to it. The hand grappled for purchase on the sink. The rest of the beast inched its way into the room and spilled onto the floor. It waved its arms and made an annoyed sound. The flies went to the ceiling in a huge, black swarm, where they rested, humming. The creature stood and brushed itself off. Its magic circled the room, buzzing in my back teeth, and making the edges of things dance.

I took a good look at the being in front of me. Beyond fight or flight, I could do nothing but stare. The beast had a goat's head and a black fur-covered body. His legs ended in hooves. A long tailed black coat covered his torso, and a priest's white collar circled his neck. He wore no other clothes. The hugest uncircumcised penis I'd ever seen hung between the being's legs.

Bile stung my throat. I wondered how appropriate it would be for me barf. The goat man and I had met before, the day I found the Mace Treasure. Goat man. The silly name made me want to belt out hysterical laughter. Wasn't there a mythological name for this thing? Rainey or Hannah would have known it right away, but I had to struggle to find it. Then it came. Satyr. Yes. That was it.

Mysti would have told me that mythology was created by humans and that humans couldn't understand what this thing was. But I needed something familiar to cling to so I wouldn't float away on a magic carpet with the last of my sanity. Oh, I was in so deep. The satyr reached back into the mirror and withdrew a huge black book covered with symbols that burned and wiggled like fire.

"We're all here." Sol rubbed his hands together. Water dripped from them, pattering on the floor. Someone banged on the bathroom door, hollering my name, but the voice sounded far, far away. Too far for me to even tell who it was. The goat man bleated at Sol, its slit-pupiled eyes resting on me. "Oh, yes. You haven't formally met—" Sol made a weird sound, but I heard "Bub."

Bub bleated. This time I understood him. "She's the one who broke up my choir."

The choir in question had been made of bloodthirsty zombies singing religious hymns backward. I bowed my head and hoped it looked repentant enough.

Bub bleated again. "No matter. I'd had some of them for centuries. They'd grown boring." I raised my head to find Bub staring at the rider on my back. He spoke to it. "What's your name?"

The rider hissed. Bub bleated and raised his book as though he was going to whomp the rider one. I sort of hoped he would, but I didn't want to get hit upside the head, and I had a feeling that was how it would end.

Sol held out one dripping arm to stop Bub from swinging his book. "No. We're going to bargain like civil creatures."

I didn't want to bargain and wanted to say so, but my tongue was stuck to the roof of my mouth. The rider's growl vibrated from within me.

Bub bleated again. My mind translated his words. "Parasite, you'll lose whatever pass you have to be here if you're unreasonable."

The rider shifted on my back. Its sharp taloned toes

dug into my sides. "I must kill this woman. Otherwise I can't go back to my master." He wrapped his spindly arms around my neck, choking me.

Master? The idea sent icicles of terror shooting through my body. The hag's half-assed attempt to strangle me was nothing compared to it working for something bigger and meaner than itself. Neither Mysti's nor my best magic had come close to beating the hag. How could we expect to beat its master?

"You can't kill her." Sol reached one waterlogged and wrinkled hand forward and pulled at the passenger's arm until it gave me some breathing room. "Her destiny and mine are entwined and promised."

I swallowed against a scream. I didn't want to be entwined with Sol. Or Bub. I wanted some semblance of normalcy. The punchline was that I'd never get it. The sad, dark thoughts the hag's claws had released circulated through my brain, reminded me I could kill myself. End it all. In death, everybody was normal. The hag shivered in pleasure at the death song running through my mind.

"You can't stop me from killing her." The passenger put his bony arm over my windpipe and began to whisper in my ear. "Death will be sweet, restful. There'll be no more uncertainty. No more loneliness."

The thought didn't sound all together bad. Death might hold the peace that eluded me in life. Nobody would ever get hurt because of me. I'd never feel like a freak again. I'd seen enough ghosts step into the light to know that was all I had to do to escape this world.

Sol snapped his fingers in my face, and the thoughts

cut off. A stream of water dripped from his too-white hand to patter on the tiles. The snap was like a cold blast of water to my face. The death fog backed away, and I saw it for the abomination it was. My thoughts had been so cold and clinical. So reasonable. Had I been alone, I might well have decided to let myself tumble into darkness, across the line of life and death. My teeth began to chatter.

Sol nodded at the change in me but spoke to the hag. "No, I cannot stop you alone. But Bub is here already. I can call in more markers. How many of us can you fight?"

"My master will send me back to darkness if I don't fulfill my orders." For the first time, the passenger sounded afraid. "I was stationed in that room to wait for her, to attach myself to anybody who might know her. Now I've found her. My orders are to kill her."

"Who is your master?" Bub asked.

The hag stiffened. "A being much more powerful than I. He commands many and is able to assume more than one form. The Kessler woman met him."

Bub and Sol stared at one another as though they were having a conversation I couldn't hear. I tensed. What now? Sol finally nodded and muttered, "I'm not sure Peri Jean will agree."

Bub bleated, but my mind translated his words like a computer. "She must. It's the only way she'll survive. This glutton will keep eating at her until she gives up." He turned to me and bleated again. "You'll negotiate for this parasite's contract from his master."

I couldn't do that. There was nothing I could offer a supernatural baddie like the one hag belonged to. The concept of a mirror shard splitting the skin on my neck sounded more and more like sweet relief with every passing second. At least it would be over. No more weird shit.

"There's going to be weird shit for you whether you're alive or dead." Bub acted as though I'd spoken my thoughts aloud. "You have destiny. Be grateful. Most don't." He stepped forward and put one furry hand on my arm. Magic pressed against my skin, and my teeth buzzed again. "As for being able to pull this off, you can. A few of my kind have gained entry into this world. They all have things they want." Bub shrugged and glanced at Sol. He opened his wrinkled lips to speak, but he never got the chance.

The hag spoke quickly. "I'm willing to bargain. I want my freedom. I'm willing to stop trying to kill her until we see if she can negotiate my release. But I'm not going to stop feeding on her until she finds me a new host," said the creature on my back.

The idea nauseated me. I'd lost control of the situation, of my life. All these creatures crowded around me negotiating. My family and friends taking turns knocking on the door. The walls seemed closer than ever. Heat from the room's light fixture beat down on the top of my head. I thought again about breaking the mirror. My father's face flashed in it, filled with disappointment. Shame heated my cheeks.

"That seems fair..." Sol trailed off.

"He's trying to convince me to kill myself." I glanced from Sol to Bub. They gave me blank stares back.

"He brings forth nothing that wasn't already present." Sol's cold gaze penetrated mine.

"Everything has to eat," Bub supplied.

"You have got to be kidding me. What is this shit? I thought y'all came to help." My voice rose. The knocking on the door started again. I spun around and slapped the door. "Will you stop that? I am trying to make a deal." The knocking cut off like magic.

"Look at surviving this as honing your gifts." Bub's snout pulled back in grotesque parody of a smile.

My temper flared. "That's not fair. I can't rescue Wade, fight off this thing trying to make me kill myself, kill King Tolliver, *and* play matchmaker for this hovering turd." I jerked my thumb at my shoulder.

The hag hissed over being called a hovering turd. *Too damn bad.*

Sol stared at the hag perched my shoulder. "Twenty-four hours for Peri Jean Mace to negotiate your freedom?" He was ignoring me. If I'd thought I could have won, I'd have beat his ass.

"Yes." The rider's body tightened with excitement.

"Now, wait just a damn minute..." This was happening too fast. A million protests crowded my mind so full I couldn't speak any of them.

"What is it?" Bub bleated.

"When does he leave?" My voice trembled. I didn't want this malignant cancer hanging off me, trying to get me to self-destruct, for the rest of my life.

"I can't survive on my own after so many years in captivity. I have to rebuild my strength," the hag shouted.

"Not by feeding off me." I whipped my head back and forth.

"You'll move to a suitable host once you've attained your freedom," Bub told the hag.

"If she can find me a suitable one." The hag sounded put out, and there was something about this bargain that didn't feel quite right. I tried to put my finger on it. Bub let out an impatient grunt.

"The two of you will find a way to work it out." The final word ended in a goaty bleat.

Sol clapped his hands together with a wet smack. "This is the deal. Peri Jean Mace will remove this parasite from its contract. In return, the parasite will choose a new host and move on immediately. Do both of you agree?"

"Yes." I waited for the hag to speak. The seconds dragged until I worried it was going to renege.

Finally its answer came. "Yessss."

Bub climbed onto the sink and threw his book through the mirror. "Good thing. I can't stand around in this shithole anymore." He climbed in after the book. Glass rippled and bent with his movements. Flies swarmed over the mirror.

Sol waited until Bub was gone and climbed into the sink. He began to shrink. "If you have problems, summon me. But remember. This call was free. The next one won't be." In other words, I better want him real damn bad before I reached out. Sol went headfirst into the drain and disappeared.

The pounding on the door started back up. I groaned.

"Peri Jean!" Mysti screamed. "Say you're okay, or I'm getting Tubman to break down the door."

I let her hammer for a several seconds while I massaged my temples. The hag's presence hovered at the base of my consciousness, a wisp of noxious smoke. I stared into the mirror and watched it materialize on my shoulders. Its liver-colored lips broke into a wide smile, revealing the fishy barbs it had for teeth.

Its thoughts met mine. *Kill yourself now. Save the misery.*

I sent back my own message. *Where's Barbie's tape? Isn't that what you were guarding when you got hold of Hannah?*

Confusion came back. *I only know the tasks I was given.*

Other than killing me, what was that? I thought at it.

I was attached to a telephone. The front desk chose when to ring it. If it was answered, the person was mine.

Holy guacamole. How many people had this thing consumed from the inside out? My skin crawled.

"Please, Peri Jean, please. At least tell me you're all right." Mysti, her voice tight with worry, tapped three more times.

I opened the door and forced a smile onto my face. "Don't worry about me. I'm just peachy."

10

—————

THE UPSTAIRS LOFT looked exactly the same as it had when I went into the bathroom. The same air from the ceiling fan feathered over my skin. The same spicy smell still hung in the kitchen. That bothered me.

Everything was different for me. My inner self was stretched to bursting with the presence of the hag. I had made a deal that felt not quite right and might end up getting me killed. This little space should somehow mirror the difference.

Cecil and Dillon sat at the table sharing a pack of mini doughnuts. The coffee maker bubbled and hissed on the kitchen counter, and the rich, almost chocolaty, smell of brewing coffee filled the small space.

Mysti and Hannah sat on the other side of the room. Hannah held a crystal in one hand. Mysti spoke seriously, probably lecturing about the benefits of the crystal.

Cecil broke off whatever he was saying to Dillon. "You made a deal." There was no question in his soft voice.

"Only for the next twenty-four hours. It has to find another host within that time period." I stopped to consider. "And it won't be anybody here."

The thing hissed in my head. I was getting tired of the hissing, ready to plug its nostrils and mouth with clay or shit. I rinsed out my coffee mug in the sink, trying to pretend there wasn't another presence in my mind, an oily, ancient presence sitting heavily on a part of my brain that didn't like being poked.

Hannah wandered into the kitchenette and stared first at the coffeemaker and then at Cecil and Dillon. "Who are these people?"

Cecil and Dillon stared steadily back, eyes blank and unwelcoming. They'd come to help me out of loyalty, not because they genuinely cared what happened to Hannah. She was what they called a townie. Townies were not to be trusted or even liked. If Hannah alienated them, they might turn their backs on the whole situation. It was up to me to find some connection between my family and my lifelong friend.

"This is my great-uncle Cecil. Memaw was his sister." I waited for Hannah to gasp and smile, maybe say something nice about Memaw, but she only gave a tired nod. I gestured at Dillon. "Dillon here is my cousin by marriage. She and her husband have two babies."

The Hannah I remembered exclaimed over children and asked to see pictures. This one only nodded again and let her gaze slip off my cousin. She got coffee from the coffeemaker, ignored the creamer I offered, and sipped it black. She took her coffee, sat at the table, and put her forehead on one hand.

"Can I have one of your cigarettes?" she muttered at the table. Wordlessly, I handed her the whole pack. The woman who made a face every time every time I smoked lipped a cigarette out of the pack and lit up with a fluid motion. She blew smoke at the table and closed her eyes. In her other hand, she squeezed the crystal Mysti had given her.

I had let a supernatural monster possess me for Hannah, and she couldn't even thank me for a cigarette? Guilt followed right on the heels of the thought, sat down, and made itself at home. I was an asshole. Hannah had been through hell these last few months. It was going to take time to get better. A true friend would find a way to understand.

I reached for the cigarettes, intending to light one, maybe to bond that way. But Hannah flinched away and shoved the pack toward me with the back of her hand. She cut her eyes at me. The pain etched in the tender skin at their edges clawed my conscience open and spit poison in it. I'd thought all it would take to get the old Hannah back was a few magic words and a little personal sacrifice. I'd underestimated the way life can beat people down.

The dark thoughts I'd had in front of the bathroom mirror came flooding back, this time armed with a new torture device. Hannah didn't want to be around me because I probably brought back every second of the horror she'd suffered at Michael Gage's hands. It would have never happened if she hadn't been my friend. She had to realize that life near me would always be chaotic and dangerous. Hannah was right to turn her back on me.

I'd never be able to hold on to anybody I cared about. They'd get hurt or killed. Just like Memaw, Chase, Eddie, and Wade. Rae, if I wanted to see it that way. My own mother had hated my guts. If I took myself out of the equation, it would stop the cycle.

That's when I realized the voice in my head wasn't even mine. It was that malignant asshole riding my back. I called on the mantle and let it squeeze the little jerk, even though it made me ache with fatigue.

The hag's oily voice came to life inside my head. *"You know I'm right."*

I let the mantle squeeze until my black opal pendant heated, and the little monster squealed in pain. Deep down, I knew the parasite was right. Because of me, Hannah might be lost forever. Even if she wasn't, the old Hannah was buried so deep in the woman in front of me, she was going to have to *want* to come back. Nothing I could say or do would force her out. The back of my neck tightened and began to ache.

Mysti motioned me away from the table. I followed her to the other side of the loft and stared through the floor-to-ceiling windows at the street below. Things looked so normal down there, a whole world where women didn't make deals with monsters, where people had normal lives. Lives with PTA meetings, insurance payments, and yoga pants. Shit I'd never have.

The tightness in my neck spread to the muscles between my shoulder blades. The parasite inside me shifted and stretched, like a snake uncoiling to soak up the sun. Its pleasure at my discomfort burned in the middle of my chest.

Mysti tugged at my sleeve. I dragged my gaze off the window and regarded my friend. She had on her teacher face. Mouth set in a straight, severe line. Eyes sympathetic and calm. Deep breaths through her nose. She smoothed down her hair, which was a rat's nest and wouldn't look good until she shampooed and got a blow dryer after it, and folded her hands in front of her. "If you want to help Hannah, let her do something that feels normal."

I shook my head and shrugged. What was normal for Hannah at this point? I took a look at my old friend. She sat hunched over the table smoking. Dillon held out a powdered sugar doughnut. Hannah stared hard at it, then took it carefully as though it might actually be a turd dipped in powdered sugar. *Oh, Hannah. How did it get to this?* Hannah, her former table manners gone, shoved the donut into her mouth whole and rubbed the powdered sugar onto her filthy jeans. An idea hit me. I gave Mysti a thank you nod and walked halfway to Hannah.

"How about some clean clothes? Tubby'll go get you some." From somewhere nearby came Tubby's snort. He'd protest, might even pull a fit, but I could make him do it.

Hannah twisted in her seat and gave me her blank stare. "I want to go to my apartment and take a shower." Request delivered, she sat up a little straighter, and some of the clouds lifted off her face.

I didn't know how to answer that. King might have sent someone to watch the museum or even to wait in Hannah's apartment. He wanted revenge and would do whatever it took to get it.

"She probably knows someone'll be waiting. This woman is no longer your friend. Kill her," the parasite whispered in my head. Its voice raised thoughts of scaly things and dark places. The words planted a kernel of paranoia in my subconscious. Images of King stepping out of one of the museum's dark corridors flitted around my brain.

Tubby came into the room and gave me an authoritative head shake. I knew the signal for "bad idea, forget it."

Hannah watched this exchange, and her shoulders dropped. "Never mind," she muttered.

"Why never mind?" I came a little closer. Nothing beats a shower in one's own bathroom. This might help Hannah realize she was out of danger for now, that she'd turned a corner.

"Because you don't trust me." She drew on her cigarette, burning it down to the filter, and crushed it in the ashtray on the table. I came to a decision.

"I'm taking her to her place to clean up," I said to Tubby but stared at Hannah. She almost smiled. Tubby spun around and hurried from the room.

Cecil spoke without looking away from Hannah. "Please don't. Too much could happen out there."

I ignored him and motioned Hannah to get up. She stood, hesitantly at first, legs unsteady as a new colt's, and then seemed to gain her confidence.

Tubby came rushing back into the room. In one hand, he held a handgun. In the other, a stainless steel tomahawk. "I won't go with you, but..." He shrugged and held out the weapons.

I reached for the tomahawk. Behind me, Dillon made a questioning noise. I turned around, weapon held aloft, and said, "I'm killing them if they're there, and I want to do it like I mean it."

From behind me came the sound of Hannah drawing back the slide on the handgun. Before her attack, she'd been quite the amateur marksman.

"You could defend yourself with your gift," Mysti said from nearby.

"They don't deserve the effort." I walked out of the room without looking back. The museum was only a couple of blocks. Minutes if we walked fast. We left the former antique store through the entrance into the alley.

No baddies waited in dark shadows. A stray cat hiding in a dumpster gave us a pretty good scare, and we ran the last half block, giggling like old times. Hannah punched in her security code and unlocked the museum's back door. A door through the back hallway opened onto Hannah's private staircase to her loft apartment.

My cigarette-infused lungs ached after two flights of stairs toward the top floor. Hannah heaved and panted beside me. She used to occasionally run with Dean and Rainey. I remembered the way she'd lit the cigarette back in Tubby's hideout.

"Quit smoking, and it won't be so hard." I wanted to get her joking, trading good-natured insults, but her shoulders rounded.

"Hard not to smoke around that bunch." She took a few more heavy steps.

I wanted to tell her she'd be back to her old self in no time, but the words sounded false even before I said them. Instead of speaking, I pressed at my side where a painful stitch had formed and followed Hannah the rest of the way to her apartment. We stood gasping on the landing, both of us with our hands on our knees. Hannah caught her breath first and pulled her loft key from behind an ugly gray sculpture that appeared to be a woman holding open her vulva.

I wrinkled my nose. "The hell is that?"

"Sheela na gig." The old Hannah would have talked for ten minutes about the historical significance of the weird thing. This one simply unlocked her apartment and pushed open the door.

I gasped at the sight. The love seat bled stuffing from large tears in the upholstery. The two suitcases Hannah used for a coffee table had been dented and smashed in. A broken whiskey bottle, glass spraying out all around it, lay near the small, open kitchen.

This made no sense. The apartment looked as trashed as it had the day Michael Gage tore it apart and kidnapped Hannah. I knew for a fact she hadn't come back home to it looking that way because Rainey Bruce and I cleaned it, repaired what could be fixed, and threw out the stuff that couldn't.

"I forgot about this." Hannah pushed around me and went inside the apartment.

"Wait. Someone might be in there." I hurried after her.

She kept walking into the kitchen where she opened the freezer and drew out a bottle of vodka. She pressed the bottle against her forehead for several seconds, then unscrewed the top and took a long pull. She shuddered as the alcohol hit her system.

I wanted to tell her not to drink, that it would just make the world look worse, but who was I to tell anybody else what to do? Besides, it would just make her angry at me. "What happened here?"

"A party." She tried to smile, but her lips trembled. She took another drink.

"*Tell her to kill herself,*" said the nasty little voice at the back of my mind. "*She'll be better off.*"

The idea sent a red rage through my head. I gathered the mantle, ready to let the little bastard have it. The monster, a being who should have been a million times more powerful than me, scuttled away. Interesting. I filed away the experience for later, went to the cabinet where Hannah used to keep sugary sweets, and pulled out a box of mini cream pies.

"Probably stale." Hannah took another drink and held out the bottle to me, something she'd not done since I explained to her why I never drank.

The ghosts. Back when I'd been so afraid of seeing them, I stayed away from alcohol because it dulled my defenses against them. Now I saw things far worse than ghosts, made deals with them, let them rent a room in my body. I stared at the bottle of clear liquid, tried to remember the last time I'd had a drink, and couldn't. I was a thirty-plus-year-old woman who didn't know how to drink.

"Maybe another time. I need to stay on my toes right now."

"Makes his voice quieter." Hannah took one last drink, recapped the bottle, and shoved it back in the freezer of her fancy stainless steel refrigerator.

"Whose voice?" I wanted to see what she'd say about the squatter.

She tipped her chin at my shoulders. "He who drains you of all hope. I didn't know what was wrong at first. I'd had flashbacks, heard voices, since Michael Gage and Nash Redmond kidnapped me. I thought the extra voice was part of that."

I nodded to show I understood, hoping to keep her talking.

"It'll learn the things that haunt you, play them over and over." She opened her freezer and stared at the vodka bottle. After several seconds, she gave her head a firm shake and let the door swing shut. "Alcohol made it not matter so much." She let out a sad chuckle. "You know, if King busted in here right now and blasted us both into the next existence, it wouldn't be so bad. The monster's gone from inside me, but he left the seeds. I feel like they're gonna ride me all the way down." She stared into my eyes, a stranger in a familiar skin. "He'll do it to you too, even if you get rid of him."

With that, she walked past me and into the bedroom. Her groan at the mess in there floated back. I wanted to offer to clean her bathroom so it would be nice for her but didn't quite dare. This hardened woman might throw the gesture back in my face, make me feel foolish. So I listened as the water from the shower began raining on the tiles and tried not to survey the damage in Hannah's formerly beautiful home.

The hag leaped and cavorted over my turmoil. I tried to clear my mind, but images of Wade somewhere hurting, probably dying, populated my thoughts. The parasite lapped up the worry, grunting in lusty pleasure. I squeezed my eyes shut and forced my mind to a blank. My stomach somersaulted as the parasite's negativity filled me, brimming over.

It'll ride you all the way down, Hannah had said. Maybe she was right.

A few minutes later, we snuck out of the Burns County Museum, a building Hannah owned free and clear, like a pair of criminals. Hannah had on fresh clothes and full makeup. She slung a soft-sided bag over one shoulder with another change of clothes inside, just in case.

We cut through the alleyways, me on high alert, Hannah strolling along as though this was an okay way to spend the last few seconds of her life. At the back door to Tubby's hideout, she put one hand on the knob but didn't open the door. "You didn't have to do this for me."

"Nope." I gripped my tomahawk tighter and glanced behind us.

"Why'd you take the risk?" Her knuckles whitened as she tightened her grip on the doorknob.

"You're worth it." The answer came fast. I didn't think much about it.

She pursed her lips and almost smiled. "Thank you. I hope you don't end up feeling like it was a waste of your time." She turned the knob and slipped inside before I could reply. I hurried after her, but she'd disappeared into the big building.

———

I GAVE Hannah time to get away from me before I went inside. Maybe a little space would ease things. The alley door led into the back half of the first floor of Tubby's building. Tubby seemed to be using it as an office with a bright floor lamp set up next to a scarred and battered desk. If I'd had to guess, and I really didn't want to, I'd have said this was where someone logged illegal shipments.

Soon as I walked into the office, Tubby vaulted out of the metal folding chair behind the desk, hurried to me, and grabbed my arm. "The hell happened to you? Y'all's gone an hour. Don't take that long to shower." He gave me a hard shake.

Anger, far too wild and out of control for the situation, flashed in my head. I jerked my arm away from Tubby. He took a step backward, skinny hands held up in a warding off gesture. The thing in my head salivated for violence. I could practically hear its stomach rumbling.

I took a deep breath, then another. "She needed a break."

Tubby sat back in his metal chair. "You know we got to get moving. Get that tape of Barbie's. Get it to King."

Hannah emerged from the shadows near the back

stairwell to the loft. "You can't. That would be a betrayal to Rainey."

I almost smiled. This was the old Hannah, ready to fight for her friends. I wanted to hug her but knew she'd hate it. I nodded. "You're right. Rainey has worked her whole career to get Uncle Jesse out of prison." There was more that I didn't say. Rainey was in love with Jesse. It would drive her crazy for him spend the rest of his life in prison for a crime he didn't commit. "But King's going to kill Wade if I don't give him that tape in twenty-four hours."

Hannah gasped and put her hand to her throat. The stark light from Tubby's lamp lit her bare arms. For the first time, I noticed the dark, finger shaped bruises on her pale wrists. *Oh, Hannah. What did they do to you?* Unshed tears stung my eyes.

"I don't understand. How'd they get Wade?" Hannah sat on the edge of Tubby's desk.

I wasn't sure how to proceed. Wade had saved Hannah, gotten shot doing it. Yet she seemed to remember none of it. "What do you remember of the last twenty-four hours?"

Hannah's eyes moved back and forth for several seconds. Finally, she looked up at me like a kid who knows he has the wrong answer. "I remember you coming into Long Time Gone and King throwing you out."

I pulled out my cigarettes, popped them against the palm of my hand several times, and pulled one out of the package. Tubby held out a lighter, its flame flickering. I leaned forward, inhaled, and closed my eyes to enjoy the nicotine rush for a second. "Yesterday evening, I got a visit from the thing we just detached from you. Tried to kill me. Not five minutes later, you sent me a text telling me to come get you at the compound this morning."

She watched me, face expressionless. "I just don't remember."

Irrational anger flared again. I'd risked the man I loved, probably lost him, to help her, and she didn't even remember.

The hag waited, eagerness swelling its presence. The malignant presence started whispering. *"You're stronger. You could scramble her brains, tear open her body, and spill her blood."* The image took form in my mind.

My fury increased, now directed at my nasty little guest. The mantle snapped inside me. The thing writhed, its screams loud in my head. I gave myself a shake and found Hannah watching. A crease had formed between her eyebrows.

Tears brimmed in her eyes. "It's killing you now."

"No. It isn't," I said too quickly and cheerfully. "Let's get back to yesterday morning. Tubby and Wade helped me conduct a raid on the Six Gun Compound."

Hannah paled. "They have guns."

"We had explosives." Tubby grinned. Hannah got even paler and put her hand over her mouth.

"We were able to get you out, but Trench Coat shot Wade." I paused here and let the urge to scream and tear at my hair pass.

Hannah put her hands over her face and rubbed her temples. "Oh no," she moaned. "Wade is so nice. A real gentleman...for that group anyway." She grabbed at the beer Tubby had sitting on his desk, gulped it down, and stifled a burp. Tubby and I exchanged raised eyebrows. Hannah took several deep breaths. "King won't let you have Wade back alive. You know that, don't you?"

I knew it was a possibility, but I wasn't ready to admit it. Tears burned my eyes, and rage heated my cheeks. There was nothing I could do to stop whatever was happening to Wade, nothing I could do to take back what got him into this mess.

Corman let out a beastly yell. "I'm dyinnnnng." Nobody bothered to answer him. "Hey, is that Hannah I hear? You wanna come suck my dick? Take my mind off it?" His words ended in a combination cackle and sob.

Hannah's eyes widened with fear, and she gripped her own wrist, right over the finger marks. Understanding flashed over me.

"If Wade doesn't make it back here," I said through my teeth, "Corman's days are gonna get real short too. Trust and believe me on that one." Hannah flinched away from my fury. I tried to rein it in, but my malignant passenger stoked the coals, showing me images of King hurting Wade.

"*Hannah caused it all*," the thing whispered in my head.

"Will you shut the fuck up?" I screamed the words and clapped my hands over my ears. The parasite retreated before I could rally the mantle.

Hannah's mouth drooped. She began shaking her head. "No, no, no. I don't want that monster to have you. Not to save me. I wasn't worth saving. There's nothing left but…" She waved a hand at the air. "Nightmares, panic attacks, and loneliness."

I wanted to tell her that loneliness plagued me too. And the nightmares were no picnic either. But never in the history of the universe has it helped someone else to downplay their wounds. So I said what I meant again. "You're worth it, Hannah. We will get this straightened out. The first step is to find that tape that King wants. You were looking for it, weren't you?"

She began shaking her head. "I won't tell you where it is just so you can give it to King." Her lips turned down in scowl. "Damn, it makes me mad for King Tolliver to get what he wants. For him to hurt Jesse and Rainey. To let him kill Wade. But I don't want to give him the tape. Do you understand?"

I ducked my chin to make eye contact with her. "Who said I'm going to treat King Tolliver fairly?"

Hannah pulled on her fingers, wringing her hands so hard the bones popped. "How will we cheat him and still have a chance of getting Wade alive?"

"We'll figure it out." It was the best I could do. "We have to get that tape. That's the price King set for us to have Wade back."

Hannah sat silent for several long seconds, eyes moving back and forth as she thought. Lines I'd never seen before appeared on her face. Finally she took a deep breath. "I'll help. But I need some coffee. I'm about half drunk."

She stood and walked toward the stairs. Tubby and I followed. Hannah poured herself another cup of black coffee and sipped from it. She sat down at the table across from Dillon and tried to smile at her. Dillon stared back until she caught my scowl.

She flashed Hannah a quick, insincere smile, pulled out her cigarettes, and said, "Papaw, why don't we go have a smoke while Peri Jean talks to Miss Hannah? I won't tell Shelly."

Cecil's wife, Shelly, didn't want him smoking because of his heart condition. Dillon's offer got Cecil to his feet faster than I'd seen him move in a while.

"I might smoke one." He gave Hannah a more sincere smile and a little wave. The two went downstairs.

I pulled a chair away from the table and sat where I could see Hannah but not too close. "So the tape."

"I stumbled into a booby trap." She sniffed her coffee and pushed it away.

I tried to smile at her reaction to the coffee. "Smell like the morning after?"

Hannah smiled back, but it was only a ghost of the smile that had made her almost famous for fifteen minutes. "Catch me up on what you know about Rainey's and my investigation."

I told her all I knew. The email. Rainey's missed meeting. Barbie's luggage getting looted.

Hannah nodded. "Okay. I remember all this. Rainey brought me Barbie's overnight case. It was one of those old-fashioned ones, hard-sided and with a little mirror in the lid. I wondered what Barbie wanted with an outdated thing like that." She held out her hand, and I put my cigarettes in them. Watched her light up like a pro. "Nothing was in it other than regular toiletries and—get this—a pink vibrator."

I laughed, nodding. I remembered encountering the nasty thing.

"I gave up on it pretty quickly and got into searching her laptop. I'm no hacker, but I'm not a slouch either." She glanced at me and winked, but quickly looked away. "I found a payment to a hotel. Scratch that. It's not a hotel. It's more of a roach motel."

I wrinkled my nose. "I thought Rainey had her PI look at the laptop. Can't believe he didn't find that. She needs to fire him."

"Oh, he probably did find it. But I'd seen that dump a dozen times driving between here and Tyler for my therapist appointments. So it caught my interest." She stopped talking.

I watched her closely. She might have decided to shut down again. I hoped not. Wade was running out of time. So was I.

Hannah took a few deep breaths and seemed to rally. "I wanted to help Rainey. She's been so caring. So I went to the motel. Just walked in the office and told them a lie about being a private investigator hired by Barbie's family. The guy handed me a key. He was...weird."

The hag had said Hannah met its master. This must have been the guy. I considered asking Hannah how the guy who gave her the key was weird, but one look at her face froze the question in my throat.

Hannah stared straight ahead, eyes dull, chewing on

her lip. Whatever she saw in her memories upset her. I wouldn't dig out of respect for her feelings.

She spoke with a sigh in her voice. "I went into the room. You should have seen this place. Shit city. Almost immediately, the phone started ringing. I picked it up and said hello."

My shoulders cranked up even though I knew the end of the story. Somehow the monster now inside me had come through the phone and gotten inside Hannah, probably through her ear.

"I-I-I thought I saw a shadow in the mirror, hovering over me." Her voice broke. "And after that, I was—I kept having these bad thoughts. Thoughts of how I was worthless and dirty. How w-w-what Michael Gage and Nash Redmond did to me tainted me for the rest of my life. It was like living through it again. I went into the bathroom and threw up."

A slew of emotions ran through me. Anger, grief, remorse. Self-loathing, which made the entity inside me shiver with pleasure. When I spoke, it was an effort to keep my voice neutral. "Then what?"

"I thought I had food poisoning, so I drove back to Gaslight City. I barely made it into the bathroom. I knocked the night case off the counter. It hit that tile floor and busted into a million pieces. When I finished being sick, I started cleaning it up. Sewn inside the lining were pictures."

"But Rainey's PI..." I was going to tell Rainey to fire this no-account.

"Rainey never gave him the overnight case," Hannah

broke in. "It somehow got separated from the rest of Barbie's belongings. Good thing. Otherwise it might have been stolen with the rest of it."

The evil voice inside me spoke up. *"Your own mother hated you. Ever wonder what that means in the grand scheme of your life?"*

The words ached, rotten and throbbing like a tooth that needed pulling. I considered stinging the little monster, but it wouldn't change how I felt. The words were true. Barbie had hated me. How lovable I considered myself always traced back to that awful fact. I shunted the thought away and turned my attention back to Hannah. "Were the pictures you found dirty pictures?"

Hannah smiled. "Not raunchy ones. They were pictures like a private investigator would have taken. The people in the pictures didn't know they were being photographed. One had King and Barbie in it. They were arguing. Another had Uncle Joey and Barbie in it. Then there were a few of you."

"Could you tell when the pictures were taken?"

"Judging by the length of your hair, I'd say the ones of you were taken around the time of Barbie's final visit to Gaslight City. The ones of King and Joey were older. Uncle Joey was actually good-looking."

I couldn't imagine. "You decided to go out to Long Time Gone because of the pictures?" The transition from puking sick to in the mood to go bar-hopping was a little odd.

Hannah shrugged. "After I purged, I felt fine. I wanted to change the channel, put the bad feelings behind me. I knew Long Time Gone had started open mic nights, and I'd been playing my guitar again. I figured I'd find a way to chat with King while having a legit reason to be there." She shrugged, the sick expression back on her face.

"Did King ever tell you anything useful?"

Hannah's cheeks got so red I couldn't even make out the freckles. "As soon as I brought up Barbie, King invited me into his office. But instead of answering questions, he had some, uh, pot." Hannah got even redder. "I hadn't smoked since college. It was really strong stuff, much stronger than I remember. Then we did tequila shots. Later one of the Six Guns had ecstasy. I woke up the next morning naked in King's bed, thinking I'd go home..."

I cut her off. She didn't need to go through this. Talk about a chapter of life worth deleting. "That's fine. I see what happened."

Hannah raised her voice to speak over me. "Like I said, I thought I'd go home. But I could smell bacon. I figured a greasy breakfast would make me feel better. I wandered into the kitchen. There was more tequila. By noon, I was drunk and had forgotten all about home. It was all a blur until you got that thing out of me."

Footsteps thumped up the stairs. Hannah jumped, her long hands fluttering over the tabletop.

Tubby's head appeared. "You have *got* to see what Dillon made Corman do." He motioned frantically, nearly jumping up and down with excitement.

I stood from the table. "You're welcome to join us."

Hannah just shook her head, her animation drained away. I remembered what Corman had said to her downstairs. Her reaction had told a story, one whose details I didn't want to know.

"All right. You know where to find me if you need me." I headed for the stairs.

Hannah's voice floated after me. "I do just fine without you."

I walked down the stairs, my skin stinging with humiliation. Good thing Hannah couldn't see my face. It would have given my pride a nice shot to the gonads. In one second, I had gone from making progress with her to pissing her off all over again. I was going to hurt and humiliate Corman and King in a way they'd never forget. Maybe that made me just as bad as them. I didn't care.

11

———

Tubby led the way down the stairs, through the building, and toward where he'd stowed Corman. I followed without much hope that whatever they'd done to Corman would help. Tubby had mentioned something with Dillon. That alone gave me a few ideas what may have happened. Dillon had the gift of persuading people, but she was young and full of herself. She had the bad habit of using her gift more like parlor trick than an actual tool.

A board creaked above us, followed by shuffling footsteps. Hannah. She'd turned nasty so quickly I didn't dare go back to check on her. I had to trust her to find herself again, emerge from the ashes, and...

The hag's voice started up again, older than time and smarter than I'd ever be. *"She'll never be better. People don't get away from me. You'll see."*

A hole opened in my chest, its emptiness sucking away all positive thought. The hag had caused train wrecks like this since the dawn of humanity. It knew how things would go. I gave my head a hard shake. No. It couldn't end that way. Hannah had to get better. Our bond, often cemented by silliness, meant so much to me. Losing that bond meant losing part of me.

"Wishes never come true. Not for a little girl whose mother hated her. Whose grandmother was ashamed of her." The cadence of the hag's words sank in and throbbed like an ant sting.

The pain gave me an idea. I concentrated on its presence and imagined the mantle as a red wasp circling the hag's head. The imaginary insect's buzz filled my ears. The hag shifted on my shoulders. I couldn't see the entity, but I guessed it was slapping at the imaginary wasp. First lesson in life for East Texas kids: never slap at a red wasp. I made the imaginary wasp swoop in for the kill. The hag screamed.

"I'll get you. I'll get both of you," the hag shouted in my head, rattling my eardrums.

My lips spread in a hateful grin. Hurting the hag had felt almost as good as eating a whole bag of tortilla chips with good, hot salsa, but it had cost me. My body trembled. Rivulets of sweat trailed down my back. I wouldn't be able to do that very many times without needing sleep or one of Mysti's potions.

Tubby halted, perhaps realizing I had stopped walking, turned around, and came back to me. "I heard what Hannah said to you there at the end, and I bet I know what you're thinking."

I didn't answer. Tubby, more intelligent than people realized, probably did know my thoughts. Tubby's insight into human nature worked only when he was playing eye in the sky. When it got down to a personal level, he didn't know when to keep his mouth shut, when to back off, or how to show love. I tensed, waiting for an analysis of my relationship with Hannah that I didn't want to hear.

"She'll waffle back and forth between loving you and hating you for a long time. But that's only because you're easy to blame." Tubby leaned to speak into my ear. At least he wasn't shouting it where everybody could hear. "She'll have to accept that what happened wasn't her fault any more than it was yours."

"It would have never happened if she didn't know me." I didn't need the hag to make me accept at least that much blame.

Tubby nodded at that. "My stepfather would have never beaten me if my mother hadn't married him. I ain't mad at her."

He wasn't. Tubby treated his mother like gold. When she said she couldn't stand Texas summers any more, he bought her a place to live in Colorado. When she said she didn't like Colorado winters, he got her a condo in Florida.

"Yeah, she's your mother though." I pushed around him and walked straight to Dillon.

My cousin-by-marriage had a Cheshire cat smile on her face. I felt a rush of love for her, leaving her kids with her husband, who might or might not let them eat bugs, to come on this risky mission just to help me. "What's up?"

She held her hands, palms facing, about an inch apart and began moving them with the first word she said. "So we're down here smoking, except for Mysti, and Corman starts up. He's hurting. He's going to get an infection from the bullet wound." She rolled her eyes as though she'd been shot half a dozen times and survived them all. I bit my lip to keep from smiling. "Tubby went over there and looked. Said the bullet passed right through. He poured some alcohol on it. Corman started hollering again." She licked her lips and locked her eyes on mine. This was the part she was proud of. "I went over there and told him to quit hollering, that he wasn't hurting. I had to tell him a couple of times, but he did what I said."

I nodded my encouragement and said, "Good job." My mind roved to the next thing. That motel. The tape and why King wanted it. How King played into this whole thing. Those pictures. Maybe King had had some kind of deal with Barbie. But what? The connection wouldn't come. Dillon started talking again, but I barely listened.

"Did you hear me?" She raised her voice.

I cut off my thoughts. "I'm sorry. Tell me again. Hannah told me some stuff upstairs, and I'm trying to figure out what to do with it." I made a point to look at Dillon's face.

"I know what you're thinking, but this might help. Corman might have the answers to all your questions." She shrugged. "I can make him tell, but I don't know what to ask."

I thought it over. Not a bad idea. The how and why of Barbie and King's connection mattered if Rainey was going to get Jesse out of prison. It might matter if I wanted to get out of this alive. I motioned Dillon to follow me and walked to the alcove where Tubby had put Corman. Just before we reached him, I pulled her to a stop. "How are we going to do this? I ask you the questions, and you ask Corman?"

Dillon shook her head. "If I can get him willing to talk, I should be able to convince him to talk to you." She turned and strutted up to Corman, so proud of what she could do, so happy to help.

The weird, exhilarating pride and love rushed over me again. Much as I hadn't wanted to help Cecil run Sanctuary, a traveling community of grifters and carnies, I had a feeling I'd found a place for myself and my magic. I glanced at Cecil. He gave me a quick wink and nod. Love for my great-uncle flooded me. Bad as this was, even if Hannah decided to hate me forever, my life had bright spots too. I went to stand by Dillon's side.

"Corman." Dillon snapped her little fingers in front of his face. "Hey. Wake up. I want to talk to you some more."

Corman rolled his head on his shoulders, the bones in his neck popping. "What?"

Dillon crouched so their eyes would meet. This seemed to be an important part of her gift. She put one hand on Corman's chest and gave him a shake. He moaned. Whatever she'd convinced him of regarding his pain wasn't lasting long. She shook him again, hard.

He yelped and opened his eyes wide. "What?"

"Listen to me, Corman. You want to help us. The only way you're going to get out of this alive is by helping us. You believe that?" Dillon stared into Corman's eyes without blinking.

"Yeah. You're right. Y'all are going to kill me if I don't help." He blinked rapidly.

"So Peri Jean's going to ask you some questions. And you're going to answer. You want to answer. Right?" Dillon had her hand on Corman's arm, the same way I'd seen her charm three different men out of their wallets one night on Austin's Sixth Street.

"Yeah." Corman bobbed his head. "Yeah. I want to answer."

Dillon backed away from Corman and nodded to me. "He's hurting, so I don't know how long it'll really work."

I knelt in front of Corman where he didn't have to raise his head to see me. "Did King try to set up a meeting with my mother recently?"

Corman nodded slowly. "Yeah. He sent me and Trench Coat. We were to not engage her but wait until she left and then follow her." He swallowed. "But Rainey Bruce showed up. We thought maybe she was working for Barbie, so we followed her. She led us to a little house off Perdido Street. Had a padlock on the door."

My mind ran its hamster wheel. Perdido Street. That was smack in the middle of Gaslight City's African American community, in an area where many houses were unoccupied and boarded up. I snapped my mind back on task. "What else, Corman?"

"Rainey sat on the floor picking through some luggage. We called Daddy to see if we should go in and take the luggage from her. He told us to wait until she left. She did, and me and Trench Coat broke in, nabbed the luggage, and took it back to King."

Smart as Rainey was, she hadn't known to watch her back. She'd been in so much danger and hadn't even sensed it. And it was all because she knew me. I didn't need the hag to remind me of that. I broke off the thoughts about Rainey's safety. I had a lifetime to worry about them. The important thing right then was what they found in Barbie's luggage. I leaned into Corman's face. "Did King find anything of use in my mother's luggage?"

Corman gave his head a slow shake. "Nothing other than he thinks she's dead now. He got really mad then and burned everything."

I suppressed a groan. "King was looking for a recording, right?"

Corman nodded and then groaned in pain. A sheen of sweat glowed on his forehead. One drop fattened and slid down his face. He needed medical attention. Denying it might cost him his life and us our bargaining chip.

I asked the next question. "Do you know what was on it?"

Corman gave me a blank stare. I considered kicking him to get his attention but pulled back my temper. Patience. Patience. I whispered the word as though it might really help.

Finally he spoke. "I think he wants something he can use to blackmail Joey Holze."

I drew in a sharp breath. We were on the right track. According to my mother, Joey helped her cover up her murdering my father and frame my Uncle Jesse for the crime. "Why does he want to blackmail Joey?"

"Several months ago, I overheard King and Joey arguing. They didn't realize anybody was in Long Time Gone with them." Corman closed his eyes and swayed back and forth. When he opened them again, they were foggy with pain. "You had just started asking questions, saying you knew who really killed your daddy and you were trying to get Jesse out of prison." Corman licked his lips, and I held a bottle of water Tubby or someone had sat by the chair up to the injured man's lips. He drank greedily.

Poor man had to be miserable. He was a jerk. No doubt there. But did he deserve this? "What did they say?"

"Joey told Daddy that if that tape gets found, some-body's gonna go down, and it ain't gonna be him. He wanted Daddy to kill you, Hannah, Rainey, and Jesse." There was enough meanness left in Corman to grin at me.

Coldness worked its way down to my feet. I'd already known King was trying to have me killed, and I knew Joey wanted me dead. But hearing Corman say it had more of an effect than I'd have imagined.

"Then what?" I almost choked on the words.

"King refused. He said his deal with Joey ended the day Paul Mace died. Joey slammed out of Long Time Gone." Corman nodded at the water, and I gave him more as I put together a timeline. Joey ordered King to kill my friends and me. King refused but later changed his mind enough to talk to Tubby about putting a contract out on my life. Then Hannah offered herself up like a birthday present, and King saw another way to blow the whole thing sky high.

Struggling to keep my voice even, I said, "What deal did King and Joey originally have?"

Corman hung his head and let his eyes drift closed. My hopes soured. He either didn't know or was too sick to talk more. This great idea was turning into one big dead end. He hadn't told me a damn thing I really needed to know.

When he spoke again, I had to strain to hear him. "See, I was only eight or so. Joey would come by the house late at night, when my brother and I were already supposed to be asleep. That was when we lived over by the haunted witch cabin." He stopped speaking, and I gave him water again, mind racing.

The place Corman called the haunted witch cabin was the site of my father's murder. And a lot of other things important to me and my history. Corman pushed the bottle away with his chin.

"I remember asking Daddy why he was talking to a cop. Because he always taught me and my brother that cops are the enemy. Daddy told me the only way he could stay out of jail and keep the motorcycle club was to help Joey."

"Do you remember how King helped Joey?" I hunched in front of Corman like a gambler over a craps table, wanting the answer to be there enough to keep trying even when it seemed hopeless.

"Daddy didn't tell me much about his business back then." Corman shook his head.

No, no, no. I wanted him to know something useful so badly I was ready to sic Dillon or even Tubby on him.

"The only thing I really remember is from when I was seven or eight years old. It was summer. Joey called for my father. Daddy rushed out the door, told me to stay put. A while later he came back with a paper bag. There was blood dripping out of the bottom of it." Corman leaned his head back and closed his eyes, grunting at intervals.

"Where'd he put the bag?" Maybe all these years, Barbie, Joey, and King had kept up a blackmail standoff. Joey had the murder file which either implicated King, Barbie, or both. Barbie had this recording King wanted so badly. It probably implicated both Joey and King. Then King had whatever was in this bag. Barbie's clothes from the day of the murder? Maybe. Maybe not. They'd each had their little insurance policy to keep the others from squealing. If one went down, they all fell.

"We used to have an old school bus behind our house." Corman watched me through half-lidded eyes. "Daddy kept it there. Told me if he ever caught me out there, he'd beat me black and blue."

"Any idea where it is now?" This bag and the tape were Jesse's ticket out of jail. If I could get my hands on one or both, my uncle would be free. Only King stood in the way. I tried to think like my Uncle Cecil, to see how to best manipulate the situation. But my thoughts ran together.

"Maybe the safe at Long Time Gone." Corman shrugged and winced. "Maybe the safe on the compound. I never saw it again."

"Okay. Thanks for your help." I turned to Tubby. "Get him a doctor or a nurse. I'll pay."

Corman leaned his head back and muttered a thank you. I turned to leave the room. Even though I didn't like watching Corman hurt, I still didn't want to spend time with him. Dillon and Cecil flanked me. I stopped on the other side of the building, next to the staircase, and filled them in on what Hannah told me. I finished with, "The tape's got to be in that motel room. We have to get in there. But after that? No idea how to find the tape."

"I might have some ideas on finding the tape." Cecil put his hand on the bannister. "But do you think Ms. Whitebyrd would be willing to join our discussion?"

Mysti stood off to the side with Dillon, probably asking about her ability of persuasion. I swear, sometimes I thought Mysti ought to write a supernatural encyclopedia. "Mysti," I called.

She turned to see what I wanted.

"Can you join Cecil and me upstairs to talk about finding Barbie's recording?"

Without answering, Mysti hurried across the room, Dillon at her heels.

We climbed the steep staircase, Cecil yawning every other step. My great-uncle was an old man. At least eighty. Maybe older. We needed to find him a place to sleep for a few hours. At the top of the stairs, I stopped so quickly Cecil and Dillon ran into me.

"What is it?" Cecil muttered and then yawned again.

I couldn't speak. I couldn't do anything but stand rooted to the top step and stare. Hannah hung from one of the exposed beams, swaying back and forth. An overturned chair lay at her feet. I let out a howl I'm sure the Six Guns heard all the way back at their shitty compound.

———

My LUNGS EMPTIED, and my scream ended. I ran to the

overturned metal folding chair at Hannah's feet, uprighted it, and wrangled it into position. Pain flashed as I ripped off a couple of fingernails. I ignored it and scrambled onto the chair.

Inside me, the hag pulled toward Hannah. I didn't understand what the little horror was up to but didn't have time to figure it out. Mysti pushed a pair of scissors into my hand and grabbed my legs to hold me steady.

I grabbed Hannah around the waist, the material of her linen blouse rasping against my cheek, and did my best to lift her. The buckle from her belt dug into my forearm. For a second, I thought I didn't have the strength.

Then I put some slack in the rope. Hannah's body flopped and swayed, limp, dead meat. With my free hand, I snipped the braided nylon rope she'd used to try to end herself. She fell against me. I overbalanced, and we tumbled to the floor. Hannah landed on top of me, and my head slapped hard against the wood floor.

The hag cast about, frantic, pressing toward Hannah with all its might. Its plan came to me in a flash. The hag would grab onto Hannah's life force through me, consume it, and be able to overpower me. That wasn't the worst part. Once the hag ate Hannah's life force, she'd be gone forever.

"Fight it." Mysti leaned over both of us, pulling Hannah off me. "Don't let it get her."

Reaching for strength I wasn't sure I had, I wrapped the mantle around the hag and held it fast with all my might. It slammed against the walls of my body. I rocked with each attempt it made to get to Hannah.

"*Let me go,*" it screamed inside my head.

"You'll have to kill me first," I managed to grunt.

Dillon appeared and yanked away the noose, revealing an angry red circle around Hannah's neck. Mysti shoved her out of the way and began CPR and chest compressions.

"C'mon, Hannah," she snapped every time she came up for air. "Peri Jean won't talk to your ghost if you let yourself die."

The hag's keening at sight of Hannah, and a good meal, made it hard to concentrate. I curled on my side, hands over my ears, and let my conscious slip into the hag's.

Through its eyes, I saw Hannah's life force rising from her still body, not responding at all to Mysti's efforts. Somehow I knew Hannah didn't want to come back. She wanted to be done with this. The hag leered gleefully at the destruction of my friend. As I watched, the life force rose further. Time was running out.

Helpless tears coursed down my cheeks and scooted down my neck to soak into the crew neck of my T-shirt. It couldn't end like this. There were so many things I still wanted to do with Hannah, so many conversations I wanted to have. But I was occupied fighting the monster inside me and could do nothing.

Don't lie to yourself. The whisper came from my elbow. Priscilla Herrera stood next to me wearing her young skin. She raised one heavily tattooed arm and adjusted her wide-brimmed hat.

My malignant passenger hissed in displeasure at Priscilla. In a flash, Priscilla's face elongated, the eyes darkening to black pits. Her mouth fell open. She let out a howl. My horrible passenger answered Priscilla's howl with a low, reverberating growl, which came out through my mouth.

My black opal heated at the proximity of so much magic. I gathered the power of the mantle, taking note of my flagging energy, and squeezed the hag harder. Instead of cowering away, it pushed an unearthly scream through my lips. It shook the room.

Mysti jumped away from Hannah and faced us. Her eyes grew. "What's happening over there?"

"You're losing her. I can see her life force." Panting with fatigue, I rolled onto my knees and crouched like a cat trying to yak on the carpet.

Priscilla came with me and whispered in my ear. *Don't you want to ask how to save her?*

Right now, I just wanted her to go away. Priscilla didn't care about me or my friends. All she cared about was her part in my destiny. She planned for me to have the full measure of the magical gifts passed through our family line of witches. Sometimes I got the idea there was more, but I didn't like to think about more duties and more misery. The point was, Priscilla wouldn't help me unless it fit into some grand plan of hers.

Right now, while I watched one of my oldest friends die, I didn't have time for Priscilla's brand of bullshit. Between her and the hag playing demolition derby inside my body, I probably had as much reason to jump ship as Hannah did.

Ninny. I want only what's best for you. This girl's death on your conscience is not one of those things. Priscilla came nearer, and her spicy scent tickled my nose. *Although you don't have full use of my gift, you can bring her back.* Her cold fingers pressed against my temple. The night I killed Michael Gage replayed on my mind's movie projector. Priscilla's freezing fingers turned my head to look at Hannah's still form. Her life force had risen almost all the way out of her but was still connected. *She's not gone yet. Wake her up. Gently.*

The hag salivated for me to go nearer Hannah. It wanted a chance to snap forward like a dog snatching a treat and suck in the life force. Once it did that, Hannah and I were both cooked. Hannah would be all the way dead. The hag would be too powerful for me to control, and it would suck me dry too. The crushing weight of helplessness came back. I spun to Priscilla, ready to give her the what-for, and found her ready for me.

Your will is as great as the thing inside you. Otherwise, he'd have already defeated you. She faded from sight, done with me. Understanding flooded over me. She wanted me to see what I could do, despite grief, despite fatigue, against risk. Tiredness ached in my bones.

Priscilla always called me a coward. Right then, I understood what she meant. Destiny isn't fairy dust and magic. It's a long, blood-stained crucible, suffused with more grief than victory. I had to try.

"Peri Jean, if you're going to do something, it needs to be now." Mysti's voice snapped me out of my own head.

I nodded, even though I didn't know how to do this. In my weakened state, I needed physical contact with Hannah. It would give me more control because I wouldn't have to push my power into her from a distance. But touching Hannah would give the hag access to her.

"Peri Jean..." Mysti didn't need to finish the thought. I knew.

I had to at least try. I reached for the mantle, intending to send it to Hannah long distance. It slipped into my exhausted grasp, trembling and tired, but there.

The hag, hiding deep inside my psyche, as though the mantle couldn't find it there, chuckled. I wanted to hurt it but couldn't without using more precious energy.

You can. With my strength, you can. Priscilla Herrera's voice came from all around me. It bolstered me, gave me the strength I needed to go on.

I got to my feet and staggered to Hannah's still form. The silver mist of her life force barely touched her now. It was ready to change, ready for the next thing. Not on my watch.

I channeled the mantle again and held my hands over Hannah. The hag leaned forward, straining against the bonds that glued us together. I concentrated on my breathing, made it the only thing in the world, and hoped what I was about to do wouldn't fry mine or Hannah's brain. Control wasn't my strong suit.

I waited until my mind was clear as a pond after a strong wind, nothing in my ears but my own ragged breathing. I split the mantle down the middle. One half swaddled the hag, wrapping it so tight the thing couldn't even make noise.

It was a temporary solution at best. There'd be no way I could hold the split indefinitely. It would fall as soon as my concentration did or when the last of my strength ebbed away. But for right then, I hoped it was enough.

I let the other half of the magic trace around Hannah's head, looking for a way in. I entered through her eye and saw the spark of life still attached in her brain. My magic circled it, warming it, nurturing it. It brightened and kindled. This was the limit of my power unless I wanted to give her the Michael Gage treatment, which would cause an aneurysm or a stroke. I withdrew.

The life force had disappeared, hopefully gone back into Hannah's body. She jerked, once, twice, her head rolling side to side. But she didn't open her eyes.

No. I must have been too late. Grief broke open inside me, cold and poisonous. I lay my cheek on her still chest. The sobs ripped out of me, one after the other, as I clutched my friend and mourned her. The hag squealed and squirmed, trying to free itself. If I had contained it with only half my magic, maybe I could kill it. I'd cry for Hannah, then I'd try.

I let my grief out in sobs and shrieks. My black opal grew hot with the force of it. Somewhere outside the window, my raven familiar cawed. The sound of his wings flapping filled the room.

Hannah's chest hitched, and she coughed. She tried to roll over on her side, but I was practically lying on top of her. I pushed off her and sat back on my legs. *Was it death convulsions?* Hannah coughed again and half rose, clawing at her neck.

"Water. Give her water." I yelled the words to nobody

in particular. The sink faucet came on, and footsteps approached.

Mysti knelt next to Hannah and put the glass to her lips. "Take it slow."

Hannah took a sip of water and spewed it. Coughs wracked her body. Dillon stepped forward and knelt in front of Hannah. "Stop coughing. Your throat don't hurt."

Hannah did as Dillon told her. Mysti tried again. This time Hannah swallowed the water and held it down. She took the glass in her own hands and drank.

Finished, she handed the glass to Mysti and glared at me. "Why didn't you just let me die? Then this would be over. I wouldn't have to..." She broke off her words with a sob.

I recoiled with shock, but then my had-enough kicked in. I narrowed my eyes at her. "You wanna kill your damn self, run off and do it somewhere I can't see you. You ain't dying on my watch."

Hannah cut off her sobs and bared her teeth at me, her face contorted with fury. I tensed, ready for her attack. The idea of fighting my best friend killed something inside me, and my magic let go of the hag. It raged around my psyche, causing as much pain as it could. A headache blossomed behind both eyes and spread into my sinuses where it leaked pain into the rest of my head. One tear streaked down my cheek.

Hannah struggled to her feet. "You have no idea what it's like to live with this." She hit herself in the chest with the palm of one hand.

I had no argument. The horror of what she'd been

through was beyond my understanding. She spun away from me and made a beeline for the stairs. Tubby went after her.

"Stop it," Hannah shouted. "Let me go." Then came the sound of flesh striking flesh, and I knew she'd slapped him.

Footsteps thumped back up the steps. Tubby reappeared, carrying Hannah over his shoulder, his mouth turned down. He dropped Hannah on a cracked leather recliner and leaned over her, holding up one finger. "Don't hit me. I'll give you that one out of loyalty to Peri Jean, but I ain't one of those men who puts up with a woman slapping around on him. I'll whup your ass if you try it with me."

Feeling the need to protect Hannah, I stomped over. Tubby held up one hand for me to stop. The menace in that one gesture stopped me where I was. And I considered this guy a trusted friend? *You could kill him without lifting a finger.* The voice wasn't my own. It sounded confident and ruthless, but it wasn't the voice of the hag either. I realized I'd heard the voice of who I would become when I took on the full measure of Priscilla Herrera's mantle. The thought froze me. "Tub? Don't threaten her, okay? She can't help herself."

Tubby spun to face me, eyes blazing, but took one look at my face and stood down.

"She can risk our whole operation." Tubby Tubman was explaining himself to me. I couldn't believe it. "Then all this trouble, all we've lost, would be for nothing."

I stared down at Hannah. She met my glare and shot

eye-daggers of her own. Would she snap out of it again? It didn't much matter. The old Hannah truly was lost. This one was all that was left. The hurt spread over me, aching and throbbing, but this time I didn't let it consume me. I stared at Hannah until she blinked and turned away.

Cecil and Dillon began straightening up the mess I'd made. Drama was over to them, and I guessed it was for me too. I drew myself up to my full height, which was pretty unimpressive, and approached Mysti.

"You kept me moving instead of letting me freeze." We hugged tight. I patted Tubby on the back. "You did the right thing."

Thanking people, and doing it in sincere way, was one of the things Cecil had been teaching me about leading people. Now I felt him watching me from inside the kitchen. I turned to meet his eyes. They were so like Memaw's my chest ached. He winked at me and gave me a nod of approval.

"You ladies ready to talk about my idea to get the tape out of the motel?" Cecil held a valise I'd watched him take out of Mysti's car a lifetime ago and was rummaging through it.

I nodded and dragged the chairs around the table. Tubby came to lean against the wall, his arms crossed over his chest. Mysti started some more of her awful smelling tea. Hannah sat alone on the other side of the room, head down, face red with anger.

I didn't know what to do for Hannah. Next time she did something like this, I probably wouldn't be there to save her. And that would be the end of a friend I truly loved. I let myself fully embrace the sorrow and then put it aside. I had business to tend to.

Wade Hill was still alive, and I'd do everything I could to save him. If Cecil had an idea that might help, I wanted to hear it.

12

———

CECIL SET what appeared to be a mummified human hand on the table. I gasped and withdrew, scenting for the telltale odor of rot.

Mysti leaned forward. "That what I think it is?" A smile played on her lips, broadening when Cecil nodded. "As I live and breathe, I never expected to see one of these."

I watched the two of them, confused. The thing was disgusting. If it was real. Maybe it wasn't real. Because if it was, we were sitting here at this table with part of a dead body.

Mysti glanced at me and giggled behind her hand. "Look at you. Big bad Peri Jean, afraid."

"It's a piece of a dead person." I glanced at Tubby, hoping for approval, but he stepped forward, blue eyes alight with curiosity.

"Hand of Glory, ain't it?" He actually grinned. Cecil smiled back. Tubby muttered, "Hot damn."

I stared at the dead hand, twisting my face in disgust.

Mysti rolled her eyes at me. "Don't you remember the ordeal you went through to take on Priscilla Herrera's mantle?"

I nodded.

She leaned forward, mirth leaving her face. "The old Peri Jean Mace died a symbolic death that day and was reborn a witch of Priscilla Herrera's line. This left you with an even deeper anchor into the realm of the dead than you already had with your psychic medium ability." I didn't react. She leaned forward and put her hand over my arm. "The Hand of Glory belongs to our kind. Do not let fear take it away."

I tried to look at the thing without my stomach rolling. Footsteps creaked on the floor. Hannah came into view, walking on her tiptoes. I studied her face, searching for the anger and resentment. It seemed to have faded for the moment. She leaned over the table.

"That thing is butt ugly." She glanced at me. For a tiny second, I saw the bond we'd shared. Then it danced away, and dull hurt took its place. She turned away from me and spoke to Tubby. "Is there another chair? Or am I allowed..."

"Of course you're allowed." I got up and found an extra metal folding chair leaning against the wall. I set it behind her without speaking and sat back down. I grimaced at the Hand of Glory. "So what are we going to do with this?"

"I'm wondering that myself. Maybe Mr. Gregg will enlighten us." Mysti didn't wait for Cecil to answer. She plowed on, her voice more scholarly with each word. "I have never even seen one of these or talked to someone who used one. My knowledge is strictly folkloric. The Hand is cut off a hanged murderer while his neck is still in the noose." She shot a guilty glance at Hannah, who flushed. "The amputated hand goes through a very specific procedure to preserve it. It is then used as a candle, mostly by thieves. It's supposed to keep the occupants of the house sleeping while the thieves rob the house."

Tubby leaned forward, grinning. "I've heard you light one finger for each person sleeping. If a finger won't light, means somebody's awake in the house."

"The person who gave it to me said to knock with this hand, and it would unlock any door." Cecil shrugged at the difference between his interpretation of the Hand's powers and the other ones.

The thing still disgusted me. "Where'd you get it?"

"My grandmother had a twin brother named Samuel. My great-uncle," Cecil said. "Uncle Sam liked gambling and women and would go off on binges of both. He came back with this one time. Sam had no children, and I was the only boy child born to our family at that time. So he gave it to me." Cecil chuckled. "My mother had a fit. That was the first and last time I ever saw her show disrespect to her elders. She wanted to take it away from me. Daddy wanted to sell it. But Samantha stood up to them both, said Samuel wanted me to have it, and have it I would."

"You ever use it for its intended purpose?" Tubby stared at the thing. His finger snaked out a couple of times to touch it, but he withdrew each time.

"No. I don't have the gift of moving energy like Peri Jean. The Hand of Glory stayed in a special cedar box most of my life." He took the box out of his valise and set it on the table. It was plain, stained cedar with sigils carved into the wood. "I'd forgotten about it, but Jadine had one of her dreams earlier this week. She woke up asking about it. Knew exactly what it looked like. I got it out so she could..." Cecil shrugged. Jadine was Cecil's adopted daughter. She possessed the gift of precognition, among other things. "Then when Mysti called asking for my help, Jadine insisted I take it."

Jadine called her gift dream walking. She saw dreams of the past, dreams of the future, even dreams of the present. It usually happened when she slept. "Did she say exactly what she saw?"

Cecil nodded. "This ought to interest you. She said she saw you in a small room with only a bed. The room had red carpet and a picture of a horse on the wall. It also had a red phone."

Hannah gasped. "That's the motel room where I picked up that *hag*." She jerked a thumb at me. We all knew what she meant.

Cecil stared at Hannah for several seconds, the lines on his face deepening. He started to say something but shook his head. He spoke instead to me. "Jadine also said she saw you using the hand to knock on the wall. Perhaps this tape is hidden in the walls of this motel room."

I still wasn't a believer. "But how would you hide something in a motel room wall? It's not like your house, where you do renovations."

Mysti spoke up. "For the room to have been guarded by the creature now inside you, there has to be something important in there. And it's still there because Hannah didn't find it."

"I agree with Ms. Whitebyrd." Cecil gave Mysti the smile he always seemed to reserve just for her. He wanted her to join Sanctuary the same way a mosquito wants blood and did everything he could to charm her. Mysti patted Cecil's hand and smiled back. I wanted to pour syrup over the both of them. Cecil leaned forward where he could see Hannah's face. "Ms. Kessler, I'd like for Peri Jean to have as clear an idea as possible about what she's walking into. This might also give us an insight into how the tape is hidden. Do you feel like answering questions?"

"I'll try." Hannah had taken the crystal Mysti gave her out of her pocket and squeezed it in one pale, freckled fist.

"You went to the front desk at the motel to ask for the key. Did the ummm...*person* manning the counter strike you as odd in any way? Make you uncomfortable?"

Hannah gave him a blank stare.

"I think I know where Cecil's going," Mysti interrupted. "Maybe his face was really narrow? Or his fingernails seemed sharp? It might have been his teeth you noticed. Or he might have smelled like swamp water."

Hannah stared at the table, wringing her hands. "There was something odd about him. But I can't..." She sat up straight. "I thought I imagined it." Hannah shook her head as though trying to clear it. "Sometimes, since my time with Michael Gage, I hear and see things that aren't there."

"This was probably real." Mysti used her reassuring voice.

Hannah swallowed hard enough for it to make a clicking sound. "His tongue. It was his tongue. For just a second, I thought it was forked like a snake's. Not surgically split, like you sometimes see, but thin and long. It flicked out of his mouth."

Cecil sucked in a breath. "I haven't seen one of those since I was a boy. A man like that came to see my grandmother sometimes." He put his hand over mine. "Listen carefully. This is who you'll negotiate the contract on your life and the rider's freedom with. He's no joke."

I thought about the forked tongue and swallowed hard. Why did I always get stuck dealing with weirdos? "But I don't know how to..."

Everybody at the table simply stared. They didn't how to negotiate with the hag's owner either. I was on my own. "The day's wasting. Better to try this than sit on our asses and let the clock run out."

Someone pounded on a door downstairs. Tubby got up. "That's the medic I called. I'll stay here with Corman. Y'all go on."

"I'm staying too." Cecil yawned again. "Do you have a bed in this building, young man?"

Tubby showed Cecil to a room with a locked door and let him inside.

———

Mysti and I gathered her witch supplies. She had a place for each thing in her witch pack. My pack was usually a messy jumble. I grabbed what I needed and then tossed it back in when I was done.

I pinched the Hand of Glory between a thumb and forefinger and lifted it off the table. The fingers twitched, and I dropped it with a clatter. Hannah giggled from behind me. I turned to face her, already smiling, but she turned away and walked into the living room. The recliner groaned when she sat on it.

Mysti stared at me with the corners of her mouth pulled down. I gave her a shrug. This time I picked up the Hand with little caution. I dropped it into Cecil's box and worked the latch. Then I slid it into my witch pack.

Mysti leaned close to whisper in my ear. "What about Hannah?"

"I can't leave her," I whispered back.

"No," Mysti agreed. "You need to keep an eye on her. Her life force was out of her body long enough for transformation to have started."

No, not that. People sometimes came back from near death experiences with psychic gifts. I didn't think Hannah could handle much more. I nodded to Mysti to show I understood and walked into the living room to find Hannah rocking in the recliner. She stared, blank faced, at the wall.

"Want to come with us?" I stood near her chair but not too near. She shrugged without looking at me. I tried again. "You were always good at puzzles."

She finally looked up. "Plus, I might try to eighty-six myself if you leave me here."

I hefted my witch pack onto my shoulder.

"You gonna force me to go?" She squared her shoulders.

"I honestly don't know what to do." The words, ones I'd have never said back at Sanctuary, just came out. Leaders always know what to do. But Hannah's situation was out of my element. So I added more to them. "I just figured... you're good at this. Smarter than me."

Hannah pulled herself out of the chair and approached Mysti, ignoring me. "Do we need wax to light the Hand? Or do we just knock without it lit?"

"All the legends I've heard talk about it being lit," Mysti answered with a glance at me.

"But that's for burglarizing a place and making sure everybody stays asleep, right?" Hannah asked.

"We could just try knocking with it. See what it opens." Mysti held up both hands and shrugged. In other words, we'd have to try things until something worked.

"Works for me." I led the way out of the loft.

"Wait a minute," Dillon called after us. I turned to see what she wanted. She gave me a hopeful smile. "Mind if I go? I ain't never seen nothing like a Hand of Glory in action."

I motioned her to come along. Mysti shot me one of her patented scolding looks. I shrank at her disapproval but didn't renege. I'd gotten used to making my own decisions over the last few weeks and liked it.

Dillon ran to join us, crowding up against my side. "You think me and Finn could use it for—"

I held up one hand to cut her off. "Later. We'll discuss it later."

Mysti stared for a long second, her expression unreadable, and then turned and went down the stairs. From somewhere near, Corman let out an ungodly scream. We ignored him and kept walking.

Mysti led the way to her dusty white Toyota sedan and used the remote to unlock it. Hannah got in the back.

When I opened the door opposite her, she raised her head, stared at me levelly, and said, "Please ride in the front with Mysti."

The hurt of her rejection almost blinding me, I stumbled to the front seat passenger side. The hag chewed on my hurt, poured some salt on it, and gnawed some more. The ache set up between my lungs. Every time I took a breath, it gave a low throb. I needed to blast the little bastard, but all a sudden, I didn't have the energy.

Dillon got in the backseat and stared at Hannah as though she expected her red hair to burst into flames. Dillon had watched and helped me do worse to people who'd done less. She glanced at me, and I gave her a slight head shake. Dillon cocked her head at me. She didn't understand me giving Hannah a free pass. Nobody but family got those in our world. And Hannah wasn't family.

"*Kill her. That's what she deserves.*" The hag's ugly voice sucked even more want-to out of me.

Mysti started the car and drove us out of Gaslight City. As we passed the green city limits sign, I wished I didn't have to come back. The wish that I didn't have to do another damn thing, that I could just die, crept into my thoughts and moved through them.

Mysti's voice cut it off. "I've been thinking about the

deal you have to make with the hag's master." She spun the radio's dial, cutting it to silence. "There's no way of knowing what terms he will offer. The hag probably doesn't even know. But my experience has taught me one thing."

I turned to stare at my friend in shock. She always acted horrified and sad when I made deals with Sol. But now I realized she probably made her own deals from time to time.

"Don't take the first terms offered. They're usually unnecessarily steep. This thing will act as though there's only one choice. But that's a lie." She stopped there and turned the radio back on.

The hour's drive to Tyler passed in tense silence, except for the occasional gasp from Hannah. I turned to see what was wrong. My friend stared out the window, eyes widened in horror. I wished so much I could help her but didn't know anything else to do.

As little girls, we'd been inseparable, always whispering secrets and wondering over the world together. Then my ability to see ghosts injected a gift-wrapped box of shit into our relationship. We weren't friends for more than twenty years after that.

Hannah had come back into my life less than two years earlier. We picked up as though we'd never left off, only this time as grownups. We shopped. Made fun of the way men looked and acted. Ate too much ice cream. Loved each other. Had us a helluva time together.

The memories brought tears, both happy and sad, to sting my eyes. But nothing lasted forever. The truth of who and what I was came to call again. This time it had done permanent damage to Hannah's body and mind.

The image of her hanging from that rafter took shape in my mind. Knowing me caused her to do that. How would she ever let me help her when I was the cause of her misery?

"*She'll never be okay.*" The hag's voice lowered to a soothing caress. "*Once I plant my seeds, they'll grow whether I'm there to tend them or not.*"

This time I gathered the mantle, ignoring the way my body ached in fatigue, and delivered a sharp shock to the horror inside me.

"*Bitch*" was its only response. Its less-than-pained response let me know I was running out of juice. I'd have to rest soon.

"You'll want to get in the turn lane now." Hannah's voice from the backseat nearly made me jump a mile. She stuck one bruised arm between the seats and pointed to a strip of depressed businesses. "It's right across from the used car lot. The big white building."

Mysti jammed on the brakes and whipped into the turn lane. "I'm glad you said something. It doesn't look like a motel." Cut into a small hill, the backs of its buildings facing the road and hiding the entrances to the guest rooms, The Rose City Inn hit me as a good place to do clandestine business.

Traffic cleared, and Mysti zipped across the lanes and up the narrow driveway. A few late model cars sat in the oil-stained and cracked asphalt parking lot. Had Hannah been herself, we'd have joked about it being a by-the-hour establishment or the kind of place you went to do things you didn't want to do in your own home. I glanced at her and caught her staring. She turned her head away.

"The admissions office is that little building." Hannah pointed again, and Mysti pulled into a parking place in front of it.

"Don't go in there and talk to the monster." Dillon rose over the back seat and gripped my arm. "We'll break into the motel room. Use that Hand of Glory thing."

I shook my head. "I have to go in and make a deal for the hag. Otherwise he'll never leave my body." I opened the car door. Dillon opened hers too. It flattered me that she wanted to act as my bodyguard, but she had way more to lose than I did. I waved one hand at her. "Stay here." I climbed out of the car before she could form an argument and went inside.

13

———

THE ADMISSIONS BUILDING had a glass entry door. The sun peeked through the clouds to glare off it, making it impossible to see inside. I took a deep breath and pushed the door open. An entry bell dinged, and the smell of lemon-scented cleaner almost knocked me back out the door. There wouldn't have been many other places to go.

The building's interior had been walled off so that coming inside trapped the customer in a tiny booth with the door to the parking lot behind them and a narrow window looking into an office in front of them. The office was empty. I rang the silver bell at the window.

Shuffling footsteps rewarded my impatience. A cadaverous man wearing black skinny jeans and a frayed T-shirt advertising a punk rock band popular when my daddy was a teenager appeared at the opposite end of the office. His hair, cut into a Mohawk and about a foot tall, vibrated like a tuning fork as he walked toward me.

How much hairspray did this guy go through to get his

hair to stand up like that? When Mohawk was five feet away from me, his natural odor broke through the lemon-scented cleaner. Maybe a better question was how often he showered. I almost had to put my hand over my nose.

Mohawk's musk smelled earthy and a little skunky. It reminded me of the smell I always associated with water moccasin snakes. I feared snakes, especially after having a shapeshifting acquaintance bite me. Cold runners chased down my back. I took a step away from the counter, my heart picking up speed.

Mohawk leaned his arms on the counter and stared at me. A faint pattern, like a faded tattoo, ran up both arms and disappeared into his sleeves. His eyes were a woody brown with no white and a not-quite-round black pupil. His head bowed out behind his ears, the same way a viper snake's did.

"Peri Jean Mace." He dragged the end of my name out in a long sssssss. "My servant found you. Was it through the woman calling herself a private investigator?"

"Does it matter?"

He smiled. The site of his human teeth, flat and small, relieved me until something flashed and I saw fangs. His mouth opened wide, and he hissed at me.

The hag, trembling in fear of its master, hissed back, the sound so loud I thought it would blow out my eardrums. I yelped and backed into the door.

Mohawk pointed one long skinny finger at me. "Why do you live?"

I took deep breaths until my mind settled. "I want to buy your servant's contract on my life and his freedom."

Mohawk's forked tongue ran out and tested the air between us. He frowned and shook his head. Tested the air again. I wanted to scream worse than I've wanted to scream in a long time. How many of these things had I walked past and never noticed? Mohawk feinted at me like a snake striking. That time I did scream. He liked that. It made him laugh. "Nothing at this establishment, including your passenger, is for sssale." His eyes flicked to the monster on my shoulder. "Kill her."

The rider's hands tightened around my throat, and its will snaked into me and ordered me to give up. I tugged the arms away from my neck. The hag didn't struggle much. It probably figured this was its only chance to get out from under Mohawk.

I tried to sound tough. "Mister, I don't have time to pull your pud and stick my tongue in your ear. Everything in the whole fucking world is for sale." I widened my stance and met his flat gaze, stomach writhing with nausea.

Mohawk ran his tongue out again. Confusion twisted his features. He leaned forward and snapped his fingers. "I've got it. I knew I recognized that smell. You're a witch of the Gregorius line. Are you not?"

Priscilla Herrera's maiden name was Gregory, and I'd heard Cecil use every possible variation of the name as his surname. Was Gregorius where it started? Maybe. I hoped so. Because it sounded like the magic running through my veins might help me for once in my life. I nodded slowly. Mohawk reached underneath the counter. Behind me, something clicked. I turned and saw he'd thrown the bolt, locking the door. Panic shot through me. I grabbed the door and yanked on it. Mohawk snickered at my back. I turned back to him, edges of my vision gray. I fought not to faint. Mohawk might eat me while I was unconscious.

"The price to buy out the contract on your life and for the rider's freedom is this: I want to sire a get from you." He pulled a yellow legal pad in front of him and began scribbling on it.

Icy pinpricks danced over my skin. A lightness spread through me. I leaned against the door to keep from spilling onto the floor.

"It's been a long time, centuries, since I've had a half-human get. But I'd think the same terms would still work." His tongue flickered out as he wrote.

I shook off the shock and made myself form words. "No. I'm not doing that." My voice sounded flat and direction-less in the small enclosure.

Mohawk stopped writing and slowly raised his head. "Yes, you are. It won't leave lasting damage. You'll be able to go on to have as many children as you like. I'll raise our child. You'd never have to see him or her again."

I swallowed sour spit and threw out what I thought was my trump card. "The doctor said I can't have children."

Mohawk tilted his head and sighed, the way someone would at a cute puppy who'd done something naughty. "Come now. We both know a good healer could fix that."

All the strength left my body. I slid to the floor. My vision blurred, and the room tilted. I woke to someone patting my face. Mohawk's long fingers were smooth and freezing cold. When had he let himself out of the office? Wait a minute. There was no door.

The better question was how he'd gotten out of the office. The only way I saw was through the tiny hole people were supposed to use to slide their credit card to him. I let out a little yelp and scuttled away from him, pressing myself into the farthest wall, which was actually only a couple of feet away. He sat back on his heels.

"Is it the conception you fear? I promise you'll remember it as the best night of your life. No human man will ever compare." His eyes, that odd, woody brown, bored into me.

"I won't," I whispered. Mysti's words came back to me. *Don't take the first offer.* With great effort, I got control of myself and sat up straight. "There has to be something else."

Mohawk stood and offered me his hand. I didn't want to take it but feared making him angry. As soon as our flesh touched, a wave of lust unlike anything I'd ever felt washed over me, buckling my knees. I nearly fell back down. Mohawk smiled. "Nothing this easy. Nothing you'll enjoy so much."

There was no way. Not even if he promised all my wishes would come true. I shook my head.

He pressed his lips together. "Fine. You'll retrieve an item for me."

I relaxed. That was all?

Mohawk gave the glass separating the enclosure from his office a tug. It swung open. He climbed back through to his stinky office, only his climbing was more like slithering. He dropped gracefully to the floor.

"What do I have to find?" I might not want to agree to this either.

"A book." His tongue flitted out again to test the air. "Millennia ago, I was worshipped as a god. I wrote on the walls of caves to instruct the faithful. Those worshipers found new gods or died out, but my word survived. Hundreds of years later, my word was found again by new initiates. These had knowledge of writing. They recorded my wisdom into three tomes." He paused to dig under the counter. While he fumbled around, ideas of how those religious sects must have risen and fallen flitted behind my eyes, the images horrific.

Mohawk tucked something into his jeans pocket. "When their time was near finished, I directed them to hide the books in three separate places, so the right person or people might find them. One of the books made its way to Texas, where its foolish user lost it. You'll locate it and return it to me."

Nobody had to tell me this book caused evil. Retrieving the book and helping to pass it on contributed to whatever got done with it. But I was locked in this room with a monster, my choices laid before me. I could allow myself to be killed. If I died, so would Wade. I could beget offspring with this *thing.* I wasn't sure my sanity would survive the conception. Even if I refused to find the book, it wouldn't stop the evil in the world.

If I agreed to find the book, how much danger would I be in? I tried to weigh the possibility against the monster standing in front of me. My mind wouldn't cooperate. It was still too busy imagining the horror of being intimate with Mohawk. Then the right question came to me. "Why can't you get the book yourself? You're more powerful than me."

Mohawk must have seen the decision on my face, for he smiled. "When the time comes, I'll give you all the information you need to find it."

I nodded. Mohawk held out his hand for us to shake. I let him take it. In a flash, before I could react, his spine bent at an impossible angle, and he bit my hand. Too late, I tried to pull away. He held me fast.

"A symbol of our contract." His tongue flicked out. This time I did yank my hand away. I spun and began to kick the glass door, ready to break it to get away from him.

"Stop that," he barked.

I stiffened at the tone of his voice and stopped kicking.

"Come back over here." He tapped the counter.

I wanted to retaliate in some way, but a lifetime of brawls had taught me to admit when I couldn't win so I could live to fight another day. I shuffled back to the counter and tried to ignore the smirk on his face. He grabbed me by the collar and pulled me close enough to see the pattern running underneath the skin on his face. "Our deal is final. If you back out, you'll be collected as a slave."

I wanted to be damn clear where I stood with this monster. "So the hag is free. The contract on my life is null and void."

He rolled his eyes but nodded.

I wasn't finished. The deal had to be certain. I didn't trust this thing any further than I could throw him. "And all I need to fulfill my end is get your book. You know it'll have to wait, right?"

"Yes. I'll be in touch at a later date." He dug in his pocket and held out a small, white envelope. "The rules of my establishment. Breaking them will result in fees."

I took it. My hand shook so hard the paper rattled. Mohawk reached under the counter. The door buzzed and unlocked. I spun on my heels, slung it open, and charged into the parking lot.

———

I HURRIED to Mysti's car and scrabbled at the door. My breath came in harsh gasps, my vision strobing along with my pounding heart.

Mysti bailed out of the car, Dillon right behind her. In unison they assaulted me with questions. "What happened? Are you okay?"

Dillon snatched the hand Mohawk had bitten. The puncture wound was shallow and had already stopped bleeding. But Mohawk had achieved his purpose. It would leave a scar on my olive skin.

I gently pulled my hand away. "I'm fine. I just didn't expect to see someone like that." Shivers jittered through me.

My passenger's hissing voice woke up. "*I am pleased and honored you succeeded in freeing me. Now we can negotiate our separation. If I don't kill you and eat your essence.*"

"If I die, I'm taking you with me," I said aloud. Mysti's and Dillon's faces fell in shock.

Hannah slowly climbed out of the car and stood a short distance away with her arms crossed over her chest, fear evident in her posture. "The man inside's not a human being, is he?"

I shook my head.

Mysti echoed my head shake. "You and Peri Jean will both see them everywhere now that you've been ridden by one of them. They all feed off the human race in one way or another."

My rider hissed at her implication. "*Nasty witch. You should burn her where she stands. You have the power.*" My anger ignited, and I saw an image of me with a maniacal expression on my face, hands around Mysti's throat.

The world wavered around me. I didn't know how I'd survive too many more hours of the constant needling from this thing. The way it played with my emotions tired me out in ways a hard day's work couldn't.

Mysti came near and put her arm around me. She pulled back immediately. "You're freezing and shaking all over."

"You want me to get you coffee?" Dillon tugged at me.

I shook her off. "I need to smoke. I'll join y'all in a minute."

"*Yes, let's have a talk.*" The rider's excitement raised the hair on the back of my neck.

I took off walking toward an alcove. The rider had promised to negotiate with me about finding a new host now that I'd secured his freedom. I wasn't sure what I'd do if he didn't uphold his end of the bargain.

"Are you really okay?" Mysti called after me.

I held up one hand and spoke without turning. "Will you take my witch pack into the room?"

"I'll do it," Mysti yelled. "Sure you don't want me to come with you?"

I waved again and kept walking. Two vending machines hummed in the alcove. One offered generic soft drinks. The other had a small selection of candy so old they were covered by a frost of spiderwebs. I leaned against the wall and put both hands over my face, so exhausted I wanted to cry. "Tell me how to get rid of you."

The rider's mood had brightened. The light of it seeped through my body, and I enjoyed a second wind. "*That's not necessary.*"

"Hate to say this, but we're going to have to break up." I clamped a cigarette between my teeth and lit it.

"*It doesn't have to be all negative. Now that I'm free, we can work together.*" The hag's voice went faster and faster. "*You'll have power beyond your wildest dreams. I'll…*"

I broke in, sick of listening. "You promised Sol and Bub we'd negotiate a new host for you if I secured your freedom."

The hag hissed its displeasure. "*Few will be as good as you.*"

The hair on the back of my neck stood up. "Are you saying you won't transfer to another host?"

"*I'm saying the likelihood of you finding a suitable one is slim. You are suitable to me.*" The cold avarice in the rider's voice sent shivers through me.

My stomach tightened into a stinging ball as the gravity of the situation unfolded in my mind. I certainly couldn't call Sol again to enforce the bargain. Not after I already owed Mohawk a hide-and-seek expedition. Owing another favor was not the answer. Bub had encouraged the hag and me to work out our differences. That left using magical force. Maybe. But only if I had a chance to rest soon. Fatigue had me feeling as though the simple act of walking was a strongman test. The hag chuckled. It knew my dilemma.

I stubbed out my cigarette and stalked toward the motel room wishing I had somebody to punch out.

14

Dillon jogged out to meet me. "Let's use the Hand of Glory to unlock the door. Mysti said it was fine as long as you agreed." I glanced at Mysti, who rolled her eyes.

I understood right away. Dillon had been pestering Mysti about that stupid hand the whole time I'd been arguing with the hag. Dillon was lucky she hadn't gotten the sharp side of Mysti's tongue. My mentor had the patience of a saint, until she didn't. With a few words, she could cut people off at the knees and rub poison in the wounds. I got closer and saw Mysti was biting the corner of her lip and straining not to laugh.

"Can we?" Dillon tugged at me, not unlike the way her toddler-aged daughter did when she was determined to get her way.

I didn't know what to tell her. Already tired, I worried about the magical energy it might take to make the hand function. But I really didn't want to go back to Mohawk and beg for the key. I raised my eyebrows at Mysti. She gave me a short nod.

Mysti set her witch pack on the concrete sidewalk underneath the breezeway. She spoke to me. "You'll have to anoint it and state its purpose since Cecil gave it to you."

I took the box with the Hand of Glory out of my pack and knelt next to Mysti. She handed me the jar of tallow and a pair of latex gloves. At least I wouldn't have to touch the nasty shit. I pinched the Hand of Glory between my thumb and forefinger. Magic heated up my black opal.

I took a few deep breaths and found the swirl of the mantle waiting inside me. "Hand of Glory, I anoint you for the purpose of unlocking any door, even secret ones hidden inside this room."

The hand jerked in my grasp. I bit back a scream. Didn't matter how many times I saw stuff like this, it still gave me the cold willies. Slowly, tendons creaking inside the Hand's husk of dry skin, the fingers curled into a loose fist for knocking.

"Can I knock with it?" Dillon hovered over me, hand already out.

"I'd think not." Mysti grimaced. "It's going to obey Peri Jean now."

"But that sucks because Peri Jean won't go on jobs with Finn and me…" Seeing Mysti's and my blank stares, Dillon trailed off.

I rose and stepped in front of the door. Lightly, I rapped three times with the Hand. The lock clicked, and the doorknob turned. The door swung open a few inches.

"You know what me and Finn could do with that?"

Dillon stayed close enough to whisper her comments in my ear.

"We'll talk on it later." I raised my eyebrows at her. Dillon took a step back, even though she could have whipped me six times over. I'd seen her get in a few scraps. She was vicious. I walked into the room, the others close on my heels.

The stench hit me, and I stopped. The room smelled like the inside of an ashtray.

"This is how you smell." Mysti gave me a light tap. "Griffin too." Her boyfriend smoked long cigarillos, which stank worse than my cigarettes ever did.

"I don't smell this damn bad." I blamed the carpet. Maroon and stained almost black in places, it probably pre-dated no-smoking motel rooms. The walls were no better. They'd probably started out a nice, soothing cream color. Now they were the color of pages in an old book. The smell of stale smoke rolled off the walls. I was surprised the stench didn't come off in visible waves.

When I thought of my ex-husband, which wasn't often, I imagined him in a room like this one. Tim would have a cigarette tucked in the corner of his mouth. It would joggle as he tried to score the next high, with the room's nasty red phone tucked between his cheek and shoulder.

The rider woke and drank in my misery. It stretched like a cat waking up from a nap. "*Your mother hated you. She built this room and contracted me to destroy you.*" Truer words had never been spoken. I'd known my mother's real feelings for me all my life. Even so, the pronouncement stung, and my throat tightened with unshed tears. The hag liked that. *"Break that mirror on the wall. Stab the other women, then kill yourself."*

The idea played through my mind. Part of me longed for the sweet painlessness of death. Tendrils of icy fear followed. They snapped me out of my funk. Death wasn't always painless or peaceful. A lifetime of communicating with ghosts taught me that much. *Just settle down and ignore the hag,* I coached myself. Bit by bit, I pulled myself together. "Hannah? You know I suck at puzzles. This is your wheelhouse. Where's the tape hidden?"

She flashed me a brief smile, but it was a ghost of her old mega-watt grin and sadness lurked around the edges. She seemed over the worst of her funk, but the next one would come. I pushed off the thought and made myself smile back. I'd have to take it one minute at a time with her if I wanted to be any help at all.

Hannah walked around the room, taking in every nook and cranny. Her footsteps echoed on the bathroom tile. She spoke to me with her eyes fastened to the carpet. "There's an in-wall toilet paper dispenser. Let's start there."

We did. I used the Hand of Glory to knock on the wall all around the toilet paper. Dillon, to my horror, produced a knife with a wickedly long blade and began prying the thing from the wall.

"Why are you doing that?" My voice got all high and sounded about as commanding as a prudish teenager.

"That hand might only open doors. This ain't no door." Dillon grunted and pulled the thing out of the wall. Nothing was behind it except for mouse droppings and old insulation.

I glanced at Mysti, eyebrows raised. She thought it over. "The door you're asking about is metaphoric. It's the door to a secret, probably magically spelled, hiding place. The hand knows that and will open it without us cutting holes in the walls. Dillon." She gave my young cousin a light tap.

Hannah led us to the sink and pointed at the mirror. I knocked on it. Nothing happened. The air-conditioning unit, positioned at the back of the room, yielded similar results.

I hand searched both the nightstand and the dresser. Several used condoms lined a bottom drawer of the dresser. I turned away in disgust.

While I'd been spinning my wheels, Hannah had been examining a paneled wall in the back of the room. A clothes rack hung off it and a luggage rack leaned against it.

She spoke to the wall instead of me. "I think there's something back here. Come see." I went to stand next to her. She took the slightest step away from me but began tapping on the wall immediately to cover it. "Listen here." She tapped a few times. "Then here." She knocked a few more times.

"It's different," I agreed. "But how would Barbie get in here?"

Mysti joined us. "I'd imagine a spoken spell opened it. Something simple probably, easy to remember even over the course of years."

I raised the Hand of Glory and held it over the wall.

"Go on." Mysti pressed her fingers to the wall. "The Hand should pop it right open."

I knocked three times, and we waited. A tiny portion of the paneled wall faded away. Inside lay a wood box carved with an old-fashioned Indian head, the kind that used to be on the baking powder tins. I reached for it. My black opal necklace gave me a hard shock. I jerked back my hand. "What the hell?" I rubbed my chest.

"Do you hear that?" Hannah stared at the ceiling.

I didn't, but I listened. Distantly, I heard a deep groaning like two pieces of wood rubbing together. It got louder as it came closer. I tensed and bent my knees, getting ready to fight. My black opal heated. From above us came several quick pops. We all tilted our necks to stare at it. The ceiling rippled like a sheet of plastic, and the wall bulged out toward us.

I slung out both arms and pushed Hannah and Mysti back just as a flash of bright blue light came out of the wall and slammed into my chest. I flew into the bathroom, screaming all the way. My legs hit the edge of the tub. My own momentum folded my knees and knocked me down. My head cracked against the wall on the way down, and I bit my tongue. Pain flashed through my skull. Blood flooded my mouth as it began to throb.

The blow to my head knocked me off-kilter. I sat there, ears ringing, tongue aching, and listened to the water dripping from the faucet. *Plink. Plink. Plink.* The longer I sat there, more hurt bones and muscles woke up and said hello. My tailbone hurt the most.

Hannah stepped into the doorway, head cocked to one side, eyes impassive. The cold eyes got me more than anything else. They held neither concern nor horror. She could have been watching this whole ordeal on TV. My friend really had been stripped away.

Wade had told me over and over that people don't survive trauma like Hannah experienced without changing. He'd been right. All the same, I hurt for her and wanted more than ever to make things right. Before her suicide attempt, I'd thought things were going well, that she just needed time. But her willingness to do herself in had left me spinning. Watching her watch me made it seem even more hopeless.

Dillon shoved Hannah aside and charged into the bathroom. She leaned over the tub and made a face. "Damn, this tub smells like a dead rat lived it in for a year. Let's get you out of it." She gripped me under my arms, but I was too dazed to help her. Dillon twisted and glared at Hannah. "I ain't Peri Jean. You don't get a free pass with me. Get over here and help."

Hannah turned and walked away.

Mysti came into the room rubbing the side of her head, a trail of blood leaking from one corner of her mouth. "You okay?"

"Are *you* okay?" We exchanged smiles. The jobs Mysti and I did together weren't the safe kind. Stuff like this happened more often than not.

"Whatever knocked you into the bathroom pushed me all the way to the door. I bit the inside of my mouth is all." Mysti looked in the mirror over the sink and used toilet paper to dab the blood off her face. "So now we know there's a magical protection guarding the tape."

I laughed even though it wasn't funny and felt the back

of my head for injury. "Give me a few minutes, and I'll get myself out of this tub."

Dillon huffed. "I ain't waiting a few minutes. Stinks like the devil's unwashed dick in this hellhole." She leaned over me, gripped me again, and pulled with her legs. She was skinny but strong, and this time I helped a good bit. She took my arm and helped me out of the bathroom.

We found Hannah hunched over my witch pack. I gasped and stumbled over to her. "Look, I'm willing to take a certain amount of your shit, but it doesn't include you going through my stuff."

Hannah kept her back turned to me. I gripped her shoulder and twisted her around. She jerked away and slapped at me, eyes glinting hate. "What's the matter? You don't trust me anymore?"

Baffled by the sudden hostility, I searched myself to make sure my malignant rider was still in place and not back with Hannah. The hag stirred as though I'd woken it and stared from my eyes. I saw Hannah as the rider did, all raw and full of hurt, fear, and humiliation. Death shadowed her like a rain swollen cloud.

I took a step backward and calmed myself. "Those are my witching supplies. They're personal to me. I don't let anybody touch them."

"Some of them bite." Mysti stood next to me, so close our shoulders brushed, her way of supporting me. Friendship was a well that only ran dry when you let it. I had a bit more to give when it came to Hannah.

"What were you looking for?" I pulled the zipper on the pack and opened it wider.

Hannah shrugged. "Something magic is protecting that box. We've seen that before. Remember how we used cast iron to get around it?"

The entity guarding the writing slope. My first step on the road to the Mace Treasure. Hannah had used a pair of iron tongs to remove a clue from it. It seemed eons ago, in a time when we'd all been so innocent and happy.

"All I have is a horseshoe." I dug for it and showed Hannah. She took it from me and knelt in front of the hole in the wall.

Mysti edged closer to Hannah. "Don't let it hurt you."

Hannah edged the horseshoe into the hole and hooked the box out. It fell to the nasty carpet and bounced. Hannah stared at it, face blank. "I'm afraid to touch it. I guess I could find a fireplace store and see if they have cast iron tongs. We could use them to crush the box and get at whatever's inside."

I didn't know if that was the best idea. No telling how long it would take Hannah to get back here. Wade's life was ticking away, second by second.

Mysti leaned over the box, holding her hand less than inch from it. "No, the protection spell is human magic. I feel the earth elements in it."

"Can we unbind it from the box?" I imitated Mysti and held my hand over the box. Sure enough, I felt what she felt, even heard the rush of the wind and smelled the seawater used to make the spell.

"Maybe. Definitely if we could get the witch who cast the spell to take it off." Mysti raised her eyebrows, no idea she was asking the impossible.

My mother had worked with one witch I knew of. They died together the day they tried to kill me. Amanda King's ghost would never help me.

"You might be surprised," Mysti said to my unvoiced concern. "She's stuck in the afterlife she created for herself and may be looking for redemption."

Maybe. Or she might be waiting for me to put myself in her path so she could try to kill me again. She'd seemed pretty intent on it the first time. "She's evil."

Mysti nodded. I knew this nod. She'd let me have my say and then present her compelling argument. "From what you told me, Amanda King got caught up in a bad situation. An affair with a married man. Married man's wife murders him right in front of Amanda. All of a sudden, she's an accessory." Mysti watched me digest all this. "Nothing is ever purely black or white. There is no telling what your mother threatened if Amanda didn't cooperate."

I wasn't so sure I bought that. Amanda had acted pretty enthusiastic about trapping my spirit to use as a spectral henchman. Or hench-woman.

"Do you want to save Wade or not?" Mysti crossed her arms. "I want to save him. He may be pig-headed, but he's a good guy. This is the only way we're going to meet King's deadline."

Hannah moved out of the corner of the room. "He won't give Wade back, not alive."

She'd said that before. I knew she was right, but I had to try. I'd never forgive myself if I didn't. "Is there no other way?" I asked Mysti, just to make sure nothing had changed in the last couple of seconds.

"If we had a week, we could figure out something else. Absolutely." Mysti nodded so hard her earrings clacked. Then she shook her head. "But we don't. We've got hours. Contacting Amanda King is our best bet."

I let out a long breath. My body seemed to deflate with it.

Mysti nodded and grabbed her witch pack. "We need to start right away."

———

MYSTI HAD me drag the rickety two-person table as close to the center of the room as we could get it. She draped an obviously old, lace edged cloth over the table. I frowned at the pageantry.

"We're going to have to go to as much ceremony as we can to attract her." Mysti put out an incense burner and stuck a white candle into an ornate candleholder.

"Why's that?" I looked on with growing alarm. Never had I gone to this much trouble to contact a spirit. They just usually came.

"Oh, let me think." Mysti's sarcasm was sharp enough to cut and edged with enough impatience to maim. "We're not where she's buried. We're not at a crossroads. Oh, and the big one. You killed her." She dug in her pack and turned to me. "Do you have wormwood?"

I didn't use as much incense in my rituals as Mysti did, so I had all the wormwood incense she'd given me to start my witch supply pack. I handed it to her and stood close. "What are we really doing here?"

"Begging for help from the one place we can get it." Mysti pulled a plain bowl out of her pack and poured purified water into it. Next came a small chalkboard and a piece of chalk. She pushed a piece of paper with some creepy symbols on it at me. "Draw these on the chalkboard with this chalk."

One of these symbols looked like a coffin with skulls on it. Another was a cross with skulls at each point. "I can't draw these. They're too complex."

Mysti closed her eyes and took a long breath, puffing out her stomach. She opened her eyes, and I saw fear. "They don't have to be perfect. You just have to do it."

Mysti set an empty cobalt bottle on the room's dresser and a container I knew held grave dust next to it.

I drew the symbols, nerves jumping in my stomach. Mysti's near panic had me out of sorts. My mentor rarely acted this way. If Mysti was scared, this had to be some bad, dangerous stuff we were doing. My jittering hand drew shapes that looked like Dillon's daughter, Zora, might have drawn them. I handed the chalkboard back to Mysti. "This stops now unless you tell me what's got up your ass."

Mysti tapped the cobalt bottle. "We'll make this a spirit bottle to open a permanent line of communication with Amanda."

My mouth dropped open. "You mean Amanda could contact me any time? No. Absolutely not. She imprisoned my father's ghost, for Pete's sake. She tried to *kill* me."

"Let me speak." Mysti held up one hand. "Contacting Amanda will either go really well or really badly. Having her here as a guest rather than a hostile witness will go a long way toward keeping her happy." She took out a container of dried bread cubes and sprinkled olive oil over it.

"But that doesn't mean she and I have to become asshole buddies." I followed Mysti back to her pack.

She spun to face me, brown eyes hard enough to make me back up a step. "If you'd recognized her for what she was earlier and befriended her, she might have banded with you against your mother. Ever think of that? And might have already told you about this room and what's in it."

Movement in the room's mirror caught my eye. Priscilla Herrera's spirit appeared right behind me. Her whisper came from inside my head. *It'll be okay. You're stronger now.*

My nerves continued to churn. I stepped away from Mysti, ready to tell her to stop and knowing I couldn't. "All right. What else do we need?"

Mysti didn't answer at first. She pointed at things, whispering to herself. She pressed her lips together and muttered, "It'll just have to do."

"What'll just have to do?" Dillon's voice, hard as she was, came out in a squeak. She stood with her hands on her hips. She might not understand what was going on, but she'd fight over it because it scared her. *Great. Just great.* My shoulders tightened.

"It would really help if we had something of Amanda's. I can use thread or wool, but a personal item helps more." Mysti shook her head. "We don't, though, and that's that."

"Uhhh..." I crept over to my witch pack and dug around, trying to remember where I put it. My fingers closed on cold stone, and I drew out the skull. Carved of some marbled black stone and small enough to fit in the palm of my hand, it gleamed in the motel room's tobacco tinged lighting. I held it out so Mysti could see. She approached warily, walking on the balls of her feet as though she might need to run.

She took the skull and held it close to her face. "Arfvedsonite. It has to do with moving forward. Some use it for psychic visions of the future. Some think it facilitates acceptance of change." She held it out to me in the flat of her palm. "May I ask how you ended up with it?"

"I filched it when we cleaned Amanda's stuff out of the clearing where Priscilla Herrera's cabin is." I thought back on the day, remembering the deep, irresistible urge to just slip it in my pocket.

"Rather than the bottle, we'll use this for her point of contact with you." She put the bottle and grave dust back in her backpack. "Consecrate the skull for spirit work. Then hold it over the wormwood smoke to create the connection. Amanda's a fairly new spirit. She shouldn't have trouble finding her way to an item she used in spell work." Mysti flicked her fingers at me, a silent order to get moving.

I got out my supplies and took them in the bathroom. The scent of the lemon cleanser and my oil relaxed me. I whispered to the skull as I worked, explaining its new purpose. By the time I took it out of the black cloth, the change in the stone rang through my arms.

I walked back into the bedroom to find Mysti and Hannah huddled together whispering. Mysti touched Hannah's arm, her face set in sympathy, and nodded. They both turned to watch me enter the room, the skull upright on the palm of my hand. Hannah moved away, eyes carefully averted from me. Mysti approached and nodded at the skull.

"We're ready. Either you get your familiar to open the gate to the underworld, since he's a psychopomp, or I have a guardian I've worked with before." Though Mysti's tone was pure business, I heard a little tremor at the edge of it. The fear in my chest wound tighter.

"I'll call Orev." My familiar wouldn't ask for much other than the cat kibble he sometimes ate. Deep inside, my mind burned with my connection to Orev. With Dillon's power here to draw on, all I had to do was step into the psychic connection. I nodded to let her know what I intended. She uncovered her raven tattoo, and I did the same. The connection came to life. Orev's cries filled the room as did the sound of flapping wings. The shadow of a huge bird, wings raised, appeared on the wall. He wasn't really in the room, but his spirit was. Good enough.

I held my arms up in imitation of his wings and spoke. "Orev, my familiar and guide, open the gates to the spirit world now."

A clang like an iron gate being opened shook the room. The smell of dead flowers and dust tickled my nose.

Mysti handed my athame to me. "Your blood on the skull."

I did as she said, grunting as I stabbed the tip of my index finger. My blood absorbed into the skull, and the white marbling in the black stone took on streaks of red.

Mysti gave me a small nod of approval and pushed me in front of the altar. "Call her by her full name."

My heart jumped. How could I voluntarily contact someone who had tried to kill me, had killed Eddie Kennedy, and had imprisoned my father's spirit for twenty-plus years? Crazy. That's how. I took a deep breath and centered myself. "Amanda Irene King, please grant us the honor of your presence." I raised an eyebrow at Mysti. She nodded and motioned me to say it again. "Amanda Irene King, please honor us with your presence."

The overhead light buzzed and went out, leaving only the candles flickering. I glanced at the mirror to see Mysti beside me and Priscilla Herrera's ghost flanking me. The hag perched on top of my shoulders like a gruesome parrot. The black opal pulsed power on my chest, its heat burning my skin.

"Again," Mysti whispered.

I opened my mouth to speak, but Priscilla Herrera's deep, commanding voice came out instead of my regular smoker's screech. "Amanda Irene King. Visit us. Dine with us."

The room's temperature plummeted. The hair on my arms raised, and the tip of my nose felt like an ice cube. Amanda appeared before me, head down, two fingers on the skull. We connected with a chiming sound. Shivers ripped through me. My teeth began to chatter.

"Peri Jean Mace." Amanda raised her head. To my relief, she looked much as she did the day I bested her and helped kill her. The phantom sound of her screams from that day echoed in my memory.

"Will you dine with me?" Amanda's dry rasp made me want to cut and run.

Instead of answering, I took one of the bread cubes and ate it. Tasted awful and stale. Amanda smiled. The rest of the bread cubes rippled green, then black with mildew, and shrank to nothing but a stain in the bottom of the bowl.

"Will you drink with me?" She smiled again, and for a split second, her face was the mask of horror she'd worn as my father's ghost pulled her underground to her death.

I took the bowl, sipped from it, and set it down. The remainder of the water slowly dissipated until a little dampness in the bowl's bottom was the only proof it had been full.

"I know why you called me here." Amanda's grating voice had grown strong enough to fill the room.

Hannah moaned from one corner, but I couldn't take my focus off my visitor. Doing so might give her another chance to kill me.

"Do you wish to help me?" I gulped.

She showed me her death face again. I held myself as still as I could. Her rasping voice came again. "Perhaps you think I owe you for my behavior the last time we encountered one another."

I shook my head no. "I wish things hadn't happened the way they did."

Priscilla Herrera's anger burned at me. *Never apologize,* she hissed inside my head. I tried to ignore her, but the hag chimed in, hoping I'd get angry and blow this situation all to hell.

"I made a great many mistakes on your side of reality." Amanda's specter floated, blowing side to side, even though there was no wind in the room. "Maybe I can soften them by helping one whom I wronged." She took her fingers off the skull and went to where the carved box lay on the floor. "Barbie chose this. She chose everything, used everybody." Amanda's harsh voice rose. "She ended my life. Put me where I am now."

I glanced at Mysti, fear pumping through me. I panted with the force of it. Amanda sounded like she was winding up to have a good, old-fashioned tantrum. Mysti pressed one hand to my back. *Stay steady,* her gesture said.

Amanda hunched forward and wept, transparent hands on the filthy carpet. She morphed into what her corpse probably looked like now. Nothing but bones and hanging strips of cloth. Her words guttural, she began to chant. "This spell I unbind. It is no longer needed. Spirits, go now, return from whence you came. Thank you for doing my bidding."

The protection spell gave a crisp snap, turned into a wisp of smoke, and shot toward the door, where it exited underneath.

Amanda floated back to the table, put her fingers back on the skull. "May I visit again?"

I glanced at Mysti. She raised her eyebrows in victory. She'd been right, and she'd never let me hear the end of it. Amanda waited for her answer. I gulped. "Yes. Please visit again."

Amanda stared at my fingers for several long moments. My athame clattered across the table toward my hand.

"More blood on the skull to seal the agreement," Mysti whispered behind me.

I took up the athame, dreading the minute prick at my finger. Annoyance radiated from Priscilla Herrera's ghost. She didn't like this one bit. I didn't either. But what else could I do? If I insulted Amanda, I'd have another enemy. I pricked my finger and spattered a few drops of blood on the skull. It absorbed them. The red in the skull's pattern deepened. Amanda left with a whisper of dead leaves and the smell of turned earth.

Mysti lit a bowl of her special banishing incense. "Have Orev close the gates to the underworld."

I raised my arms as wings again. "Orev, close the gates to the underworld." The metal clang rattled the mirror in its frame.

Mysti smiled at me in congratulations. Hannah rushed over to the box and popped it open. Inside was an outdated micro tape recorder. A plastic baggie of batteries lay beside it. I came to stand beside her, wanting to help, but didn't quite dare. Hannah shoved the batteries into the tape recorder and turned it on.

The sound of a noisy, public place dominated the scratchy recording. My high hopes fell a few inches. It was easy to forget how nice digital recordings sounded compared to the older tape kind.

"There's his car," Barbie muttered. "Get lost but stay where you can see me. Don't let them drag me out of here."

A scared female voice that barely sounded like Amanda said, "O-o-okay. But I can't believe you're—"

Barbie's hiss cut her off. "Here he comes. Go on." Several seconds passed. Then Barbie said, "Well, well, well. Is this a new sheriff I see?"

The recording scratched and muffled. I imagined Joey and my mother hugged. Gross to the power of gross.

"That election wadn't nothing but a formality." Joey's phlegmy, nasty voice sounded exactly the same as when I knew him.

Footsteps approached, and a chair scraped. "This is the last time I'll meet the two of you in public." King sounded younger but no less mean.

"Whatever you say, Tolliver." I thought I heard a smile in Joey's voice. "Let's negotiate."

"Ain't nothing to negotiate." King's voice lowered to a growl. "I got Barbie's clothes from the day she killed Paul Mace and the murder weapon. Joey, you got the file saying the knife found at the crime scene wasn't the murder weapon. You kept that fact out of the mix because Jesse Mace confessed. Ain't that so?"

Joey mumbled something I couldn't quite hear because a group of people walked by talking at the top of their lungs. I bit back the urge to shush them.

"You're right," King said. "Don't matter now. He's in prison. But ain't neither of you turning on me. Way I see it, we in a standoff. I don't want no more bullshit from either of you." He hit something, the table from the sound of it. "No more coming to my house and scaring my boys. And you, hell bitch, just stay the fuck away. Or all of us is going to the death chamber together. Hear me?"

A chair scraped back. "Fuck this," Barbie said. Her heels tapped across a floor, and a door squeaked open. The tape ran as she got into a car and started it. The engine revved, and someone began to pound on the window. The brakes squalled, and a car door opened and closed.

"You can't just leave me here." Amanda sounded out of breath.

"Did you just run across that restaurant like a fucking moron?" I knew the tone of Barbie's voice. It was the one that meant she was about to really pitch a fit. The tape cut off.

So this was what King had wanted enough to hold Hannah hostage. I'd ram it so far down his throat it would be next Christmas before he shit it out.

15

———

I HELPED Mysti gather her things. She'd hang around a nasty place like this an hour past what she had to in order to do it her way. Not me. I just threw things together and fixed it once I got home. Or didn't. Dillon got in on the act, asking Mysti what every single thing was for.

I got tired of listening to Mysti's patient explanations and went to tend to my own belongings. The tape recorder sat on the bed. I reached for it. Hannah nabbed it before I could touch it.

"Who gets it? King or Rainey?" Hannah feinted away from me, recorder held to her chest. "Rainey needs it to get Jesse out of prison."

"She's going to get it," I promised. Hannah's face relaxed, and I did too. "It wouldn't hurt if we added the clothes Barbie was wearing the day she murdered my daddy."

Hannah edged a little closer. "How do you think you

can get that? King's not going to let you go digging around in his stuff."

I zipped up my pack and closed the distance between us. I lowered my voice to a whisper. "When we go to meet King to hand over the tape and get Wade, he's going to try to kill us. We'll either win or die. If we win, we'll get Barbie's murder suit. If we die, it won't matter."

She gave me a grim nod. Our eyes met, and we understood each other for the first time since I'd rescued her from King. Neither of us thought death such a fearsome thing anymore.

I pointed at the tape recorder. "Use your phone to make a copy and send it to Rainey. Also tell her King has Barbie's clothes. Tell her there's a safe both at his compound and at Long Time Gone. Could be in either one."

Someone knocked on the door, hard, three times. We all froze and stared. The knock came again. Three more times. Something croaked, "Housekeeping."

Bullshit. A place like this was more likely to have free penicillin shots than housekeeping. I put the chain on the door and cracked it open. At first it seemed nobody was there. Then a withered face, so deeply wrinkled it appeared featureless, appeared in the crack. I sucked in my breath and took a step back. One silver eye stared past me. The other eye socket was empty, nothing more than a slitted hollow.

"Oh god. What is that?" Dillon cried out.

The thing acted as though it hadn't heard. "Don't try to leave. Management's on the way." Its voice, expressionless and dry, came from inside the room with us. I slammed the door and leaned against it, lightheaded, trying to process what I'd just seen.

"That was a corpse pushing around a housekeeping cart and talking. What the fuck?" I spoke to Mysti, the most reasonable person in the room.

Mysti nodded and pushed past me to stare out the peephole. The dead thing outside started knocking again, pausing every three knocks to repeat its message. Mysti backed away from the door.

"What is that?" I repeated.

"Heard of zombies, haven't you? There's no telling what kinds of monsters that monster in the front office has lurking around this place." Her chest rose and fell with her panicked breaths.

Mohawk's threat of collecting my soul resurfaced in my mind. Would he turn me into something like the monster outside our door once he was done with me? I began to tremble. The zombie, or whatever it was, continued to knock on the door and deliver its message over and over.

Dillon went into the bathroom and turned on the light. She came back in a few seconds. "Ain't no window in there, but we gotta go. I can't handle this no more."

The hits on the door got harder and then stopped. I let out a sigh of relief. "Okay. Let's try to make it to the car before—" The door slammed open so hard the knob embedded in the wall.

Mohawk rushed into the room and grabbed me by the arm. "How dare you vandalize my property and render it useless?"

Dillon and I exchanged a quick glance. She launched herself onto Mohawk's back and hooked one arm around his throat. I gathered my magic until it bubbled and shot it at Mohawk's silver earrings. They turned bright red, then orange.

Inside me, the hag jumped up and down like a spectator at a dog fight. Inhuman lust for violence and the pain of others. The being's reaction bled into my emotions, increasing my enjoyment of the moment. Then I realized what I was doing, what I was becoming. All the coffee that day bubbled in my stomach, acid burning the back of my throat. I had to get rid of this thing, and I still had no idea what to do. Mohawk snatched at me with a hand that had grown ugly claws. I jumped out of the way and refocused.

Mohawk let out a high-pitched scream. I kept pouring magic into the earrings. They went blue, and his ear started to smoke. He let go of me to clap one hand to his ear, staggered backward, and slammed Dillon into a wall. She slid to the floor but crawled to her feet, fists out, ready for the next round.

I tossed Mysti's pack at her and grabbed mine. "Run!" I threw open the door. There stood the thing Mysti had called a zombie. This time I got a good look at her withered arms. The smell of her dead flesh gagged me. She opened her mouth and let out a howl louder than a dog shitting a brick. We were trapped. I slammed the door in the crone's face, locked it, and went to stand in front of my friends.

Mohawk's ear, burned black from my magic, fell off his head and bounced twice on the carpet. A new ear grew back in its place within seconds. He lowered his chin, head flattening and elongating. The faint pattern I'd noticed on his skin surged forward and turned to snake scales. "I used this room to collect human souls. You broke it with your stupid fucking magic. Taking one of you as a slave is fair exchange. I pick the Gregorius witch."

In other words, he picked me. I blurted out, "I pick your mama." The mantle built like a coming storm. I held it inside, knowing I'd need to unleash it all at once just to stun the creature in front of me.

Mohawk's throat widened like a cobra's. He hissed and lunged at me. Unable to shoot magic at him fast enough, I let out a weak yelp and jumped back into Hannah.

She steadied me and kept a grip on my arm. "He can take me. I'll never be normal again," she whispered.

No way. The idea scorched my ass. No matter how Hannah viewed me, or whether she wanted to be my friend again, I'd die fighting for her.

"Hell no. This prick's just being a low rent asshole. I'll burn him where he stands if he fucks with me any further." I pointed one finger at Mohawk and pretended it wasn't shaking. "You're gonna get that dead thing away from the door, and you're going to let us go. I got business to take care of."

"What part of 'you destroyed my property' are you too trashy to understand? You owe me, witch."

"Amanda Irene King is dead. Barbara Willis Mace is dead. Neither of them needed the spell on this room or that box anymore." Explaining myself wouldn't make an iota of difference. When somebody's decided they've got their panties in a twist, physical pain is usually the only thing that'll dissuade them. I could hurt Mohawk, but I doubted I could maim or kill him.

Mohawk straightened, and his head went back to sort of human proportions. "Let's talk about this like grownups. I knew of Amanda King's death. And Barbara's. Their deaths changed nothing." He rested his weird colored eyes on me. "This establishment runs on two basic levels. I have deals with the people, like Barbara and Amanda, who need to hide something here. The deals I make with those people serve a set of needs—mostly my own." He took a step toward me, and his tongue flicked out. I leaned into Hannah hard enough to feel her shaking. Mohawk came closer, smiling. "People who come here seeking what's hidden in the rooms serve another purpose. My slaves, like the one on your shoulder, have to eat. The humans who don't get eaten are repurposed into slaves like the one outside this door." He crossed his arms over his emaciated chest.

I forgot my disgust and took my weight off Hannah. "But I already agreed to find your stupid book. So you're getting that in exchange for releasing the hag on my back from your service."

He fingered a chain he'd padlocked around his neck. "This is a separate debt, incurred by the damage you and your friends caused to my property." He stared at each person in turn. I'd have bet he knew their deepest wishes, their darkest secrets. He thought for several seconds, his tongue testing the air at intervals. "I still want to sire your firstborn."

Hannah made a sound of disgust.

I jerked a thumb in her direction. "I agree with her. It's still a no."

Mohawk's long skinny hands went up and patted the air between us. "You're perfect. One of a strong line of witches." He moved toward me, weird pupils pulsating with his heartbeat. "You realize I can take what I want. You're in my debt." He moved, too fast for my eyes to track, and grasped my shoulders. "I could imprison you right now."

I let my magic loose. The walls wavered, and the flapping of wings filled the room. Orev, still in spirit form, came back with friends. Their gray shadowy forms lighted on every surface, including my head. Their caws began, deafening, maddening, so loud I felt them against my skin. These spirit ravens were almost as intimidating as the real deal. Mohawk took several steps away from me, face tight with worry.

"Enough," I shouted. They quieted, but the shadows hovered all around the room, their intent clear. They'd fight for me.

"The gatekeepers are yours?" Mohawk stared around the room, jumping each time one of the shadows moved.

I nodded.

Something changed in Mohawk's face. The amusement changed to greed. "I'll pay you more money than you ever dreamed existed to sire your firstborn."

I shook my head and let the magic build again.

Mohawk smirked. "I enjoy volunteers more, but I could convince you this is what you want."

I let the magic go again. It blasted into his chest and knocked him backward. His leather jacket began to smoke. Though he didn't seem hurt, he nodded. "What do you suggest to clear our debt?"

"You need this room to be operational, right?"

He nodded.

"I can bind a ghost, a really mean one, to this room." I licked my lips and waited for his refusal.

"Do you have it with you?" Mohawk's gaze slithered over me.

"No. He's not dead yet."

A smile crept over Mohawk's face. His eyes flicked between human and snake, and he rocked back and forth. "Fresh?"

I nodded and gulped.

Mohawk's movements became more and more sinewy. His face flashed to a snake head for just a second and then back. "So full of possibility. There could be online postings to lure people here. The internet is a virus, you know."

I shuddered at the idea of how he'd use the spirit I planned to deliver and glanced at Mysti. Maybe she had another way out of this. Like any good teacher, she read my intent and gave me a sad head shake. I was on my own. Pretending to be bored, I stuck my hands on my hips and heaved a big sigh. "We got a deal or not?"

He smirked and clasped his hands behind his back. "It's done. Have the spirit here by this time next week."

I nodded my understanding. "It'll be tomorrow. If I don't come, I'm dead."

Mohawk cocked his head in mock concern. "If you'd like to negotiate for my help—"

One word flashed in my mind. Never. I shook my head before he could finish. He nodded and wound through us to get to the door. It clicked closed as he left.

"Let's go right now." I grabbed my witch pack with shaking hands and shouldered it. "Hannah, get started on that recording as soon as we get in the car." I had more to say, but I opened the door of the motel room because I couldn't stand to be in there another second. Whatever I'd been about to say died on my tongue. Four Six Gun Revolutionaries sat on their bikes right in front of the room. One by one, they got off their bikes and sauntered toward us, grinning the way I figured a crocodile would once he had his prey cornered.

———

A SIX GUN I knew as Hundred Proof walked in front of the rest. King must have put him in charge of this little mission. I had no hope of sweet-talking Hundred Proof. He'd always looked me over with a curl of his lip and then called me a devil worshiper after a few shots of his favorite hundred proof rum. Three other Six Guns flanked him. Of them, I only knew Jugs who'd gotten his name from his man breasts. The other two were young, hangers-on who hoped to become Six Gun Revolutionaries someday.

Hundred Proof smiled at Hannah. "Hey, little pistol. You ready for some more wild times?" Hannah stiffened and managed to shake her head.

Fury spurred my heart to pound hard. My blood pumped so fast it made me lightheaded. "Leave her alone, shitlord."

Hundred Proof's face turned red. My mouth went dry. Why hadn't I just kept my mouth shut? The hag laughed and danced inside me. It would love it if I got killed here. Then it could soak up my life essence and jump into one of the Six Guns. Lots of evil to mine there. I pressed my lips together and hoped nothing else came out.

Hundred Proof's face split in another, nastier grin. He pulled a revolver the size of a small cannon out of his pants and pointed it at me. His thumb hooked over the hammer and pulled it down. "All right, you smart ass bitch. You wanna talk? I'm gonna axe you some questions. Wrong answer'll get you dead. First question. You see that fucking snake crawl out of your room?"

Having a gun pointed in my face killed a lot of my smarts. Hundred Proof's question could have been in another language. My brain didn't absorb a word of it. All I could think about was what would happen to Wade if I died here. I put my hands up, wishing like hell I could go back in that nasty motel room and lie on the stinking bed. Anything to get away from this ugly little scene. Where'd Mohawk go? If he was so interested in me, he could have stayed to help me fight these bullies off. Coward.

Hundred Proof closed the distance and pressed the barrel of his gun to my forehead. The cold metal burned a ring of reality into my skin. My bowels went loose, and my knees turned soft. Would the bullet feel cold or hot as it cut a rut through my skull? Hundred Proof lowered his voice. "I axed you a question, whore."

I shook my head, unable to concentrate on anything but the sight of his finger through the trigger guard. Wade always said to never put my finger through the trigger guard until I was ready to fire my weapon. Did this guy follow the same rules? If so, I only had a few seconds to live. What would happen to Mysti, Hannah, and Dillon after I died? Oh, I had to think of something. Problem was, I couldn't form coherent thoughts.

My black opal heated, pulsing with the thuds of my heart. Hundred Proof's liquor-tinged body odor found my nose and became the only thing I smelled. Each wiry black hair on his finger stood out. From somewhere came the squeal of the housekeeping crone's cart. Why didn't she come help? I'd have let anybody help me at that point.

"I axed you a question," Hundred Proof screamed.

My thoughts fractured again. I couldn't remember the question, not looking down that barrel.

"We didn't see the snake." Hannah's voice trembled, but underneath the fear lurked fury. And Hannah's fury was almost as bad as mine.

"Weird ass looking thing." Hundred Proof spoke as though he wasn't holding a gun to my head. "Had this black stripe all the way down its back. Solid white other-wise. Six feet long if it was a goddamned inch. Never seen nothing like it."

I waited. I didn't know what else to do. My black opal thudded against my skin, but I couldn't think enough to ask myself why.

"I don't like snakes." Hundred Proof paused as though expecting a chorus of agreement. He got it from his cronies. My group didn't say a word. "They always kinda sneaky. Ready to bite you when you ain't even seen 'em. Like the way you came in our compound and tore up shit. Turned Mojo against us." Mojo was the Six Guns' nickname for Wade. My head got light at the thought of him. "Then you shot Corman. Just like a fucking snake." Hundred Proof's finger tightened on the trigger.

I waited for the blast, with sick questions of how long I'd be aware before I died racing through my mind, and tried not to piss my pants. Grief for my friends bubbled up and fizzed over. I shook so hard Hundred Proof's revolver vibrated. The hag leapt and cavorted with joy. Too bad the little shit didn't have a kazoo to blow along with his victory dance.

Hundred Proof chuckled. "All right. Here's the money question, bitch. Right answer, and I'll kill you with one shot. Where's King's goddamn tape?" Hundred Proof dug the pistol's sight deeper into my forehead. The skin popped as the sight punctured it. Blood dribbled down my forehead, over my nose, and dropped.

The pain cleared my thoughts. The black opal's pulsing meant magic was nearby. I clenched my teeth and concentrated on it. Ravens cawed in the distance. The shadow ravens who'd come to help in the motel room couldn't help now. This wasn't a supernatural matter. I needed real, flesh and blood ravens to claw at eyes and peck faces. And they weren't close. This would be over with before they could get here.

What else was there? The mantle swirled at the base of my back, weakened from me showing off for Mohawk, but still there. I was too tired to draw it together. How untalented was I? Cecil had picked the wrong person to be his right hand. These people surrounding me had put their trust in the wrong witch and medium. The thought sent shame rolling through me. I realized I had an answer for Hundred Proof.

"I ain't got the tape." And I didn't. Hannah had it. Another, more awful thought crossed my mind. What if they ended up killing Hannah for the tape? I couldn't live with that. If that happened, they might as well just go on and kill me too.

"Bullshit, you ain't got the tape. You were in that room too long not to have it." Hundred Proof shifted foot to foot, the gun moving my head.

"Didn't you see the guy with the Mohawk? And the old lady with the cart?" Mysti sounded calmer than I could have, but panic spiked the ends of her words. "They took the tape from us."

"Listen to me, dumb bitch number two." Hundred Proof's voice lowered. Pretty soon he'd start pulling the trigger. "We been following you since Gaslight City. There ain't been no man with a Mohawk nor any old lady with a cart. Now you got to the count of ten to give me that tape. One." Hundred Proof shouted each number with a pause between it and the next one.

I didn't know what to do. He was going to kill us all whether we gave him the tape or not.

"Eight," Hundred Proof yelled.

"S-s-stop." Hannah barely got the word out. "She doesn't have the tape. I do." She rummaged in her bag.

"Drop that thang." Another Six Gun rushed over with his pistol pointed at Hannah. She let her purse fall to the concrete sidewalk. He knelt and rummaged in it. Didn't take him any time to find the tape recorder. He shoved it in his pocket and backed away from us, still pointing his pistol at us.

My hopes, already trashed, plummeted to the depths of hell. King had out-snaked me in every way. Even if they let me live, there was still no chance of getting Wade back alive. I'd thought King might wait to kill Wade in front of me, just to show me he could, and I'd have a chance to save him. That was gone. Jesse would spend the rest of his life in prison while two nasty old men, King and Joey Holze, held the key to his freedom. I'd known life wasn't fair before, but this whole situation just highlighted the ways it sucked. I started to get pissed.

The underling passed Hundred Proof the tape recorder. He took the gun off my head. Mysti grabbed me and pulled me to her. I put my arm around Dillon. She vibrated against me. Whether it was from rage or terror, I didn't know. Hannah stood apart from us, hands on her hips, eyes narrowed.

I couldn't take my eyes off her. The old Hannah would have been cowering by now, mad or not. She'd have hidden behind me and hoped my experience with these types would save us. Not now. She was the only one of us not shaking. My dear friend had risen from the death of her trauma tougher than I'd ever be. She held herself as though she knew exactly how this whole thing would play out and didn't care.

Hundred Proof slipped the tape into his pocket without listening to it. "Don't kill Hannah-banana. King said he ain't done with her."

Jugs marched over, man tits jiggling, and gripped Hannah's arm. He yanked her toward the motorcycles. A hard-edged dread flattened out her lips and dulled her eyes. The other men raised their pistols and pointed them at us.

I'd poured my share of gasoline on fires, both literally and metaphorically. That was what happened to my emotions right then. Anger and disappointment locked horns and rose to tower above everything else, belching fire. I'd lost everything. The chance to get Jesse out of prison. Wade's life. Mine and my friends' lives. The more I thought about it, the madder I got. The hag ate it up like caviar.

The mantle swirled again. The natural components of everything around us sang out to me. The cries of the ravens came from all sides. They'd made it after all. Hundred Proof lowered his pistol and spun around to assess the threat. The first bird swooped down, feet open wide, and sank its talons into Jugs's face. He let go of Hannah. She reared back one foot and kicked him so hard it knocked her onto the asphalt. Jugs probably didn't even feel the kick. He was too busy worrying about the raven trying to puncture his eyeballs.

"Shoot the goddamn bird," Hundred Proof screamed at the others.

The younger of the hangers-on pointed his pistol but put it right back down. "It'll hit Jugs."

I focused on the power coursing through me and opened myself to the metal in the guns, the fire used to forge them, and the possibility of fire in the gunpowder.

The first gun to explode belonged to the hanger-on who'd pointed his gun at Jugs. It blew up with several quick blasts and a flash of light. The hanger-on jumped around screaming, holding up the stump where his hand had been. Hundred Proof and the other hanger-on stared, guns still out, but too shocked to react.

I put my effort into Hundred Proof's and the hanger-on's guns, full of doubt I'd be able to make anything happen. Making the first gun explode had exhausted a great deal of my power, and I was already spent from the hag's influence. The guns began to smoke. Hundred Proof yelped and tossed his away. Hannah ran over and picked it up. She barely flinched at the heat. She began pumping slugs into Jugs. He screamed when the first bullet punched into the middle of his chest. He clapped one hand over the wound, and Hannah shot again. She kept pulling the trigger until she clicked on an empty chamber.

The other hanger-on was tougher than Hundred Proof. He kept his hold on his weapon, even though the smell of burning flesh filled the air. Sweat hung on his face in beads, and his mouth trembled from the pain. "It's the damn witch doing this." He pointed his pistol at me. I shot my power into it right about the time he pulled the trigger.

The blast blew off most of his head. Brains and blood spattered the ground like thick rain. The guy ran three steps and then collapsed. The hag cheered as though it was a sporting event. I stung it in the ass and smiled at its cry of pain.

Pulling desperately at the last of my power, I walked toward Hundred Proof. I had to get that tape recorder from him. Hundred Proof scrambled away from me and ran for his motorcycle. I focused on the gas in the tank, felt all the elements the gasoline and the metal tank had come from. All I had to do was pull down some fire. I set myself to call for lightning and stopped. If I burned up Hundred Proof, I'd lose the tape recorder. Hannah hadn't had a chance to record the contents of the tape. There had to be another way.

Hundred Proof swung his leg over his motorcycle and started it. I gathered the mantle and tried to send the feeling of fire to his body. It would distract him enough for us to get him off the bike. I pushed the fire at him, but nothing happened. The mantle gave an exhausted little sputter and refused to cooperate. I pushed again, head aching with the effort. Still nothing happened. I was spent.

Dillon ran out from behind me, screaming at Hundred Proof. "You don't want to leave yet, you..." She trailed off as the bike peeled out of the parking lot, taking with it the tape and the last survivor to tell the tale. "Fuck." Dillon kicked one of the dead bodies.

I glanced at Mysti, looking for guidance and comfort. My friend stood with her hands over her face, shaking all over. Hannah had pointed the pistol at Jugs again and began pulling the trigger onto the empty chambers. Ravens milled all over the parking lot. One lighted on the neck of one of the dead men and plucked out his eyeball. My stomach turned. The hag tried to goad me into vomiting. The push and pull of sensation and emotions had my head spinning. No wonder Hannah got like she did.

Mohawk came running out of the office, waving his arms. "What the fuck are you people doing out here? Having a war? You're going to pay for these damages."

I nudged Mysti. "Go start the car." I went to get Hannah. She struggled when I tried to pull her away from Jugs's body, but one hard jerk and the rage faded from her face. Her legs folded, and she began to bray big, ugly sobs. Dillon came to help me with her.

"Did you hear me?" Mohawk rushed to my side, waving his long skinny arms around like a teenage girl at a boy band concert. "You're going to pay for these damages."

I turned to stare at him. "Shut up and get away from me. You smell like snake."

Mohawk went still mid hand wave. His mouth dropped open. "You…"

I pointed at the three corpses lying on the pavement. "I'm sure you can find a place to get rid of those."

Mohawk gaped as we dragged Hannah, whose body now vibrated, to Mysti's car and shoved her inside. Mohawk didn't try to stop me. We exchanged one glare as I got in on the passenger side. He was still watching as we sped out of the parking lot.

16

———

I WATCHED the rearview mirrors as Mysti drove us back through Tyler, expecting to see flashing lights and hear sirens. We never did. Once we were safely out of town, passing acres and acres of farmland, I doubled up one fist and slammed it into my own thigh hard enough to hit a reflex and make the leg jump. The hag leapt with glee.

"Don't." Mysti took one hand off the wheel to grab at me.

"How could I not have known they were watching and waiting?" I hit myself again. This one was more the hag's doing than mine, but I didn't really disagree. "I deserve this for being stupid. They were going to kill us. And we were going to be lucky if that was all they did." Anger heated me to the point of sweating. King had played me like a stupid little girl. And I fell for it.

"Y'all, Hannah ain't doing too good." Dillon's voice came from the backseat. I twisted to peer over the back of my seat at Hannah. She stared out the window, eyes glazed, still shaking all over. Her lips moved in silent conversation with herself.

I faced forward again to think. How could I trust myself to make a good decision now? This whole situation had slipped beyond my control. I'd thought I was doing so well dealing with my gifts and helping Cecil, but the way I'd handled all this proved I had a hell of a lot to learn. A clicking sound came from the backseat. I pulled down the visor and stared into the mirror. Hannah had quit talking to herself. The sound was her teeth chattering together.

"Next chance you get, pull over." I kept my voice low and gave Mysti a light tap. She nodded, changed lanes, and put on her blinker. A convenience store came up. Mysti swung into the parking lot and drove around the side where nobody could see us.

I unbuckled my seatbelt and knelt on the seat facing backward. Hannah jittered, unaware of my attention, unaware of anything except her private misery. Ever since her attack, Wade and I had argued about her ability to get better. He'd maintained the position that she couldn't. I'd told him he was wrong over and over. Now I'd been with her less than a day and was already terrified by the extent of her brokenness.

"*Use your magic to kill her. It'll be a mercy killing. She's miserable anyway.*" The hag's reasonable tone infuriated me. I tried to sting it but was too tired. It laughed at my effort, heaping self-doubt into my emotions by the double handful. I shook off the minor failure and turned my attention back to Hannah.

She didn't seem to know we'd stopped. Her head

tracked movement we weren't making. She'd start at the left, and her head would slowly track to the right. Then she'd go again. A low moan vibrated in her throat. Her hands clenched into fists and released.

Helplessness froze me in my seat. All I could do was stare at my friend, deep sadness working its way through me. The hag shivered with pleasure.

"Her circuits are probably overloaded. She's been through so much in a few short months." Mysti turned to watch Hannah too.

Hannah's moan got louder and louder until it was a scream. "Stop! You're going to hit."

I realized she was looking at the highway in front of us. Cars sped past, none of them showing any signs of being about to wreck. The high whine of a motorcycle, one of the low slung sport bikes that Wade called crotch rockets, cut through the low roar of engines. The driver zipped onto the shoulder, whizzing past cars as though they were standing still. A brown SUV whipped onto the shoulder to turn into the convenience store where we sat.

"Oh no," Dillon muttered. "He can't stop."

The hair on the back of my neck stood up, and the skin on my arms tightened into chill bumps. Time slowed down. It felt like I could get out of the car and tell the motorcycle rider to stop. But I couldn't. It had been too late from the first moment I'd glimpsed him speeding down the shoulder.

I tensed my body, anticipating the crash, but nothing prepared me for the awesome explosion of screaming metal. Nor was I prepared for the way the motorcycle rider's body went airborne and flew a good twenty feet. He fell on his head. I don't see how it was possible, but I heard the crack of his neck as it broke.

The motorcycle rider's ghost rose from his body. He shook off the wreck and ran for his ruined motorcycle, which still hugged the back of the SUV like a mashed bug. His arms went through the crumpled machinery again and again as he tried to pull it off the SUV. He hadn't yet realized he was dead. He just thought he'd ruined his bike.

I stared back at Hannah. She'd known, or seemed to. But how was that possible? Then I remembered what Mysti said about Hannah's life force, how it had already started the transformation into death. Nerves clenched painfully in my stomach. Hannah couldn't take another traumatic change. Worse? Having seen how she was, I didn't think I could help.

A horn blowing snapped me out of my thoughts. Traffic had stopped behind the wreck and started to back up. People climbed out of their vehicles. A man ran over to the motorcycle rider's body and checked the pulse. After a few seconds, he removed his hand, backed away, and got on his phone, likely calling emergency services. We had to get out of here.

"Get going," I said to Mysti.

"But someone might need help." She pressed her lips together, the way she got when she thought she'd seen an injustice.

"The motorcycle rider is dead. His ghost's over there trying to peel his bike off the back of that SUV. The people inside it are going to be okay, and he's still going to be dead. There's nobody we can help." I settled my gaze on her face, hardened my voice to the one I used on the people in Sanctuary. "The cops'll be here soon. You want them in your face?"

"But Hannah…" Mysti trailed off and started the car. She had to angle around the growing traffic jam to get out. Some guy yelled at us as we got back on the road. Dillon gave him the finger. I started laughing. It poked at the ball of stress lodged in my chest, making it hurt worse, but I kept on until tears streamed down my face.

Someone else's laugh joined mine. It felt good to laugh with somebody, so I laughed harder. My sides hurt. My belly ached, but still I kept on laughing. Then I realized it was Hannah laughing with me.

I turned to look at her and saw she was laughing and crying at the same time, tears flooding down her face. Dillon had pressed herself against the other side of the car. I unbuckled my seat belt, crawled in the back with Hannah, and put my arms around her. She struggled at first. I held her tighter.

I hugged her and rocked her and stroked her hair. Our laughter turned to weeping and faded away in hitched breaths and deep sighs. We finally let go of each other. Dillon stared on, eyes taking up most of her face. I shook my head to let her know I wasn't about to have a breakdown. After I asked Hannah if she'd foreseen the wreck, I might wish I could escape, even if it meant losing touch with reality for a while. The hag basked in all the emotion, stretching toward it like a flower in the sun. That snapped me back into control.

"You saw that crash before it happened." I used the hem of my sweat jacket to wipe the last of the tears off my face.

Hannah nodded, her mouth working. "I saw how Little Ricky was going to die too."

I frowned at the name.

"The prospect who blew his hand off." Hannah wiped at her face. "I saw it when we were back in the motel room. But I didn't know why I was seeing it. Then as soon as he died, I saw myself shooting Jugs and you killing Holden."

"Death-warning. That's what it's called." Mysti glanced in the rear view mirror. Tears streaked her cheeks. I wondered briefly what people saw as they passed this carload of crying women.

"Did it start after your attack? Have you been seeing this stuff all along?" I hated to bring up Hannah's time with Michael Gage, but if she'd been having these awful death visions the whole time, no wonder she hadn't gotten any better.

"No. Today. After I hanged myself." She stared at her lap. "I was seeing stuff all the way to Tyler, but I thought it was just...the PTSD. Little Ricky was the first one where I realized what was happening."

More sadness sank deep into me. Hannah could see the death warnings because she'd died for a few seconds. I knew someone else that had happened to. He'd survived death only to wake with a psychic gift. It had driven him to madness and murder. I couldn't let that happen to Hannah.

Hannah pulled on her fingers, wringing them like she

was milking a cow. "I'm sorry I did that. Hanged myself. I was just so mad at everything, and I didn't want to deal with it anymore." She gulped back another sob.

"*Tell her it's too bad she didn't succeed,*" the hag crooned.

"I'm not mad at you. Just scared for you." I put my arm over her shoulders.

"I saw your friend Chase while I was lying there on the floor with Mysti doing compressions." Hannah hitched out a sob but got control again. "He said to tell you he's proud of you. He's the one who sent me back. He pushed me, and I woke up."

I hung my head. The pain of Chase's loss still ached like a rotten tooth. Not a day went by that I didn't see something I wanted to tell him about or make a joke only he would understand. Tears welled up in my eyes, and I swiped at them.

Dillon handed me a tissue from the box Mysti kept. I passed it to Hannah. She gave me a grateful nod and mopped at her face.

"Do you think Chase did the right thing? Sending you back?" I wanted her to say yes. I willed her to say the one little word. Because if she didn't believe she could get better and keep on living, she couldn't.

She took a deep, trembling breath. "I don't know."

We passed a huge pasture with a house on a hilltop overlooking it. Hannah pointed at the house. "The lady who lives there'll die tonight. She'll go outside and step in a hole. When she falls, she'll come down on a rake that her son left outside."

My heart sank, and I allowed the truth to sink in.

Hannah wouldn't get better. Too much death, too much tragedy, too much sadness. She'd never be able to escape it. This new gift would haunt her until she took her own life.

Dillon leaned forward until she could see Hannah. "I got this gift of persuasion. I can see if it'll help you feel better. Only problem is, it wears off. But I might be able to give you a break when things get really bad."

Hannah nodded, focused on the seat in front of her. She didn't look too enthusiastic.

"And something like your being able to know when people are going to die could be great," Dillon continued, talking too fast, trying too hard. "We could use it at Sanctuary." She glanced at me for approval.

I nodded without believing it. Dillon knew how much I wanted Hannah to find a way back to herself. We'd spent too much time going over my guilt and my hopes for her not to. She only wanted to help, no matter how misguided the effort.

We drove through a tiny town and passed a nursing home. Hannah face stilled. "One person in the next hour."

Civilization petered out, leaving only stretches of farmland. Hannah watched it go by, her lips sometimes moving. Finally she turned to me. "You think maybe I'd have quit seeing people die if the Six Guns hadn't followed us? And I hadn't seen what was going to happen to Little Ricky? Or maybe if I hadn't killed Jugs?"

I shrugged. This game wasn't worth the time or the effort it took to play. Shoulda, woulda, coulda never helped anybody. I glanced at Dillon. She tipped her head at Hannah.

She wanted to try to persuade Hannah. I was too tired to think of why she shouldn't. I'd been up more than twenty four hours and desperately needed more than a catnap.

Dillon leaned over me and tapped Hannah. Once she got the other woman to look up, she caught her eyes and said, "This stuff about people dying is something you only know if you want to know. Even if it comes when you don't want it, it don't bother you none."

Hannah blinked twice. The tension around her eyes cleared a bit, and the lines bracketing her mouth relaxed.

"Probably won't last long." Dillon sat back. "But I can do it again."

Hannah's shoulders relaxed. She took a deep breath. "Thank you." She leaned her head back and closed her eyes. I hoped she'd sleep long and dreamless, maybe let me take her to stay with Dean and his wife once we got back to Gaslight City. I didn't want her to be part of this anymore.

Dillon began tapping on her phone. She frowned. "Finn says he can't get in touch with Papaw. Says he been trying the better part of an hour."

Tension coiled in my shoulders. I tried to play it off. "Cecil said he was going to take a nap when we left. He may have turned off his phone."

Dillon shrugged and sent that back to her husband.

Hannah's head snapped up, her eyes wide. "King attacked them. That's why he wasn't with the ones who came to get the tape. He went to rescue Corman." She closed her eyes and shook her head. "I was so focused on my own drama, it didn't even hit me. But that's exactly what King would have done."

I whipped out my phone and tried Cecil. It went straight to voicemail. "Papaw," I shouted into the phone, voice shaking. "Please call me if you get this. We're worried about you." I hung up and called Tubby. His phone went straight to voicemail too. I set the phone in my lap and rubbed my quaking stomach. The engine screamed as Mysti hammered down on the accelerator. We passed a sign that said Gaslight City was ten miles away. I ground my teeth. It was too far, and we were too late.

"*They're dead, they're dead, they're dead,*" the hag chanted.

I hoped it wasn't right.

———

MYSTI BARRELED through downtown Gaslight City with no care of the speed limit. She ran three stop signs but had to stop at a red light or hit crossing traffic. I scanned the quiet buildings and empty streets, a sick feeling spreading along my already frazzled nerve endings.

I'm not sure what I expected to see. Maybe men wearing bandanas over the lower half of their faces, hands resting on gun belts. But nothing seemed amiss. Most of the businesses had closed for the day. Now that Dottie's was closed, people who wanted to eat an evening meal out had to go to one of the new restaurants across town. Downtown was all but deserted.

For some reason, that was worse. We passed Silver

Dreams Antiques. The glass front door hung open, its windows shattered. King had been here. He'd busted in and done God knows what. My stomach cramped. For a second, I was sure I was about to blow chunks all over the backseat. Mysti slowed.

"Don't park out front. Go through the alley." I leaned forward, arms resting over the back of the front seat, spit flooding my mouth.

Mysti obeyed. The alley parking lot was empty. The back door hung open too.

Mysti stopped but didn't park. "What do I do?"

I wanted to scream at her that I didn't know. Fear beat at my chest, begging me to lose control. But I no longer had luxuries like that. I calmed myself by pushing all the thoughts from my mind and letting my muscles relax. "Somebody might be in there waiting for us. Go to Bull-frog's. Park in the back."

Mysti took my directions through the back alleys, the space between some of the buildings so narrow there was barely an inch clearance between her Toyota sedan's mirrors and the brick buildings. We came out in front of Bullfrog's Billiards.

I stared at the pool hall. Was anything wrong? Damn it all to hell, I wasn't savvy enough to know. Wade or Tubby would have. But not me. The front door had been propped open with a cinderblock. Music blasted onto the cracked sidewalk. The usual garbage of crumpled beer cans and cigarette butts littered the curb. Only one way to find out. I nudged Hannah. "Let me out."

She took her time about opening the door and

climbing out of the car. I crawled from the backseat, brushed down my jeans, and headed for the front door. Hannah stayed on my heels. I turned to her. "Go back to the car. Dillon will protect you. Tell her I said so. And tell her I said to run if it comes down to that."

Hannah's eyes widened with disbelief, then narrowed. They smoldered in irritation. "I don't need your protection. The fucking worst already happened."

I took a step closer. "Cut the shit. I can't protect you. I used my magic too much back in Tyler."

"I can take care of myself." She pushed past me and continued toward the open front door.

I hurried after her, but her legs were way longer than mine. She passed through the door and into the darkness. I ran to catch up and nearly plowed right into her back.

"What do you mean I can't come in here?" Hannah yelled into Bullfrog's pockmarked face.

"I mean get the fuck out," he yelled back. "You're with the Six Guns, and I don't want my establishment shot up."

I came around Hannah's side. "We're just looking for Tub. Where is he?"

Bullfrog's face went blank. "He don't want to see you. You're going to get him killed, you keep on."

I relaxed a little. Tubby was here. He wasn't dead. If Cecil was with him, he was okay too. Dillon and Mysti hurried inside, both breathing hard as though they'd been running.

Bullfrog groaned. "What is this, ladies night? All you wore-out bitches, get the fuck out."

I took a closer look around the bar and realized there

wasn't a legitimate customer in the place. Every man here worked for Tubby, and they were all armed. One man had a deer rifle propped against his leg. Another held a tire iron. They were ready for action.

"Who you calling a wore-out bitch, you flabby old slug?" Dillon advanced on Bullfrog, too busy flying off the handle to see what was going on.

Bullfrog reached into his back pocket, where I knew he had something deadly, probably a knife. And I knew he'd use it because I'd watched him kill someone a lifetime ago.

The hag snapped to full attention. I wanted to kick it in the ass. Exhaustion worked its way through my bones. Fatigue settled in and made itself at home. All I wanted to do right then was walk out of Bullfrog's and forget all these people and their problems. Instead, I got my hand up like I was an ace sorceress and raced at Bullfrog, shouting, "Pull a weapon, and I promise I'll melt your brains."

The sound of a dozen pistols having their hammers pulled back filled the room. Someone pumped a shotgun. Cold sweat broke out on the back of my neck.

Bullfrog's puffy face turned even paler, and his piggy eyes widened as much as they could. He held up both hands. "Y'all stand down. She means it."

So he knew about me. Good. A mean kind of joy, one the hag loved, spread through me. I got closer to Bullfrog. "Tell me where Tub is. Now."

Bullfrog reached again for his weapon. My skin tightened. I didn't want to be stabbed, not today. Wade wasn't around to heal me. Hell, he might never be around again. I dug deep, finding the shining thread of the mantle and latching onto it. A sheen of magic dropped over my vision. I saw through Bullfrog, saw the tar of evil inside him. I pulled on the magic a little more, trying to force it to my fingertips. Even if all I could do was give him a little shock, it would be enough.

"What the Sam Hill is going on down here?" Tubby rushed into the room and slid to a stop. His mouth dropped open, and he looked like he'd seen a ghost. Then he launched himself at me, laughing, and wrapped his skinny arms around me. He clutched me to him and planted a gross, wet kiss on my mouth. He let go of me and hugged Mysti. She flinched but managed to pat his back. He even hugged Dillon and Hannah. Tubby was so happy he was almost crying. He poked Bullfrog in one fleshy arm. "Why didn't you let me know they was here?"

"You said they was probably dead." Bullfrog crossed his arms over his beer belly.

"But you see that they ain't dead." Tubby waved one arm at us. Bullfrog shrugged. Tubby gusted out a sigh and turned to me. "Cecil thinks y'all are dead. Get on upstairs and show him you're fine."

Oh no. Cecil had a heart condition. What if he'd had a heart attack? I ran for the back storeroom and raced up the stairs, the others' footsteps thundering behind me. Worst case scenarios had my stomach roiling and ready to purge by the time I got to the door and twisted the knob. It was locked. I slammed my shoulder into the wood, ignoring how much it hurt. Tubby pushed the key into my hand. I unlocked the door and shoved it open.

Cecil sat in the recliner staring at the wall. He slowly

turned to see who it was. He frowned at me, blinking rapidly, and stood. He kept his distance from us. Then it hit me he may have thought us dead. Cecil could sometimes see ghosts just like me. His power had faded over the years of bad health, but he had his moments.

"It's me." I rushed at him. "We beat them. Killed all but one." We embraced.

Dillon's arms went around us. "I'm so sorry, Papaw. We tried to call you, but it went straight to voicemail. Why didn't you answer?"

A tear streaked down Cecil's face, and he wiped at it. "My phone's dead. Forgot my charger. Tubman lost his phone in the alley. Nobody's found it yet. Neither of us know your numbers by heart."

I stepped out of the group hug. "How'd you and Tub make it out of Silver Dreams?" The Six Guns had snuck up on us, cornered us like the predators they were.

"Jadine called to warn me." Cecil smiled, proud of his adopted daughter. "She said for me and Tubby to get out. Some bad men were headed our way."

"'Bout that same time, I got a call from my inside man in the Six Guns telling me about the same thing." Tubby grinned at the look on my face. "Come on, Peri Jean. I got people ever'where. Including inside the Six Gun Revolutionaries Motorcycle Club. How you think I ain't dead right now?" He giggled. "My man said some Six Guns was on the way to kill you women, and King and the others was coming to rescue Corman and kill Cecil and me. We barely had time to get out before they came in. I just panicked is all." A flush crept out of Tubby's collar.

"Tubby picked me up and carried me most of the way here." Cecil looked none too happy about this development. "That's when he lost his phone."

I nodded and glanced around the tiny studio. No signs of Corman. My muscles clenched, and the urge to scream fought for control. The hag lapped up all the negative feelings and keened for more. I tried to speak, to ask the question whose answer I didn't want to hear, but I couldn't form words. Sharp gasps came out instead. Colored dots appeared in front of my eyes. I leaned over and grabbed my knees.

Tubby came closer. "What is it?"

"Corman," I whispered.

Tubby's smile dropped. He shook his head. "The Six Guns took him. He's gone."

That meant Wade was gone too. Forever. I sat down hard on the floor, unable to hold myself upright any longer. Tears slipped down my face. Understanding dawned on Tubby's face.

"Aw shit. Wade." His shoulders dropped, and his face turned red. He'd missed an angle. "I didn't think about him. All I thought about was you. If you're dead, that's both my best friends from childhood." He swallowed hard. "I wad'nt ready for that."

Tubby's mention of Chase poured more coals onto the fire of misery burning in me. I put my hands over my face and cried, long howling sobs. I curled into the fetal position on the dirty floor and let the sobs rip out of me. The hag sucked on my sorrow, drawing out more emotional poison to ache in my chest.

"Wade and Chase are probably happier dead," it told me. *"All the times you've cheated death, you've cheated yourself of peace."*

The hag's reasoning was laughable, but I had toughed it out all I could for one day. Its words hit home and burrowed. No wonder this thing had hurt Hannah so much. Before the hag attached itself to me, I'd never seen my death as a positive occurrence. But now I did. I sobbed harder, holding my stomach.

"Your death wish will always be waiting to surface. End it now and never feel the despair again." The hag laughed.

The idea of listening to another second from this otherworldly asshole infuriated me. But I was tired. Just so tired. Little by little I got my crying under control. Tubby handed me a paper towel. I used it to wipe my face, picked myself up off the nasty floor, and sat in the straight-backed chair Tubby usually used, not even caring how filthy it was. My eyes stung with more tears. Wade couldn't be dead. Not while we had unfinished business. But King Tolliver played for keeps. No other course of action made sense.

"The Six Guns took Corman, and they've got the tape. Wade is likely dead. What do we want to do?" I sat hunched over. The weight of it all was just too heavy to make myself sit up straight.

Hannah came closer but still kept her distance from me. "We can't let King get away with this. We attack."

I liked the idea, but it could have just been the hag's influence. The Six Guns outnumbered us, and they were tougher. The attempt would probably kill us. The hag would love that. "What do you think, Papaw?"

Cecil and I stared at each other, the way we did when there was a decision to make. When he spoke, his words were slow and deliberate. "I say we walk away while we can."

I put my hands over my face and began to moan. Sour disappointment coursed through me, but I knew he was right.

He softened his voice even more. "Jesse is my blood, just like you, Peri Jean. I want to see him out of prison just as much as you. And Wade Hill risked his life to help our family just weeks ago. Leaving him to die feels like a betrayal. But you're responsible for the people of Sanctuary, sweetheart. You have to go back to them." He locked his dark eyes on mine. It was one of his better intimidation techniques because it made me feel about as big and tough as a bug.

The hag started up. "*Go fight the Six Guns. Go out in a blaze of glory and take as many as you can with you.*"

This was the first time the hag's ramblings made good sense. Did that mean it was driving me crazy? I rocked back and forth, seeking some kind of comfort. This had gotten so big and ugly. I felt like I was drowning in the deep end and had no idea how to stop it or to minimize the damage.

"You can't just let this go. You have to do something." Hannah came nearer.

Before I could formulate an answer, my phone buzzed with a text message. I picked it up and saw King's name.

He'd sent a video. The face in the freeze frame belonged to Wade. My thumb hovered over the play button, but I was scared of what I'd see. Tubby crowded close, studied the screen, and hit the play button.

Wade wheezed like he'd been running, and he grunted after every breath. "Peri Jean? That you?"

The camera spun around to show me King's ugly mug. He grinned. "Surely you ain't chickening out like a little bitch. Wade's still alive. Don't you wanna come get him? I've named my price. Bring cash to the compound." The screen went black. I let the instrument slip from my grasp and drop to the floor.

That damn invoice. I didn't even have that kind money. But if I did, I'd shove it down King Tolliver's throat and set it on fire. Maybe I'd substitute some used toilet paper. I grabbed my phone and prepared to tell King just that. Tubby snatched it and held it out of my reach.

I leapt off my chair and ran into the squalid little room where Tubby crashed with his skanks. I collapsed onto the bed and put my hands over my face. My already raw throat ached with the need to cry some more, but I wouldn't let it come. I lay there with my jaw clenched and my chest shaking.

17

FOOTSTEPS ENTERED THE ROOM, and the door closed. I took my hands off my face, expecting Cecil. He'd comfort me, tell me walking away was the mature decision. Instead I found Tubby leaning against the door, skinny arms crossed over his chest. "I can put fresh sheets on the bed, you wanna rest. Or get you some food."

I shook my head. "I want to kill King, but Cecil's right. They'll mow us down like tall weeds." I got a whiff of my own fear sweat and grimaced.

"My men's at your disposal. That'll even things up a bit." He lit one of his nasty unfiltered cigarettes.

"They're tweakers." I massaged the back of my neck, but the stress headache I'd had since I'd rolled into Gaslight City a day ago didn't budge.

"And that makes them think they're invincible. They'll take chances you and I won't." Tubby dug in a beat-up nightstand and found an ashtray.

"You can't tell me you think Hannah's solution is the right one. She's off the rails." I lit a cigarette.

"She's right but for the wrong reasons. Just 'cuz we walk away don't mean it's over. King and the Guns'll hunt us down and shoot us like fish in a barrel." Tubby watched me through the haze of cigarette smoke we'd generated.

I thought about what he'd said. Death didn't scare me. The shadow side the hag had scratched open had indeed been the true me, the one who secretly hated her life and wouldn't mind leaving it behind. What scared me was seeing people I loved die. Tubby was right about one thing. King was going to come for them whether I went to fight him tonight or not.

"We go tonight, at least I'll go down fighting." I leaned back against the dirty wall, hollowness spreading through me.

Tubby leaned against the wall next to me. "One last stand?"

I nodded my agreement. He held his fist out. We bumped.

Tubby pinched out his cigarette butt and dropped it into the ashtray. "Let's plan this thing. They're at the compound, expecting you. What do you do?" He closed his eyes and leaned his head back against a greasy mark on the wall. It must have been a regular spot for him.

My mind was a roiling mass of darkness. I took deep breaths and tried to focus. An idea floated out of the void. "What about a distraction? Just like when we went to get Hannah, only using my talents?" If I was going to die tonight, I might as well pull out all the stops.

Someone tapped on the door. "Who is it?" I yelled.

Mysti and Dillon stepped inside the room, both of them fidgeting so much it looked like they were trying to tap dance. Finally Dillon couldn't stand it anymore. "Are you really going to stand down?"

"No. But you can go back to Finn. Take Cecil with you." I nodded at Mysti. "You go back to Griff and Brad."

Mysti shook her head. "I'm helping."

She had her chin stuck out like she was going to war. Too tired to argue with her, I explained the only plan I had, which used the only talent I had. Mysti began to smile. She put her phone to her ear and turned her back. Dillon got out her phone and did the same.

Tubby smoked, squinting at the smudged wall near the door. "Your plan's good. It'll make 'em run. But if I was King, I'd leave my men to fight and hopefully kill you while I waited with a select crew in a safer place."

Tubby had a point. A bunch of outlaws could definitely outfight me, some grifters, and Tubby's meth head army. "We could split up."

Tubby didn't give me a chance to say anything else. "But where on that fifty acres would King go to hide?"

I blew smoke rings to quiet my mind. The answer came. "Get Hannah. She'll know any additional places on the compound where King might hide."

Mysti, off the phone by now, spoke up. "She's downstairs taking shots with Tubby's...friends."

Tubby snatched my phone, called the bar, and told Bullfrog to send Hannah up.

Hannah came in pulling her fingers, the effects of her

drinking session non-existent. She'd redone the makeup she cried off on the way home from Tyler and looked a tiny bit like her old self with her expensive clothes and diamonds winking at her earlobes.

"Sit down." I motioned at a cracked vinyl and rusted aluminum chair. Hannah did what I said.

"Is there anywhere else on the compound or nearby King might go for safety? You were there a good bit, right?" I had about a pack's worth of cigarettes jamming the ashtray but I lit another.

"Can I have one of those?" Hannah reached out without waiting for an answer.

I got up, gave her a cigarette, and lit it for her. Her smoking now was almost funny after how much she'd hated me doing it. I kept my feelings to myself.

Hannah inhaled deeply and turned a little green when the nicotine hit her. "Yeah. There's an old cabin with no electricity right in the middle of the property." She set her cigarette down in the ashtray.

I gave her a scrap of paper and a pen. "Draw a map to it."

She shook her head. "I want to show you where it is." She shoved the paper back at me.

"We're probably going to die." Finally speaking the thought I'd been having on loop felt surreal.

Her face reddened, and that slow burning fire came back in her eyes. "I'm ready."

My hate for Michael Gage and Nash Redmond raged. If I could have gone back in time, both of them would have died slower, screaming for mercy that never came. Hannah watched me. We exchanged a small nod. I'd been trying to get on the same page as her since I'd rolled into town. It had taken a mutual death wish brought on by the hag's asshole ministrations to do it.

"While I'm creating a distraction, you'll take Tubby and Bullfrog to the cabin. You're going to be alone with them." I had to give her the out if she wanted it.

"I'll do it." She nodded and left the room without a word.

Mysti and Dillon had been whispering in the corner. Now they came to hover near the bed.

Mysti spoke first. "Griff and Brad are on the way."

"Tell 'em not to come. Too dangerous." I glanced at Tubby for support, but he just shrugged.

Mysti turned on her authority voice, the one she used to win arguments. "No. They want to help Wade." She made a sour expression. "I do too. He's a good man, even if we don't do things the same way."

I issued my own line in the sand. "You can only stay until after the distraction is in motion." Mysti shook her head. I held up my hand. "Save it. Go home if you can't do what I say."

She flushed but nodded.

Dillon shoved her phone in her pocket and sat on the edge of the bed. "Finn's staying with the kids, but some of the men from Sanctuary are coming to help the family. They're only a couple of hours away."

I shook my head and started to refuse. She held up one hand. "They've finally accepted you as a leader. You'll insult them."

A wave of fatigue rolled over me. I had to sleep. Otherwise I wouldn't be doing any magic tonight, and we'd lose most of our advantage. My eyes fluttered. Tubby stood and ushered them all outside.

"Wait a minute. You need to help me decide what to tell Cecil," I slurred.

"Rest," he said. "I'll talk to him and do everything else that needs doing." He shut the door with a soft click.

Just staying upright was difficult, but I twisted on the bed until I could see myself in the cheap, full-length mirror Tubby or someone had hung. The hag rested on my shoulder, bigger than ever. We stared at each other.

"You've drained me, kept me fighting myself all day," I said aloud to the creature.

It shrugged its bony shoulders and curled its tail around its gnarled feet. I wanted to get angry with it, hurt it again, but I couldn't even do that. Priscilla Herrera appeared behind me in the mirror.

It was funny how things changed. A year ago, I'd have gasped and spun around, terrified at having a ghost at my back. Now I nodded a greeting in the mirror at my triple-great-grandmother.

She spoke to my back. "I am energy. You may draw from me at any time. I'll show you." She came around to stand in front of me. At this angle, she was transparent and radiated cold like an open chest freezer.

She put one cold finger in the spot between my eyes. "Now pull, just like you pull on the gift of power that I gave you. And don't let your passenger drink." Her voice sharpened on the last words, and I knew if I failed to perform, she'd berate me.

I focused on the feel of her ghostly fingers and let my senses move beyond, into Priscilla's form. The room went away. A ball of energy turned and burned in front of my eyes, sparking every once in a while, limitless as the energy inside me. I watched it for several seconds, awed by its beauty. I let my own ball of energy move toward Priscilla's. It inched forward, almost too tired to move. The two balls finally touched. A flash pulsed behind my eyes. I saw in that second all of Priscilla's knowledge. It flashed by too quickly for me to grab. But the energy hovered right there.

"Now pull. Just as you'd access your gift." Priscilla's voice pushed its way out of my mouth.

I connected to the spark the next time it lit up and held on for dear life. The energy stores I'd expended over the day with the fights and the worry began to refill. The hag rolled over inside me, straining to get its nasty claws into the energy so he could grow even bigger. I used the mantle to block myself from him. He howled and thrashed around, scratching at my most tender insecurities. I steeled myself as best as I could.

Priscilla's energy, now part of mine, whispered in the most hidden parts of my brain. "*Well done. Now we can talk. When I lived, I called things like the one inside you* cauchema." The word rolled off her tongue like an exotic song. "*You know that* Cauchema's *goal is to kill you and eat your energy before moving on to the next victim. You must expel it and then force it into its next host before it weakens you further.*"

I interrupted. "But what about the agreement I made with Sol and Bub?"

"Cauchema *tricked you all. It never plans to agree on a suitable host. In truth, any host is suitable.*" She paused as though I might argue. I didn't. I couldn't wait to get rid of the thing. "*Do not think about the way you'll do this. Control your mind.* Cauchema *is waiting to outsmart you or turn you against yourself.*"

I laughed, high and hysterical. "I can't plan anything because I don't know what to do."

Priscilla's impatience swam behind my eyes. "*Pay careful attention to those around you. They'll tell you how without knowing. I'll influence them.*" She disconnected so quickly my ears popped. Whatever we'd done left behind the scent of ozone in the small room.

The wall between my nasty passenger and me tumbled. Much as I wished I could keep it up, it would drain too much energy. I'd have to tough it out. My specialty. The rider and I glared at each other in the mirror. It snarled, showing its tiny, spiked fish teeth. I flipped it the bird.

The smell of cooking meat drifted up through the old floorboards. How long had it been since I'd eaten? My stomach growled to let me know it had been too long.

My phone buzzed with a text message from Tubby. "Got you a burger."

I WENT IN THE BATHROOM, washed my face, and walked

down the stairs, amazed at how refreshed I felt. The pool hall was more full of smoke than usual. A familiar voice belted from the jukebox. Chase Fischer. Tears sprang to my eyes. It was the one album he'd managed to make. Of course Tubby had a copy on his jukebox. He might have been a shithead, but he'd loved Chase in his way.

Love mattered because we all screwed up a lot. We did and said things we wished we could take back. Without love, there'd be no chance for redemption. Tonight I had a chance to make things right and to settle some scores. It might kill me, but there was no more worthy cause than fighting for those I loved.

"*Death would be peaceful for you*," the hag crooned. I rewarded it with the magical equivalent of an ear twist and sat at the bar. Tubby put my hamburger in front of me and wiped his greasy hands on his stained apron. "I remembered the way you like it. Hot sauce and tomatoes. A deviled egg on the side."

Tubby still cared enough to remember. Tears filled my eyes. I blinked them back, realizing what a shitty friend I was. I knew next to nothing about Tubby's preferences, except for the unsavory ones. If I survived this night, I'd learn more about him. Be kind and considerate when he needed it.

"Thanks for remembering." I ate the deviled egg in three bites and moaned in pleasure. I bit into the hamburger. Better than I'd expected from Tubby. I became so intent on enjoying the greasy sandwich that when Tubby spoke again, I almost dropped it.

"Ever time I boil eggs, I think about something Bullfrog

used to say when we were growing up." Tubby leaned on the counter, putting our faces close together so I'd hear him over the din of noise.

"Mmm?" I wiped hamburger juice off my face. Memaw would have swatted my behind for pigging down this food like an ill-mannered hooligan.

"Bullfrog claimed you could put a frog in a pot of cold water, and if you increased the heat real slow, the frog wouldn't realize he was in danger and would boil to death." Tubby handed me more napkins. Behind Tubby, a shadow moved.

I focused long enough to see Priscilla Herrera standing next to Tubby, her hand on his arm. Chill bumps had formed on Tubby's arm at the point of contact. Priscilla's words came back to me. She'd said her idea for getting rid of the hag would come from my friends. Quickly, I pushed the thought away before the hag latched onto it and set my mind to ignore Priscilla. At the moment, the monster was focused on my gluttony, enjoying my filling belly, and pushing me to eat more, to get overfull.

"Don't tell me y'all tried it." I took the last bite of hamburger just in case Tubby was getting ready to tell a grody story. Tubby raised his eyebrows and shrugged. So those two jerks had tried it. Poor frog. They might not be beautiful, but they served a purpose in the great wheel of mother nature's cycle. "How'd it go?"

Tubby laughed. "Well, we caught the biggest bullfrog we could find. Got him in the boiling pot and turned on the stove real low. Water didn't even get very hot before that bad boy come jumping out and latched itself onto

Bullfrog's face." Tubby squeezed his eyes shut and giggled. He opened them again and fanned his face. "Looked like that space movie with Sigourney Weaver. You know the one I mean?"

I did, so I nodded, giggling in spite of myself and trying hard not to think about what Priscilla wanted me to get from this.

"That ain't the best part." Tubby, into his story and laughing so hard he could barely talk, put both hands over his face. "Bullfrog started stumbling around the kitchen, knocking shit down, and hollering, 'Get it off! Get it off!'"

It might have just been the stress or the fear of not knowing what was next, but Tubby's antics tickled me. I threw my head back and laughed, pounding the bar with one fist.

Tubby clapped me on the shoulder and walked away. I waited for everybody else to finish eating. When conversations started back up, I stood on the bar and began to speak. Nobody argued with my plan. I told them to be ready at midnight, went back upstairs, and took my long overdue nap. I jerked awake, full of worry and regret, but I forced myself to shake it off.

We pulled out at midnight on the dot. The dark highways leading out to the Six Gun Revolutionaries' compound seemed to stretch out forever. The ten-mile drive felt like a million miles by the time Tubby pulled his beat-up pickup off the highway and cut the headlights. Hannah and I climbed out. Bullfrog climbed out of the bed of the truck and brushed off his pants. He'd refused to squeeze into the cab, citing that Hannah and I made him sick.

"I'll go ahead and make sure the security camera's taken care of." He slipped into the darkness.

Mysti, Brad, and Griff parked behind us and met us halfway between the cars. The darkness was so complete, all I could see were the whites of their eyes.

"You ready?" Stress tightened Mysti's voice. The contents of the bag she held rattled together. Fresh spirit bottles, seasoned with urine and fingernail clippings. The gross contents made the ghosts think they were still alive and attracted them to the bottles. Brad carried a bag of salt in case things got out of hand.

I nodded, afraid my voice would shake if I spoke. This summoning, one without the protection of a circle, was the riskiest we'd ever attempted. I thought the risk necessary. We needed the ghosts to leave the place they were summoned so they could scare the life out of the greatest number of Six Guns.

Hannah sidled up beside me. "Do your best. That's all you need to worry about." She squeezed my arm and went to stand near Tubby, holding out her hand for a cigarette. He handed it to her and lit it for her.

"Where's this graveyard, Tubman?" Griff gripped his grave dowsing rods in his fists.

"Been a long time since I been to it, but I think it's just off the back gate over there." Tubby gestured at the closed gate, where Bullfrog stood with his arms crossed over his beer baby.

We walked to the gate. I took out the Hand of Glory,

which now glowed a sickly green, and knocked three times. The gate's lock clicked open. Tubby led the way in, the beam of his flashlight bright in the complete blackness.

He pointed the flash at the woods and took careful steps, branches cracking beneath his feet. He found the path and motioned us to follow. We picked our way through the brambles and into a cleared area. A few leaning tombstones skirted the edges of the space. According to Tubby, these were King's ancestors who first settled here in the early eighteen hundreds. The rest of the ground was full of unmarked graves.

"All right. We gonna go find this cabin." Tubby took Hannah's arm and pulled her along between him and Bullfrog. I watched her back, expecting her to give me a nervous glance over her shoulder. She didn't. *That Hannah is dead*, I reminded myself.

I searched for the mantle and found its shifting power deep within me. The rider dug its talons in deep. I winced at the discomfort and walked toward the marked graves. These were the oldest spirits here. They'd be the hardest to raise.

I lit my candles and dropped to my knees, raised my arms over my head, and called my magic. Power came from the dirt and the water beneath the dirt. It came from the slight breeze drying the sweat on my face. It seeped out of the trees, making their spicy scents stronger. But mostly it came from me. The candle flames jetted and hissed. Everything was ready. I didn't need a magic spell to call the dead. This was what I was made to do.

I let my power drift down into the dirt and found the used-up remains lying in a rotted wood coffin. This had been King's great-great grandfather. I saw the line of fate and DNA connecting them and latched onto it. Then I said the words, the only words I needed, "Rise now."

The dirt moved underneath me, and I got out of the way. Spectral bones edged out of the dirt, inch by inch, until there was a translucent hand. I grasped it, cold throbbing through my arm, and pulled it to the surface.

Brad came near with the bottle and the summoning incense. The ghost went into the bottle without any urging. I moved to the next grave and the next. Then we needed Griff and his dousing rods to find the unmarked graves for us. We collected souls until all but one of the spirit bottles were full. I saved back that spirit bottle for something I'd need to do later.

I turned to Mysti. "This is it, sister. Y'all get as far away from this place as you can."

Mysti swallowed hard, lips trembling, and shook her head. "No. I can't leave you. You're my student and my friend."

Griff and Brad appeared on either side of Mysti. I'd already told them to drag her away if necessary, and they'd agreed.

"Thank you all." I choked on the last word. This could be the last time we were together. I wanted to say something meaningful but couldn't quite figure out good enough words for these people who'd given me a chance and loved me when they didn't have to.

Brad came forward first and wrapped me in a hug. "You

be careful," he murmured. "Come back to us." Mysti and Griff came nearer and wrapped their arms around Brad and me.

"We don't have to leave." Griff's voice shook.

"Please do. This is no longer your fight." A selfish, scared part of me wanted them to insist on staying, but they didn't. I cupped Mysti's face in my hands and pulled her close. "Do what I say, this one time." Her hot tears ran over my hands. She nodded. I let go of her. My friends, some of the truest I ever had, said their final goodbyes and faded into the shadows. Mysti's sobs floated back to me. I stood alone in the cemetery until I heard the car start and drive away. Then I called the number Tubby had given me for the leader of his meth militia.

"This's Don." The nasally twang almost puckered my eardrum.

"Where are you?" My voice trembled with fear, but I didn't have time to be afraid. Tonight was for keeps.

"Waiting on you by the truck, just like Tubby said."

"Come inside the gate. It's time."

18

───────

THE METH ARMY and I took the final curve, walking as softly as possible. King's house, still smoking from the fire, came into view. I'd been smelling it for the last several minutes. Now the smell overpowered me. I wanted to cough but pushed a hand over my mouth.

Don, who'd been creeping along next to me, didn't have the brain cells left to do that. He coughed several times, then gagged.

I turned to him, just about to cuss him, when the first voice rang out. "They're here. Let's light 'em up boys."

A gunshot cracked the night. Because I wasn't stoned out of my gourd, I hit the ground. The meth heads did not. They started shooting, hurrying toward the danger.

"Stay here," I hissed at them. They did as I said but kept shooting. I took one of the carefully sealed bottles from my otherwise empty backpack and used my pocket knife to break the seal. The awful smell of death and piss floated out. I winced away from it.

"Rise," I whispered. The wind picked up, and a glowing wisp rose from the bottle. "Take form," I breathed. A human form took shape. This must have been someone the Six Guns decided to take out. One side of his head was caved in. I poured a little more power into him until he looked solid. Then I said, "Go."

More spirits rose from the bottle. It took major juice to do it, but I made them look almost, but not quite, solid. The effect would have won awards in a horror movie. I sent the spirits to find the men shooting at us. The first scream came before I'd even gotten to the second bottle.

Ignoring the screams, fighting fatigue, I continued my task until more dead than living walked the grounds of the Six Gun Revolutionaries' compound. Gunfire and screams came from the darkness. One man ran past us, his hair standing on end. A motorcycle started up and took off, only to crash in a rattle of metal a few seconds later. It burned bright. The guy who'd been riding it screaming high and pure for at least a minute.

"Jesus," Don said next to me. The firelight allowed me to see him clearly for the first time. High cheekbones stuck out of his emaciated face. His white goatee and scraggly grayish hair put his age over forty. "Do me and my men go in now? Kill the rest of 'em?"

My body stiffened, and I swallowed hard. I'd never get used to this. Ever. I forced myself to nod but couldn't form the word kill. "Do whatever Tubby said. Okay?"

"What about those, uh, ghosts?" Don listened to the screams with wide eyes.

"Don't let them scare you or make you hurt yourself. At dawn, they'll go back where they came from."

Don got up and motioned to his little army. They disappeared into the dark. More gunshots started up.

I took out my phone and called Tubby.

He answered on the first ring. "You're at King's house." His voice was dead and flat. "Go back to the burned-out mobile home and take the path running in front of it. Follow it 'til it ends." He hung up.

I stared at the phone. Did this whole situation have Mr. Cool rattled? Sure sounded like it. I got up and started walking, still pondering the way Tub's voice had sounded.

The ground next to me crunched, and a figure stepped out of the darkness. I held up my flashlight, and Dillon squinted at me.

"What the hell are you doing here?" I hissed. "I told you to stay with Cecil and the guys from Sanctuary. They're your ticket out if things go south for me." The Sanctuary crew was my escape plan, and we'd outlined it down to where we'd stop for coffee if we needed it. None of those plans included Dillon coming to find me here. I'd wanted to keep my people as safe as possible.

"Put the light down." She raised one arm to ward off the brightness.

I kept the light where it was. "Who's going to take care of your kids if you get killed tonight? Go back." I pointed at the trail behind her.

"I owe you the world, and I am gonna help you." She shook her finger at me. "We are family, and you will accept my help." She edged in close enough for me to see the anger on her face. Her words from earlier came back. My refusal of their help was taken more as insult than hero- ism. I threw my arms around her and thanked her, all the while begging the universe to spare her any harm.

We marched down the trail in front of the old mobile home. It wound deep into the property, away from the electric lights set up near King's house and the Six Guns' clubhouse. After a walk so long I was sure we'd somehow gone the wrong way, I saw the glow of the lamplight through the trees and held out my arm.

"Where's Tubby?" Dillon whispered.

Steps came from behind us. The way Tubby's voice had sounded came back to me again, finally making sense. Dread clawed the pit of my stomach. I turned slowly. My flashlight found Trench Coat's ugly face. It was set in a sneer. He had his shotgun pointed at us. Dillon and I raised our hands without bothering to go for the guns Tubby had given us.

This wasn't a pissing match. Trench Coat would kill us in the blink of an eye. His finger tightened on the trigger of his shotgun, and he smirked at me. "Tubman's in the cabin. Go on in." I hesitated. Trench Coat stepped forward, shotgun pointed at my chest. I'd be dead if he pulled the trigger at this range. I'd likely be dead if I went in the cabin. The only plus to going in the cabin was I had some time to try to figure out a way to take Trench Coat with me. I turned and went inside.

Soon as I stepped inside the old log cabin, the odor of mildew made me sneeze. Light flickered from a camp lantern hissing in the corner. It caught Hannah's red hair.

She stared blankly at the lantern as though mesmerized by it.

I rushed to her, eyes adjusting as I went. Tubby came into focus. He sat a few feet from Hannah, face stony. Bullfrog sat next to him, arms draped over his knees, eyes hooded and bored. Dillon grabbed my hand and squeezed too hard. We clung to each other. I couldn't believe this was how it all ended, with no vengeance or setting things right at all.

"Sit on the fucking floor, all of you." Trench Coat waved the shotgun.

"Where's King?" I hissed at Tubby.

He shook his head and turned away. My nerves sang soprano. I was missing something big here.

Hannah turned to me, fear deadening her face. "Trench Coat was waiting for us. He knew we'd come."

Bullfrog snickered. I spun to face Tubby. He turned his back to me. I reared back and hit him in the back as hard as I could. He grunted but didn't face me again.

Trench Coat laughed. "Lemme call King, see what he wants done with all 'a you."

I leaned my head against the wall. Hot tears streaked down my cheeks. Trusting Tubby had been stupid. Now people I cared about would die. At least I wouldn't live to regret it long.

The hag sang songs of joy inside me, drunk on my despair and the likelihood that I'd die soon. At least the entity would invade one of these murdering assholes and destroy them from the inside out. The small silver lining did little to soothe my fury at myself and the regret brewing inside me.

Trench Coat spoke a few words into the phone and hung up. He came over and unlocked handcuffs tethering Tubby and Bullfrog together. "Tubman, Bullfrog, disarm Peri Jean and her cute friend. Put the guns on the table."

Tubby and Bullfrog went about their task. Bullfrog made no effort to avoid my death glare, but Tubby sure did. His bony shoulders hunched nearly to his earlobes.

I glanced at Dillon, nodding my head at Trench Coat. Couldn't she tell him to shoot himself in the head or something? Understanding what I wanted, she shook her head, lips turned down and blinked rapidly. I got it. She needed to make eye contact for her magic to work. Perfect.

Trench Coat came to stand over Hannah, Dillon, and me. He dangled two sets of handcuffs from his finger. "Y'all make a little lady chain. King's waiting on y'all. Told him I had the main course, plus a side act." He liked his joke so well he laughed.

I kicked at him as hard as I could. Faster than I imagined a man his size could be, he snapped out one hairy arm and grabbed me by my ankle. He lifted me by my leg until I was off the ground and then kicked me in the face. I heard Tubby shout "no," and the world went black.

I woke up some time later, my mouth and throat full of blood. My body rocked with the motion of a vehicle moving.

"You okay?" Dillon whispered.

"Yeah." My voice came out all clotted. "I need to spit."

"Well, I'm in front of you. Don't spit on me." Hannah

sounded tougher than I felt at the moment. Evidently she'd hardened herself against whatever waited at the end of this ride.

I swallowed hard and held back another retch. She'd probably strangle me if I barfed on her.

"We had to carry your sorry ass all the way to this van," Hannah barked. Her tough act was about half past old.

"Look, Hannah, I apologize things went to shit. I told you—" I cut off my own words. Reminding her she could have stayed away wouldn't help matters, so I changed the subject.

"What happened with Tubby and Bullfrog? Did Trench Coat let them go in exchange for double-crossing us?" Tubby's betrayal was a hollow throb in my chest. How could I have trusted him? Stupid.

"Oh, we're here." Tubby sounded more disgusted than scared.

Dillon spoke up, her words running together. "After Trench Coat kicked you, Tubby tried to get the gun away from him. Bullfrog pulled him back and said they'd done their part and could they go. Trench Coat said King had had enough of both of them. Said they'd taken a dead end road tonight, and the end was coming up fast."

The van rolled to a stop hard enough to send the three of us sprawling together. A grunt came from the other side of the van. It sounded like Bullfrog. I wished I had the energy to fry his brains right here, but my trick with the ghosts back at the compound had drained me. I needed all the energy I had left to fight Trench Coat and King. Footsteps crunched outside the van. I stiffened and held my breath. A screen door slammed. King's voice raised in greeting.

"I got 'em," Trench Coat crowed.

I nudged Dillon and spoke in a whisper. "We get inside, tell Trench Coat to shoot himself. I'll do the rest." I prayed for luck, strength, and wisdom but figured I'd be lucky to die first so I didn't have to watch Dillon and Hannah die.

"Come here," Tubby hissed.

"So you can betray me again, Judas Tubman?" I glared into the dark in what I hoped was Tubby's direction.

"No. Hell no. I got a handcuff key in my sock. I'm cuffed too, so I can't get it, but you could. Get yourself loose."

I crawled toward Tubby, forcing Hannah and Dillon to crab walk along with me. I bumped into his knees.

"Your left," he mumbled. "Look, I'm sorry things went this way." Tubby did sound sorry. He sounded like he was about to cry. "I really did want to help."

But when it came down to saving himself, Tubby did it. I pulled off his boot and dug down into his sock. The key was on a piece of thread tied around his ankle. I guess he figured it was better than nothing.

"Just snap it." His voice, completely absent of his usual swagger, was actually nice. I hooked my finger underneath the string and did what he said.

Voices came from outside the van. A key turned in the lock of the van's cargo doors.

I shoved Tubby's boot back on his foot. We women scooted back to our side of the van. The door swung open, and I saw that I was right back at Wade's little cabin by the lake.

King leaned into the van, grinning. He winked at Hannah. "Sugar, I am so glad you're here. This is where it gets fun."

Hannah tightened her body and snarled at King. He laughed at her defiance.

"Look at the other one." Trench Coat gestured at Dillon.

Dillon leaned against my arm, body stiff with fear. Tough as she was, she knew we'd stepped in some stinky shit this time.

Trench Coat grabbed her by the arm and hauled her out, dragging me and Hannah behind her. He didn't give her time to climb out of the van and just threw her on the ground. It nearly yanked my arm out of socket. I held onto the handcuff key, but only out of stubbornness. I nearly fell on top of Dillon. Hannah did fall on top of me, knocking the air out of me.

King hauled me up by one arm and spoke into my ear. "You gonna *know* you're dead by the time I'm finished."

19

THEY DRAGGED us into Wade's cabin. It still smelled like mildew, but now the tang of bacon hung in the air too. I looked for Wade but saw him nowhere. *Probably dead.* I swallowed a sob.

Corman came out of the room I assumed was the bedroom. One arm was in a sling, and white bandages covered his shoulder. He slipped me a nasty wink. "And here are our guests." Pistol gripped in his good hand, he sauntered to where King stood and echoed his father's posture.

"Get 'em seated." King jabbed a finger at the floor.

Trench Coat came up behind me and kicked me in the back of the knee. The force of the blow traveled up my body like an explosion. I yelped, and one leg went out from under me. Trench Coat forced me to the floor. I dragged Dillon and Hannah with me. The three of us sat in a row. All we needed to do was reposition our hands and we'd be like those see-no-evil monkeys.

Trench Coat left the room to fetch Tubby and Bullfrog. The door closed behind him. A few seconds later, someone gave it a hard kick. From outside, Trench Coat yelled, "Open it." Corman hurried over and opened the door. Trench Coat hauled Tubby and Bullfrog into the room.

"Over here." King pointed at an empty spot near the kitchen. "Give 'em a good view of the action." Both men laughed.

"Get on your knees, boys." Trench Coat pulled on Tubby's arm.

A sheen of sweat stood out on Dillon's too-young face. I bumped her arm and pressed the handcuff key into her palm. She nodded and closed her fingers around it. When the time came, she'd unlock herself and persuade Trench Coat to shoot himself.

From across the room, Tubby watched us, ignoring Trench Coat's increasingly irritated order to kneel. When Tubby saw he had my attention, he lowered his head like a bull about to charge and slammed his forehead upward into Trench Coat's chin. The big man shouted in pain.

"Hey!" King shouted, wrapped one fist around Tubby's arm, and yanked him away from Trench Coat. Tubby turned around and bit King. Corman ran over to join the melee, waving his one good arm.

This was it. I turned to Hannah. She stared at me, dead-eyed as King. "Now," she mouthed.

I nudged Dillon and nodded at Trench Coat. She gave her wrist an expert twist, and the handcuff fell off. She dropped the key on the floor next to my hand. I picked it up and uncuffed Hannah from me. Before I'd have told her to get out, to run for her life. This time, I gave her the same good luck nod I'd give anybody else.

Dillon stood and rushed at Trench Coat. She kicked him in the shin to get his attention. Knots of fear tangled up with new doubts. Watching Dillon kick Trench Coat showed me how unprepared we were for this. It was like seeing a toddler attack an adult. I wanted to call her back but it was too late. Trench Coat spun, eyes wide with surprise. They locked on Dillon's. Her mouth quirked into a smile that sent a chill down my body.

"Shoot yourself in the head. Now." Her raspy smoker's voice, not too different from mine, sounded like thunder coming down. I waited for Trench Coat to paint the wall with his brains.

He laughed. "How'd you get loose?" He grabbed her by one arm and pulled her close.

The last wisp of hope I'd held floated away. Our gifts weren't a hundred percent. Sometimes they didn't work. What a bad time for Dillon's gift to go on vacation. Or maybe Trench Coat was too inhuman to fall prey to her. Either way, we were cooked.

King twisted away from Tubby, who was snapping at him like an angry dog. Tubby latched onto to King's neck. Corman, finally doing something useful, drew his pistol.

"Not yet. Hit him in the head," King yelled. Corman did. The sound of the metal hitting bone nauseated me. Tubby, hands still cuffed behind his back, crouched to one side and spat out blood. His legs wobbled and bent. Corman slammed the pistol into his head again. Tubby collapsed, dragging Bullfrog down to kneel exactly where Trench Coat had been trying to get them to kneel before it all started.

Trench Coat, Dillon dangling from one hand, spoke to King. "Ain't she cute? You got to let me have first go at this one."

King slapped Trench Coat on the back. "You saved my ass tonight. You can have first throw at all five of them."

My mind scrambled for a new plan. I even tried replaying Priscilla's appearance behind Tubby when he told me the boiling frog story. None of it would connect. The ideas burned to ash and then rose out of my reach. There was nothing to do but kneel there on the floor, waiting for our fates to find us. This was how it ended. No bang whatsoever. Just a bunch of beat-down rejects fixing to die badly.

Dillon stomped Trench Coat's foot. He leaned down into her face.

"S-s-shoot yourself in the head." Her voice didn't sound so sure now. I wasn't so sure either.

Trench Coat used the hand not holding Dillon's arm to grip the back of her neck. He gave her an open-mouthed kiss. My stomach plummeted. *No. This is all wrong.* Dillon lost her cool and screamed against Trench Coat's lips, her yell ending in a sob. He broke the kiss and dragged her toward the couch. She locked her legs and swung her fists, panicked blows glancing off his arms. He threw her onto the couch. She tried to get up, but he pushed her back down. Her terror-filled eyes locked on mine.

The rider dug its talons deeper into my shoulders,

lapping up the fear and sadness I felt and begging for more. Its thoughts crowded into mine.

"This is even better than you killing yourself. You're so afraid. Maybe I can even collect more spirits than just yours." The nasty monster's words sped up until they ran together.

My black opal pulsed magic, and some of the fear left me. I remembered what I was and reached for the mantle. I'd make Trench Coat burn from the inside out. Show him who I was and what I could do. My magic crackled in the small room, touching each person. When it hit King, he raised his head and walked toward me with his pistol raised.

"Suck it in, witch. I won't just blow your head off. I'll bring you over here to the couch for a front row seat." He stepped closer, put one booted foot on my calf, and began to press down. He hit a nerve and shot pain up my thigh. He bore down until I whimpered. Then he took his foot off me and spoke into my ear, his humid breath contaminating my skin. "Sit still."

I kept my eyes on the dirty floor. *Think.* There had to be a way to get out of this. Finding it was my damn job.

Corman watched the scene with glazed eyes, a smile playing his lips. His gun hand hung limp by his side. The sight of him infuriated me. I'd been ambivalent about Corman until I'd bumbled into playing hide the salami with him one boring day when I worked at Long Time Gone. Afterward, he'd humiliated me at every turn but still expected we'd become an item. I had reacted poorly. He'd gotten pissed. But bad as Corman was, he wasn't soulless.

He loved his little nephew whom he was raising. He loved his father, awful as he was.

The big question was could Dillon get through to Corman? I turned back to find her crying with her mouth closed, eyes wide with fear, as Trench Coat, pants around his knees, held her down with one hand and tore at her clothes with the other. I had to take a chance. I glanced at King. He still had the gun pointed in my direction, but he wasn't watching me. He stared at Trench Coat and Dillon, the front of his pants bulging.

The sight spurred me into action. Anything was better than watching this scene play to conclusion. I let out a loud cough, gaze flicking to King to see if he reacted. He didn't. I coughed again. Dillon rolled her eyes to me. I glanced at Corman and then back at Dillon and gave her a nod.

She took a deep breath and turned to Corman. She locked eyes with him. "Shoot him in the head."

Slowly, as though he was dreaming, Corman raised his gun hand. His hand tightened around the gun, and his finger squeezed the trigger.

King realized what was happening a beat too late. He took his gun off me, shouted, "No!" and tried to shove his son.

The gun went off with a flash of fire. Trench Coat's head jerked to one side before I heard the crack of the gun. Blood and brains hit the floor in a liquid splat. The big man dropped to one knee, hand scrabbling madly, probably for his gun, which lay on the floor next to him.

I climbed to my feet, handcuffs dangling from both

wrists, and staggered across the floor to kick at the Trench Coat's hand before he used up his last seconds of life shooting Dillon in the face. Trench Coat fell to one side and lay still. Dillon ran to cower behind me.

"What the fuck?" King screamed at his son.

Corman, blank faced, slowly lowered his gun.

"Fucking witches." King snatched the gun from Corman's hand and looked around for Dillon. He saw her cowering behind me and simply pointed the gun at me. "Your mother was right about you." His finger tightened on the trigger. "Nothing but trouble."

Cold spread over me. In my worry about having enough energy, then of King shooting me for using my magic, I'd almost waited too long. I grabbed at the mantle and sent the invisible ants to roam all over King's body. My favorite trick. The horrible man frowned at first. One foot twitched. Then the other. The tap-dance sped up until he tripped around the room, clodhopper boots drumming on the floor.

Hannah marched toward him. "Dance, bitch, dance," she yelled, wagging her hips, her face red and angry.

King spun to stare at her and lost his balance, eyes flashing fury. His gun thumped to the floor. Dillon dove for it, checked the safety, and pointed his own gun at him. Her finger curled around the trigger. She meant to kill him if she got the chance.

I opened my mouth to tell her to shoot him but stopped. An idea took form. This might be my chance to get rid of the hag. "Dillon, hold off," I called.

"I don't have to settle for him. You can't get rid of me yet."

The cold, scaly whisper slithered around my brain. It felt like the greatest truth ever spoken, and that was how I knew it was a lie.

King lunged at Dillon. I gave him even more ants and burned them hotter. I savored the way he twitched with mild discomfort a few times before he screamed and slapped at himself. Hannah kicked him in the ass when he stumbled too close to her. I laughed.

"Bitch," he hissed at me. That's when I decided he was getting the hag if it was the last thing I did.

"Your mama." I smiled.

Bullfrog chuckled in the corner of the room. I glanced at him and remembered Tubby's boiled frog story. Again, I puzzled over the way Priscilla had stood next to him, seemingly guiding his words. An idea flashed. Before it could take root, I used some of my precious energy to put up a wall between the hag and me, so it couldn't see what was coming.

Priscilla Herrera's spirit came into the room with a blast of cold air. She hovered near, wordlessly offering her energy. I drew from her and first unbound the hag. Then I set loose just a few of my spiritual fire ants to crawl all over the hag.

The entity shifted but dug in tighter. "*That's not going to work.*"

"There are two hosts in this room for you to choose from. Go now." I gave it a shove, wishing it would see reason and not turn this into a cat fight.

"*Never. I want you.*" The thing's purr raised the hair on the back of my neck. I added a few more ants to the first wave. The hag laughed at me. I ignored it and kept adding ants until they covered the hag. Then I poured all the energy I had into making their bites sting like the wrath of God.

The hag bounced around inside me, trying to find somewhere safe. I blocked off the deepest parts of me and held on tight. It felt like there was a tennis ball bouncing around inside me. Then a heavy weight formed in the bottom of my throat and began working its way to my mouth. It scraped against tender membranes and ripped open spots to claw its way higher. It blocked off my airflow. I tried to cough, hoping that would push it out. My lungs began to scream for oxygen.

"I will never forget this betrayal, you duplicitous witch. One day you will know my power. I will find a way to... What's she doing? Make her stop!" The hag actually sounded scared.

Long skinny arms went around my sides, and I smelled a mixture of sweat and Hannah's perfume. "It's okay," she breathed into my ear. "You're not going to die." Her fingers touched my belly button. She formed a fist, rolled it up, and then pushed in and up.

The hag flew out of my mouth and went straight for King, attaching itself to his face. I slumped with relief and took a deep breath. For the first time since the hag had bestowed itself on me, the air I breathed felt fresh and clean. My mind, clear of the hag's hate and poison, calmed. My thoughts untangled and quit hurting so much.

The seeds of destruction the hag planted, the wishes for my own death, glowed fire hot for a second, then died down. They stayed out in the open. The hag had promised they would. But maybe I could control them. At least I'd have a chance to be okay. I took my focus off myself and watched King's little show. A nasty smile grew on my face.

King staggered around the room, clawing at the hag, which had shrunk in size to barely as big as a Barbie doll. King kept his lips pressed shut against the hag. I needed to get that mouth open so the hag could get in.

"Where'd you hide Barbie's murder clothes, King?" I came close but kept up my magical defenses to keep the hag out of me. Surviving another round with it was beyond my pay grade. "I need those clothes so you and Jesse can exchange places in the pen."

King ignored me, eyes rolling wildly in their sockets. He must have realized that opening his mouth was doom. There had to be a way to get him talking. I remembered Tubby telling me the only thing King cared about was his motorcycle club. "I guess this is the end of the Six Gun Revolutionaries. I killed most of those pussies back at your compound. Now all that's left are you and Corman. You're going to prison. Corman's too stupid to run things by himself."

"Stop right there," Hannah yelled. I twisted to see her pointing a pistol at Corman. He lunged, and she fired. Corman clapped one hand over his midsection and sank to his knees, his face going ghost-pale. "You shot me, you stringy whore."

"You deserved it, syphilis breath." She didn't miss a beat and kept the gun pointed at him in case he wanted another one. This tough Hannah had her uses.

I followed King, talking to the back of his head.

"Scratch that. Corman'll probably die. The Six Guns'll die with him. You know what I'm gonna do before the cops get here? I'm gonna piss on all your jackets and burn the motherfuckers."

Of all the things I'd said, that was enough. King spun to face me, took his hands off the hag, and reached for me. "No, you ain't. I'm gonna kill you."

The hag slid into his mouth. King bent at the waist and let out a deep, coughing retch. I gathered the mantle and lent power to the hag as it burrowed deep in King's soul. I leaned into King's face. "I hope you two assholes enjoy each other."

Realization brightened King's eyes with hatred, but it was too late. The damage was done. He tripped over Corman and sprawled on the floor with Trench Coat's corpse. He lay there panting, eyes rolling in fear.

I staggered away from them, but Dillon rushed over and got in King's face. "You really wanna confess to the cops. Tell them where the tape is. Where the clothes are. You don't want Jesse Mace in prison no more. You know it's your turn."

King stared at her, hand still on his chicken-skinned throat. She repeated her message again and again until he began to nod. He took out his phone and pressed three numbers.

Corman raised his head. "What are you doing? Don't call them. Call the damn doctor."

King ignored him and pressed the phone tighter to his ear. Corman struggled with his father.

Tubby rose and snatched Hannah's gun away from her.

He must've gotten the handcuff key from the floor and freed himself. He slammed the gun into Corman's head. He did it again and again, the clank of metal on skull just as disconcerting as it had been when Corman had done it to him. All the while, King spoke into the phone, eerily calm, explaining the day he'd helped Joey Holze cover up Paul Mace's murder, telling them where the tape and clothes were and how to find us. I hoped the 911 operator was recording the whole mess.

Tubby's arm went back for another slam at Corman's head. I caught it midair. He turned to me, lips pulled back from his teeth, frightening and fierce.

"Help me tie them up. In a few minutes, King won't want to confess."

Tubby nodded and went back to where Bullfrog was sitting against the wall, hands still cuffed behind his back. Tubby's handcuffs lay on the floor. He kicked them at me without turning away from Bullfrog.

He raised the gun and spoke to Bullfrog. "You went behind my fucking back. I can't trust you no more."

So it had been Bullfrog and not Tubby who'd betrayed us to the Six Guns. Shame filled me. I'd thought the worst of Tubby the first chance I got. I owed him an apology.

"But I saved us..." Bullfrog's icy eyes tracked around the room. Before Bullfrog could continue, Tubby shot him in the head. The man's body jumped once and slumped over to the side. Bullfrog's eyes blinked as the blood pooled around his head. Tubby leaned over the dying man, unlocked his handcuffs, then shot him again in the chest.

Shock rooted me to my spot. I stood there, ears ringing,

handcuffs dangling from my hand. Seeing Tubby do what came naturally to him chilled me several degrees. He was what he was, friend or not. I needed to never forget that. Dillon took the handcuffs and gently convinced King he wanted to handcuff himself. He set his phone down and did exactly as she asked.

Tubby went back to Corman's unmoving form, cuffed his hands behind his back, and turned to glare at me. "Had to kill Bullfrog. He'd 'a done it again."

I couldn't do anything but gulp in response and take as narrow breaths as possible. The room reeked of two violent deaths. Light shimmered in the corner nearest Trench Coat's body. Right. Mohawk expected delivery of Trench Coat's spirit in the next few hours. I shoved what I'd seen Tubby do into a dark little room in my mind and locked the door on it.

I approached Trench Coat's spirit. The spirit, scared and confused, backed against the wall. Across the veil, moans and screams echoed, coming closer with each second. No bright light would come for Trench Coat's spirit. The darkness would claim him and drag him into whatever afterlife waited for lost souls like his. I uncapped the spirit bottle and said words that made me sick inside. "Hear that, Trench Coat? It's the darkness coming to claim you. Come with me, and you won't have to go." My stomach churned at the wrongness of what I was doing.

My talent was helping the dead move on, not condemning them to slavery at the hands of a shapeshifting monster. But choices existed in shades of gray. I'd started this quest to save friends and family. This was what had to be done to finish it.

After I coaxed Trench Coat's spirit into the bottle, capped the bottle, sealed it. Hands shaking, I dug in the dead man's pockets and chose a focus object. He'd had a keychain with a wicked looking spike fastened to the loop. I figured it would do fine.

Now I could take care of the most important thing. I knelt down in front of King. "Where's Wade?"

King's lips stretched in a slow smile. His eyes glittered. "Dead. I shot him in the head right after I sent you that video."

The world narrowed into a pinpoint focused on King's ugly, malicious face. The ringing in my ears blotted out all other sounds. I got up from the floor, stumbled into the kitchen, opened a drawer and found a butcher knife. It would do.

Back in the living room, I stood over King and adjusted my grip on the knife. I'd have to stab hard if I wanted to hit his heart. I raised the knife over my head. Behind me, someone was screaming for me to stop, but I didn't have time for them. Putting all my force behind the knife, I let it swing downward.

A strong hand closed around my wrist and jerked me away from King. The hand squeezed harder, grinding the bones of my wrist together. I yelped and dropped the knife. Tubby let go of my wrist and cupped my chin, fingers digging cruelly into cheeks.

"Did you hear what Hannah said?" he screamed.

The world snapped back into focus. Hannah stood on the other side of me, red-faced, sweaty, and panting.

"Did you see Wade's ghost?" she managed between deep breaths.

I bent to grab the knife and get back to my task. King needed to die. He'd hurt too many people. Hannah curled her fingers in my hair and yanked my head back so we were face to face again.

"Did you see Wade's ghost?" she gritted out through clenched teeth, her grip tight on my hair.

The pain in my scalp snapped me out of my rage. I thought about her question. "No. I didn't." And Wade would have come to say goodbye, maybe even offer some last advice. A tiny glimmer of hope sparked.

"I didn't see him die." She raised her eyebrows.

"You think King is lying?" I didn't. He'd never lie about something so hurtful.

"I ain't lying," King bellowed. "I shot that motherfucker dead."

"We have to find him." I ran to the only other room in the cabin, the bedroom through which Corman had entered the room. The bed was mussed, but nobody was in it.

I raced to King. "Where is he?"

He worked his mouth and spat at me. I went back to where I'd dropped the knife.

Dillon hurried alongside me, talking fast. "Forget him. The cops'll be here soon. Wade might still be alive, but he's probably running out of time. If we wanna find him, we gotta go now."

20

I RACED out of the cabin to the van that had brought us here, yanked the door open, and saw Trench Coat had taken the keys with him. I dug in my pockets and retrieved the spike keychain I'd stolen from his corpse. The first key didn't fit. Neither did the second one. Frustration built in me.

"Those are the wrong keys," Hannah said from behind me. I spun. She handed me a keyring with one large key on it. I climbed into the van's driver's seat and started it up.

"Wait a minute. I'm going too," she said over the rumble of the engine and went around to the passenger side and climbed in. Dillon clambered into the back, Tubby right behind her. I did a U-turn in the cabin's tiny front yard and flew down the little dirt road, ignoring the screeching of limbs dragging against the van's sides and the sound of the van bottoming out on the road from time to time. I came to the highway and stopped. I didn't know where to go.

Hannah seemed to read my mind. "Okay. Slow your mind down. Think about that last video King sent, the one where Wade was calling your name." I moaned, my body aching with the misery he must have been in. Hannah gripped my arm. "No. Put that part away. Think about what you saw."

I saw the smoke blackened walls, as though the room had burned at some time. "King's house. The Six Gun Compound." Even as I said the words, they felt wrong. I searched my mind, but no better answer came. Wade could be running out of time. I screeched out onto the highway and drove toward the compound. The feeling of wrongness continued, growing stronger and stronger. I let off the gas and pulled onto the side of the road near a row of rural mailboxes.

"What is it?" Tubby's voice came from the darkness behind me.

"I'm wrong. I can't tell you why, but I know it." Sweat ran into my eyes, burning, and I swiped at it. I patted my pockets, looking for my phone, even though I'd already noticed the absence of its familiar weight. Trench Coat must have taken it, and it was probably back in that cabin in the woods, the one with no electricity, at the Six Gun Revolutionaries' compound. "If I could watch the video again…" I didn't even finish the sentence.

Next to me, Hannah opened the glove box and dug around in it. She began setting phones on the van's dashboard. I stared at her, openmouthed.

"They used to do it to me all the time. Take my phone away so I couldn't leave." She stared into the darkness as she said the words. "Sorry I didn't think of it sooner." She picked her phone out the jumble and stuck it in her jeans pocket.

I grabbed my phone, went straight to the text messages, and played the video again. Hannah unbuckled her seatbelt and crowded next to me.

"You're right," she said. "That's not King's house. See the walls? King has that cheap eighties wood paneling. Even burned, it wouldn't look like this. This is some kind of log cabin. See how thick the wood is?"

I played the video again, this time muting the sound so I wouldn't hear Wade's pitiful voice calling me. Hannah was right. The walls had rounded humps like a log cabin's walls. "Maybe the bunk house?" I had never been out there.

Hannah shook her head. "It's sheetrock out there."

Tubby and Dillon crowded next to our seats. I played the video again. Dillon leaned so close her breath fogged the screen. I started it over.

Tubby and I spoke at the same time. "The smokehouse."

Hannah made a face. "The one beside Long Time Gone?"

Without answering, I spun the van around and sped in the other direction. After too many minutes, I bounced across the parking lot of Long Time Gone and jerked to a stop next to the smokehouse. I fell out of the van, scrambled to the smokehouse door, and flung it open.

The smell of infection hit me, sharp and sour. A dark

shape lay still against one wall. I forced myself to approach it. "Wade?"

It was so dark inside the tiny room I couldn't see if it was him. Someone pushed a flashlight into my hand. I turned it on.

"Oh god," Hannah moaned and backed out of the room. Her running footsteps sounded over the dirt as she fled.

"Hannah?" Dillon called after her and trudged off, grumbling.

I couldn't move or breathe. I couldn't even process what I saw.

Wade lay still, dark circles under his eyes, his face pale around his beard. Near his hairline on the left side was a spattering of black dots surrounding a dark pit. Blood had matted his dark hair to the side of his head. I put my hand on his chest, expecting to feel nothing but stillness and chilled skin. But fever warmed my palm.

"He's alive," I said to nobody in particular. I called to the last bit of my power, trying to remember Wade's healing words but realized they didn't matter. Only intent mattered.

"Wade Hill, I call this infection out of your body and back into the earth from whence it came. I call for your head and brain to heal any damage." Unlike Wade, I couldn't look into a body and see the sickness. I didn't know how bad the head wound was. Still I pulled for everything I was worth. Maybe I wouldn't kill him in the process.

The wood the smokehouse was built from, old wood

grown right in this pine forest, came to life, its gentle vibration working its way through my shoes and up my legs. I drew on its power, and the spark of magic mixed with science in the flashlight's glow. It flickered and buzzed like a dying bug. "I call the infection and the injury to come out of this body."

Wade stirred. His chest heaved. He choked. I knelt on the nasty floor and pushed on him. Tubby appeared next to me and helped, both of us grunting. It was like trying to push a car out of a mud bog. I pulled on the magic again, the sore muscles crying out for mercy. Wade finally rolled. I stroked his filthy hair, most of it stiff with dried blood. "Go on. Let it go."

He coughed again but nothing came up.

Magic. I needed more magic to get the sickness out of him. Dillon should have stayed. I could have combined our magic. Too late to call her back now. I focused on the little breeze in the room until it ran in a steady warm stream. "Infection and injury, come out of Wade Hill."

Wade coughed again, gagging this time. He puked up a gout of foul smelling pus. The shakes hit him. Tears began to leak out of my eyes, and I began to pray even though I doubted there was any help out there for someone like me. *Please, please. Let him live.*

Wade's hand closed over my wrist. He rolled his eyes, bright with fever, up to mine. "I'm dying. Call my sister, Desiree. My phone's in the garbage can in King's office inside the bar. Her number's in it." He swallowed, and his eyes fluttered.

"Peri Jean?" Hannah's voice came from the doorway. I

twisted, afraid to take my eyes off Wade. She swigged from the bottle of vodka she gripped before she spoke. "I've called Dean. Told him to get out here now. The bag with the murder clothes was in the safe inside King's office. So was the tape." Her eyes lighted on Wade and flicked away. "I'll go get Wade's phone out of the trash. I saw it and wondered what it was."

Tubby yelled for Dillon. She appeared as though she'd been waiting right outside the door. Maybe she had. For the first time since I'd met her, she looked as young as she was, wide-eyed, scared, and overwhelmed by this night.

"Back the van right up to the door," he ordered. Then he spoke to me. "Let's get him into the van. You can drive him to the hospital quicker than an ambulance can get out here."

The three of us hefted Wade off the floor of the smoke-house. His yell of pain scored into my memory so guilt could call it up next time I was having a bad day. Hannah found some blankets inside the bar. We used them to cover and cushion him as best as we could. I climbed into the van and started it. "Get in," I told Tubby and Dillon.

Tubby backed away. "Po-lice is about to get involved in all this. Ain't none of y'all seen my sorry ass tonight." He winked at me, turned, and disappeared into the woods behind Long Time Gone.

"If it's gonna be the po-lice, I just can't." Dillon ran after Tubby. She feared cops the way some people fear wasps and bees. I let her go. We'd find each other later.

"You coming?" I asked Hannah and moved the van's gearshift to drive.

"I'll wait on Dean, make sure he gets the evidence against King." She held my gaze. "I don't see Wade's death. Just get him to the hospital."

I couldn't let myself feel relief or hope right then. Everything seemed too precarious. "Will you call Rainey and let her know it's over?"

She nodded and stepped away from the van, a sure signal she wanted me to go. I drove out of the parking lot but took one glance in the rearview mirror before I turned onto the road. Hannah stood silhouetted against the huge, bright moon, swigging from her bottle of vodka.

———

I DROVE Wade to the hospital. The emergency room workers acted more concerned about the events that got Wade there than helping him. Until I started stinging them with magical fire ants. Then they ran around glancing at me like a dog who couldn't be trusted. It was their own stupid fault.

I went outside and called Desiree on Wade's phone. She'd been waiting for my call, said Wade called her most days, even just for a minute or two. Another thing I never knew about him. She knew something was wrong when he went quiet. Desiree promised to leave within the hour and said she'd be at the hospital by morning.

Dean's unmarked white cop car pulled into the lot and made a beeline for me. He parked at the curb and stood over me with hands on his hips.

"Did you get the tape and the murder clothes?" I asked,

as though I hadn't pulled a jackass fit in the emergency room and used magic to get my way.

He nodded and sat down next to me with a tired sigh.

"You gonna arrest me?" I kept smoking, wanting to get as much tar and nicotine as I could before he took me in. Smoking was probably outlawed in the fancy new Sheriff's Office downtown.

He smiled, and I remembered why we dated. He was still gorgeous. "I said I wouldn't, and I won't. As far as the law knows, Mr. Tolliver got into a war with a rival motorcycle gang and was so scared by it, he decided to confess to an old crime to get police protection."

I shook my head. "You seriously blaming it on a rival motorcycle gang? That sounds so TV."

Dean shrugged. "The Six Guns needed to be over in this county. Nobody'll miss them."

"What about Bullfrog?" He wasn't in a motorcycle gang, Six Guns or otherwise.

Dean frowned for a moment before realization dawned on his face. "You mean Jeremiah Pike?"

I shook my head. "Was that his real name?"

"That's him," Dean said. "We will just assume Mr. Pike somehow got caught in the crossfire. His running afoul of the law goes back many years."

I watched Dean's face, looking for remorse or shame and saw none. The harsh parking lot lights could have been to blame, but I didn't think so. "Don't tell me you're becoming a crooked cop." I knew I was shitting my own bed, but Dean had bitched endlessly about his predecessor's dishonesty. Now he was acting the same way.

"Depends on what you think a crooked cop is. I'm protecting the citizens of this county from a menace. Besides, I..." He stared out at the dark parking lot, choosing his words. "I guess I felt like I owed you. I'm not sorry we broke up, but I am sorry for the way I acted. Can we call it even?"

I nodded my yes. "Where's Hannah? I figured she'd come on to the hospital."

Dean shook his head and rolled his eyes. "She downed half a bottle of vodka while I was with her. I took her to the museum and got her into her apartment. She was snoring when I left."

I took the news silently, even though I was hurt she hadn't called and explained. It was a clear signal she wanted nothing to do with me right now. It could have been because she couldn't take any more tonight. But I thought it was just that she didn't want to be around me. Things I could have done different flooded my thoughts and made me wince.

Realizing Dean was watching me, I said, "Good luck on fatherhood. You're gonna do great." I stood, eager to be away from my ex. We'd both changed, good and bad.

Dean stood with me and gripped my arm. "Don't come to my house again, okay? My wife was pissed."

We grinned at each other. I gently pulled my arm away and walked back into the hospital. It was obvious the workers didn't want me there, but they were too scared to try to throw me out. Not too long ago, I'd have felt ashamed. Now I didn't much care.

A nurse wearing scrubs with cartoon puppies on them

took the time to tell me Wade's head wound was non-fatal, but he had a concussion and they didn't know how bad it was yet. The older gunshot wounds in his back were so infected they would require serious antibiotics or his organs might shut down. She said to check back in an hour to see if they'd gotten him into a room yet.

I went back outside, lit yet another cigarette, and called Rainey. She answered the phone squealing about the downfall of King and the recovery of the evidence that would help Jesse get out of prison.

She stopped speaking and let out a yell. "I'm getting Jesse out."

"Don't get too excited," I warned. "King'll probably deny knowing about any of it."

Rainey snorted. "The county prosecutor's been advising me for years on getting Jesse's case reopened, and we've already talked. He says the evidence is going to make a difference. Either Joey Holze or King will break. Maybe they'll turn on each other. All I know is Jesse's getting out." She yelled this last part and let out a mad cackle. A tear, both of joy and grief, slid down my cheek. I let it run to my jawbone and splash to the concrete. I took a deep, shuddering breath.

"Where are you?" Rainey stopped laughing.

"Hospital." I explained about Wade.

"Do you want me to come?" She didn't want to. I could hear it her voice. She wanted to keep celebrating and getting ready for the last leg of her longest marathon. I didn't begrudge her a bit.

"Naw. I got it under control." Tears leaked from my eyes

in a steady stream, and I had to strain to keep my voice even. Rainey and I said our goodbyes. I went back into the hospital to wait for news of Wade.

When they finished treating Wade and moved him to a room, I stationed a chair outside the door. The nurses didn't like it, but none of them wanted to fight me. Not long before dawn, through a haze of half reality, I thought I saw an angel with a halo of blond hair step off the elevator. She had with her a younger angel. They came to a stop in front of me.

The blond woman, who was unnaturally tall the way I figured all angels probably were, leaned over and shook my leg. "Peri Jean?"

I jerked awake at her foggy smoker's voice. The woman and girl slid into focus. They weren't angels. Obviously mother and daughter, both with blond hair, long legs, and hourglass figures. I pegged the daughter in her late teens. The woman's age wasn't so easy to guess. She had a web of fine lines around her eyes and mouth, indicating at least forty years on earth, but her eyes looked thousands of years old.

"Desiree?" I had expected Wade's sister to be a female version of him and not so...feminine.

"Yep. We're here." She pointed at the room. I nodded and stood, smoothing down my filthy blue jeans. Desiree tried to smile, but worry chased it off her face. "I hope you'll not take offense, but this is a family matter. We'll deal with him alone."

I blinked and took a step backward, hands up. I needed a cup of coffee anyway. I took off walking but never made it to the cafeteria. Cecil and Dillon met me in the lobby of the hospital. Mysti, Griff, and Brad stood slightly behind them. I rushed to them, arms out. They circled and hugged me, all asking questions. We went into the cafeteria where I told them everything I knew and drank numerous cups of coffee.

When I couldn't stand it any longer, I went back upstairs to check on Wade. His room was empty.

Too shocked to move, I stood holding the door and staring into the room. Footsteps came toward me. My paralysis broke.

I hurried into the room and shut the door. Wade's hospital gown lay over the footboard of his bed. Blood-stained bandages stuffed the trash can.

Hurt welled up, tightening my throat. I pressed one hand over my mouth to hold back the sob trembling against my lips. Wade couldn't be gone. This wasn't how things were supposed to end between us.

How did they heal him? It was a good question, a good way to put off accepting the truth in front of me. Wade's healing power came from his being the seventh son of a seventh son. His sister and niece weren't sons at all. They shouldn't have been able to heal him. So there.

Grief expanded in my chest, tightening it. I swallowed hard and let some of the truth seep in. It didn't matter how Wade's sister and his niece had healed him. Witchcraft. Blond-chick power. The result was the same. They'd healed him, and he'd left without saying goodbye. I took a trembling breath, walked the few steps to the bed, and put one hand on it.

An envelope that looked like it had been around the block a few times sat on the pillow. My name was written on it in Wade's uneven scrawl.

I snatched up the flimsy paper with trembling hands and nearly tore it taking out the sheet of paper within. A grocery list? What the hell? Then I turned it over. Words covered the whole page.

Peri Jean,

I figured I was going to lay there and die in that stinking smokehouse. Thank you for saving my life. I'll never forget it.

Gaslight City is over for me. Has been for a while. It's time for me to move on.

It's also time for me to let you walk your own path. I think I've put you in more danger than I have helped you.

I love you with all my heart and wish things could be different.

Godspeed.

—Wade

I stood numb and still. The coffee gurgled on my stomach. I made myself pick up the envelope again and hold it open. My mojo bag, the one that let Wade know when I was in trouble, in need of his help, lay in the bottom of the envelope. I slipped it into my pocket. Hands quivering, I folded the note and put it back inside the envelope. Then I stood there, numb.

If Wade and I no longer had our connection, how would he come when I needed him? He wouldn't. Ever again. But I could know when he was in trouble.

I knew enough about magic now to make my own mojo bag. And Wade had left all the stuff I needed behind.

I rushed to gather a few strands of his long black hair off the pillow and liberate a few of the bloody bandages from the trash can.

The door clicked open. I shoved the mojo bag supplies into my pocket and turned, expecting to see an angry nurse, wondering where her patient got to, but it was Tubby.

My mouth trembled, and I held up the note.

Tubby nodded. "I saw two blonds helping him across the parking lot. The hospital must have shaved part of his hair off. How does he get all the women, even looking like that?"

I shrugged. Tubby put his arm around me and steered me toward the door. "Your people's waiting downstairs. Best get to 'em."

Tubby led me through the halls. I walked with my head down, dependent on him to keep me from falling on my face. He did his job. We got back down to the lobby.

Just as Tubby promised, my family and friends sat waiting for me. Griff and Cecil had their heads together. Had the two of them worked things out? Neither looked mad. Mysti sat, Dillon's phone in hand, exclaiming over pictures of Dillon's kids. Brad gave me a wave and a smile. I started toward them, but Tubby caught my arm.

He kicked at the floor, face reddening. "Bullfrog had the double-cross planned before we left the bar. I never even knew. Trench Coat met us in the woods. It was either go along or die right there."

"You did what you needed to survive." I didn't expect any different from Tubby. He lacked Wade's selflessness and Dean's need to be a hero. Didn't make him bad. Tubby was just cut from a different cloth.

"That mean you'll be back in Gaslight City sometime soon?" He looked hopeful. Did he really have so little to look forward to?

I shook my head. "I think my business here in Burns County is finished for good." I hadn't realized I felt that way until the words came out. But my business was finished here. After everything, I shared a little of Cecil's superstition about the badness of this place.

Tubby nodded. He jammed his fists in his pockets, head down. He looked so lonely.

"But I'll be traveling all over Texas with my family this summer." I said the words quickly before I could change my mind. "Come visit us. You've got a lot in common with my cousin, Finn."

He raised his head smiling, leaned forward, and kissed my cheek. "*Hasta luego,* beautiful." He waved and walked out into the softness of the early morning, whistling.

I WENT to my friends and family. Nobody wanted to hang around longer than necessary. We gathered up what was ours and prepared to leave town. I bundled my stuff into the big truck I'd stolen off a dead woman.

"You sure you want to ride by yourself?" Dillon's forehead creased with concern. She needed to quit doing that. Her fair, freckled skin would remember those wrinkles and stay like that all the time.

"You go on with the others. Papaw shouldn't be by himself." Cecil wasn't really my Papaw, but it felt good to call him that. It felt good to have Dillon standing at my back. I pulled her into an impulsive hug. She squeezed hard and whispered that she loved me. I told her I loved her too.

I drove past the museum on the way out of town. A "Closed" sign hung in the door, but the lights were on in Hannah's upstairs apartment. I wondered if she would open the museum today. *Not my problem.*

I turned left at the next stoplight, away from the museum and away from Gaslight City. My next business was in Tyler at the Rose City Inn. I dreaded facing Mohawk again and even felt a little bad for what I was going to do with Trench Coat's sprit, but a deal was a deal.

At the Tyler City limits, it hit me that I hadn't said all I had to say to Hannah. I pulled over and called her phone. I wasn't surprised when it went to voicemail.

I left a message. "Hannah, I'm sorry things ended up the way they did between us. Your friendship has saved my sanity so many times. I guess I hoped my friendship could save yours. Maybe what I did gave you one more chance for a fresh start. I'll leave you alone from here on out. Life's hard enough without the past coming back to haunt you. I love you and wish you the best life has to offer. Watch out for dead ends." I hung up. Ten minutes later, I pulled into the Rose City Inn's lumpy asphalt parking lot and cried until I wanted to puke.

Someone tapped on my window. With as much dignity

as I could muster, I wiped off my face with my T-shirt and got out of the car.

Mohawk didn't ask what was wrong. Their kind didn't seem to care much about human feelings. I suspected they saw us the same way most humans see animals. It seemed fair in the grand scheme of things. Besides, Mohawk was the last person—thing?— I wanted to spill out my sorrows in front of.

He said, "Are you prepared to fulfill your end of our deal?"

I nodded and followed him to the room where I'd leave Trench Coat's spirit for eternity. Mohawk unlocked the door and held it open for me.

He sniffed my hair as I passed. I tightened with disgust but tried to hide it and set my witch pack on the bed. I dug out Trench Coat's keychain and tossed it on the bed beside my pack.

Mohawk came close and picked it up. He began to smile.

I preened a little in spite of myself. "It's either that or the mirror for the focus. Otherwise, he won't be able to attach himself to people."

"I know how magic works." He rolled his eyes.

I dragged the rickety table out in the open and spread the lace tablecloth I'd borrowed from Mysti on top of it. The same candles she'd used only a few hours earlier went on top of that. I put my hands on my hips and waited for Mohawk's decision.

He tossed the spike keychain in his hand several times. "Your ghost can't travel the way the hag could, especially once he's dedicated to this room. If I choose the mirror, he'll be confined to the room." It wasn't a question. He was thinking things over, so I didn't bother to answer. "You have enough skill and power to trap him in this keychain?"

I nodded. The confidence felt like an ill-fitting coat, too expensive and heavy for someone as plain and unimportant as me.

"If someone were to touch the keychain, pick it up, could he attach himself and go home with them? Haunt them, scare them? Maybe get them back here for the big finale?" Mohawk's greedy smile sent chills running over my skin. It reminded me of the hag's cold avarice.

"If I tell Trench Coat to do that, he will." I'd had most of a night and the drive over here to recharge. Beyond that, I could always draw energy from Priscilla Herrera's spirit, who I felt watching this transaction a little too gleefully. She wanted this for me. Realization of power was everything to her.

"Fine. That's what I want done." Mohawk crossed his arms over his emaciated chest.

I went about consecrating the keychain and naming it for its purpose. Mohawk helped me call a circle, which was stronger and better than any I could have called, and stepped inside with me.

"To watch closer." He flashed his snake fangs at me.

I set the spirit bottle containing Trench Coat's spirit on the table next to the newly consecrated keychain and poured a ring of sea salt around them. Beyond that, I sprinkled a ring of holy water. I didn't want Trench Coat's spirit to get out and attack me. I had a feeling he'd want to finish our private war.

"Here we go," I muttered to myself and cracked the seal on the spirit bottle.

Trench Coat's spirit came out in a foul mist, evil radiating from it. As a person, he'd had a shell that made him look sort of like the rest of us. Now he was stripped down to pure, soulless evil. Mohawk inhaled deeply and hissed behind me. I turned to find him with a dreamy smile on his face. He nodded for me to continue. I raised both arms and pointed my athame at the swirl of spirit.

"Gerald Raymond Hendry, Trench Coat, I bind you to this keychain where you'll stay until you're picked up..."

"Or stolen," Mohawk added.

"Or stolen. Once this keychain is touched or taken from this place, you may torment the thief in any way you see fit. When the victim is weak, bring them back here to this man behind me." I focused on the swirl of Trench Coat's spirit and pushed it at the keychain. The spirit rushed at me, hit the wall of the circle, and bounced back. Hate emanated from it.

Trench Coat's voice came to life in my head. *"I'll get you."*

I poured more energy into making him connect with the keychain. In the end, Trench Coat went into the keychain because it was familiar and had belonged to him in life. The keychain jittered against the table for several seconds, then stopped.

"It's done," I told Mohawk and broke the circle around the keychain. He took the keychain and carefully set it at the base of the lamp on the nightstand. He winked at me and motioned me to follow him.

Outside he led the way to his office and held open the door. "Please go inside. We still have one matter to discuss. You promised to find an object for me."

I nodded my yes, stomach starting to churn at the idea of being back in that office with Mohawk the Snake Man. I followed him inside. The wild odor of the room surrounded me. I forced myself to take shallow breaths. Mohawk sat down behind a desk and leaned back.

He began playing with a cat's eye marble. "When I bit you, I gave you a bit of my venom. Not enough to make you sick, but enough to forge a bond between us." He handed me the cat's eye marble. "When I've gathered the information you'll need, I'll use this to contact you. Failure to respond within twelve hours forfeits our deal. If that happens, you'll belong to me to do with as I wish."

My stomach tightened at the thought. I took the marble and dropped it in my jeans pocket. It had a warm, alive feeling that made my head swim. "We square?"

Mohawk jerked a nod and opened the door for me to leave.

I got the hell out of there as fast as my short little legs would carry me. I shook until I crossed the Texas/Louisiana border.

21

———————

Ｏne Ｍonth Ｌater

Outside Austin, Texas

Summer lurked in the May sun, waiting for its chance to burn our asses for another season in hell. A bead of sweat popped out on my scalp and rolled slowly toward my eye. I wiped it away just before it hit.

"You can't stop yet." Zora's wail hung perilously close to tantrum territory.

"I ain't stopping." I waved the little makeup brush at her. "This sweat gets in my eye, I won't be able to make you into a *Dia de los Muertos* girl." I glanced at Dillon, silently asking if she wanted another turn. She shook her head, eyes wide.

Much earlier in the day, in what seemed like a brighter, simpler time, Zora saw a piece of art with a beautiful woman whose face was made up like a sugar skull. She informed her mother and me of her desire to wear similar makeup. She insisted, regally, like a queen bestowing favor, that we also make up her baby brother Zander.

Zander's makeup had taken a half hour. The little boy had been easy to please. He didn't know the difference between good and bad and had run off laughing to show his daddy.

Zora, on the other hand, wanted her makeup to resemble something from the Sistine Chapel. Now she sat in my lawn chair, chubby arms crossed over her chest.

"Get it right this time, Peri Jean." She pooched her lips out at me.

I knelt down in front of her, saying to Dillon over my shoulder, "After this, you gotta try again. My hands are cramping."

Dillon let out a snort from behind me. I knew that sound. She'd had enough. If I couldn't make Zora happy, Dillon would tell her it was over. The tantrum would then ensue. At least we were at the back of Sanctuary's camp. Maybe nobody would think we were killing Zora.

Cecil's golf cart buzzed into our little area and parked under some trees several yards away. I stopped painting again. Zora let out a frustrated wail.

"Let's see what Papaw wants." I held up my hands. She kicked her feet. I dodged out of the way.

It wasn't Cecil who got out of the golf cart, though. The hot sun shone on red hair, brightening it to the color of flames. The woman walked toward us, head down, face in shadow. My heart flipped over and then back again. I recognized that walk. And the hand wringing. I stood and wiped the makeup off my hands.

Hannah stopped several feet from me. But it was close enough to see clarity in her caramel colored eyes. She tried to smile, but her mouth just trembled.

I stood rooted to my spot. Had she come all the way to the hills outside Austin, Texas to tell me we'd never be friends again? I stiffened myself against the rejection. She took a few more steps and held out her arms. We ran at each other, wrapped our arms around each other, both laughing and crying at the same time.

"You look a lot better." I pushed her away from me. "How are you?"

She frowned. "Sober. Thinking clearly. You know? Every day is a chance for a good day."

I nodded. Maybe I knew what she meant.

"I'm sorry for the way I acted. Especially for my disappearing act there at the end. No telling where I'd be if you hadn't come to help." She hugged herself. From somewhere behind me, Zora called my name and told me to hurry. Dillon shushed her.

"I had an ulterior motive. I wanted to get my uncle out of jail." I'd been talking to Rainey almost every day. It looked like Jesse was really going to get out of prison. King was locked away in jail, and Corman had disappeared from the hospital. I tried smiling at Hannah, but I was too close to tears to do anything but grimace. Tears brimmed over the edges of her eyes. She dabbed at them before one could sully her perfect makeup.

"Did you hear Uncle Joey keeled over dead of a heart attack when the cops came to his door in San Antonio with a warrant?" Hannah's shoulders slumped. The fatigue and sadness I'd seen on her before darkened her face for just a second, but then she straightened and shook her head. "But I'm not going to let that ruin today. I came here to thank you."

I shook my head. "Forget it."

She ignored my words and gripped my shoulders. "I wouldn't be here if you hadn't kept after me until you saw me face to face. When you found me, I wasn't going to last much longer." One single tear escaped and rolled down her cheek.

"That hag riding your shoulders wasn't making your recovery any easier." I wondered how the rider had fared with King, or if he'd even stayed with King. The hag was free now. It didn't have to stay with King if it found another host it liked better. The thought made me shiver.

Hannah licked her lips. "Things were bad for me before then. Otherwise, that hag wouldn't have dragged me down like it did." She swiped the tear track off her face. "People think the worst thing that can happen is you die. It isn't. The real tragedy is surviving. Especially when you survive what I did." She sniffed.

"It takes way more strength to live than it does to give up." I stood with my arms crossed over my chest. I'd never look at Hannah and not think about my fault in what happened to her. But I'd also never look at her and not remember the effort it took to save her.

"You find something to live for." Hannah wiped underneath her eyes and snorted. "After I hanged myself and came back seeing when people would die, it changed things. It made me see life for what it is—a gift. But the only way it's a gift is if you share it with the right people." She glanced around the grouping of campers, caught Dillon's eye, and waved. "I was wondering if...now that I'm like you...if I could—"

I wrapped her in a hug before she could finish. We wept in each other's arms until my eyes were raw and my chest ached. But it was good pain and good tears, the kind that come from something being right. Some friendships are just for a season, but some of them are for life. My friendship with Hannah was like that. We finally released each other and stood laughing and crying and wiping our eyes.

"You can stay in my camper while you see if you like it here." I gestured at my camper, the door open, a fan buzzing inside. Orev perched on the canopy. He cawed in welcome.

"Actually, I bought my own RV. It's near the check-in office. I wanted to make sure you still wanted me as a friend." Hannah dragged her hand over her face, smearing her elaborate makeup. "I sold the museum—and my gorgeous apartment—to Benny Longstreet. You're not in Gaslight City anymore, and I don't have any business there either."

"It's like Sodom and Gomorrah. You don't want to look back." We both laughed at that, but a look exchanged between us. Those awful thoughts the hag scratched out of me still came out to play sometimes, said I had nothing to live for and ought to just kill myself. Did that happen with Hannah too? I said nothing. Talking about thoughts like that seemed to give them more power. The moment passed.

"I'm tired of waiting to have my makeup done," Zora yelled. Dillon shushed her again.

Hannah walked toward the little girl, smiling her old smile. "I bet I can do a better job than Peri Jean Mace."

Hannah's steps had a tentative little shuffle, but I hoped she'd someday leave it behind. She squatted in front of Zora and dug in her handbag, which looked like it cost as much as my camper. She took out a black eyeliner pencil and began drawing a recognizable flower around one of Zora's eyes. It was quite a bit better than what Dillon or I had done. The two of us exchanged a smile and a shrug.

I watched Hannah put makeup on Zora, both of them giggling, my throat tight with tears. I went to sit next to them. Hannah glanced at me out of the corner of her eye and pushed her purse at me. "Get out my sapphire eyeliner."

I dug around in her purse and grabbed the first blue eyeliner I saw. After all, how many blue ones could she have? Hannah never even wore blue eyeliner. I handed it to her.

Hannah glanced at it and handed it back. "Not the teal. The sapphire. There's a difference."

"No, there ain't. You're just being picky." And the argument went from there. I made sure to sound outraged. But inside, where it counted, I couldn't have been happier.

Life didn't come easy. It beat a person into the dirt. Took away their dreams. Left them bleeding and hurting.

Hannah would never be the same. Hell, would any of us? Didn't matter.

Life was facing the storm and getting up after it demolished everything. Surviving to fight another day. That, and staying away from dead ends.

Keep reading for a sample of the next Peri Jean Mace Ghost Thriller.

Chapter 1

The dead lady whispered in my ear, "Tell him my wedding band is in the cookie jar on top of the refrigerator, but don't tell him his father killed me."

I broke my connection with the spirit and gave the cowboy across from me what I hoped was a mysterious smile. "Your mother says her ring is in the cookie jar on top of the refrigerator. And that she loves you."

"S-s-seriously? I been looking for that thing for the better part of a year now." The cowboy was young, early twenties at most. Lean, hard body in tight jeans. Sleeves of his western cut shirt rolled up to reveal tanned, muscled forearms. He'd have been cute if it hadn't been for his buck teeth. Less than two years ago, I'd have come on to him just to see what happened. But I'd changed since then. The cowboy leaned a little closer. "Lemme axe you something.

Was that real? All them shadows moving behind you? The way the room got cold?"

I pushed away the defensiveness I felt when they asked this question. They meant no harm. They were just responding to something they didn't understand. "I didn't see the shadows since they were behind me, so I don't know if they're real or not. As for your mother's spirit? Sure. She was real. Redhead, right? Pretty eyes?" I didn't mention the way the side of her head was dented or the gash on her face.

The cowboy's face paled beneath the smooth, tanned skin. "Yep. Died in a car wreck eighteen months ago. Somebody ran her off the road."

The hair on the back of my neck stood up, and a shiver rolled through me. I itched to tell him his father had something to do with it but knew I wouldn't. It wasn't my business. We never interfered with townies. It was the unspoken rule of Sanctuary, the traveling community of grifters and magic practitioners I helped lead. Instead, I'd close the transaction and let him go.

"Sir, are you satisfied that I answered what you came in here to find out?" I pushed the silver jar toward him.

He dug in his pocket but stopped short of getting out his wallet.

My stomach hardened. I'd had a few people try to cheat me. Here, surrounded by friends and family, all fiercely loyal, that kind of thing wouldn't fly. But the fights were nasty.

The cowboy cleared his throat. "I know the price you

gave was just to contact my mother and find out where the ring was, but can you tell me if asking Harley to marry me is the right thing?" Those buck teeth made him look like a brown rabbit.

"Sir, I could take your money and tell you something, but I don't have the gift of precognition." I glanced behind me as though my great-uncle Cecil or his wife, Shelly, were about to rush out of the shadows and scold me for turning down money. That didn't happen. They were both busy with their own jobs.

The cowboy, eyes downcast, took out his wallet and peeled off the agreed upon amount, plus one dollar, and dropped it into the jar. The last of the big tippers.

I bit back a smile, thanked him, and followed him out, closing the flap of my tent and hanging up a "Be right back" sign. Summoning his mother's spirit had taken a bite out of my energy. She'd been a sad spirit, and she hadn't wanted to cross the veil. I needed a spike in my blood sugar if I wanted to last the rest of the evening. The freaks came out on Saturday night, which meant a chance to earn big money.

People moved past my tent, most barely giving me a glance. Finn, my cousin, called them sheeple. The rest of my family, still new enough to me to seem mysterious and exotic, called them townies. I'd resisted the classification but had gotten where I classified people within a few minutes of meeting them. Thrill-seeker. Wanna-be mystic. On the grift. Too stupid to live. On a Saturday night in the rural part of the Texas Hill Country, an hour minimum from any large city, Summervale Carnival was the best show for miles.

I stepped into the throng, determined to eat and feel more human. Hot, dry July wind ruffled my hair, drying the sweat on my face and powdering it with dust. A chaser of rancid grease and burnt sugar hit my nose. My appetite shrank. I lit a cigarette and strolled, coaxing myself to force down some kind of sustenance. Anything other than carnival food sounded good.

Sometime in my few months of traveling with the carnival, the honeymoon had ended. But Cecil had contracted Sanctuary to work the Summervale Carnival through Labor Day. We had our own little area in a hidden corner people seemed to find no matter how out of the way it was.

In addition to the spirit work, I sold spells that worked so well they scared the smart-ass out of the people who bought them. But money wasn't the only reason to be out here.

As long as Oscar Rivera's soul remained, he constituted a threat not only to me and my family, but to the world in general. Oscar Rivera, known as the Coachman, had been a nasty man and a nastier ghost. Neither my family nor I would be truly safe until I banished Oscar from the living plane. Otherwise, he'd eventually find a way to get revenge for the way I'd stomped his ass a few months earlier.

The search brought us to the Texas Hill Country because, in a vision, I'd seen Oscar hide his soul in what looked like a cavern. This part of Texas was known for its underground caverns. My best friend, Hannah Kessler, and I had been scouring newspaper archives and stories of old murders, trying to find a trace of Oscar during his human life. Our luck hadn't hit yet, but I held out hope it would.

I stopped walking, letting people stream around me, and sucked in a deep breath of the dry Hill Country air. I tilted my head upward to stare at the sky. So huge, so many stars. Unfettered by the branches of tall pines we had in East Texas, the sky here opened up and stretched out into eternity. The summer heat was as unforgiving as a brimstone preaching evangelist. But at night, like now, the stars seemed closer and sharper, like I could reach out and cut my finger on them. The energy flowed from them into me.

Tired as I was of Summervale Carnival, I wasn't tired of the Hill Country. This place grabbed me and held on tight. It had a different feel than East Texas, sort of an Old West vibe. The sight of actual cowboys on their way to work at nearby ranches captivated me. Germans had been the ones to settle much of this county, and their influence still colored the style of buildings and the local restaurants. And the country itself. Breathtaking. The land stretched out into hills and valleys covered by clumps of hairy looking grass and squat, gnarled trees.

My stomach rumbled. Accepting the inevitable, I stopped at a booth selling tropical punches made out of "100% real fruit." The owners sold moonshine out of the back of the booth. They'd said it came from a recipe in the family for three hundred years.

"Ms. Peri Jean." The female half of the couple who owned the booth passed me a cup of punch with a slice of pineapple garnishing the cup's edge. I dug for my money. She raised her chin. "Nope. On the house. That spell you sold us to increase our business really worked."

I nodded my thanks and cut back into the crowd, guzzling the drink. My tent and maybe more customers awaited. Before long, I reached the row of tents belonging to the traveling community of Sanctuary. Made of a heavy vinyl-coated material, the tents rattled and flapped in the hot wind.

A shadowy figure leaned out from the edge of one of the tents as though taking a peek at me. That cowboy's mother's ghost. I groaned.

Some of the spirits I contacted for money weren't so eager to go back where they came from. I had learned to deal with them in a businesslike way and to act confident.

Spirit, be gone. I drew on my magic and gave it a hard push. The spirit disappeared. I rejoined the throng of drunk townies, wild-eyed thrill seekers, and bored parents walking the dirt path through the makeshift carnival and walked past my family's row of tents.

I stopped at the sound of Dillon's husky smoker voice ringing out of the first tent. The sign outside read "Stop smoking with HYPNOSIS! $75 per person." A peek inside showed me she had a full house.

A Sanctuary member stood just inside the entrance taking a wad of money from a woman whose wizened skin made her look like an advertisement for quitting smoking. The Sanctuary woman, on the run from an abusive husband, raised her brows in question. I smiled, backed out of the tent, and peeked into the next one.

My cousin Jadine sat staring into a crystal ball. Inside the ball, a mist of smoke moved around. The sign next to Jadine read "See into the future. Ask Mistress Jade for a reading."

"Peri Jean, I need to talk to you." Jadine raised her head and stared in my general direction. Her accuracy still amazed me, especially since she was blind.

"How'd you know it was me?" I stepped the rest of the way into the tent.

"Your soap. And you coughed a couple of times." Jadine took her hands off the crystal ball, and the mist stopped moving inside it.

"I think you like catching people off guard." I moved close enough to give her a playful nudge but didn't sit at her table. My butt was tired. "What's up?"

"I'm not sure I should tell anybody this." Something in her voice raised my drama antennae.

I'd sounded that way too many times not to recognize it when I heard it another woman's voice. "What is it?"

"Brad's asked me to marry him." A little smile hovered on her lips.

I swallowed my first response, which was incredulity. Brad Whitebyrd loved playing the field, loved thinking he was a ladies man. Had Jadine stolen his heart? I counted how many times he'd visited camp, even going as far as to work while he was among us. His actually doing work convinced me. "What'd you say?"

"That he'd have to ask Papaw. What do you think

Papaw'd say if Brad asked for my hand?" I thought it over. Cecil would be brokenhearted that the only child he'd raised to adulthood thought herself ready for marriage. His heartbreak would come out in anger and admonitions.

I had my own misgivings. Jadine was only twenty-one. She really ought to date a bunch of guys and make a more informed choice.

But what did I know? I'd married young, divorced quickly, dated a bunch of guys, and still spent every night alone, the man I loved completely cut off from me. By choice.

"Peri Jean? Are you saying nothing because I ought to tell Brad no?" She clenched her hands in the lap of her brown, flowered dress.

"Just thinking." I came close enough to put my hand on her shoulder. "You're old enough to do what you want, no matter what I or anybody else thinks."

She grinned, and I thought I knew why Brad White-byrd would swear off bachelorhood for Jadine. She was gorgeous. "So you think Papaw won't get angry?"

"Oh, I didn't say that. He'll scream. He'll cry. He'll tell you not to do it." I giggled, and Jadine joined me. "But once he gets over it, he'll welcome Brad into the family. He's a pretty accomplished energy witch. Cecil will want him in Sanctuary after he thinks about it."

"I can see us being happy together." The look of hope on her young, untested face made me want to laugh and cry at the same time.

I'd have never told her she was wrong. Sometimes you just know when somebody's the right one. I'd leave the persuasive speeches to Cecil and Shelly. Jadine's adoptive parents, especially her mother, would probably drive her crazy. Shelly viewed her daughter as a princess and thought she'd marry a prince. Brad Whitebyrd was more like a spoiled frat boy.

"Will you go with Brad to talk to Papaw?" Jadine twisted in her chair. I knew this request came from Brad.

"Nope. If Brad's big enough to get married, he's big enough to do the hard stuff on his own." I leaned down and slowly pulled my cousin into a hug. She squeezed tight and let go of me.

"There's something else. I had a vision, a real one." Jadine plucked at the rayon of her dress.

My breath caught in my throat. This might be the break I needed, the thing that would make all these weeks with Summervale Carnival worth the effort.

"Something with Oscar Rivera?" I willed her to say yes. The worry about what I was going to do when I found his soul and could dispatch him was eating me up worse than just finding him and fighting him.

She shook her head, frowning. "It was a man asking about us, like he was looking for us. He was in San Antonio at that RV park where we stayed."

I quickly calculated. Our stay in the city of San Antonio had been two weeks ago. "What did he want with us?"

"I don't know. But he had a snake for a necklace." She made a face.

My guts twisted as I considered all the people or *things* who might wear a snake for a necklace and might be looking for me. Anybody from Sol, my contact across the veil, to a topside supernatural overlord and slave trader I'd nicknamed Mohawk. I turned my attention back to Jadine. "Tell me more about this man."

She shook her head so hard, her blond waves whipped back and forth. "That's it. Then the vision flashed to you. You had a hole right here." She tapped herself on a spot above and between both eyes. "Bright light was streaming out of it." Her breath came faster. "Those runes—the Coachman's runes—were floating around you, and they were glowing." She gulped.

I took a step away from her, freaked out by what she'd seen and unable to make sense of it. Sometimes Jadine's visions were symbolic. This one would take some thinking.

"I did a search on my phone for the part about the light coming out of your head." She gave me a sly little smile. I wanted to thump her. Brad Whitebyrd had probably taught her how to talk to her phone and make it talk back.

"Find anything interesting?" I did all I could to keep the amusement out of my voice.

"I found stuff about an evil eye and stuff about a third eye." Jadine shrugged. That was the extent of her knowledge, which was more than she'd have been able to access on a smartphone a few years ago.

"Okay. Thank you for letting me know. If you think that man is getting any closer, or if you somehow sense him here, come get me. Immediately." Feeling eyes on my back, I glanced at the tent's flap, only to see the shadow pull back quickly, as though to avoid detection. That was it. I'd banish this damn spirit as soon as I got away from Jadine. I turned to go. "Good luck with Cecil and Shelly."

Jadine blew me a kiss and went back to her crystal ball.

Available now.
Order Dark Traveler from your favorite bookseller.
ISBN: 978-1-947462-17-5

Visit Catie's website:
www.catierhodes.com

Find Catie on Facebook:
http://www.facebook.com/catierhodesauthor

Follow Catie on Book Bub.
https://www.bookbub.com/authors/catie-rhodes

Join Catie's email list:
http://smarturl.it/lrdenewsletter

ABOUT THE AUTHOR

Catie Rhodes writes southern-fried urban fantasy with a strong dose of horror and a side dish of humor.

She is the author of the Peri Jean Mace Ghost Thrillers. Her short stories have appeared in *Tales From The Mist, Let's Scare Cancer to Death, and Allegories of the Tarot.*

Catie was born and raised behind the pine curtain in East Texas. She comes from a family of world champion liars.

Their tall tales molded Catie into a purveyor of her own brand of lies and legends. One day, she found the courage to start writing down her stories. It changed her life forever.

Catie Rhodes lives steps from the Sam Houston National Forest with her long-suffering husband and her armpit terrorist of a little dog.

Find Catie online:
www.catierhodes.com